BY JILLY GAGNON

#famous

All Dressed Up

Scenes of the Crime

Love You,
Mean It

Love You, Mean It

A NOVEL

JILLY GAGNON

DELL
NEW YORK

A Dell Trade Paperback Original

Copyright © 2024 by Jilly Gagnon

Published in the United States by Dell,
an imprint of Random House, a division of
Penguin Random House LLC, New York.

DELL and the D colophon are registered trademarks of
Penguin Random House LLC

LIBRARY OF CONGRESS CATALOGING-IN-PUBLICATION DATA
Names: Gagnon, Jilly, author.
Title: Love you, mean it : a novel / Jilly Gagnon.
Description: New York : Bantam Dell, 2024.
Identifiers: LCCN 2023027474 (print) | LCCN 2023027475 (ebook) |
ISBN 9780593722961 (trade paperback) |
ISBN 9780593722978 (Ebook)
Subjects: LCGFT: Romance fiction. | Novels.
Classification: LCC PS3607.A35855 L68 2024 (print) | LCC PS3607.
A35855 (ebook) | DDC 813/.6—dc23/eng/20230616
LC record available at https://lccn.loc.gov/2023027474
LC ebook record available at https://lccn.loc.gov/2023027475
Printed in the United States of America on acid-free paper

randomhousebooks.com
randomhousebookclub.com

2 4 6 8 9 7 5 3 1

Book design by Alexis Flynn

To my grandmother, Janice Peglow,
a tough old bird with the most fiercely loving heart.
I miss you.

Love You,
Mean It

One

"Oh, but what about the mortadella? I hadn't even thought about that. Though I suppose you don't carry a good mortadella, do you, Ellie? Rose never will buy it here . . ."

Ruth Pinsky looked up from the deli case, eyes pinching with preloaded skepticism about the quality of my mostly-pork-fat, the small twist of her head sending the hairspray-regimented battalions of her hair helmet shivering. I took a small, twisted pleasure in noticing that her roots hadn't been touched up for at least a month, a half inch of grizzled salt-and-pepper mounting a rear attack on the permed, brassy blond front lines.

"I think it's excellent mortadella, personally. Would you like to try a slice?" I managed, hoping my gritted teeth looked something like a smile.

"That's probably best. Jimmy's so particular. And some of what I've brought back in the last few weeks really hasn't been up to par."

Rictus in place, I bent to haul out the mortadella, sliced a paper-thin strip onto a piece of wax paper, and handed it across the counter to Ruth. She nibbled at it thoughtfully, as though she hadn't sampled every fucking deli meat we carried five times over.

Actually no, that's not fair. She never tried anything "exotic," which apparently referred to the turkey and chicken options.

"Hmm . . . no, I don't think so." Her mouth pinched with distaste as she *finished the entire slice.* "Thank you, though."

"Of course."

I glanced over my shoulder not at all subtly at the retro wall clock mounted on the black-and-white-tiled wall that ran behind the deli counter.

"I don't mean to rush you, Mrs. Pinsky, but we're closing soon."

"Oh, of course. I suppose . . . the spicy salami? I *think* Jimmy liked that last time."

"That sounds like an excellent choice," I said, reaching for the massive log of cured meat. "And we'll always be here tomorrow if you want something else. Half a pound?"

She nodded, the skin around her eyes still twisted with a mix of disdain and vague worry. All this for half a pound of sandwich meat.

"A little less, actually. Jimmy's doctor told him to watch his weight."

And yet, salami.

"I wonder . . ." she murmured. I started up the slicer and pretended not to hear. Ruth Pinsky didn't know what she wanted on the best of days, and we'd just passed the five-sample mark, so clearly this was *not* the best of days. The whirring of the machine almost managed to drown out the rhythmic thud in my ears, impatience raising my blood pressure. Within seconds, I was weighing the salami, wrapping it, handing it to Ruth.

"That'll be five ninety-two."

I waited, tendons in my jaw tightening as she counted out the coins.

"And . . . ninety-two." She nodded curtly as she handed over the last penny. "Thanks so much, Ellie. See you soon."

"Can't wait, Mrs. Pinsky."

I managed to make a show of wiping the counter for five whole seconds before running after her to flip the sign to Closed.

Jesus *fuck,* why was life filled with so many Ruth Pinskys?

Ma would have told me to be charitable. Ever since her youngest boy had finished college and set up in Boston, Ruth, a lifelong homemaker and mother to three smothered sons, hadn't had their every movement to fret over. So instead, she fretted over salami. Three times a week at least. Oh, and occasionally the weather—god help whoever she managed to buttonhole on days when snow was moving in, *They say there might even be a bombogenesis. Have you ever heard anything so terrifying-sounding? I sent Jimmy to Costco to stock up on canned goods and gas for the generator . . .*

I mean, at least find a hobby. Or if you don't want one, drive to Boston and burden your own offspring with your endless, pointless, judgmental dithering. It's under an hour if traffic isn't terrible. Though who really knew, if Ruth's driving was anything like her meat selection.

Play nice with the regulars, Ellie, they're what keeps this place afloat. My dad's warnings may have fallen on pop-punk-deafened ears when I'd first started working alongside him in the shop, but now, without him around to sparkle for the customers—his genuine interest in their home repairs and children, his endlessly repeated jokes, blinding them to my eye rolls and sniffs—I actually tried to take the advice, if only because I liked how it made Dad feel so close I could almost hear his voice. Well . . . tried as hard as I could. A woman has her limits, after all.

I let myself dissolve into the closing routine, double-wrapping the meats and cheeses in the deli case, pulling out whatever was too small or had been sitting a few days for the volunteers the soup kitchen sent by every morning before we opened, bagging the half dozen baguettes that hadn't sold and propping them up in the fraying wicker day-old basket near the register (the focaccia was coming with me to Mimi and Grandpa's, with a pint of whipped red pepper ricotta). I'd just finished my check on the stock of tinned fish, artisanal oils, spices, crackers, pestos, and high-end pastas that crowded the shelves around the customer side of the store, when the bell rang again.

"Fair warning, I got Pinskied *right* before closing," I said, not bothering to look up from the trays of sides squeezing into the far corner of the deli case. Maybe the roasted beets with gorgonzola and pine nuts for tonight? After however many decades of living off deli leftovers, the entire Greco clan could use a little more veg in their lives.

"Oh my *gosh,* Ellie, what if it wasn't me?" My cousin Bella's already large brown eyes had grown so wide her lashes grazed her brows, and her rosebud mouth was open in a perfect little o. I couldn't help but smirk. We'd known each other all our lives— technically all *my* life, she was a whopping seven months old by the time I appeared on the scene, an age gap I'd always resented since it put her a year ahead of me in school—but she was still so easy to tease. Mimi called us Sugar and Spice when we were kids. Guess which one I was.

"Then I'd be calling the authorities. If you were ever more than two minutes late without texting to explain, foul play would have to be involved." I cocked an eyebrow at Bella. We both knew I was right, she was *pathologically* punctual. Maybe she'd gotten it from her dad's side of the family; it definitely wasn't in the DNA we shared.

It was just one of our many obvious differences, and yet Bella and I had somehow always managed to balance each other out, my overdeveloped fire tamped down at crucial junctures by her breeziness, other times acting as the vital line of defense her gentle nature was incapable of mounting on its own.

"Okay, that aside, Mrs. Pinsky's a regular. That counts for something."

"I have dozens of lovely regulars for whom I am *endlessly* grateful," I said with an exaggerated bow. "With Ruth . . . what counts is what she *pays* me."

"I think it's sweet that you're part of her routine. She must really care about this place to make the trip that often."

"Or they blacklisted her at every other grocery store and deli in a twenty-mile radius."

"Can they do that?" Bella looked genuinely shocked.

"I think they'd invent it just for her."

"I suppose she can be a little . . . unaware of herself at times," Bella conceded, "but she doesn't mean any harm."

"And yet none of that gives me back the hours of my life she steals." I finished scooping the beets into a four-quart tub, closing the lid with an emphatic snap. Bella was frowning, trying to find an excuse for Ruth Pinsky, no doubt. The usual prick of guilt at seeing her much-better-personness in action flickered through me as I flipped off the lights in the deli cases one by one.

"Is that a new top? It hangs really well on you." I gestured at the emerald-green boatneck blouse Bella was wearing, delicate seaming through the midsection and a flouncy peplum giving low-key corset vibes. It was clearly off the rack, but it seemed made for her particular shape, clinging without pulling or sagging anywhere. Honestly . . . I wouldn't have even bothered tailoring it if she'd brought it to me.

Bella rolled her eyes, repressing a grin.

"I'm sure you could make a better version . . ."

"Take the compliment, Bell."

"Well . . . thanks. I liked it." She shrugged, pleased. Which made me feel slightly better about my general saltiness.

"I cannot *wait* for Mimi's lasagna. I think it's going to be restorative."

"Oh, is she making lasagna tonight?" Bella's eyes lit up. Of all the many fabulous Italian dishes our grandmother produced for the weekly Greco Sunday dinner, lasagna was understood to be her masterpiece. The secret was somewhere in the spiced lamb, but so far, I hadn't been able to replicate it. Which was probably for the best. I already spent my entire working life surrounded by pork-fat-stuffed pork products, after all.

"If she isn't, there will be hell to pay, mark my words." I flipped off the last of the lights and joined Bella at the front door. "On that note, let's get out of here before Ruth realizes I charged her for the Genoa salami instead of the spicy hard."

"Not on *purpose,* though?" Two vertical lines of worry appeared on the preternaturally smooth, light brown skin of Bella's forehead. Somehow, the faintly anxious expression accentuated her high cheekbones that much more; she really did have unfair advantages in the looks department. I widened my eyes meaningfully as I set the alarm just inside the door.

"Bella, she asked for *five samples.*"

By the time we made it to my grandparents' sturdy robin's-egg-blue cape on the edge of town, the rest of the family had already arrived.

Grandpa was installed in his worn leather armchair in the corner of the living room, Auntie Susan flanking him, her birdlike figure perched at the very edge of the overstuffed scroll-armed brown velvet couch that dominated the space. She leaned in to say something directly into her father's oversized (but underfunctioning) ears, the thicket of dark hair that had long since migrated off the top of his head to their interior perhaps dampening their abilities.

"You don't need to do that, Susan. We're fine." He frowned, waving a hand through the air, eyes glued on whatever game was playing on mute on the massive, boxy television.

"Dad, we *want* to. Anyway, the man who shovels our walk said he'd throw it in for practically nothing."

"Auntie Susan, stop trying to make Grandpa feel old," I said, moving over to drop a kiss on his liver-spotted head. He smiled vaguely at me, laying his hand over the one I'd rested on his shoulder. "Until he actually breaks a hip, he can shovel his own snow."

"Don't be morbid, Ellie." Auntie Susan pursed her lips, annoyed.

"I'm not the one worried about Grandpa handling a shovel." I raised an eyebrow, gratified by Grandpa's low chuckle. He wasn't wired to stand up to people—especially not the women in his family—so at some point, I'd elected to take on the role for him.

At the other end of the couch, my uncle Bill, Susan's gentle giant of a husband, was trying to carry on a conversation with their son, Max, who was resolutely focused on his phone screen. Max was sixteen but still had that overgrown-adolescent-boy scrawniness, arms and legs spidery in the fitted, vaguely goth clothes he'd started wearing when he hit high school. I felt a general solidarity with Max—all manner of "alternative" kids got stamped as weirdos in Milborough, and I'd been similarly . . . *disaffected* during my theater-kid teenage years. But talking to him felt like pulling teeth.

"Hey, Max," I called out. He glanced up through the spiky *keep out* gate of dyed-blacker hair on his forehead. Man, lately he even *looked* at odds with Bill. Max had the same olive-skinned Greco coloring I'd inherited—our genes seemed to override all attempts to input new DNA, including Bill's Midwestern sandy-blond pallor. "Have any new music recs for me?"

He frowned, thinking, then his face lit up briefly, in a way that made him look like the sweetly nerdy kid we all used to actually enjoy.

"There's this synth-pop band that's kinda cool, Pistachio Dream," he said, tapping at his phone more urgently. "I just sent you a link to their latest video."

"Sweet. Anything else you think I might like, let me know. I'm too busy to be cool anymore." Max scrunched his face in a *way* too quick expression of grim agreement.

"Ellie, Bella, is that you?" Ma's voice rang out from the kitchen, and I quickly shed my shoes and retreated through the entryway, Bella lingering to say her hellos. Ma was still in scrubs, pulling together a salad at the center island, the Formica top slightly discolored with age but otherwise spotless. Mimi hadn't updated the house since the eighties, but she sure as shit cleaned it twice a week, top to bottom. I perched on a stool at the counter, stretching to snag the bottle of red wine at Ma's elbow. She raised an eyebrow as she sliced a mushroom against the pad of her thumb, even strips dropping onto the fluffy pile of arugula in the bowl.

"Don't start, Ma. I spent the last half hour at the shop choking down Ruth Pinsky's thoughts on the quality of the mortadella."

"Where does she think she'll find a better mortadella?" Ma's wide blue eyes narrowed to slits. I couldn't help but notice the crow's feet the expression pulled out. She always claimed she was going to start slowing down at work, but I had yet to see any sign of it.

"Exactly." I poured a generous glass of wine, then tilted my head at another glass, eyebrow raised. Ma turned her face heavenward and sighed, her unspoken yes. I poured a glass for her, then one for Bella. I was already a good third of the way through my own when Bella joined me at the counter.

"There's my favorite niece!" Ma reached across to cup Bella's cheek with one hand before returning to the salad. Bella's mom was Ma's sister. Laurie and Dave had moved to Nashville about five years back so he could take a teaching post at Vanderbilt, but Bella was established in Boston by then, and she'd kept coming to family dinner every week, even during my brief stint in New York. Taking over the deli when Dad died won me a brief wave of goodwill from the family elders, but Bella was still the favorite Greco of our generation by *far,* and she wasn't even a Greco. Frankly, I couldn't blame them.

"How's the big city treating you, Annabella?" Ma said, pausing between vegetables to take a small sip of wine.

"About the same." Bella wrapped both hands around the bowl of her glass.

"I don't know why you don't just come back here. Rents in Boston are out of control, I was reading about it in the *Globe* just last week."

Bella gave a gentle smile. We played this out pretty much every week, and somehow it never seemed to bother her.

"When Milborough's got a good marketing job for me, it'll be top of my list."

"You girls have both always been so ambitious," Ma said, her tone suggesting it wasn't entirely a compliment.

"Pretty sure that only applies to Bella." I reached across the counter to pluck a cherry tomato off the salad. Ma slapped my hand playfully. "In case you forgot, I hung all that up to run the family deli."

"But look at all the changes you've made! I just saw something about how 'on trend' tinned fish was, how restaurants are charging fifteen, even twenty dollars for some sardines and a few crackers. I never would have believed it."

"You *didn't* believe it. You and Mimi basically tried to have me committed for bringing in brands that cost more than a dollar."

"Well, I'm a big enough woman to admit when I'm wrong. The point is, you've really put your stamp on the place. Classed it up!"

It's not that I wasn't glad she appreciated the changes I'd made—it *was* nice to take more ownership over the deli, even nicer to see the people I cared about most genuinely proud of me. At some point that I couldn't put my finger on, I'd even stopped thinking of it as Dad's or Mimi's—my responsibility but the family's *thing*—and started thinking of it as *my deli*. And it was; the shop it was today wasn't the one Dad had run, or Grandpa and Mimi before him.

Still, I'd always hoped to achieve more in my life than "caught the trend in tinned fish at the right time." I tried to smile—Ma meant it as a compliment; there was no point in making her feel bad. Besides, I was the one who'd practically insisted on giving everything up to run the place.

"What can I say? I'm basically the Martha Stewart of meat slicers."

"*That's* what you think classy is?" Bella giggled.

"Okay, the . . . Grace Kelly of . . . giardiniera?" I tried.

"Her royal highness of ham?" Bella retorted.

"You girls are so *strange* sometimes."

"Yeah, but you love us," I said, relieved that the moment had passed without her noticing. I bent to haul out the food I'd brought from the deli, the slight heat from the wine melting the surface layer of permatension in my neck and shoulders. "Do we have another cutting board? I brought beet salad, but we also had a leftover focaccia." I waggled the square of bread in the air before plopping it on the breakfast bar.

"Did you think to bring—"

"Red pepper ricotta spread to go with it? What do you take me for, Linda?"

"Have I ever told you how much I love you, daughter of mine?" Ma fluttered her eyelashes exaggeratedly. "Look in the cupboard," she added, pointing with her knife to the narrow cabinet where Mimi kept cutting boards and cooking trays, separated with cheap tension rods so they "wouldn't get all jumbled." Margaret Greco, the O.G. of Pinterestable home organization hacks. Which begged the question . . .

"Where's Mimi?" I said as I pulled a scarred wooden board from the cupboard.

"At the town council meeting. Don't worry, I made sure your grandpa got the lasagna in the oven."

"Still? They must have had a hell of a lot of crosswalks to fight over."

"Don't. I think it's lovely your grandmother stays active in the community."

"*I* think it's lovely that she gets to argue someone else into submission on occasion," I said. As though to punctuate the point, the side door shot open and Mimi burst into the mudroom, stamping her feet far more aggressively than the dusting of snow on her boots called for. "Speak of the devil . . ."

"Don't you start with me, Eleanor," Mimi grumbled as she plopped onto the bench to wrench off her shoes, her legs barely reaching the floor—Auntie Susan and I had both inherited Mimi's trim, compact frame, all ropy strength with *zero* tits. "I'm in no mood. Frank? *Frank!* Get in here, we need to talk!"

I grimaced at Bella. We teased about how definitively Mimi wore the pants, both with our grandfather and most every other person she met, but she'd always had a marshmallow center. It just happened to be hidden under a very thick shell of hard work studded with crunchy bites of judgment. Mimi never hesitated to let you know her very clear views on how things ought to be done, whether you were talking about a moral obligation or how to make red sauce. It was just what passed for fun with Mimi; she liked sparring with someone who didn't back down. I'd inherited her throw-the-first-punch nature right alongside my washboard chest.

My grandfather shuffled in from the next room, vague worry corrugating his forehead. "Everything alright, dear?"

"No, everything is very much *not* alright," Mimi snapped, standing with a grunt. She was closing in on eighty, and her once dark hair was now mostly white, her familiar face striated in all directions. But her dark brown eyes still glittered with fierce intelligence, and she was probably in better physical shape than I was. Since she and Grandpa had stepped back from actively running the deli about ten years ago, Mimi had not only taken up local politics, she'd also leaned into both nature hikes and a very serious yoga practice. We used to joke that she'd outlast us all, though that hit a hard stop once Dad died.

She made a beeline for the wine, pouring herself a generous glass and taking a huge gulp before thrusting it toward my grandfather with such ferocity the wine nearly sloshed over.

"They're trying to run us out of town."

"Who do you mean, dear?"

"The entire goddamned lot of them! The traitors!" She slammed the glass down on the counter so hard my mother winced. "After how many decades? But of course that means nothing compared to some hoity-toity city shop . . ."

"Mimi, why don't you sit down, you're obviously upset." Bella stood to pull out a chair, flashing me a *what the fuck?* face. I shrugged. I couldn't remember ever seeing Mimi like this.

Mimi sucked her lips in, face tautening as though it was preparing for an explosion, then exhaled loudly and took the seat Bella had offered. I hurried to place the half-sliced loaf of focaccia and the tub of cheese between them. No one loved the R. J. Pegg focaccia we stocked at the deli more than Mimi. She scraped a thick blob of ricotta over an end piece and tore into it fiercely.

"Why don't we start at the beginning." Ma used the slow, careful tone she usually reserved for the angry patients and patient-spouses who thought bullying a nurse would somehow get them better care. "Did something happen at the meeting?"

"*Yes,* something happened. All our neighbors just *happened* to sell us out without even a second thought," Mimi fumed.

"We're gonna need a few more details, Mimi," I said, raising an eyebrow.

She turned her fiery glare on me, but I just raised my eyebrow another quarter inch. She wasn't the only Greco woman used to striking fear into the hearts of lesser mortals with her temper alone. After maintaining the standoff a second or two, Mimi took another bite, chewed furiously, then closed her eyes, presumably channeling her yoga breathing or some such. Finally, she turned to my mother.

"You know the old Taylor's department store, down on Jefferson?"

"Of course. It's a sporting goods shop now, isn't it?"

"It *was* until about a month ago. Phil Bray is retiring to Arizona, and his kids don't want to take over, so they're selling off the stock."

"Oh, that's too bad," Bella murmured reflexively. I was ninety-nine percent sure she'd never been inside Bray's. Her workouts consisted of Pilates at her fancy gym and occasional aerial yoga, and while I loved hiking in the woods around Milborough, we both shared a deep abhorrence of camping, which was most of Bray's raison d'être.

"It's about to get worse," Mimi said, jaw set grimly. "Do you know what that prick Ted Taylor plans to do with the place?"

"Margaret . . ." my grandfather murmured, frowning. As long as I'd known her, Mimi had had a foul mouth, but it always seemed to startle Grandpa. Still, she wasn't *wrong*. The Taylors had been among Milborough's wealthiest families for over a hundred years, and somehow they managed to add to their pile with each new generation of country clubbers. Ted Taylor had always strutted around Milborough as if he owned the place. The fact that these days he *did* own a lot of it somehow only made it more galling.

Mimi ignored Grandpa, turning to me to deliver her next pronouncement:

"He's trying to bring in Mangia."

I gaped, stomach plummeting so fast it almost made me dizzy.

"Like the . . . what would you even call them, a food department store?" Bella said, the worry lines appearing on her forehead again.

"That's the one." Mimi nodded grimly. "And if they pull it off, mark my words, it will mean the end of Greco's Deli."

Two

We all stared at Mimi in stunned silence while her words sank in. When Mangia came to Boston, it had been major news, the multi-story emporium of all things Italian—from artisanal oils and obscure brands of torrone to wines from every region to multiple miniature restaurants—a definitive point scored in the one-sided fight it was perpetually waging against New York.

Clearly the company was looking farther afield these days. It made sense; it wasn't just city dwellers who wanted the fantasy Mangia sold. Even *I* understood the appeal. You could take in a brief lecture on the food history of Umbria, meet a friend for lunch, and finish all your grocery shopping without ever leaving the premises. Shit, they probably had entire deli cases given over *solely* to mortadella. Ruth Pinsky would have a field day.

I swallowed hard—my mouth had started to flood nauseously with saliva.

"You said he's *trying*. The Taylors haven't sealed the deal yet, right?"

"It's just a matter of time. They've 'been in talks' for months," Mimi said, crooking her arthritic fingers into derisive air quotes.

"What did he say about the timeline?" I pressed.

"*He* didn't say anything, the chickenshit." Mimi's lips pursed with disgust. "He sent his son to do his dirty work."

"Wait . . . do you mean Trip?" Bella blinked, tilting her head to the side. A hazy memory of Trip Taylor briefly stepping into her relentless rotation of high school boyfriends breached the roiling waters of my mind.

"He called himself Theo, but I'm sure that's him. Slick as can be. Rain would probably bead up and slide right off that smile. Do you *know* him?" Mimi narrowed her eyes at Bella.

"He was the year above me in school," Bella said, eyes darting to mine for a fraction of a second, *Don't you dare say more.*

"Yeah, everyone knew Trip Taylor," I said. Bella would never hold up under concerted interrogation, and the fact that their romance lasted about a minute more than ten years ago would *not* count as a mitigating factor with Mimi in her current state. "He was on lacrosse, right? King of the bros? I think there was a brother a couple years behind me, too. But forget the douche report, the town is letting this happen?"

"The town was practically drooling at the prospect. Moira Lythikos didn't even mention the parking issues. *Moira.*"

"But even if they do come in, it's not the end of the world, Ma," Auntie Susan said, glancing around for support. "We don't *know* the deli would go under."

"You don't know the business, Susan. Ask Ellie, *she* knows I'm right."

Everyone turned to me. I was still so gut-punched I couldn't fully process.

"There's no way to stop this?" I finally managed.

"It was a preliminary vote, but if it's any sign of the way the wind's blowing . . ." Mimi blinked hard and wriggled her nose against the sparkle of tears filling her bright brown eyes. "Half of them have shopped at our store since they were kids. They didn't even take five minutes to decide that wasn't worth a slice of old bologna if it meant getting some fancy-pants food mall. Five generations in this town out the window," she spat, rubbing fiercely at the crepey skin around her eyes with a knuckle.

"Nothing's decided yet," Ma said, stretching to lay her hand over Mimi's. The fact that Mimi allowed it without so much as a sniff spoke volumes about how deeply this was wounding her.

After a few long moments, Mimi shook off my mother and exhaled a sharp breath.

"Nothing we can do about it, I suppose. Ellie, I hope you brought something besides bread to serve with the lasagna. Green salad gives me the trots."

Dinner was a subdued affair (at least by Greco standards), and by the time Bella stood to go, conversation had mostly tapered off.

"Thanks for the lasagna, Mimi. It was incredible, per usual." She bent to squeeze my grandmother's shoulders. Mimi patted her hand distractedly, not bothering to return the hug. "Grandpa, you owe me a cribbage game next week."

"Only if you promise not to skunk me," he said, rising from the head of the table to wrap Bella in a warm hug, voice characteristically quiet. Where Mimi was sharp, Grandpa had always been soft, the one to slip you a candy after a scolding with a finger to his lips. A yin and yang thing, I suppose. "I'm too old to bear the shame."

"Pretty sure I'm the one who needs to worry about the skunking. Alright, I should go before it gets too late. Love you all." I followed Bella to the door, slipping my feet into the black chef's clogs I wore on workdays—hopelessly unfashionable, but I was way past the point of valuing trendy footwear over a functioning lower back. I tilted my head at the door, widening my eyes, *Let's talk outside.*

I waited until we reached her car to speak.

"Mimi's right. If Mangia comes in, that's it for the deli."

Bella heaved out a huge sigh, leaning against the vehicle and wrapping her arms around herself for warmth.

"We don't know that . . ."

"Bella. We *absolutely* know that. I need to stop it somehow." I shook my hands at my sides, bouncing on my toes, anxiety buzzing through me like a physical current. Mimi was right, the deli wasn't just a job, it was our family legacy. It was the reason I'd moved back from New York after Dad died. Mimi and Grandpa had insisted they were up to running it themselves until they found a replacement, but I knew how relieved they were when I straight-up ignored that and broke my lease. How could I do anything else? It was the strongest, most tangible connection I had to Dad, every corner the site of some happy memory. Even five years later, it was the one place on earth that he still felt *present*. And other than the house we'd just walked out of, it was the only place that really felt like home. I swallowed hard, forcing the thoughts down. Bella didn't need to know how maudlin I was getting over a *storefront*.

"For Mimi," I added. "You know what it would do to her and Grandpa if this went through." I frowned as a bulwark against the threat of tears. *They* were who I was really worried about . . . right? God, how much wine had I drunk?

"It sounded like things were pretty far along," Bella murmured, tugging at the tip of a curl and letting it spring back into place once, twice, three times.

"I have to at least *try*, Bella." I jutted out my lower lip, trying not to let it tremble, and she nodded.

"Okay. What's the plan?" Gratitude surged through me. Bella might not think this was possible, but she would be in it with me until the bitter end.

"Getting in touch with Trip Taylor is as good a place to start as any. Do you still have his number?"

"Are you just gonna cold-call him?"

"I don't know. Maybe?" With effort, I forced my shoulders to drop. "I mean I'd text, I'm not a monster."

"Okay, just . . . try not to come in too hot, yeah?" I opened my mouth to respond but Bella lifted a hand. "Not because of you, although it is *totally* fair advice on that front." She tilted her chin down, pinning me with a knowing look. "I'm saying it because of Trip. People change, obviously, and we were just kids when we dated, but he tends to . . . not take criticism well?"

"A rich white man that doesn't like being criticized? *No.*" I pulled a faux-shocked face.

"Okay, but if you want to win *over* that rich white man . . ."

"Fine. Noted. Kid gloves only for the easily tarnished silver spoon."

Bella smirked as she found the old contact and sent it to me. Then she wrapped me in a tight hug. Despite myself, I dissolved into it. Unsurprisingly, Bella was an *excellent* hugger, enough so that she occasionally made me rethink my entire stance on the practice.

"Let me know anything I can do. Boston's really not that far."

"Don't make promises you can't keep."

She laughed and released me, moving around to slide into the car. She turned to me before closing the door.

"It'll be okay. I promise. Even if . . ." She licked her lips slowly, considering. "It'll all turn out for the best." I nodded, and she closed the door, waving once before driving off into the night. I stood there for a long time after she was gone, just outside the sparkling glow the porch light scattered over the snow that covered my grandparents' lawn, shivering in the winter night.

Bella was wrong, and we both knew it. Unless I did something to stop this, nothing would be okay.

If only I had any fucking clue where to start.

Three

I stared at the phone, the three thousand, four hundred and twelfth attempt at the text glaring back at me in the cold blue light.

To: Little Lord Doucheleroy

> Hey, Trip. It's Ellie Greco. Not sure if you remember me, I'm Bella Hill's cousin?

Did I not know I was her cousin? I deleted the question mark and bit my thumbnail, reaching blindly for the glass of whiskey on my end table. Opening sallies with the enemy required something stronger than wine.

Should I say more? Lay it all out from the start? No, this was good. Neutral. Best to see if he'd respond at all before I sent a novel.

I sipped the whiskey, letting the smooth, caramelly burn run down my throat, clicked Send, and forced myself to focus on the nature show I'd turned on when I got back to my apartment. Trip might not have his phone on him all the time. Maybe he was one of those people with "digital boundaries" whose phone went into a jar by the door the minute they got home.

I forced my eyes back to the TV, letting David Attenborough's plummy voice flow over me.

The grown python can stretch to as long as twenty-six feet, but it's adapted camouflage that keeps it invisible until the moment prey happens by. Its rapid strike stuns the unfortunate mammals, which it kills by wrapping its muscular body around them before swallowing the creatures whole.

The phone buzzed—oh thank *fuck*. I snatched it up before it could even go dark.

> I go by Theo

My jaw tensed, but the dots said he was still typing, so I forced myself not to respond.

> Sure I remember you. How is Bella?

> She's great

> Glad to hear it

> Any reason you were texting?

I bit my thumbnail again. This was it. The plea I'd rehearsed spilled out with only a handful of typos.

> I'm not sure if you know, but I run my family's deli. It's been around in one form or another since the 1920s. We were all really concerned to hear your dad was planning to bring Mangia into Milborough and worried about how it would affect businesses like ours

I stared at the screen, sucking first one lip, then the other through my teeth. Finally I clicked Send.

The three little dots appeared . . . they kept blinking for ten seconds, twenty . . .

Then they went away. I gripped the phone a little tighter. What could that mean?

They started again. Okay, so he was thinking about what to say. Maybe he hadn't considered our deli. Hell, maybe he didn't even know it existed. People like the Taylors probably had groceries flown in from Switzerland or some shit, right?

Stopped again.

I was staring so hard now I could practically feel my eyelids attempting to recede into my skull. Maybe he was composing his own novel. But was that good? Trying to find the words to apologize for *destroying someone's family business* probably takes a lot of time. My breath started coming short as I willed the dots to come back. He had to say *something,* didn't—

Oh god, the dots! My whole body tensed as they blinked, blinked, and then . . .

And?

Wait . . . seriously?

I hunched over the phone, molars sanding each other down as I furiously typed.

> And I know you're a spoiled dick whose lucky grandpa was born first but for some people HAVING A LIVELIHOOD actually fucking matters

I was *so close* to hitting Send, then I thought of Mimi hunching over the breakfast bar in . . . not quite defeat, but the closest approximation of it I'd ever seen in her. I closed my eyes, breath-

ing deeply—*in through the nose, out through the mouth*—the way
Bella had told me the 0.1 times I'd attempted to meditate with
her.

I held my thumb over the Delete key, grimacing as I forced
myself to type something Bella-approved.

> And I was hoping we could meet to
> discuss it before anything is finalized.

The dots barely flashed before his response appeared.

> I'm not sure what good that will do,
> negotiations are fairly advanced.

I was about to fury-text for real this time when the dots appeared again.

> But if you want to talk about it
> anyway, I'll be at the property
> tomorrow to meet with some
> contractors. You can meet me there.

Relief flooded through me, so intense I felt a little shaky.

> Sounds great. What time?

> I'll be there at 8 sharp

> See you then

I hesitated a moment, then added.

> Thanks for taking the time

> NP

I set the phone down, feeling triumphant. It was just step one, but I'd managed it. I was doing *something*. And tomorrow I'd take step two: I'd channel Bella's way-more-zen energy, and I'd explain to Trip—Theo—whatever the fuck he went by—how important small business was to our community. How important *our* business was to the town's history. Maybe, just maybe, I'd find a way out of this.

I turned back to the TV, turning over what I could say to convince him—other businesses would be affected too, maybe that was a way in? The Taylors held commercial properties all over town; getting Mangia in but gutting the downtown core would have to affect their bottom line. Other folks might just see dollar signs flowing into town—no one else was as *directly* competitive with Mangia as we were—but the coffee shop near me wasn't that convenient if you had no reason to head downtown in the first place. Joe's Pizza was good but not great, they'd definitely suffer. Maybe other business owners hadn't realized what this would really mean, yet. If they'd gone to the meeting at all.

I briefly toyed with the idea of rallying them . . . but that could take weeks, and by then it might be too late. For now, the play was going to Theo directly and trying to hit him the only place it might hurt: in the money. Even if the Taylors could afford to lose the rent from every other shop and restaurant and whatever else they owned, stripping Milborough of the charm that made it appealing in the first place would have to have long-term consequences. Mangia was the kind of play that was banking on Milborough continuing to gentrify, but without the cluster of cute shops, restaurants, *delis* even, it was hard to distinguish from Burnton (closer to the freeway) or Andrew's Point (wealthier overall, but without the character). Without the quirky cute–factor, the exodus of Bostonians might redirect toward one of them, or even Amherst or Salem. Sure, some of those people would visit Mangia occasionally, maybe even often enough to keep it open, but surely the Taylors didn't want *all* their eggs in that retro wire-and-wood basket. There had to be an argument in there that would work, even with Trip—no, *Theo*, don't fuck that up—Taylor.

The nature program showed a bunny, its trembling making it extra adorable.

The python's strike is so fast that by the time the marsh rabbit senses him moving overhead, the giant snake has already wrapped himself around the smaller creature, in preparation for swallowing his meal whole.

Four

I glanced at my phone again, foot tapping out my annoyance. I'd been waiting for fifteen minutes outside the old Taylor's department store—it had been Bray's since the late nineties, but locals all still referred to it that way, an unintentional reinforcement of the Taylor family's sway over all of us—and still there was no sign of Theo.

I wrapped my arms tighter around my body, the cold prickling through my winter jacket. The windows of the building were soaped over, so I couldn't tell whether the contractors were inside. I sure as hell wasn't going to risk setting off some alarm—annoying Theo before we even started wouldn't help. But I was freezing, and the deli was just sitting there closed while I stood here like an idiot (I would *not* risk this meeting getting back to Mimi by calling in one of our handful of part-timers), and a not small part of me was starting to wonder if this was some kind of prank. Seriously, where *was* this asshole?

I was finally turning to leave, muttering curse words under my breath, when a shiny silver BMW rolled up to the curb, windows tinted so dark you could barely make out the silhouette of a driver. It parked in the loading zone, and out popped—of course—Trip (no, *Theo,* try to remember it's *Theo*) Taylor.

He had his phone to his ear, so he didn't seem to notice the daggers shooting out of my eyes in his general direction. Though his armor of money probably would have deflected them anyway.

He'd always been tall, somewhere over six feet, but he'd filled out since high school, his ropy, athletic frame broader now, more masculine. He'd stayed in shape—the trim cut of his obviously expensive blue shirt and gray wool slacks made that clear. His once blond hair had darkened, and was cut long on top, swept back now but probably always falling just over his eyes in a way that made women want to tuck it back for him. What I had to believe was a very deliberately cultivated two-day stubble accentuated the strong lines of his jaw. Even beneath a slightly heavy brow, his eyes were startling, a steely dark blue that reminded me of lake water, tiny flickers of browns and greens hinting at things hidden beneath the surface.

In high school he'd been cute, in that smirking jock way, but I had to admit it: He'd grown into full-blown handsome. And really, why not tack that on, he'd already won the white-male-with-money lottery. Still, everything about him—from his just-too-long hair, to his expertly tailored camel cashmere overcoat (left open with a plaid scarf draped inside the collar—cold couldn't touch a *Taylor*), to his polished black Beatle boots—just screamed *dick.* Seriously, if I'd been trying to broadcast "entitled arrogance" during my stint as a (failed) theater costume designer, I couldn't have put together a better look.

I could feel my eyes bugging with fury. I sucked in a fiery breath, digging my nails into the butts of my hands. *Stay calm, Ellie. You need this dick's help.*

He bent to grab a tray of coffees, then made his way to where I huddled in the entryway, at no point really looking at me.

"I don't know what to tell you, Ryan. We've got three other offers on the space, and you've known about the deadline for a month. I like your concept, but if you're not willing to float a few months while you sort out the licenses, we can't keep holding it for you . . . Okay . . . Sure, talk then."

He clicked the phone off and turned to me, one corner of his mouth twitching up in an amused smile that accentuated his sharp cheekbones. I hated that I noticed the fucking cheekbones.

"Ellie. You made it."

"I did. At eight." I kept my face almost aggressively bright, tilting my head to the side and cocking an eyebrow. If anything, he just looked more amused.

"And you decided to wait here instead of going in? You must like this weather better than I do. Shall we? I've got a really busy morning."

My body trembled with the effort not to spit fire as he opened the unlocked door—of course it was unlocked, why hadn't I even *tried* it?—and swept into the building. I hurried after him, practically running to keep up with his long strides. I knew the height difference wasn't technically his fault, but trotting after him like a child just annoyed me further.

As we made our way to the elevator at the far back wall, I glanced around the space that had, until recently, been stuffed with tents and kayaks, hiking boots and dehydrated meals. A few shelving units were scattered around the massive room, but otherwise it was empty, and it was surprising to see how vast it was. The ceilings were high, maybe twelve feet, and ornate crown molding ran around the edges, the swirls and folds reminiscent of cake frosting. Every so often a fluted column sprouted through the floor, its crown blooming lavishly at the ceiling. Bray's had been carpeted, I was pretty sure, but the contractors had already ripped all that out, revealing dark-stained hardwood floors. They were scuffed and dull with age, but you could tell they'd be beautiful refinished. It wasn't hard to imagine the lovely space Taylor's must have been when it opened in the early 1900s, a glamorous temple to the gods of consumption, the sumptuous setting stoking religious zeal even in those who hadn't walked through the doors as believers.

"I never realized how pretty it was in here."

Theo turned to me, his smile looking genuine for once.

"It's got incredible bones. Bray's didn't really take advantage of that."

He pressed a button on the elevator and I focused on the details: the subtle diamond-patterned coffering of the ceiling, the airiness of the space when dozens of kayaks weren't leaning against the walls, the vaguely deco brass surrounds on the elevator itself. Mangia couldn't have found a better location if they'd tried.

The elevator arrived and Trip (no, *Theo*) thumbed four, the top floor. I frowned, trying to remember the last time I'd been in the store. At least a couple years ago, probably to buy something simple—running shoes, or leggings.

"Was Bray's really four floors?"

He shook his head.

"The third floor they kept for admin and extra stock. The fourth we rented out separately as office spaces. Frankly, it was hard to keep them filled."

"I'm surprised you didn't boot Bray's out earlier."

His lips pursed but he didn't turn to me.

"No one booted anyone out. They had a long-term percentage lease, and the business was solid. They were good partners. But Phil Bray's ready to retire, so that's that." He turned to me, holding the tray out. "By the way, is black okay? I wasn't sure how you take it, but it seemed like a solid guess."

Heat rose to my cheeks as I accepted the cup.

"You didn't need to get me coffee."

"It's the least I could do. You were coming to me, on my schedule, all the way across town from your deli. I'm sure this wasn't convenient. So? Did I guess right?"

"Actually, I usually take three sugars. In fact . . ." I dug around in my pocket, fingers closing on a single square of paper. The sugar packet was beat up, the words worn away, but it was still intact, thankfully. I pulled the lid off the coffee, tore the packet with my teeth, and dumped it in. "Better than nothing."

"Really, three sugars?" He raised an eyebrow, amusement flickering over his lips, on the thin side, but somehow perfect for his face. "No offense, but that seems off brand. The sugar hoarding, obviously, since you're not eighty, but also just the order itself."

"None taken. Especially since we don't know each other well enough for you to know my 'brand.' As far as the sugar, I run a deli. I always have random condiments on me."

"Fair. I just thought all the artsy cool kids took their coffee black."

Somehow that just made me feel more embarrassed. The idea of Trip Taylor thinking any of the kids I hung out with back in the day were *cool* was ludicrous, but it was a kinder description than I would have expected. I took a few deep breaths. He was clearly going out of his way to put me at ease—I could at least try not to spew acid from the start.

I tried a sip of the coffee to reorient. Even with less sugar than I liked, it was good, smoother than the stuff I made at the deli, with a chocolatey mouthfeel. *Just one more thing Taylor-level money can buy.*

"After you." He spread his arm wide as the elevator doors opened.

The fourth floor was in a state of much greater chaos; a handful of tarps heaped with debris was visible from the elevator, and skeletons of walls past stalked across the floor, bits of plastery flesh still clinging to their corpses. Powdery dust coated everything, including the inside of my nostrils pretty much immediately. A largish hole gaped in the dropped ceiling just outside the elevator doors, hints of the building's entrails gleaming through it, and I moved to one side, skin prickling anxiously.

"Watch your step. Especially if your tetanus boosters aren't up to date," Theo said, gingerly stepping over a pile of nail-studded two-by-fours before continuing past shells of rooms of varying sizes, some more or less intact, others stripped to the studs. I followed, sticking close behind to avoid the various construction obstacles. A lone brass plaque, coated in a grayish film, clung to a remnant of drywall to my left, the gravestone for FRASER AND PHIPPEN ACCOUNTING SERVICES.

We curved around the elevator block toward the northeast corner of the building. If the area around the elevator was chaotic, this was postapocalyptic. Much more of the ceiling had been pulled away, and a tangle of ancient-looking wires and dingy pipes and vents had colonized the space above. With the ceiling tiles ripped out, you could see how far up the space went—another few feet, easily, the building's various systems strung loosely through the center of it.

A double-height ladder rose out of the middle of what must have once been one of the larger offices, chunks of broken building materials, ragged curls of wire, and various tools littered around its base. The man on it was fiddling with something on a ceiling beam, the back of his head just barely visible between snaking tubes overhead.

"Jaime, how goes it?" Theo called up. The ladder wobbled precariously as Jaime turned to face us, crouching. He was in his early twenties, but the wide grin he broke into when he spotted Theo made him look even younger. "Coffee? Double cream, right?"

"Oh hell yes." He stretched to take the coffee cup Theo was offering. "Thanks, Theo."

"Of course. Where's Mike?" Theo frowned, looking around.

"He went with Don to pick up supplies. You wouldn't believe what they did up here. There are these giant metal boxes around half the wires, we have to pull them out to even see what the hell is going on. I've never seen anything like it."

"Wonderful. Always the news you want to hear from your electricians."

"Don't worry, we've got you. Anyway, you knew it was gonna be a big job."

"A big job that I expect to stay below the very big estimate Don quoted."

"That's above my pay grade. I just do what I'm told." Jaime grinned and sipped his coffee.

"I'll let you get back to it." Theo turned, tilting his head for me to follow, and started making his way around the back of the building, not bothering to wait to see if I was following.

About forty feet along, an empty doorframe opened onto a mostly intact office (which is to say, it still had walls and a ceiling). A single folding table stood in the middle, a few folding chairs scattered around it. Theo set the tray down on the corner of the table, sliding his laptop bag off his shoulder and placing it in the center. He took a chair on the far side.

"Have a seat." He gestured at the nearest chair, its cracked vinyl surface lightly coated in the same dust that was floating through the air. I swiped at it with the sleeve of my coat (it immediately striped gray) and sat.

Theo pulled out a sleek silver laptop, flipping it open and scanning the screen as he reached for the coffee tray, plucking one of the two remaining cups free.

"So? You have my undivided attention, at least until Don gets back," he said, scrolling on the computer.

I took a deep breath, forcing my annoyance down. This was my chance to convince him.

"I run Greco's Deli across town. We're small, but we've been there for decades. Since the forties in that building, but longer as a business. It's a Milborough institution."

"You mentioned that." He scrolled a couple times, eyebrows moving toward each other, then typed out a quick sentence, clicking decisively on the trackpad before turning to me. I was once again startled by the deep blue of his eyes, the robin's-egg shirt making them appear brighter against his fair features. "What's that got to do with me?"

I blinked rapidly, trying to remain calm. *This is the dick you need to win over.*

"It has everything to do with you, at least if you're set on bringing Mangia in." He stared, waiting. "It will run us out of business! And not just us. It could change the entire face of the town."

"That's not our intention, I assure you," he said, then took a slow sip of his coffee. "But it's also not my problem." He shrugged, the tiny movement of his shoulder like flint against my core. I could almost feel my tinder catching.

"Well, it *will* be your problem if half the shops downtown are boarded up within the year. This building isn't the only place your family owns," I spat, leaning forward in the chair.

He raised an eyebrow, a hint of a smile twisting his lips.

"That's true. But it is one of the largest *single* holdings in our portfolio. And finding a retailer to lease the space on terms that work for everyone isn't as simple as you'd think."

"Terms that make the Taylor family richer, you mean." I sniffed derisively. "Because owning half the town isn't enough?"

"Sorry, are profits not important to *your* business?" he pulled an exaggerated "confused" face and took another long sip of his bougie-ass, probably-five-dollars-a-cup coffee. The arrogant prick.

"They're not the *only* thing that's important to us, no." I was gripping the chair seat now, body rigid as I leaned even farther forward. "*Some* people actually care about Milborough's history, about the people who live here, not just the ones who parachute in from Boston to drive up housing prices. Some of us actually love this town. Not just what we can wring out of it."

His nostrils flared, a muscle in the side of his temple jumping.

"Are you done?" He leaned back in the chair, wreathing his fingers together behind his head. The pressure in my head shot so high it felt like my eyes might burst all over him. "Because believe it or not, I didn't agree to let you interrupt my workday just so you could call me a money-hungry asshole."

"I never said that," I forced out between clenched teeth.

"Not in so many words." He drew in a long breath, eyes fixed on mine. "But I think we both know what you *meant,* yes?"

Fuck this arrogant little shit and the daddy's money he rode in on.

"If the brand-new BMW fits, *Trip*. Or sorry, *Theo*. Because you're *so* different from your dad, right?" I slammed my body back, folding my arms across my chest. His lips pursed and I felt a warm burst of triumph. I'd struck a nerve somewhere. "Hats off, you've really blazed your own trail. Let me guess, he's a Mercedes man?"

"I think we're done here," he said sharply, turning back to the laptop. "Let me finish this email and I'll see you out." The tight set of his jaw and the stiff way he was holding his shoulders was unmistakable now. He might have been toying with me before, or maybe he just didn't care enough to feel invested, but now he was *pissed*.

Shit. I'd been trying to listen to Bella, I really had, but he was just so goddamned *annoying* that all my good intentions had flown out through one of the many holes in the ceiling. I took a small sip of coffee, trying to let the acid brew mask the taste of the pride I was gulping down.

"Theo . . . I'm sorry. That was"—I closed my eyes tight, *god,* I hated apologizing, especially to someone like *him*—"unkind. I don't usually lose my temper, but this whole situation is incredibly stressful."

"Don't you?" The corners of his lips quirked slightly. "Weren't you the girl who threw all those bocce balls at Pritchard's head?"

"You *heard* about that?"

"The whole school heard about that. It's not every day that a sophomore reduces a middle-aged man to tears in the middle of the soccer field. Plus, he was out for blood. You should have heard him when the guys brought it up at practice."

Dear lord, let one of the ceiling holes open up *beneath* me and drop me out of this place. Of course Theo had heard about it— Pritchard coached lacrosse. The fact that he'd never outgrown the entitled eighties bully vibe he'd probably honed during his *own* high school days—I mean, what kind of adult man takes a cheap swipe at a teenager's *chest size?*—probably didn't change how the team saw my . . . let's call it a snap decision. I licked my lips, genuinely unsure how to play this.

"In my defense—"

"Oh, you don't need to defend that. Pritchard was an absolute jackass. I can't believe he hadn't been sued out of the school years earlier." Theo's nose wrinkled in disgust. "I'm just sad you didn't actually hit him." His lips curled slyly, eyelids lowering in a way that somehow intensified his deep blue gaze. A startled laugh escaped me.

"Sorry. My aim's better when I'm not being sexually harassed by my elders."

Theo's shoulders twitched in another tiny shrug, though this time it was far less infuriating. As his smile faded, he sighed, leaning onto the table.

"Listen. I hear you about the Mangia deal. I know what it could mean for businesses like yours. Honestly . . . I said the same thing when Ted first floated it. I even have my own reasons for wanting to keep them out of this building. But you have to understand—"

A piercing shout interrupted us, followed by a series of sharp clatters and a heavy thud. Before I could process what was going on, Theo had bolted up, eyes wide, and was running past me into the hall.

"Jaime?" Theo's voice was high and tight. *"Jaime."*

By the time I'd managed to start after him, Theo was under the electrician, arms wrapped around the man's middle in an intense bear hug. Jaime's head and shoulders were hidden by the tangle of building systems, but it was clear that until Theo had arrived, he'd been dangling from some hidden part of the ceiling. The ladder had tumbled to the side, various tools spread out around it, the remnants of the coffee splattered across the floor.

"I've got you." Theo widened his stance and bent his knees. "Let go."

Theo grunted as Jaime complied, crouching to absorb the man's weight and carefully lower him to the ground. He took a step away, resting his hands on his thighs and taking a few deep breaths as Jaime shook out his arms. A few drops of blood spattered across the floor from a cut in his hand.

"You alright?" Theo said.

"Yeah, I'm alright." Jaime nodded slowly. "I don't know what happened. One minute I'm reaching for the screws on the far side of the ceiling beam, the next I'm hanging on by my fingertips." Jaime blew out a breath so large it inflated his cheeks. "Lucky you were here."

Theo stood, still breathing heavily as he pinched the bridge of his nose between his fingers. When he released it, his brow had dropped low, anger clouding his handsome features.

"What were you *thinking*?" Theo pointed overhead. "Why stretch to reach something when no one was here to spot you?"

"I know, it was stupid. But it was just a fluke thing. Anyway, I probably would've been fine, I was scared more than anything." Jaime shrugged.

"Probably would've . . . you don't *know* that!" Theo barked. I could see color rising in his cheeks as he thrust a finger at Jaime. "And where's your fucking hard hat?"

"Whoa, Theo, settle. Nothing happened."

"But it *could* have. You could have broken a leg, or fallen onto something sharp." Theo's lips were turning white they were squeezed so hard. "And look at your fucking hand!"

Why was Theo getting so worked up about the not-even-an-accident? Sure, the guy could have wound up with a broken ankle if he'd been *really* unlucky, but it wasn't that big a deal. Since when did Theo Taylor—the kind of jock who jumped off porch roofs into backyard pools drunk, last I'd heard—care this much about the possibility of minor injury? Jaime, looking as baffled as I felt, spoke carefully.

"I scraped it on a loose screw. It's not deep. I can find the first aid kit if you want."

"This is why we have protocols. You can't just *ignore* them, Jaime. You can't just act like—"

And then a large metal cage fell out of the ceiling and hit Theo, *thunk,* on the back of the head. He crumpled to the ground, limp.

"Oh fuck . . ." Jaime's eyes went wide as he stared at Theo. I rushed over to kneel beside him.

"Theo? Theo!"

His eyelids fluttered briefly, but they didn't open. I turned to Jaime, adrenaline coursing through me.

"What the fuck is wrong with you? Call an ambulance. Now!"

Five

I stayed next to Theo, one hand on his shoulder, the other gripping his wrist, as Jaime paced, fingers threaded through his dark hair, murmuring curse words. I hovered my hand over Theo's nose and mouth—for the fifth time at least—but he was still breathing, slowly but steadily, and I could feel his pulse.

God *dammit*. We had just been getting somewhere, I could feel it, and then he had to go and get *knocked out*. Would he blame me for that? Most likely. Even if he didn't, he'd probably be in a hospital bed somewhere while his father chugged along with the Mangia deal, and by the time I'd have another chance to reason with anyone, it would be too late. A tiny voice at the back of my brain (probably Bella's) tried to chide me—*This man is out cold, he could be seriously injured, you're really thinking about* yourself *right now?* But I couldn't help it—this stupid freak accident could cost me my family's *entire legacy*.

A wail through the windows told us the ambulance had arrived. The elevator doors were just pinging open when Theo's eyelids fluttered again.

"Where . . . ?"

He winced, trying to raise a hand to his head. Even that small motion seemed to set off a wave of nausea, and he gulped heavily, his color draining.

"Shhh. Just stay still. The paramedics are here," I said. He turned that intense blue gaze on me, frowning with the effort of piecing things together. His eyelids drooped again as the EMTs descended on us, rolling him onto a portable stretcher, hoisting him onto the gurney, checking vitals and notating things, and soon they were going to be hauling him away and then when would I have a chance to talk to him again? I wasn't exactly going to make his hospital visitors list.

"Where are you taking him?"

"Burnton General." They were already wheeling him toward the elevator, kicking aside piles of debris. Any second they'd be out the door and that would be that, my grand plan to save the deli KO'd in the first round.

"Can I ride along? He'll . . . want to see me." Not likely, but possible. For all I knew, getting chewed out by random former classmates was his kink.

"That's only for family."

"But I *am* family," I said, getting desperate. I could just catch Jaime's confused stare in my peripheral vision. "Or . . . almost family. I'm his . . . fiancée?"

Jesus Christ, Ellie, where had that *come from?*

The EMT at the foot of the bed turned to the one at the head, eye-talking rapidly—even their unspoken communications were highly trained and efficient. Then he turned back to me and nodded once.

"Alright. Are you parked nearby? You can follow us."

"Right. Okay." I ran back to the office to grab my purse, turned to go, then decided to scoop up Theo's laptop bag and my coffee as well. I would need to be caffeinated to pull this off. By the time I'd darted back out to meet the EMTs, the elevator doors were opening.

And before I knew it, we'd crammed inside, then we were hurrying across the empty first floor, and loading Theo—passed out again, it would seem—into the back of an ambulance, and *what the fuck had I been thinking this was not going to end well.*

"What did you say it was that struck him, Miss . . . ?"

"Greco," I said, eyes darting to the hospital bed. Monitors beeped softly over Theo, breathing steadily beneath the rough hospital-issue sheets. "It was like . . . a metal cage?" I mimed a box about a foot wide with my hands. "It had been protecting the wiring. I think Jaime grabbed on to it when the ladder fell. It seemed pretty heavy duty."

"Sounds like."

"Will he . . . be okay?" I gulped. The magnitude of my impulse lie paired with the hospital smell was spiking my anxiety. Dad's heart attack had been sudden and massive—he was gone before I even made it home from New York, let alone to the hospital—but after that, Mimi had insisted that Grandpa finally get the bypass doctors had been recommending for years. It had gone as smoothly as possible, but those visits were all wrapped up in losing Dad, anxiety sharpening the chemical odors of cleansers and medicines, none of them strong enough to completely eradicate the faint hint of decay they were fighting.

The choking feeling overtaking me wasn't really for Theo, but it must have seemed like it to the nurse, a middle-aged woman with faded red hair and reading glasses that kept slipping down her broad nose. She gave me a gentle look.

"Don't worry, sweetie, your fiancé's gonna be just fine." Hopefully she thought my pained look was for his sake, not at the f-word. "He's concussed, but the scans don't show anything scary. With any luck, he'll be awake within the hour."

"Okay. Thank you." I nodded rapidly, eyes glazing over as I stared at the thicket of tubes and sensors.

I'd officially given up on opening the deli for the day—Mondays were slow, and I'd texted Lauren, who owned the vintage shop next door, asking her to tape a sign to the entrance letting customers know we'd be back tomorrow. *Already driving them into Mangia's arms.*

But that's why I couldn't leave. If I had any chance of salvaging this, I needed to talk to Theo, and after the complete disaster of a morning, I doubted he'd give me another chance, if only out of vague superstition. He might know *logically* that I had nothing to do with his injury, but he'd probably still associate me with it, like when you get food poisoning and unfairly blame the last thing you ate. Not to mention I'd told the hospital staff and one of the electricians he worked with that we were engaged, which . . . might not help things if he heard that without context.

With any luck, he'd wake up and find me there, the good Samaritan just so *worried* about him, and I could play up my role in getting him to the hospital, and then if he had a single decent bone in his body, he'd at least agree to reschedule our—

"Sorry . . . don't I know you?"

I startled back to the moment to find Theo squinting at me from the bed. He pressed the button to raise the back, frowning.

"I'm in the hospital?"

"You are. How are you feeling?"

"Weird. Actually . . . not great." He reached for his head, wincing as he made contact. "Aren't they supposed to give you painkillers in the hospital? Like . . . *real* ones?"

I laughed in spite of myself.

"With a head injury? Not so sure that's the best call."

"I'll take my chances." He flashed a conspiratorial look that was surprisingly catching—clearly he could be charming when he wasn't trying to decimate your family business—then sat up straight, eyes widening. "Ellie! Ellie Greco, right?"

I exhaled, relief flooding me. For a minute, I was worried I'd have to walk him through the entire morning. But if he remembered me—and wasn't shouting *Get out, you murderous bitch!*—maybe there was a chance we could pick up where we'd left off.

I mean, not *immediately*. Even if he'd wanted to scrap the Mangia deal that very second, the pamphlet on concussion protocol recommended zero screen time, and forcing the issue felt like it could backfire. But soon.

"But . . . sorry, what are *you* doing here?"

"I was there when you got hurt. At the old Taylor's building. Do you remember?"

"You mean Bray's?"

"Well sure, until recently."

"So . . . were we shopping or something?"

A little tendril of dread started unfurling in my center.

"Do you remember our meeting, Theo?"

"Theo? Man, I kinda like that. Maybe I should start going by Theo, what do you think?"

My mouth dropped open, the dread bursting into full, ghastly bloom. Meanwhile, Theo was frowning hard, clearly trying to sort through something.

"I mean, I remember you obviously, you're Bella's cousin. And you said you were there when I got hurt, but . . . why are you *here*? Like in the hospital. Not to be rude, but . . . we don't really know each other, right?"

The red-haired nurse bustled in just then, the picture of cheer as she crossed to check Theo's monitors.

"Of course you do, silly. This is your fiancée!"

Theo turned to the nurse with an expression approaching horror. Which, c'mon. Like *he's* the loser in this setup?

"My . . . Wait a second, I have a *fiancée*? But how can it be . . ."

His eyes darted between the nurse and me, doubt creeping in at the corners.

I stared at the nurse, mouth hanging open, stomach all slithering creatures, completely unsure how to play this, the moment they found me out. Was it *illegal* to lie about your relationship to a patient? Even if it wasn't, it was highly sketchy, bordering on creepy-stalker. Was there any way I'd have a chance to explain *why* I wanted to be there when he woke up? I couldn't even imagine a version of that going well . . .

But the nurse just turned her motherly smile on me.

"Don't worry, memory loss isn't uncommon after a head injury like his. Once the swelling goes down, things will start coming back to him." She turned back to Theo. "Let me ask you a few questions. How old are you?"

"Twenty-four." His eyes darted to me. "Right?"

I grimaced. This was worse than I thought. *Dear lord, Ellie, get out while you still can.*

"How old am I really?"

"Thirty," I said. Which I wasn't actually certain of, but he'd been a year above Bella, so two years above me. I had to be *close.*

Theo's face went slack with shock.

"Thirty? That's . . . Is she serious?" He turned back to the nurse. She nodded.

"That's right."

"But . . . how can I forget *six years* of my life?" He jerked around to look at me again, wincing at the sudden motion.

"Easy, don't go pulling out your IV." The nurse fixed him with a scolding look and he sat back slightly, face still tight with something approaching terror. "Like I said, it's not abnormal to experience memory loss after an accident like yours. But it's only temporary. There's no bleeding or extensive damage, just some swelling. You're very lucky your fiancée was with you. Things might have gotten worse if she hadn't brought you here so fast."

"Thank you," he murmured robotically, eyes going unfocused.

"I know it's scary, but things will start coming back to you soon. They do for almost everyone. In the meantime, just try to rest."

Almost everyone? Jesus, way to bury the lede.

Theo took a deep breath, seeming to force himself back into his body, and looked straight at me.

"So . . . you're really my fiancée?"

It felt like a drain had opened in the middle of my stomach and my entire physical being was being sucked down it. This was not a good idea, I should not stick to this, but the nurse was watching, *what other choice did I have?* I forced a weak smile.

"That's right . . . babe." Theo gave a confused frown at that. Apparently he was as much the "babe" type as I was.

The nurse was smiling pityingly at the two of us when the door whipped open and a woman pushed inside.

She was tall and slim, with long honey-blond hair that she'd either spent hours meticulously coaxing into gentle waves or that somehow just naturally had that made-for-reality-TV style. Her crimsoned lips were pinched tight, large brown eyes wide with anxiety, but somehow it just threw her pretty features into sharper relief, the lip purse pulling out the high cheekbones, the worry widening her eyes further. Though she looked a little rumpled, her tight high-waisted faux leather pants, shiny red heels, and airy white blouse were all obviously expensive. Especially the blouse; the stark simplicity of its lines signaled "luxury" more surely than any amount of ornament could (I should know—patterning shirts like that took twice the time of more intricate-seeming multipieced affairs). She was familiar, in that vague "Maybe I saw you grabbing coffee once" way, but I couldn't place her.

I wished I could, though. She gave off the sort of high-proof, full-throttle energy that I always seemed to jibe with, a crisp confidence threaded through with a hint of sharpness that wasn't everyone's cup of tea. But I loved it. What use is a dull knife to anyone? I didn't spot it very often—not that I'd been looking particularly hard for new people to slot into my life since I got back to Milborough—but when I did it was almost a guarantee that I'd at least respect a fellow human embodiment of *no bullshit,* even if we didn't wind up besties.

The pretty woman turned to me, offering a confused attempt at a smile.

"Sorry . . . I thought . . ." She licked her lips slowly, then her eyes hooked on Theo. He was sitting up straighter, mouth hanging open slightly.

"Sam? What are you doing here?"

"You're welcome for racing all the way from Boston. Anyway, I could ask you the same thing." She arched an eyebrow. "Most of the VPs I know manage to avoid massive concussions at *their* desk jobs."

Theo grinned sheepishly, hand going to the back of his head automatically. He grimaced again.

"This? It's from my MMA side gig."

"Ahhh, that explains it."

"I'm sorry, Miss . . ." The nurse squinted at Sam, then at the chart in her hands.

"Lindsay. Samantha Lindsay. Sorry, probably should have led with that." Sam flashed a smile too brief to count as apologetic. Of course she had two first names. Women who showed up at hospitals looking like that were practically *required* to have two first names.

"Miss Lindsay. Clearly you're acquainted, but we do need to limit visitors."

"Of course," Sam said, her air of polished professionalism reappearing all at once, like an atmosphere forming around her. "Theo's obviously doing fine without me. But I *did* get a call from the hospital, so I assumed it was fairly urgent?"

"You got a . . . Dear lord, this must be Arden again." The nurse's face pinched with annoyance. She turned to me, apologetic. "The new girl on reception keeps crossing her wires. Let me just check a few things . . . but you'll probably have to go, Miss Lindsay. Visitors are family only right now."

"But she *is* . . ." Theo stopped suddenly, drawing his chin back to his neck, as though to pull back the offending words, then turned to me, eyes widening. "I mean . . ." He blinked, glancing between Sam and me slowly. Something I couldn't read passed over Sam's face, but it was quickly replaced by a calm smile.

"You mean you should have changed your emergency contact years ago? Couldn't agree more. Especially since I have a call with my CEO in an hour and you've totally salted my prep time."

"Sure, but who was I gonna put on there instead, Chase? He'd probably stop on the way to the hospital to get stoned."

Sam stiffened, face going slack, all her polish stripped away in a moment.

"Chase? Theo, are you . . ." She turned to me. "Sorry, how bad was this injury?" She shook her head, trying to collect herself. "Actually, bigger sorry, I didn't even introduce myself. I'm Sam." She extended a hand and I rose to take it, her height even more apparent as I stared up at her.

"Ellie Greco. Theo and I are . . . I mean I'm . . ."

"Ellie's Theo's fiancée," the nurse supplied as she flipped through the chart. Sam blinked rapidly, clearly surprised. Which . . . same. "As far as the injury . . . Ellie, is it alright if I explain?"

"Oh, sure . . . please do." The nurse gave me another motherly smile.

"Theo's scans all came back clear. Temporary memory loss is common in cases like this. We're prescribing rest, hence the family-only directive. And on that note, I'm going to speak with Arden. I keep telling her to check the intake forms *before* she dives into patient records." The nurse bustled out. Sam glanced at Theo again, real fear tightening the corners of her eyes.

"It sounds like I should get out of your hair before the nurse comes back and really cracks the whip. Besides, I'm sure you two don't need me hovering. Theo, feel better. And for god's sake, update your emergency contact forms." She smirked at him, then turned to me. "Do you have a second?" She tilted her head toward the hallway, gaze intense, and I nodded, following her out of the room, a hint of subtly woodsy perfume, cedar and spices I couldn't place, marking the trail. She strode around the corner to a little waiting alcove, moving to the far wall and turning to face me.

"Be honest, how much worse is this than they're saying?"

"I mean . . . I think they're telling us everything they know."

"But he's completely forgotten about Chase." She tilted her chin down for emphasis. "That's not just run-of-the-mill memory loss . . . it's full-blown *amnesia*."

"I don't know about that . . ." I murmured, screwing my face into something between worry and gas pain. Hopefully that was the correct emotion for whatever Chase had to do with everything? *Dear god, I was in so far over my head.* Sam squinted in disbelief, her perfectly sculpted brows furrowing.

"What else would you call it? I mean, you two are engaged, you must know how deeply the accident affected Theo. And there was so much guilt tied up with it . . ."

"Of course. I just meant . . ." I licked my lips, stalling for time. *Who was Chase?* More important, if I owned up to this now, would she slap me, or just walk off in a huff . . . and then file a lawsuit later? *Fuck, fuck, fuck,* this was what I got for going with my spur-of-the-moment "flash of brilliance." Who fakes being someone's *fiancée?* Jesus, what if Sam and Theo had been *currently together?* The idea gripped tight around my stomach, clammy and cold.

"It's just . . . not the only major thing he's lost," I said weakly, dropping my eyes in a futile attempt to shield myself from the moment when she saw right through me.

"Oh my god, he's forgotten *you two*." Sam lifted a hand to her mouth. "I didn't even think . . . but if he can't remember Chase . . . God, I'm such an asshole." She rolled her eyes to the dropped ceiling, sighing heavily. I just nodded. Her inference wasn't *untrue*.

"I guess I'm just hoping this will pass quickly," I finally said.

"Of course it will. Ask anyone, I'm a total catastrophizer. Zero fun at amusement parks." She pulled a goofy, wide-eyed face and I laughed in spite of myself. Once more I felt that flash of camaraderie I'd had the moment I saw her. Bella always got on my case for not making more friends, but the problem was that I was waiting for this—that same spark of connection you got with romance. I'd perfected my pointless small talk over years of working at the deli, but I was fundamentally too introverted to crave interaction with anyone who didn't lock into place with me almost immediately.

"On that note, I'm *actually* going to leave now." She smiled reassuringly, gripping my shoulder briefly. "By the way, congratulations. Theo's a really great guy. And I'm guessing he's even luckier to have you."

With that, she whisked off down the hall, leaving me alone with the faded chairs and lackluster selection of magazines on the coffee table. *Could I just leave now?* No, I'd gone too far. Theo believed I was his fiancée, so did the staff, now this Samantha did. Something about spreading the lie to her, someone who not only clearly cared about Theo but who also fell into the narrow sliver of "people I might actually like, given some time," felt particularly icky. Even though I could practically *see* this thing spinning out of my control, it was way too late to turn back. Bracing myself, I walked back to the room, clenching my hands to stop them from shaking. When I got there, the nurse was clipping Theo's chart onto the bottom of his bed.

"There she is," the nurse said, smiling. "I'll give you two some privacy. But remember, it's important that Theo rest." She flashed a warning look at each of us. "Focus on getting better, okay? Everything will come back to you in time."

"Definitely," I said. *In fact maybe I should* also *just give you some privacy until you're totally healed or maybe until never, how's never talking again sound to you, Theo?*

With that, she hurried off to her next patient, leaving me alone with Theo and the lie I'd told . . . which, apparently, he now believed.

Six

Theo and I stared at each other, neither of us sure where to start.

"I'm sure you have a lot of questions," I finally managed. "Do you want to talk about what happened? Or—"

"How did we meet?"

"Excuse me?"

Theo pinched his eyes tight.

"I mean, I know we met in high school a couple times. Obviously. But . . . how did we get together?"

"Oh. Umm," I cast around wildly. What was the right answer to this? Where would a guy like Theo hang out? Shit, when had he even moved back to town? Trying to buy time, I forced an unconcerned look. "We don't need to go into all that right now. You heard the nurse."

"I need to know." Theo fixed me with his piercing stare. "Things might come back to me easier if you tell me some of this stuff."

I stared at him, sucking my lower lip between my teeth. Honestly, my brain was short-circuiting a little. I hadn't expected him to wake up missing six-odd *years,* extra hadn't expected to have to sell the lie to a woman who, whatever she was to Theo now, had once known him well enough to be the person he'd want there if anything bad happened. I was improvising as I went, which is why I said:

"We met at Major MacLeod's."

"Seriously?" His entire face pulled back in disbelief. "Why would I be somewhere like *that*?"

Right. I'd gone and named the . . . not *divey*, per se, but definitely townie bar a couple blocks from the deli. It was the kind of spot where the bartenders knew your name and order the minute the bell over the door pinged, and if they didn't, you probably weren't getting served for a while.

"I think maybe you and your friends were there, like . . . ironically?"

Theo nodded—*That makes sense*—and my fingers curled into fists of their own accord, because *of course* he thought he was too good for Major MacLeod's.

"And we . . . started talking?"

"Actually, I beat you at pool." Why not. I was already in *so* far over my head. And he looked so damned smug about my favorite bar.

Theo laughed.

"You seem like you'd be good at pool."

"What's that supposed to mean?"

"I don't know. You've always just had that . . . 'Who gives a fuck' attitude, you know? That artsy cool kid thing. People like that are always good at pool."

For a moment that stopped me short. It was the second time he'd called me a cool kid. And this time he was operating with only half a functional brain. Did Trip Taylor *actually* remember me from high school? And weirder yet . . . have a not terrible opinion of me? It was possibly stranger than the memory loss.

"I don't know about that," I said. "But I'm definitely better than *you*."

Theo grinned widely.

"Sick burn on the head trauma patient."

"Not brag, just fact." I mirrored his grin despite myself.

"Okay, so that was when?" He leaned forward, serious again. I could almost see him flip back into business mode as he tried to spreadsheet our "lives together." It surprised me—Theo was one of those automatically popular kids in high school, with looks, money, athletic ability. Usually those kids never really *tried*. Especially when Daddy had a business ready-made for them to fall into.

"A few years ago."

"Two? Three?"

"Theo, we can't go through our entire history now."

"Why not?"

Because it's all made up.

"Because you have to rest."

"Ellie, I told you—"

"No, I'm telling *you*. This can wait. In fact, I think I should head out so I'm not such a distraction." I started gathering my things. "That reminds me, I don't think they've called your dad, but if you want, I can—"

"Don't call him." A shadow of the Theo I'd seen in the meeting overtook his face, jaw set, blue eyes freezing over; it was the face of a man used to having his orders followed.

"Are you sure?" Not that I had Ted Taylor on speed dial, but I could probably manage *something* if I had to.

"Positive." His eyes narrowed. "You really think I'd want *him* here?"

Apparently the Taylors belonged to Tolstoy's hordes of uniquely unhappy families. Which honestly piqued my interest. Theo worked for his dad, he was Ted's spitting image, both genetically and by choice (no one *forced* him into that camel coat and scarf combo), but he seemed to have the same general feeling about the man as I did. *Just one more reminder of how unprepared you were for this shitstorm you strolled right into . . .*

"I thought a head wound might qualify as an exception." Luckily, that seemed to appease his suspicions.

"If things take a serious turn for the worse, we can revisit this."

"If we want to avoid that, you really should rest, okay? I can explain everything when you're more yourself."

Theo's face tightened with frustration, but when he tried to sit up fully, the motion set off what I had to imagine was splitting head pain—he gasped and leaned back heavily, his color draining.

"I know this must be really hard. It's hard for me too," I said. Pretty much the only true thing to pass my lips since the accident. "But you need to listen to the doctors."

"O-*kay*," he said. The petulant tone was almost endearing, like a little kid finally resigning himself to bedtime.

I started toward the door and he called out.

"Ellie, wait." He was frowning at me in a mix of hurt and confusion. "Aren't you going to say goodbye?"

That drain opened up again, body sucking itself inside out, but what could I do? I should at least wait until he was semifunctioning to explain the snap decision; if I did it now, it would just confuse him more. I crossed the room and took his hand in mine, squeezing once. He'd better not expect a kiss.

But he just squeezed back, an earnest look softening his features as he gazed up at me, eyes roaming over my face slowly, as if he was trying to commit me to memory.

"Sorry I don't remember us yet, but I will. And thank you. I do know I'm lucky you were there."

"Of course . . . babe."

Theo frowned.

"Do we really call each other that?"

I laughed, squeezing his hand another time before letting go.

"Definitely not. I don't know where it came from."

"Okay, good. I was starting to worry."

By the time I made it back to my apartment, my head felt like a kicked hornet's nest. I slipped my shoes off, crossing to the sewing table in the nook opposite the kitchen to throw my purse and coat over the top. Usually I felt a little pang of guilt for using it as a coatrack—I hadn't made anything new in months—but today I was too buzzy to even fully register it.

I sleepwalked into the kitchen and pulled a box of generic Cinnamon Toast Crunch out of the cupboard, eating it dry by the handful as I tried to order my thoughts.

It took me half the box to realize that wasn't going to happen without outside intervention. I pulled out my phone, opened my texts, then thought better of it, clicking the telephone icon in the corner.

"Ellie? Is everything okay?" Bella's voice was tight with worry, and a little echoey. It sounded like she'd ducked into one of the bathrooms at her work.

"Yes. I mean, no one's hurt or anything. Or, well . . . no one *really* important." If Bella wasn't over Theo ten-plus years on, that was her problem.

"Okay, good. Jeez, you scared me. Who *calls* in the middle of the day?"

"I know. But . . . it's kind of an emergency. I . . . may have convinced Theo Taylor that I'm his fiancée?"

"Sorry, *what?*"

I ran through the barest outline of the details.

"Wow. Okay. That's . . . okay."

"Yeah," I said. "So . . . what now?"

"Let me finish up a few things. I'll be there as soon as I can."

I hadn't exactly calmed down by the time Bella arrived, but I had effectively quieted the brain buzz through constant application of reality TV. Theoretically I could have opened the shop for a few hours, but the idea of trying to manage small talk with the Ruth Pinskys of the world actually set my teeth on edge.

"Sorry it took so long, I figured we'd need fuel," Bella said from the doorway, balancing a gigantic pizza box on one hand as she heeled out of her trendy black booties.

"Veschio's?"

"What do you take me for?"

Thank god Bella understood priorities. They made by *far* the best pizza in a twenty-mile radius, but they were at the very edge of that radius and refused to deliver to me, no matter how many times I tried to bribe them with deli leftovers. I crossed to the dated kitchenette.

"Wine?"

"Yeah, we're gonna need a *lot* of wine," Bella replied from the entryway. "I'll sleep over if I have to."

Fifteen minutes later we had settled into the squishy cushions of my faded hand-me-down sofa, the entire pizza box open on the scarred wooden coffee table, our wines perched at opposite ends.

"So he just . . . *believed* you were engaged?" Bella's second slice had sat untouched for several minutes now, the little grease pools in the pepperoni slowly turning waxy.

I nodded, stuffing a huge bite into my mouth. Clearly we reacted to stress differently.

"But why didn't you tell him you weren't?"

"Because the nurse was right there! And then this Sam woman came in and the nurse told *her*." My chest tightened uncomfortably as I remembered the genuine fear on Sam's face when she realized the extent of Theo's memory loss. Her so clearly *caring* about him made the lie feel a million times more uncomfortable. But I pushed that thought down; it was too late, and she'd left pretty fast. Odds were there hadn't been any real damage done there . . . right? Regardless, I didn't have time to worry about some stranger, there were more immediate concerns. "What if they'd . . . I don't know, called the cops on me or something?"

"I don't think they'd do that."

"No offense, but it didn't seem like the time to trust to everyone being good at heart or whatever. I mean . . . can *you* imagine Theo just taking that in stride?"

"No, probably not." She frowned, taking a meditative bite of pizza. "But you have to tell him sooner than later."

"Okay, I've been thinking about this all day, and I guess my response to that is . . . What if I didn't? I mean, it's not like I'd sleep with him or anything, I'd just let him believe we were a thing until the Mangia deal was off, then——"

"Ellie!" Her eyes went so wide I couldn't see the lids. "No! You'd be manipulating him, badly. He doesn't deserve that."

"You've met him, right?"

Bella's lowered brow expressed her disgust far more eloquently than words could have. And yes, I'd known it was a Hail Mary, but a tiny sliver of me had hoped she'd come back with "Interesting . . . and clearly a wise and considered option, allow me to help fill in the details of Theo's personal history to help the cause." After all, even Ted Taylor wouldn't be able to justify driving his son's fiancée out of business, right?

Actually . . . considering Theo's reaction to the mere possibility of phoning his father, I probably shouldn't be so confident about that. I pinched my eyes tight, leaning over my knees to scrape my fingers through my hair.

"Okay. Heard. But . . . what do I *do*, Bella? Once he realizes we're not together, he'll probably make it his life's work to shut down the deli just out of resentment toward the plebe who somehow caused the ceiling to fall in on him and then lied about being his fiancée."

"Ellie, Theo's not some comic book villain. You can explain that it was an impulse decision. You wanted to make sure he was okay!" Bella had one of those pitifully hopeful pained smiles on her face that practically screamed "You're fucked."

"And then, best-case scenario, I'm back where I started. Which, in case you forgot, is on the precipice of losing the deli forever. The one place Dad still feels real to me." I paused to blink aggressively.

Even putting it into words felt like someone shredding my chest with a rusty hacksaw. Bella laid a hand on my shoulder.

"It hasn't happened yet, okay? There might still be a way to save it."

"Sure." I didn't need to tell her it was a lie, we both knew it.

I was sorrow-munching my way through another slice when my phone lit up.

"Little Lord . . ." Bella frowned, then rolled her eyes. "I think Theo's calling."

"Fuck. Okay." Reluctantly I picked up, bracing myself as though he could reach through and slap me a return concussion.

"Ellie? Please say it's you, if the nurses dial Sam for a third time I'm going to lose my shit."

"No, it's me," I said with a weak laugh. "How are you feeling?"

"Fine. Even the headache's mostly gone."

"Does that mean your memory's back?" I tensed preemptively. *Here it comes . . .*

"Well . . . no, actually." The frustration in Theo's exhale was palpable. "Which is why they're forcing me to stay overnight. But the nurse *promised* I'd be out by tomorrow at noon." Theo's man-used-to-lackeys-doing-his-bidding tone told me he was fixing some poor nurse with an *or else* stare. "Could you pick me up then? If it's not too much trouble, that is."

I squeezed my forehead tightly between my thumb and forefinger, sighing. I'd hoped I'd have a *slightly* longer reprieve.

"I can make that work. Hazel's been looking for more hours, she can probably cover at the deli."

"Thank you. The nurse won't let me leave on my own, and the only other person I'm sure could do it is . . ."

"Don't worry, I won't make you endure your dad in your fragile state," I quipped, somehow certain that's who he was referring to. His relieved laugh told me I was right.

"If I didn't already love you, I would now," he said, then paused uncomfortably. "I mean . . . Well, I'm assuming . . . Anyway, thanks.

It means a lot." There was a scraping sound, then muffled conversation. "Okay, the nurse is trying to enforce her fascist sleep regimen again. See you tomorrow?"

"I'll be there," I said, dread oozing through my entire chest cavity as I hung up. Bella filled my wine glass, handed it to me, and squeezed my shoulder.

"It'll be better to just get it over with."

"Sorry, not buying it."

"Well, then, it's better than the alternative." I glanced up, eyebrow raised incredulously. A mischievous smirk tweaked Bella's full lips. "Didn't I ever tell you? Theo's a very . . . *physical* person."

"Wow, ew. Did I do something to piss you off?"

"Not yet. But if you do, I *will* go into more detail. Now, do you want me to tell you his order at Dottie's, or are you planning to go in empty-handed?"

Seven

"Remember, no screen time until this time tomorrow at the *earliest*. We're only letting you out this early because you're a good test taker." The red-haired nurse flashed a stern look at Theo. I had a sense they'd already waged this battle.

"Yes, I know. Talk to text only."

"I'm serious. You don't want to exacerbate your symptoms."

"Don't worry, I've got his laptop," I said. He glared at me, but the nurse seemed appeased.

"Alright, then you'll sign your discharge paperwork, the doctor will stop by for one last look, and you'll be free to go. But I expect you to come back if your symptoms worsen, deal?"

"Yes, yes, we've been over this." He gestured impatiently at her to bring him the papers. With a sniff, she dropped them on his tray and walked out, leaving us alone.

"Are you hungry?" I said, shaking the paper bag I'd brought with me. "I stopped at Dottie's."

A surprised smile spread over Theo's face as he pulled the still steaming egg-and-pepper-jack croissant sandwich out of its foil wrapper, a smear of the brown mustard Bella had somehow re-membered he topped it with oozing out the side.

"How'd you—" He stopped, then rolled his eyes exaggeratedly. "Right. *Fiancée*. Of course you know my order. Though Dottie's goes best with . . ."

"Hot coffee? Don't worry, I've got you." I picked up the card-board tray that was the second half of my weak attempt at a bribe and passed it to him. He plucked out a cup and took a long, grateful swig, then pulled the top off the other, dumped in three of the sugar packets I'd thrown into the tray, and swirled it before handing it over to me. I took a fortifying sip. I wasn't really holding out hope that his favorite breakfast sandwich would be enough to smooth over the steaming pile of betrayal I was about to heap onto his hospital tray, but at the very least I should have my wits about me.

"Thanks again for picking me up. I know it shouldn't seem like a big deal—we're engaged, you'd have to have a pretty solid excuse *not* to show up at my hospital bedside. Call it a side benefit of the amnesia, I'm way more appreciative of the little things right now." Theo flashed a mischievous smirk.

"Totally," I said, trying to smile through the rollercoaster stom-ach drop. "But there's actually something we should talk about. About us, I mean."

"If you're going to suggest eloping, the answer's yes."

"Not exactly." I gulped, nauseated, as saliva flooded my mouth. "The thing is—"

The door swung open and a middle-aged doctor shuffled in, thick-framed glasses trained on the chart in his hand.

"Theo Taylor? How are we feeling today?" The doctor smiled absently at Theo, then at me, before moving to Theo's bedside and lifting his wrist to take a pulse. "This is the fiancée, I'm guessing?"

"The one and only."

"Beautiful *and* thoughtful. Contraband food is a sign of true love as far as I'm concerned." The doctor dropped Theo's hand, noting something on his chart. "You're a very lucky man, Theo."

"Trust me, I know. Even if I don't remember all the reasons why, yet." Theo turned a painfully loving gaze my way, the deep blue eyes I was used to seeing in storm-on-the-ocean mode morphing into a gentle visual caress. I gulped more coffee to cover my queasy expression, focusing on the pain of the sweet-bitter liquid burning my esophagus. Maybe if I endured an actual physical injury, the conversation would somehow be less bad? Karma *should* work that way.

"Alright, everything looks good on my end. If your memory isn't back within the next few days, you need to call us."

"I *know*," Theo said in a teenage groan. "Trust me, the nursing staff has been very clear on that point."

"They've also been very clear with *me* that I should deputize your fiancée on this in case you decide that you know better than the entire medical profession. Ellie, if there's no change and he's too stubborn to call, please reach out."

"Of course." I nodded so fast something in my neck twinged. The coffee churned in my stomach.

"In that case . . . good luck, you two. Hopefully I won't be seeing you soon."

With that, the doctor rushed out. Theo stood, wincing slightly and reaching for his head, then started gathering his things, moving with exaggerated care.

"Theo, we really should talk," I said, heart crawling up my throat. Here goes everything.

"Can it wait until we're in the car? I hate hospitals, and I'm afraid if we don't leave now, they'll force me to stay another night."

"Sure," I said weakly. That, at least, I understood. We made our way downstairs and across the parking lot.

"Is this . . . my car?" Theo frowned as I slid into the driver's seat.

"No, it's mine." I placed my phone in the holder, nudging it so it wouldn't spring loose.

"Good. I was worried." He grimaced as he took in the interior of my Camry.

"Why?" Sure, it was a few years old—okay, close to ten—and it wasn't the luxury model, but it was perfectly serviceable.

"Because this would *not* make a good impression on clients."

"Luckily, deli shoppers are a little more forgiving on that front."

"So that's what you do? Work at a deli?" He looked at me with polite interest.

"Yes, I run my family's deli. Technically my grandparents own it, but I took over."

"Interesting." He frowned. "Weren't you in New York for a while after school? Doing something artsy?"

"A little over a year, yeah. Doing costume design. Not that I had any success at it." Had Theo actually given two shits about me back then? Interesting.

"And how did you wind up back here?"

"My dad died," I said tightly. "If I hadn't come back, I'd have forced my grandparents out of retirement."

"Oh. Okay." His eyes widened. "Sorry, I didn't mean to offend."

"You didn't." I sighed. "It was five years ago. Anyway . . . where to?"

"My place. You know where it is, right?" He looked at me expectantly and my stomach bungee jumped again. Somehow I'd allowed myself to briefly forget about the task in front of me.

"About that . . ." I licked my lips, took a sip of coffee to buy myself a few more precious seconds of *not* having Theo Taylor as my enemy.

That's when it hit me: He'd poured in *exactly three sugars*.

Theo knew my coffee order. Which meant his memory—at least some of it—was back.

My skin tightened all over, panic vising my lungs. Fuck fuck *fuck*. I hadn't exactly been looking forward to coming clean, but at least I'd have control over *some* portion of the narrative. Now he probably thought I was keeping up the lie on purpose.

But if he knew . . . why let the doctor think we were engaged? The Theo I thought I knew would have had a lawsuit ready before

I even walked into his room. Instead, he'd kept up the cute-couple charade for the benefit of complete strangers.

Questions flitted around my head too fast for me to catch their tails, but one settled down in the center of my brain and stared straight at me, the points of its teeth showing beneath a Cheshire grin.

Theo knew. And he was keeping up the act. For fuck's sake, *why?*

"Ellie? Were we planning on leaving, or . . ."

Theo's face was perfectly blank, a handsome, unreadable mask. Whatever was motivating the lie on his side, I wouldn't find it there.

Which meant the little shit was testing me. No, *toying* with me. He knew I was lying, and now he was trying to see . . . what, whether I'd say something actionable? If this was all going to explode in my face, I sure as shit wasn't going to let him think he'd outsmarted me. And besides, I had to find out *why* he would fake this. Just because he hadn't sicced a pack of lawyers on me—yet—that didn't mean the option was off the table. I started blinking rapidly, doing my best to mime fighting back tears.

"Sorry, I just . . . I'd hoped you would have remembered."

"Remembered what?"

"We live *together,* Theo. Obviously." I shook my head slowly, swiping beneath my eyes for effect. "But I know it's not your fault. It's just . . . hard to see the person you love look at you like you're a total stranger."

I glanced over just in time to catch his eyes narrowing before the expression melted into an aww-shucks shrug. Oh *I see you,* Trip Taylor. He was good . . . but not good enough. Though, to be fair, he was a little brain-damaged at the moment.

"I'm sure you'll be the first thing that comes back to me. Please know . . . I *want* to remember us." He glanced down at his feet, clearly aiming for wounded puppy, but nope, not gonna fly here, *this* woman isn't so dazzled by your jawline that she can't see through your frankly flimsy attempts to play her.

"Really?" I narrowed my eyes as though I was deep in thought, shaking my head slowly. "I guess it's hard to believe you're at a *total* loss on that front. You know, since you remembered how I take my coffee."

Theo stared at me hard for a moment, then his lips curled into a smirk.

"I was wondering if you'd catch that."

"Believe it or not, you're not the superspy you apparently imagine yourself to be," I spat, turning the key in the ignition emphatically. Unfortunately, I still didn't know where we were going, so peeling out dramatically would have to wait.

"I figured either you wouldn't notice, and I'd have more time to figure out your angle, or you would, and we'd cut to the chase."

"So?" I planted my fists on my hips, striking my best seated power pose. "What is this?"

"You tell me. You're the one who tried to convince me we're engaged."

"*Convince* you? Get over yourself, Theo, it was just crappy timing." He raised an eyebrow, every inch of him dripping *smug*. Apparently that had come back with his memories, too. "I told the EMTs that so they'd let me into your hospital room. I wanted to make sure you were okay—it didn't seem ideal for you to wake up in the hospital alone, with a head wound, and not have anyone there to even . . . I don't know, tell the nurses what had happened?" I relished his brief flash of shock. He hadn't planned on my motives being *good*. And I had walked in that morning planning to come clean, so it counted. "I didn't expect you to wake up without any memory of the last *six years*."

"That doesn't explain why you didn't tell me afterward."

"I panicked, alright? Is that what you want to hear?" I rolled my eyes as hard as I could, *Well done, jerk, you caught me.* "You were confused, the nurses all thought that's who I was, then that woman came in, Sam? And the nurse told *her* I was the fiancée . . . Which reminds me, who was she, even?"

"Sam's my ex." Of course he had an ex like that.

"Right, so . . . not the easiest audience. The point is, before I even had a chance to clear things up, they were getting complicated, so I just . . . went with it. I figured it could wait until you felt slightly better. And in case you didn't notice, I've been trying all morning to find a moment to tell you what happened."

"Fair."

I blinked, stopped short. I'd been expecting him to escalate things. We sat for a moment in silence. When it got awkward, I asked him for his address and typed it into the GPS. We were pulling out of the parking lot before Theo spoke again.

"Could you . . . tell me what happened yesterday morning?" Theo's gaze was fixed out the passenger window. He was clearly uncomfortable showing even this tiny sliver of underbelly. I bit my lip, staring briefly at his forehead, as though I could see what was going on inside.

"What's the last thing you remember?"

"A loud noise?" Theo's face scrunched with concentration. "We were talking in that room off to the side, there was a crash . . ." He sighed, shaking his head. "Then it's a blank until I woke up in the hospital."

"With six years of your life erased. Which is such a random amount of time—do you think there's a reason you lost those years, specifically?" I glanced over, intrigued despite myself.

He attempted a shrug, but his neck was so tight the tendons showed. Clearly he didn't want to discuss this further. I could press—a not small part of me really wanted to, after all, who gets *amnesia?*—but there was a more immediate concern.

"So your memory came back sometime overnight." Theo nodded. "And the first thing you decided to do was play happy couple for the medical staff?"

"Actually, the first thing I did was plan ways to destroy your life."

"Wow, scorched earth." Not that I would have played it differently, but I made sure to pull my most appalled face. Theo might remember meeting me, but he didn't *know* me.

"You can't blame me for being angry. I assumed you were trying to take advantage somehow."

"Not everyone's trying to take advantage of you, Theo." Trying to make sure he was okay so he wouldn't blame me unfairly for his head injury hardly counted. Besides, I'd made Jaime call the ambulance and everything. Even checked his pulse.

"Call it force of habit." He flashed a wry look that felt somehow intimate. "Lucky for you, the nurses meant it when they said they wouldn't let me out on my own." His eyelids lowered in languid annoyance. "And since looking at my phone for more than thirty seconds made it feel like there was an ax in my head, calling around until I found a better option wasn't going to be easy."

"So what . . . your urge to murder me just evaporated?"

He broke out into a genuine grin.

"I didn't say *murder*. I'm a Taylor. We litigate."

"Same difference," I retorted, mirroring his smile in spite of myself. "Anyway, what changed? I don't see any packs of lawyers."

"I couldn't get out on my own, and you were already planning to show up by noon, so I decided to use the morning to sort out *why* you might make up this lie."

"I just told you—"

"I'm simply explaining my thought process. Unless you'd rather not hear it?" He cocked an eyebrow, his entire arrogant *Of course you'll want to listen to what* I *have to say* expression belying the words. I gritted my teeth and forced myself to nod.

"Like I was saying . . ." *Oh for fuck's sake.* "I was trying to work through what you might get out of the setup. It certainly wasn't the pleasure of my company."

"I've never said—"

He flashed a knowing grin.

"Trust me, my ego can handle it. Suffice to say we're both . . . *strong* personalities." I shrugged acknowledgment. "Since that wasn't the likeliest motivation, it had to be something else. The answer I kept coming back to was Mangia."

Oh. Shit.

"What do you mean?" I said, trying my best to channel Bella, *I can't even* follow *your thinking it's so far from what was actually going through my head.* Theo's smirk deepened.

"I mean that if you *were* my fiancée, I'd hardly bring a direct competitor into the market."

"Oh . . . I guess that makes sense."

"Which is where my proposition comes in." I frowned as I nosed the car into the parking lot of Theo's condo building.

"If you want some sort of tithe for getting you to the hospital safely, you're out of luck. Especially since I'm gonna need to save all my pennies for the moment you drive me out of business."

"Actually, I think that's something we might be able to avoid . . ."

"Oh? And how's that?" I pulled into a visitor spot near the building entrance, turning to Theo. "Let me guess, we'll show up to your office with a tray of sandwiches *so good* even your dad's heart will melt, and he'll choose amazing capicola over millions of dollars?"

"Don't be silly, Ellie, Ted wouldn't be at the office." Theo smirked. "My plan is much subtler. And likelier to succeed. Come on, you *must* see it." He raised an infuriating eyebrow. I shook my head once.

"Enlighten me."

"It's simple, really." Theo's eyes sparkled with repressed glee. "We *stay* engaged."

Eight

"I'm sorry . . . you want us to do what now?" Whatever I'd expected Theo to say, it wasn't this.

"Come inside and I'll explain. I think you'll see it makes perfect sense for both of us." Theo tilted his head toward the gigantic Greek Revival building, its central peaked roof balanced by small domed cupolas on either wing. It had been a municipal building through the fifties or sixties, its functions absorbed into the brutalist behemoth over in Andrew's Point, a consolidation of the state that felt very visually symbolic in retrospect. They'd chopped *this* building up into condos in the nineties, but I'd never seen any of them. Honestly, I was a little surprised Theo inhabited one. I'd pegged him as a brand-new-build sort of guy, or maybe a gigantic-loft-apartment-with-exposed-everything type—one of those places that were obviously expensive but totally devoid of personality.

"Yeah . . . no. Not really how I was planning on spending the day." Yes, I *had* proposed a very similar plan to Bella just last night, but I hadn't really *meant* it. Besides, if Theo wanted it, there was no way it was going to benefit me.

"That's not what you told the doctors."

"I'm sure you can manage getting to your couch without me."

"Humor me. After all, if you don't make sure I'm safe and sound, I might have to call Ted. And if he has to schlep down from the house in Stowe, he might accelerate the Mangia deal out of spite. Toward me, in case that wasn't clear."

I sniffed in annoyance. There was no way Theo would call his dad and we both knew it; whatever their relationship looked like, it clearly wasn't close. But beneath my irritation—it was incredible how much smug Theo could pack in around those well-formed lips—a strong current of curiosity was already springing up. If nothing else, I needed to know why Theo *didn't* want Mangia. Even if I passed on the fiancée setup, there might be something there I could use . . .

"Fine. But only because I'm an incredibly good Samaritan."

"I'm sure that's the first thing everyone says about you."

We made our way through the columned portico into a wide, airy lobby. A heavy wooden doorframe showed a glimpse of a tidy mailroom to the left. Closed doors to the right bore brass plates I couldn't make out.

"Theo, my man! I've been looking for you." A short, solidly built man in jeans and a worn work shirt emerged from a hallway at the back of the lobby, smiling broadly. He was fiftyish, with a bushy mustache and a thick shock of salt-and-pepper hair, his broad face deeply tanned and creased with the array of wrinkles you got for smiling too often. "I managed to get ahold of my buddy, he thinks he found some doors like what you wanted."

"I knew I could count on you." Theo grinned and leaned into the man's handshake-cum-backpat. "Hopefully Ellie likes them as much as I do, otherwise he'll have to resell them for me. Ideally at a profit."

"Oh yeah?" The man looked at me with mild interest. "You a decorator?"

"Not by trade . . . but she *does* get final say." Theo pulled me into a sideways hug, smiling affectionately. "Gotta stay out of the doghouse."

"Ahhh, so you two are an item."

"Wait, have I really never introduced you?" Theo pulled away, feigning shock. "Mike, Ellie's my fiancée. Ellie, this is Mike Delmonico, the best building manager in Milborough, and an excellent middleman for all things reclaimed."

"Fiancée? Holy shit, bro, you didn't tell me you were engaged!" Mike's mouth fell open in cartoonish shock.

"I didn't?" Theo's forehead creased with confusion. "Well . . . I suppose it's pretty new. At least I think that's what you said?" He turned to me expectantly. I blinked, unsure what Theo wanted me to say.

"Don't you . . . know?" Mike's bushy brows caterpillared toward each other.

"I mean . . . I *will* know, all the doctors promised me that, but . . . Ellie, you tell him. It's a little hard for me to talk about." Theo turned away, eyebrows tenting with pain.

"Oh, well . . . there was an accident yesterday," I said cautiously. Theo nodded tightly, which I was *fairly* sure was a signal to continue. "Theo took a pretty serious hit to the head. He's been experiencing some memory loss."

"Holy shit, like . . . amnesia?" Mike's mouth dropped open again. I nodded and his eyes went wider yet. "Fuck, dude. I see that in the movies, but I've never *known* someone that happened to."

"Apparently it's more common than you'd think," Theo said with a dramatic sigh.

"Do you have to get knocked on the head again, or . . . I mean, that doesn't seem safe. All that stuff you hear about football players and concussions . . ."

"No, his memory should come back on its own soon," I said. "Most of it's already back. There are just a few gaps that still need filling in." Mike nodded dazedly, still gaping.

"That's wild. So you're saying . . . you forgot your fiancée?"

"No, no, just the proposal." Theo flashed a pained smile. "Which I'm hoping will come back to me soon. It sounds like I really swept her off her feet."

"That's right. We were out in the Berkshires for a little mini-vacation, and Theo rented out an entire inn so my family could be there. It was like something out of a cheesy movie." I turned a fawning look on Theo, batting my eyelashes for good measure. "But that's Theo, you know? He loves a *spectacle*." Theo's jaw tightened slightly, but he nodded along.

"Sounds like him alright," Mike said with a laugh, clapping his meaty hand on Theo's shoulder. "Well, shit, man. Congratulations. To both of you. Ellie, I'm sure I'll be seeing you around. And if you don't like the doors, you just tell me and they're gone. Happy wife, happy life, that's what I always say." He tilted his chin down, poking Theo in the chest as though he were imparting deep, unique wisdom, then headed back down the hallway he'd emerged from. I waited until the doors of the elaborately framed elevator had closed on us to turn on Theo.

"I never said I was in on this 'fiancée' scheme."

His smirk was infuriatingly superior. He swiped a fob over the black pad at the bottom and pressed the 4L button.

"And yet you just told Mike our engagement story. Thanks for making me sound like some Hallmark movie lead, by the way. Rented out the whole inn? Invited your family?" He wrinkled his nose in disgust.

"It seemed like your style."

"Well, I suppose that's the story we're sticking to now." He sighed. "Too bad you weren't the one with the bout of amnesia. Then I could gently remind you that I'm not nearly so basic."

"Okay, back up. Why are you pretending to still have amnesia? And why tell Mike we're engaged at all?"

"I mentioned the amnesia so we'd have an excuse if we contradicted each other. I thought that would be obvious." Theo flashed another maddeningly superior expression.

"Is that part of your *brilliant* fake engagement plan? Because it sounds kind of tedious to maintain."

"Not long term. I just figured we could use it as a stopgap today. From here on out, I'll remember every glittering moment of our whirlwind romance. Which, by the way, *needs* to have been fast. No one will buy it otherwise."

"Trust me, Theo, no one will 'buy it' regardless."

"Oh, I don't know about that. Especially considering how much Mike loves to gossip. Once enough people know the same story, it tends to take on a life of its own." Somehow his smirk grew even more self-satisfied. How Bella had ever dated this princeling was beyond me.

The doors to the elevator opened, and Theo gestured for me to go first. I emerged in a narrow hallway that eventually let out into a high-ceilinged kitchen in black and white, somehow simultaneously modern and classic, half trendy real estate design blog, half ancestral manor.

But as much as my fingers itched to try out the Wolf range gleaming at the back, my eyes were drawn to the left, where the ceilings opened up to cathedral height. A stone-fronted gas fireplace running from floor to double-high ceiling anchored a seating area, the furniture clustered around a generous Oriental rug in front of it an eclectic mix of clean modern styles and ornate antiques. Everywhere I looked there was some interesting detail—original molding running up a wall, maybe meant to frame out a judge's bench; elaborate carving along the heavy wooden ceiling beams; double-height windows with intricate paneling that cast tessellated shadows across the honey-colored wood floors. I followed Theo to the seating area and perched on the edge of the couch. He sprawled across the other half, infuriating smirk still in place.

"Well?" I finally said. "I believe you were going to explain why I'd agree to keep up this little farce?"

"I think it's obvious why *you'd* agree." He sipped his coffee casually, eyeing me over the top.

"Yes, we both know I'm not psyched on Mangia. But you are."

"No, I'm not. Mangia's Ted's idea."

"He runs the company. If it's what he wants, it's what will happen, right?"

"He's on the letterhead." Theo's gaze darkened. "He hasn't *run* anything in years. He just swoops in occasionally to tell us peons to scrap everything we've been working on and do whatever bullshit out-of-date idea popped into his head in the infinity pool that afternoon." Theo sniffed. "I happen to think that building could be put to much better use. But Ted's made sure I don't have the authority to make that decision. None of us who actually *work* there do."

That sounded . . . messy. And familiar. Bella used to have a Boomer boss who operated on much the same "functionally retired but unwilling to let go of the reins" principal. It was a big part of why she eventually left that job.

"What sort of use?"

"Does it matter?"

"I'm your fiancée, Theo. Don't I have the *right* to know?" I gave him a simpering, eyelash-fluttering look. He sniffed out a laugh.

"Fine. I'd like to preserve the architectural beauty of the space. Initially I was thinking luxury condos, but honestly, residential development isn't something I'm interested in pursuing, and it's outside the company's current purview. Lately I've been thinking . . ." He inhaled deeply, as though steeling himself. "Mixed use. First floor commercial, and a private renovation to turn the rest of the building into a single-family home. It's still in the ideas phase."

"I mean . . . obviously I don't know what you're imagining, but why *would* Ted agree to that?" I tried to keep my incredulity off my face but failed. There was no way it would be as profitable. Plus, who in Milborough could even afford a home on that scale?

"Trust me, there are very good reasons he should at least consider it. Especially when his remaining—" Theo swallowed hard, eyes clouding over with something that almost looked like pain. "That is, since I'm the one asking. But family never has meant much to him, he's proven that *very* definitively." Bitterness curled Theo's lip.

I frowned, unsure how to respond. Clearly something else was swirling beneath the waters of Theo's "preserve the architectural details" plan, but we barely knew each other, and it felt uncomfortably personal.

"As is, he refuses to bring my idea to the board for a vote," Theo said brusquely, his tone a definitive door slam on any deeper motives. "But that was when my idea was battling unarmed against a Mangia-sized payday. Even he would have a hard time driving my fiancée out of business."

"You sure about that?"

"No, but it's our best shot." He sat up, pushing away self-doubt through force of posture. He was near enough that I could smell him, a deep note of leather mixed with the slightest hint of pine needles and a whiff of fresh laundry. "Here's what I'm proposing. You and I *stay* engaged for the time being. It won't be easy, obviously. Getting the word out through Mike was a good start, but we'll have an uphill battle convincing . . . well, *anyone,* really."

"True. Everyone I know is aware of what I think of people like *you,*" I said between gritted teeth. Theo's eyebrow shot up in mute agreement.

"Still, if we play this smart, and we have a tiny bit of luck, I think we can both get what we want out of the arrangement."

"Play it smart?"

"Well for one thing, we can't go around saying we've been together *a few years.* I mean . . . come on, Ellie."

"I'm sorry, next time I'm panicking about you getting knocked out on my watch, I'll make sure to work out our fake-dating timeline more clearly in advance."

"No need, I've already thought it through. If we lock down a few major details—a six-month dating timeline *tops,* for example— I think we'll be able to convince people." He scooped up the coffee jauntily. "So? Are you in?"

"No. Hard no. I'm gonna chalk it up to the head injury, but this is a *terrible* idea," I said. We had nothing in common. I didn't even *like* him. There was no way it could work . . . right?

"Why?" Theo gazed at me over the rim of his coffee cup.

"For one thing, we don't know each other, like . . . at *all*."

"How well do people ever *really* know each other?"

"Name one TV show I've binged recently. Hell, name literally anything I've liked ever."

"Studded black leather chokers."

"What?" I squinted, genuinely confused. "Is that supposed to be like . . . a bondage reference? Because I have *zero* intention of telling you what I like in bed, with or without this asinine setup."

"Honestly? I'd probably have an easier time guessing what you like in bed than what you binge-watch." Theo flashed a startlingly intimate smile. A warmth flared between my legs, which was frankly traitorous, but those lips were objectively *perfect*. "But as it happens, I was referring to your fashion sense. You used to wear them in high school. The chokers. They were part of your whole . . . *look*."

"Wow, okay. Unfortunately all my chokers got sent to Goodwill around the time I packed for college."

Theo waved a hand, in what I was starting to realize was a very characteristic—and maddening—gesture.

"You're missing the point. No one's going to quiz us on what we're watching. And anyway, we'll iron out enough of those details to fake it. Anything we forget to cover . . . well, one of us gets to create the canon. Like you did with that awful engagement story." His face twisted with disgust. I couldn't help but laugh.

"I'm not sure it's that simple," I said slowly. Meanwhile, a tiny bud was shooting out of the soil in the very darkest, most tucked-away region of my mind. *Why* couldn't *it be?* After all, we didn't need to make it down the aisle, we just needed to make it through a few weeks.

"I say it is. Any mix-ups from the last couple days we chalk up to the lingering effects of the accident. My hospital discharge papers specifically *mention* amnesia, who could argue with that?"

I pinched my eyes closed, shaking my head rapidly to clear the haze of some part of me actually starting to agree with him.

"Okay, but it's not just anyone we have to convince, right? Don't you think your dad will see through us?"

The corner of his lips twitched at the "us" that had slipped in when I wasn't paying attention.

"I see Ted at quarterly board meetings and whenever he decides to swoop into the office to impress a golfing buddy. The man's delusional about plenty of things, his business acumen not least among them, but even he knows better than to think he's up to date on my personal life."

"If things are that . . . strained between you, how would this help us?"

"Ted cares a lot about appearances. Hence refusing to actually retire, despite not putting in a full day's work in years. It might make him seem *old*." Theo rolled his eyes. "Trust me, he won't push Mangia through if my 'fiancée' would be directly affected, at least not until he can come up with some tortured explanation for why it's actually better for everyone. Think how it would *look*."

"If you hate him so much, why do you work with him?"

"I don't actually have to work with him very often." Theo shrugged, attempting—but not quite managing—to look unbothered. "But trust me, he'll hold off on the deal until he can figure this out. Which buys us time to lay track. And the more people that know about our relationship, the more pressure Ted will feel. Even if *he* might be willing to fuck you over, he wouldn't want the whole town to *think* he'd do that."

"And what about Sam?" The words popped out before I'd even considered them, but as soon as I'd spoken, I realized she was the thing still nagging at me. The look on her face in the hospital, the deep anxiety when she'd realized how bad things were. Lying to Mike had just been a logistical concern, but what about the people nearer to our respective orbits? Could we really do this to them?

"What about her?"

"She dropped everything to rush to the hospital. You two obviously have history."

"We do," Theo affirmed with a tight nod. "And like most history, it's in the past. If anything, Sam would want to *help* us pull this off. She knows what Ted's like." A rueful smile stole over his face. "So? Any more straw men you want to raise?"

I took a sip of my coffee, long since gone cold, mainly to avoid Theo's incisive blue gaze. I shouldn't do this. If *Trip Taylor* wanted it, there had to be a catch, one that certainly wasn't going to hook on to *his* slick exterior.

But what choice did I have? The idea was beyond crazy, it was almost guaranteed to blow up in my face, but if I didn't try it, and Mangia came in . . . could I ever forgive myself? Even thinking of closing the doors on the deli—Dad's deli—made my throat constrict. And really . . . what was the alternative?

"Let's say I'm considering this," I said. "I have some conditions. If either of us decides it's not working, we pull the plug, no questions asked."

"Of course."

"And I get to tell my family what's going on." He could take whatever risks he wanted with Sam, I was *not* keeping the people I loved in the dark.

"If you think that's wise, I can't stop you." His nose scrunched involuntarily.

"And—"

"Ellie, you have to trust me."

"No, I don't."

"Then trust that we both want this to work. I mean . . . I could have just sued, right?" A twinkle of mischief flickered across the surface of his blue eyes.

I sucked my lips between my teeth, looking for the loophole he was going to slither through at the last second, but I couldn't find it.

"Fine. I'm in."

"Good. Then why don't we break for now, and you can meet

me back here tonight. There's a lot to go over, we should get started immediately."

"What's the rush?"

"I've always been a firm believer in tackling the absolute worst tasks on your to-do list first. Which means introducing you to Ted by the weekend. So? Reconvene at seven?"

The arrogant tilt of his lips set a tendon in my jaw twitching, but I didn't have prior plans to cancel, and besides, he was right. I nodded.

"Excellent. I think this will work out very well for both of us." He extended his hand. I gripped it hard enough that he'd know not to fuck with me.

"By the way, I prefer being on top."

"Excuse me?" A quizzical look overtook his strong features.

"In bed. I like to be on top. I know I said I wouldn't tell you, but if we're *engaged,* you should probably know what you're getting into, right?"

Theo stared at me for a long second, the flush creeping past his collar giving me a perverse sense of satisfaction.

"Noted. And for the record? I'm happy to wear a studded leather choker occasionally. Just to spice things up."

Nine

"Holy *shit*."

I'm not sure what I expected the Taylor family home to look like—a ten-thousand-square-foot modernist monstrosity, maybe, or why not an actual castle, they certainly *thought* they ruled over all us plebes—but all my ridiculous fantasy versions paled in comparison to the stunning mansion we were pulling up to, set far enough back from the street and ringed round with a tall enough tree barrier that it couldn't be sullied by commoners' eyes. Yes, the house *was* huge—if it had been ported away from its expansive lawns to my part of town, it probably would have covered half the footprint of my apartment building—but it was annoyingly *tasteful*.

It was a weighty-looking colonial, wide stretches of molded white trim on all the windows, walls, roof, crisply offsetting the butter-yellow color. The front entrance connected to another at the right-hand side via an expansive stretch of porch, imposing two-story columns surrounding both the unseen side door and a second-story balcony. At the corner of the porch, an elegant stone firepit was surrounded by loungers that probably each cost more than my rent.

Everywhere you looked were little architectural details, the kind you only saw in homes with real history: lattice-paned fanlights tucked beneath the dormers; a delicate stained-glass porthole above the columned entryway; a goddamned *widow's walk* on the central roof. As if anyone whose husband died in this behemoth would have anything to wail to the heavens about.

No wonder Theo had been so charmed by the condos in the old courthouse. He'd grown up in a homier version of the *entire* courthouse.

"Is something wrong?" Theo glanced at me from the driver's seat. I'd offered to meet him here—I didn't particularly like being chauffeured, it felt unpleasantly . . . *dependent*—but he'd insisted that "explaining away" my car would derail us, even after I'd tried to pull the recent-major-concussion card. Now that I was seeing his child-hood home, I understood his thinking.

I gazed at the perfectly landscaped walkway, somehow lush even in late winter, the holly bushes bordering it practically bursting with waxy green leaves and red berries.

"I just . . . understand you better now."

Theo's eyes narrowed as he threw the car in Park in front of the three-carriage garage, since tastefully converted for modern needs.

"That sounds suspiciously like an insult."

"How could I ever dream of insulting my dear *fiancé* here at his *ancestral manse*," I sing-songed, fluttering my eyelashes Theo's way for effect.

"If that's how we're playing it, we should probably do another quick rundown of the rules," Theo said, flashing a wry, close-lipped smile. It ignited something in my chest—the pleasure of sharing a secret, maybe.

"We've been over this a million times."

"Which means a million and one can't possibly be that hard. Besides, we've only had two days to cover everything."

"Three." If you counted today.

"Humor me."

I rolled my entire head—eyes were not enough here. I'd learned, *very* quickly, that Theo was a strong believer in thoroughness.

"Rule one," Theo started, ticking on his fingers. "We don't bring up Mangia."

"Yes, yes, don't lead with the business." I huffed out an exasperated breath. "Rule two, cheek kisses *only*."

That had been my addition to our game plan. Trying to mime real passion not only felt like a surefire path to being found out—there was a reason I'd wanted to design costumes, not strut across a stage—it was just uncomfortable. But absolutely *no* physical affection would be an even bigger tell.

"I've been thinking about that. Are you okay with some light touching?" Theo's business negotiation face, all strong jawline and the barest hint of a frown, felt extremely at odds with the words coming out of his mouth.

"Such as?"

"Hand on the small of the back. Reaching for your hand occasionally." He demonstrated the movement, stretching across the center console to take my hand in his, squeezing once as he gave me a surprisingly believable look of tenderness. I blinked down at our entwined fingers, trying not to focus on the dry warmth of his skin, the way his large, strong fingers seemed to slot into mine, the perfectly gentle pressure of the squeeze—I'd always despised limp handshakes, but a bone-crusher was even worse.

I cleared my throat and nodded.

"Just don't overdo it."

"Wouldn't dream of it. And the most important thing to remember is—"

"The four-month timeline. We've been over this, Theo."

"Actually, I was going to say that Ted's almost definitely going to throw some barbs my way, but act like you don't notice them. And we're going over it because it's important, Ellie. I think our story works. Ted knows he and I aren't close—considering how little he's involved with the business now, I probably only sit in the same room with him half a dozen times a year—but maintaining the *appearance* that we are is important to his self-image. I think he'll believe that I'd propose without telling him about you, especially with the timeline, but it will annoy him to feel out of the loop, so expect a minor temper tantrum. It's something we have to accept to have any hope of keeping Mangia out. Oh, and he'll—"

"—be suspicious if we bring it up right away. Theo, I *know*. The word *mangia* will not pass my lips. Even though I am an Italian American whose life's work revolves around food and eating."

"Okay, but—"

"No buts. You have to trust me."

"Do I?" The dim light of the car interior sparkled across his deep-blue eyes. "Do I really have to trust the woman who became my fiancée *during* my concussion?"

"*Another* thing we've been over more than once." I raised my hand as he started to speak. Dear lord, it was exhausting being around someone as used to dominating a conversation as I was. "I'll remind you, this was your idea. Plus, now that we're doing this, I need it to work. This is life and death for me."

"So I should trust your killer instinct?"

"Trust that I have much more on the line than you do if we don't pull this off."

He held my gaze for a long moment, lips curling with a hint of amusement. That same heat bloomed in my chest as he leaned closer, taking my hand in his again and pulling it toward him, rubbing a thumb over my palm in a way that gave me shivers. He bent closer, until I could feel his warm breath tickling the hairs at the nape of my neck, his voice barely a whisper as he murmured:

"Good. Because I'm sorry to tell you, we are now officially under scrutiny."

I started to turn, but he caught my cheek with his other hand, leaning in to press his lips against it. My movement put him slightly off course, and they landed just where my jaw met my throat, their pressure soft but insistent. I forced myself to stay absolutely still, entire body tingling with anticipation . . . or something else. *This* was why we had rule two. Bodies just *responded* to certain things.

"We're being watched?" My voice sounded breathier than it had any right to.

"We are." The words hummed over my skin. "But I think we're passing the first test. Well done, Ellie. This will make sure we pass the second."

He opened the center console, pulled out a small box, and handed it to me. "Ted might not notice if you're not wearing this, but Marta definitely will."

I frowned and pulled it open. Inside was a small ring box, and in that . . .

"Seriously?"

The diamond nestling on the pillowy satin had to be at least . . . what do I know about carat size, but it was *big,* the flourishes of gold scrollwork punctuated with smaller diamonds on either side barely noticeable next to its heft.

"I believe it's considered traditional to propose with a ring," Theo said.

"Okay, but this must cost . . . Actually, I have no idea *how* much this would cost."

"Me neither. It was my mother's, I don't know what it appraised at last."

"Your mother's? Theo, what if I . . . I don't know, lose it in a pot of sauce or something?" I dropped the box into his hand and shied toward the door, trying to physically distance myself from the far-too-expensive object.

"Then fish it out." He smirked. "It's a ring, it's not nuclear. Millions of women wear them every day without incident. Here."

He plucked the ring out and put his other hand out expectantly, gazing at me from beneath lowered brows. Unsure what else to do, I extended my left hand. Theo took it carefully in his, squeezing ever so lightly. Even though I knew it was fake, that this was just my costume, a warmth spread outward from my chest as I watched him solemnly slip the ring onto my finger. My gaze felt drawn to his as he finished, and I found him looking at me intently, something unreadable in the swirling depths of those dark blue eyes. For a moment, we just stared at each other, then, with a small cough, he dropped my hand, nodding once, sharply. I frowned at the ring from a couple angles until the weirdly vertiginous feeling swirling through me dissipated, then waggled my fingers. As promised, it stayed put. In fact, it somehow seemed to fit perfectly.

"Oh . . . *fine,*" I said, rolling my eyes as I tugged my hand away. The warmth of Theo's touch lingered on my skin. "But if something happens to it, you can't blame me."

"Noted." I sucked in a breath that I hoped didn't sound as shaky as it felt, flipping open the visor mirror and making a show of checking my makeup until my heartbeat finally felt close to normal. "So? Are we just going to sit here, or are we going to convince Ted I'm his soon-to-be daughter-in-law?"

Theo grinned, pressing the button to turn off the engine and getting out in one smooth motion. Before I could stop him, he was opening my door. I should have found it annoyingly patriarchal, but there was something touching about how automatic the gesture clearly was.

"It's that sparkly personality that made me so *sure* you were the woman for me, Ellie Greco."

I couldn't help but laugh as he presented his arm. I took it, grateful for the stability on the slightly slick stones (heels are *not* a big part of the routine in a deli), and together we walked to the door, both pointedly ignoring the silhouettes in the room to the left of the entryway.

Theo barely had a chance to press the doorbell—and I'd had no time to comment on his ringing the doorbell at his family home—when the door opened on a tall, slender woman, her long auburn hair tousled in that casual way that took hours to achieve. She was extremely pretty, with wide eyes and plump, glossy lips, but she felt very . . . *effortful.* I, for one, had never bothered with false lashes for a weekday family dinner.

I knew it wasn't his kid sister—Cat looked more like Theo, plus her vibe was more ripped band tees and tattoos, less Real House-wives of Milborough. But I couldn't place her, which was . . . concerning.

"Theo. How lovely to see you." The woman wrapped him in a perfumed hug, rich with vanilla and sandalwood. His entire body stiffened as he lifted one hand to her back, fingertips barely grazing the fabric of her simple but elegant dress, the draped neckline and three-quarter sleeves allegedly demure while the full-body cling of the bias-cut silk left nothing to the imagination. It was impressive construction, actually. The seamstress still buried deep inside me couldn't help but wonder how, precisely, it had been patterned.

Eventually, she released Theo, and he stood, his approximation of a smile not quite reaching his eyes.

"Marta. Nice to see you again."

"*Ohhh,*" I said before I could catch myself. Marta was the stepmom—of recent vintage, and off social media, so I hadn't had a "cheat sheet" photo to work from. Theo hadn't said much about her—it was clear from his clipped tone when he mentioned her that he wasn't her biggest fan—and one of the extremely pertinent details he'd left out was that she couldn't have been older than thirty-five (and if she *was* thirty-five, it was an extremely-well-maintained plumped-and-Botoxed thirty-five).

Marta turned to me, a questioning look on her face.

"Is everything alright?"

"Yes, definitely, I just . . ." My eyes darted sideways to Theo. His amiable expression hadn't slipped but his entire body had tensed. ". . . really love your dress. I'm not sure if Theo told you, I design clothing myself. Not professionally, but . . . well, I know enough to appreciate something that well made."

"Oh, thank you so much!" I exhaled as she smiled widely, eyes flicking over my own outfit, visible through my open coat. I'd opted for a vintage mod dress I'd picked up at Lauren's store, navy velvet with white rickrack trim. Even with tailoring to move the shoulders in, so that it draped better over my even-too-flat-chested-for-the-mods figure, it didn't fit me anywhere near as well as Marta's dress fit her. "It's McQueen."

"Of course." As though I had any idea what a McQueen dress looked like in real life.

"But come in, come in," she said, voice warmer as she held the door open. "Ted will be so excited to see you."

We followed her inside, leaving our coats in the capacious entryway closet before heading into the room to the left.

Unsurprisingly, it was stunning, and *massive*. On the far wall, a gigantic fireplace with a picture-perfect blaze crackling inside was surrounded by a carved-wood mantel, shelves on either side filled with a handful of books and the sorts of *objets* that clearly cost a mint—slightly abstract bronze statues; a gigantic, weathered buoy with the name of some ancient vessel hand-painted along its side; a smattering of photos in elegant frames. The display was eclectic but tasteful, in a way that felt slightly staged . . . which shouldn't have been surprising, considering how long the Taylors had been in commercial real estate.

The furniture was festooned with ornate Empire-style swoops and curls, the printed satin, brocade, and velvet upholsteries absolutely pristine. The only out-of-place piece was a single deep leather chair just next to the bar cart, its crystal decanters all filled with brown spirits.

Sitting comfortably in said chair with one leg thrown over his knee, lowball glass in hand, was a man who could only be Theo's father—he was older, the skin on his face creased and browned by years on a golf course (I assumed), but the resemblance was striking. And next to him, perched prettily on the edge of what I *think* counted as a "settee," was . . .

"Sam?" Theo's voice betrayed genuine surprise. This we *hadn't* planned for.

"Theo. Ellie. Nice to see you again." She smiled at each of us in turn. "I'm sorry, I didn't mean to intrude on your family dinner."

"That's no problem, you're practically family." Ted's avuncular tone sat awkwardly on his crisp, suited shoulders. Theo's grip on my

hand tightened. "And I'll gladly let you go if you'll give me a decision . . ."

"I haven't decided, but you've given me a lot to think about,"
she said, a professionally noncommittal smile on her red lips.

"What are you two scheming about?" Theo said.

Sam gave him a long, assessing look, then turned it on me ever
so briefly before replying.

"Until I've thought about it, I'd rather keep it under wraps. Either way, I really should get going." Before Ted could stop her
again, she rose, flashing me a "*That* was awkward" grimace as she
passed. From the entryway she called out, "Ellie, I'd been meaning
to ask about next weekend, do you have a sec?" Smiling apologetically at Ted, I hurried after her.

"What about next weekend?" I said as she shrugged into her
coat.

"There is no next weekend, I just wanted to check how Theo's
doing. I doubt he'd appreciate my calling it out in front of Ted," she
said with an amused smirk. It was too bad my entire relationship
with Sam was premised on a lie—I legitimately *liked* her.

"Better, though he's still getting headaches. The doctors want
him to take it easy, but his memory's back at least."

"That's great." Her gaze went distant as she nibbled at her
lower lip. "Does that mean he'll have to drop out of the sailing regatta this year? Seems risky, especially if there's any weather."

"Oh, umm . . . TBD. The doctors aren't keen on it, but you
know how Theo can be when he's set on something," I said with a
loving eye roll. Thank god she'd specified *sailing* regattas. For all I
knew, Theo might be the type who rowed competitively. It felt like
lacrosse's natural counterpart. Sensing a chance to make up some
lost ground, I decided to lean in a little harder. "Though I will be
sad if we can't get out on the water at *all* this summer."

"Do you two sail a lot?"

"I wish. By the time we got serious, it was way too cold. But he
promised he'd take me out as often as I want come summer."

The sound of my name briefly drew my attention to the other

room. When I turned back, Sam was staring at me, something inde-finable flickering behind her eyes. *Hurt, probably. Because whatever Theo might say, you* know *this woman cares about him in the present, not the past.* But I couldn't let guilt derail me, tonight was too important. She wasn't my responsibility, and it was too late to turn back regard-less.

"You should probably get in there." She tilted her head toward Ted.

"Right . . ." I grimaced. Sam smirked knowingly.

"Don't worry, you've got this. Just . . . be yourself." She held my gaze a moment longer, then turned to call out. "Thanks again for the drink, Ted. We'll talk soon."

"I'll hold you to that, Samantha."

She opened the door, mouthing *Good luck* before heading out into the cold night.

Back in the main room, Theo was bent over the bar cart, two glasses in hand. He quirked an eyebrow, crystal tumblers raised in query, and I nodded fiercely, the desperation hopefully not *too* obvi-ous on my face. Lips twisting in amusement, he cleared his throat, busying himself with the ice bucket as he spoke.

"What was Sam here about?"

"Possibilities," Ted said, swirling the liquid in his glass and tak-ing a long sip, eyes boring into me in an unapologetically assessing glare. "I'm guessing we'll be seeing a *lot* more of her around here. But I'll let her share the details when she's ready."

Theo rolled his eyes at the bourbon but said nothing. When the silence started to crawl around the back of my neck I coughed.

"It's so nice of you to have us over for dinner."

"It's the least I could do if you're *really* going to marry my son." He stared at me a few seconds longer, then, without moving an inch from his recumbent position, extended his hand languidly. "Ted Taylor, by the way. But I'm guessing you knew that."

I gritted my teeth as I crossed the room to take it. One of the more dickish power moves, that.

"Elle, isn't it?" he said, squeezing my hand in an almost-bone-crusher.

"Ellie, actually. Ellie Greco." I tried to force a happy expression as I endured the handshake. "Nice to finally meet you, Ted."

"It's hardly *finally*. Didn't the two of you only meet a few months ago?"

"Well . . . yes. But now that we're engaged . . . it seemed important."

He raised an eyebrow in what could have been mild amusement or tightly controlled annoyance. Now that I was really looking, the resemblance to Theo was startling, as though someone had slotted him into one of those digital aging programs police departments used (all this *and* the Taylors get to age that well? Unfair). They shared the same strong jawline and brow, the same trim, athletic frame, and the shape of Ted's mouth, though more sharply drawn, with a hint of coldness in its twist, was reminiscent of the curves of Theo's annoyingly attractive lips. You could even tell that Ted's hair, lightly salted now, had once been the same brownish-blond as Theo's. But Ted's eyes—a flat brown bordering on black, their narrowed gaze calculating to a degree that felt almost predatory—couldn't have been more different. I had a sense that no matter how slickly pleasant Ted's expression, they never sparked with warmth.

"Usually I'd ask guests to join us for the cocktail hour, but it's nearly time for dinner." Ted's eyes flicked to the hefty gold band on his wrist that I'm sure he referred to as a "timepiece."

"Oh, I didn't realize—" I started.

"I told you we couldn't be here until seven, Ted." Theo handed me my bourbon before slipping an arm around my waist. Somehow I managed not to startle at the warmth of it, apparent even through my velvet dress and thick winter tights. "I wasn't going to ask Ellie to close her shop early."

"Yes, *shops* can be demanding. In any case, we should head in. I'm sure Betsy's waiting on us."

He rose and, without a backward glance, strode through the double doors at the back of the room, Marta clicking along just behind him—she clearly wasn't slowed down by *her* strappy stilettos. Ted and Marta turned left, and Theo guided me after them with a hand at the small of my back, bending to whisper as we passed a gigantic marble-everything bathroom.

"You're doing great, we knew he'd be . . . prickly. Just remember the rules."

Instead of responding, I gulped down some bourbon just before we turned in to another expansive room, the walls covered in an elaborate navy-based flowers-and-vines wallpaper. A weighty dining table dominated the space, long enough to easily seat twelve. A gigantic gold chandelier sparkled over the center, an upside-down wedding cake hung with hundreds of teardrop crystals.

Ted seated himself at the head, and Marta was waiting behind the chair at the opposite end. Theo dropped his hand from my back, flashed me a single determined grimace, then moved to the left side of the table, leaving me to slide into the seat opposite. Ted barked out a laugh.

"I like to wait for the hostess to sit. But I suppose that's not *everyone's* custom."

"Oh . . . sorry, my family's pretty informal."

"You don't say?"

I stared at him wide-eyed, then at Theo, who simply shook his head once as everyone else sat in quick succession.

We waited in awkward silence as the housekeeper, Betsy, poured water and wine, then served wedge salads studded with Roquefort and bacon. As she set mine in front of me, I turned to catch her eye.

"Thank you."

She frowned, then nodded once and retreated rapidly. Apparently we didn't talk to the "staff."

"You have such a lovely home," I ventured as I sliced into the lettuce, a lava flow of bleu cheese dressing oozing over it.

"Thank you," Marta murmured, taking one tiny bite before pushing the plate away. "I've been working on updating the décor, but it's such a long process."

"Marta has a background in interior design," Theo said, sipping his wine. "She actually used to work for the company. It's how she and Ted met."

I couldn't help but wonder how old she'd been when they "met." Not to mention what Ted's marital status had been at the time. God, I'd have *so* much gossip for Bella once I dragged myself through this.

"Well, you clearly have excellent taste." Marta flushed slightly, saving her smile for the leaves she was shuffling around the salad plate. I had a depressing sense that she didn't receive many compliments about her skills. At least not the ones she'd put on a résumé.

"I agree, of course. But I must say I'm more interested in *you*." Ted stabbed a chunk of lettuce. He still wore that same politely disinterested smile, but his gaze felt like a threat, a wolf who'd spotted a wounded bunny. "You're a *butcher*? Do I have that right?" Exaggerated incredulousness dripped from every feature.

"Umm, no," I laughed, the awkwardness so thick I could practically feel it congealing around me. "I run a deli. It's here in Milborough, Greco's Deli?"

"Hmm. Doesn't ring a bell." He shrugged, pushing his plate to the side and leaning back, wine glass in hand. It was clearly a signal, because Betsy bustled over to clear all our salads. How very lord-of-the-manor. "Have I seen you at the club?"

He could only mean Belle Glen, the country club of choice for Milborough's upper crust. Like most of the towns nearby, Milborough had a fairly even mix of the generationally wealthy and the generationally townie; Belle Glen was very much the enclave of the former.

"Not yet, no." I stretched my grin as far as it would go. "Though Theo's promised he'll teach me to golf one of these days."

"He'll have to. We Taylors have always been avid golfers. Theo practically grew up on that course. It's where you and Sam first connected, isn't that right?" Ted said, feigning casual. "I'm sure you know they were an item, Ellie. Before Theo let her slip through his fingers, that is. Though . . . maybe you didn't know that, this whole thing has been fairly rushed." He gestured between us, lip curling.

"When you know, you know," I said, smiling weakly.

"Who could have guessed *my* son would 'know' in just a few months?"

"Ellie's family has been in business over a hundred years, isn't that right, Ellie?" Theo tipped his head toward me, studiously avoiding his father's eyes.

"Yes, that's right. We've been in our current location—it's downtown, just off Washington—since the nineteen-forties. But before that my great-great-grandfather had a door-to-door business."

"How quaint. Theo always has loved small-town charm." Ted sipped his wine lazily. "Isn't that why you're so attached to the old Taylor's building?"

"Not primarily. Though I think you know that." Theo's Adam's apple bobbed rapidly, but Ted just shrugged. Whatever was going on between them, it did not seem likely to ease the tension in the atmosphere.

"We're really proud of it," I said, trying to channel Bella's cheery *all friends here* tones. I downed a huge slug of my own wine, too-bright smile never slipping. "Of course it's nothing compared to your business," I added. Seeming impressed with Ted's prowess had to count for something, no?

When I glanced at Theo his eyes glinted with some message I couldn't decode. I took a few deep breaths to steady myself. *Just ignore the vibes and keep trying to win him over, even if you'd rather claw your own eyes out,* I reminded myself. *Don't let him get under your skin.*

Betsy came around with the next course, filets with asparagus and an artful swoop of mashed potatoes, béarnaise sauce glistening over the top. I sliced into my meat to find the center deeply rare.

"And the two of you met at a bar?" Ted's eyes were on his steak, making it impossible to read his expression.

"Yup!" I tried to push some liveliness into my voice. "Major MacLeod's. I beat him pretty badly at pool." Theo and I had decided that element of the story I'd panic-spun in the hospital worked well enough that we shouldn't mess with it.

"Come on, I put up a good fight." Theo grinned at me.

"Keep telling yourself that, Taylor." I stuffed a bite of steak into my mouth. I wished it wasn't so good, especially since I knew for a fact it hadn't come from my shop.

"And how long ago was that?"

"Right around four months ago."

"I love a whirlwind romance," Marta said with a gentle smile.

"Theo, none of this feels *hazy* to you?" Ted said, turning to his son with a raised eyebrow. I took a sip of wine, grateful for the brief reprieve. "You mentioned some memory loss just after the accident," he added, mouth twisting with a hint of disgust.

"Luckily, it was limited. And brief," Theo said, expression rigorously controlled.

"I just wish his awful taste in music could have been permanently erased," I said lightly, hoping my tone felt spontaneous, though the interjection had been strenuously rehearsed. Apparently Ted liked women with "spunk," so light ribbing was highly encouraged in tonight's little performance. To think I'd assumed Theo was overstating Ted's . . . *Tedness*.

"Matter of taste," Theo quipped back.

"I'm just saying, we're not playing any frat boy faves at the wedding."

Theo laughed genially. He'd insisted on mentioning the memory loss—*It never hurts to have some extra cover*—but we'd agreed it was wisest not to led Ted think he'd been seriously incapacitated. Still, I could feel my armpits going damp in the close-fitting velvet dress. Could Sam have told him anything? I'd given her a different timeline in the hospital. And Ted seemed to have an awful lot of questions about our "history" . . . though that could just be because, according to Theo, their only reliable interactions were the semi-annual board meetings Ted swooped into town for.

Luckily, instead of pushing back from the table and bellowing *J'accuse,* Ted simply sighed.

"I suppose that's lucky." He raised a bloody bite to his mouth. "We'll just have to hope it's not impacting your long-term decision making."

"But the engagement happened *before* the accident, isn't that what you said, Theo?" Marta said from the other end of the table. Ted's head jerked up, but she was focused on slicing a thin strip of steak.

"That's right. Just last weekend, actually." Theo swallowed hard, then pasted on a dazzling smile. "When I booked the trip I'd only been thinking about a romantic getaway, but . . . I suppose I just couldn't help myself."

"Can I see the ring, Ellie?" Marta held her hand out expectantly and I placed mine in hers. *Smart thinking, Theo.* "Oh, that's *gorgeous.* Ted, isn't it gorgeous?"

"It looks like you've spoken to your mother about this." Marta glanced up and, noticing Ted's simmering fury, she quickly dropped my hand, lowering her eyes to her plate. Not exactly a loving father's response, but Theo's quick nod my way told me we were on track. Apparently this fell within the expected range of *Ted.* Exhaling shakily, I focused on my food again. *This wasn't going* so *badly . . . considering . . .*

"Mom gave me the ring years ago, Ted. You know that."

"You must have swept my son off his feet." Ted skewered a piece of asparagus. "Proposing in just a few months with a family heirloom? It's certainly . . . unexpected."

"To me, too! Though I don't know if it was *me* doing the sweeping." I chuckled, not quite sure where this was going.

"Oh, I just assumed." Ted stabbed a chunk of filet and held it a few inches over the plate as he leaned across the table to peer at me. The meat bled slowly onto the porcelain below, *drip, drip, drip.*

"Why do you say that?"

"You're just so different from the other girls Theo's dated." He stuffed the meat into his mouth, chewing slowly. "So much more . . . *salt of the earth*." His eyes dragged over my dress, which fuck right off, vintage mod clothes are cool even if they *are* obviously polyester. "And of course we actually *met* them before Theo went so far as to propose."

"One of my favorite things about Ellie is how down to earth she is," Theo said, not bothering to make eye contact with his father. I couldn't tell whether he was chewing, or if biting back his words had become a physical endeavor.

"Don't get offended, I'm just surprised. Would you ever catch Olivia at Major MacLeod's? Or Sam?" Ted laughed at the absurdity of that idea—clearly Olivia, whoever she was, was *far* above my local. Sam . . . I could have guessed that.

"You met Olivia what . . . three times? In two years? I'm not sure you know her as well as you think you do, Ted." Theo tossed it out so casually it was clear he always referred to his father by name, even to his face. "Anyway, all the more reason to change up my MO. Clearly the approach I used in the past wasn't working."

"Maybe. I sometimes wonder if you didn't simply give up too soon," Ted mused. Wow. Didn't even bother to look at me as he slipped that knife under my ribs.

"Have you been by the club lately?" Marta said softly. "There's a new chef in the dining room, we really like him."

"No, Marta, it hasn't been high on the priorities list," Theo snipped.

"Oh, well . . . when you have a chance." Marta's smile looked strained. She was clearly doing her best to redirect us toward casual dinner conversation but . . . "uphill battle" didn't even begin to describe it.

"All I'm saying is I'm surprised you two 'knew' in such record time," Ted said, pointing his fork between Theo and me, eyes fixed firmly on me, "when you're so clearly outside each other's usual circles."

I dug my nails into the top of my thigh, swallowing hard. Hopefully I hadn't snagged my tights. We all chewed in silence for a few minutes, my heart rate *very* slowly descending as I focused on the food, the flavors of the rich cabernet, *anything* that could keep me from actually baring my teeth at this—Mimi was dead on—complete prick.

"I'm sorry, I just can't get over how fast you two are moving." Ted leaned back and threw his leg over his knee. "You're sure you're not rushing into this?"

"We're sure," I said, hand tightening around my steak knife. I forced myself not to stare at Marta. If *those* two had been "together" for more than a year before Ted put a ring on it—affairs don't count—I'd eat my hat.

"And you don't feel . . . *out of your depth?*"

"Ted, what are you—"

He cut Theo off with a raised hand.

"Our world can be overwhelming to someone who wasn't raised the way you were, Theo. Different sets of rules, different social cues . . ."

"Don't worry, the existence of country clubs isn't as hard to understand as you might think." My lips were twisted so tightly I knew it had to look like a throwdown, but I couldn't, for the life of me, manage to unwind any. *Keep your temper,* the little Bella in my head said. But *god,* he was so *infuriating.* No wonder Theo made a concerted effort to keep his distance.

"Don't get worked up." Ted raised his hands in mock defense. "I'm only trying to look out for *you.* Once the honeymoon phase passes, it can be very difficult to build a life with someone you don't have much in common with."

"Just look at you and Mom, right?" Theo said, voice flat. "Though you really didn't come from such different worlds, at least not at the start. It was only later that the club became such a *part* of us." Ted's jaw bulged.

"I'm simply warning you, as your father, against rushing into something that's very difficult to extricate yourself from. I'd think the example of your mother and me would make you think long and hard about jumping into marriage too quickly. Forgive me, but if she's really 'the one,' why is this the first time we're meeting her?" He flung his knife my way, still not looking at me.

"Maybe because you're never around, *Ted*." Theo's voice was even, but I could see a vein popping out on his temple. "Anyway, I wouldn't dream of cutting your time at the lodge short. I know how much you hate missing out on the Stowe *season*. And before that was your annual Maldives month. The directive at the office was 'Do not disturb unless the ship's sinking.' I didn't figure this qualified." Theo's lips formed the approximation of a smile, but his eyes flashed dangerously.

"*Our* relationship isn't my concern, Theo. Proposing inside of four months . . . I suppose Ellie really *must* have hidden charms." Ted raised an eyebrow, tapping a finger on the rim of his wine glass. Silently, the housekeeper moved over to refill it.

"I like to think my sparkling wit and incredible pool skills are obvious," I said, doing my best to pull a Marta and get this back on track but sensing that this Hail Mary was too late. "Anyway, we really aren't rushing. We haven't even set a date." I could feel my pulse throbbing in my neck. My family could be a pain in the ass, but this smooth-smiling death by a thousand passive-aggressive jabs was nothing I'd ever encountered before.

"But you two are resolved to continue down this path."

"I mean . . . yes?" I squinted at him.

"We're engaged. The important thing is how much we care about each other," Theo said.

"See, that's where we disagree. Forgive me for saying so, *Miss Greco*, but when someone like *you* winds up with someone like my son, especially when the timing is recklessly fast, the first question that comes to mind is what you're after." Ted shrugged, a *Someone had to say it* look on his still handsome features. The smugness made me want to spit fire.

"I'm *after* finding someone who makes me happy."

"Oh? And you just happened to find that with my son, who's poised to inherit a multi-million-dollar company—"

"Ted," Marta said, eyes widening.

"No, let's spell it out. Clearly Ellie isn't the type to pick up on subtext."

"Jesus, Ted, what is *wrong* with you?" Theo shook his head, blatant disbelief on his face.

"What's wrong with *you*?" Ted turned his ire on his son. "You've had serious relationships with several women who would fit into this family perfectly. For you to bring home this . . . this *butcher,* and tell me you're planning to *marry* her the first time she even deigns to meet us . . . Is it meant as some sort of rebellion? Or is this all just a result of that head injury?"

"For god's sake, be civil. Be happy for us."

"I'll be happy for you when you give me a single reason to believe this is a good decision." He turned to me, narrowing his eyes. "Or answer me this, why avoid meeting us sooner? You must have known we'd see through you, even if Theo was too infatuated by your . . ." His eyes raked over my body, the implication crystal clear. *"Charms."*

Who the fuck did he think he was to talk to me that way, like I was some gold-digging slut, just because he'd managed to make a few dollars? I could almost *feel* my blood bursting into flame, the oil slick of Ted's thinly veiled contempt catching all at once.

I slammed my knife and fork down, dimly registering Marta's startled jump.

"Actually, avoiding you was *his* decision," I spat, disdain dripping off every word. "Frankly, he would have avoided this forever if I'd let him. Now I understand why."

"I'm not sure I take your meaning."

"Oh? So no one has ever told you what a pompous, self-impressed *asshole* you are to your face?" I feigned confusion, eyes wide. "That surprises me. Since you clearly can't turn it off for even a single fucking *dinner* with your *son*."

Ted's forehead clouded with anger.

"How dare you speak to me that way in my own home?"

"How dare *you* speak to your son's fiancée like she's some money-grubbing piece of trash? Fuck that, how dare you talk to Theo like he's some idiotic child?"

"Ellie, I don't need you to—"

If there was a warning in Theo's tone, I was too far gone to hear it. I leaned forward, teeth bared.

"News flash, Ted, Theo and I get along precisely because I'm *nothing* like the people you'd choose for him. And I love him because of who he is, not how much money he's set to inherit. Not that you'd understand anything as *quaint* as that." I lifted my wine glass and gestured around the room, on a roll now. "And by the way, congrats on Grandpa and Daddy getting you this house. They must have been so impressed with what a great job you did staying rich."

"We're done here." Ted pushed back from the table abruptly, his face so red it was shading purple. "See yourselves out."

And with that he strode past us, and past his guppying much younger wife, her little bleats of "Honey? Honey . . ." ignored as he disappeared down the hallway.

"I'll just . . . check on him," Marta said, face frozen in deer-in-the-headlights shock as she scurried after her fuming husband.

Without Ted there to stoke my rage, the flames quickly guttered, leaving nothing but sickly, sooty shame behind.

"Theo, I'm sorry . . ." I reached across the table, trying to catch his attention more than his hand, but he just shook his head once, sharply, lips pressed tight.

"We'll talk in the car."

With that, he rose, his physical movements eerily reminiscent of his father's, and strode out the way we'd come, leaving me to slink after him, embarrassment and anxiety surging through me on a geyser of flush.

For someone who needed this more than she could even fully admit to herself, I was doing a remarkably good job of fucking things up as much as possible.

Ten

Theo held my coat out for me, and opened the doors of the house and the car, but he wouldn't meet my eye or speak a word as we pulled out. Had I ruined everything because I couldn't endure an hour of passive aggression from Ted Taylor? All I'd had to do was bite my fucking tongue, and instead I'd—

Theo rolled to a stop as soon as we were out of sight of the house. His hands gripped the wheel tightly, knuckles a white-capped mountain range, gaze trained on the BMW logo between them.

"Theo," I started. "I know that didn't go how we planned. But you have to understand—"

And then he burst out *laughing.*

"*Wow,*" he choked out. "That was just . . . *wow.*" He shook his head, tears glistening in his eyes.

"Are you . . . alright?"

"Are you kidding? This is the best I've been in *years.*" He wiped at his eyes roughly, laughing even harder. "Did you see his *face?*"

I bit my lower lip against the grin overtaking my face.

"Honestly? I was worried he was going to have a stroke."

"It would serve the fucker right, he's caused enough of them." Theo exhaled heavily as his laughter petered out. "I mean, Jesus, even for *him* that was intense."

"Yeah, I think we can safely say that I am *not* Ted's ideal daughter-in-law." I flashed Theo a sheepish look. "And that was before I ripped him a new one."

"Well, I'm glad you did. Not only did he one hundred percent deserve it, it was the funniest thing I've seen in years." Theo shook his head as the two of us exhaled a few last chuckles. "Seriously, though . . . I'm so sorry. I had no idea he'd be that bad."

"Really?" I squinted in disbelief.

"He's self-important, obviously, and he's got a lot of bullshit ideas about the *right* way to do things, but even for him . . . Honestly, the way he went after you?" Theo's eyebrows went sky-high. "I'm really sorry for making you go through that. If I'd known . . ."

You didn't know because you've never tried to force someone from the wrong side of the tracks on him before, I somehow managed not to say aloud. Slicing deli meat, nursing, those weren't Ted's idea of *high-end* careers, even if you could live very comfortably off them, even in a place like Milborough. It shouldn't have surprised me that this hadn't occurred to Theo, but it was the kind of blind spot only someone with as much as Theo had always had could afford.

Still, right now it felt like we were on the same team—Ted hadn't exactly spared his son, after all—and disaster though the night had *clearly* been, that felt like a win worth preserving. *See, Bella? I can control myself . . . sometimes . . .*

Theo was reaching for the gearshift as the wispy curl of dread crept back in, smoke off an approaching fire.

"Theo." I put my hand on his wrist to stop him. He turned to me, eyebrows raised in question, and I quickly pulled away. "I know it was kind of funny, but . . . was that *smart*?"

"What do you mean?"

"Pissing your dad off like that." I pulled my lips between my teeth, frowning. "I mean . . . the point is to keep Mangia *out,* and now that he officially hates me . . ." I couldn't finish the sentence. We both knew Ted Taylor was *exactly* the type to drive someone out of business as petty revenge.

"Ahhh . . ." Theo sat back in his bucket seat, angling himself toward me. In the dim light of a nearby streetlamp, his expression looked soft, gentle even, despite the knife's-edge cheekbones and jawline. He stared at some point just over my shoulder, considering. After several seconds, I couldn't take it anymore.

"You do think I've ruined it, don't you? Fuck, why can't I just control my *temper*?" I raked both hands through my hair, frustration pulsing through me. *What was* wrong *with me?*

"No, I really don't," Theo finally said, shaking his head slowly. "You certainly haven't convinced Ted to join your fan club, but we didn't really *need* that. And honestly . . . it was never going to happen anyway."

"Thanks for the vote of confidence," I muttered, voice teenage sulky.

"It's not a referendum on *you*," Theo said, chin tilting down in a way that was intrinsically a little patronizing. "What you're failing to understand is how important family is to Ted."

I laughed sharply.

"Did we just sit through the same dinner?"

"I didn't say *happy* families are important, but blood is. He may not like you, but our coming here at all means I've chosen you, and he knows that."

"Pretty sure he's set on doing anything he can to make you *un-*choose me."

"Maybe. But he's tried to force the issue before, and it's never worked. Appearances matter to him. The more people who know we're together, the worse he thinks it looks if things don't work out. Especially after what happened last time." Theo sniffed out a mirthless laugh.

"Last time?"

I tried to keep my voice casual. I couldn't help but be curious about the exes who had clearly managed to win Ted's favor. In fact, some part of me, deep down near the base of my spine, felt a little . . . *prickly* about them. I tamped it down—we weren't actually a couple. Hell, Theo was pretty much the *last* man I'd ever want to wind up with. Clearly the noxious atmosphere in the dining room had permeated enough to cause mild hallucinations.

"It's a long story," Theo said, flicking "last time" aside with his hand. "The point is, Ted wants to present a united front, regardless of what he actually thinks about this, or you. Honestly? I'm starting to think that that was the best way we could have played tonight. I'm surprised I didn't think of it earlier."

"How do you mean?"

"I mean . . . clearly we're not the Cleavers. Ted can pretend he was surprised I didn't bring you around before proposing, but he knows as well as anyone that family dinners for the Taylors are usually some sort of business necessity."

"How often *do* you all get together?"

"Do client dinners count?"

"Of course not."

"Then once, maybe twice a year."

Obviously I knew family didn't mean the same thing to Theo as it did to me—I'd just witnessed *very* strong evidence of that—but the idea of a family that all lived within spitting distance seeing so little of one another didn't quite compute. Mimi laid into someone at the dinner table every other week, but it would never have occurred to anyone to stop showing up. Or even to hold on to the anger past the end of whatever tiff happened over the tiramisu. That was just *family* . . . right?

Theo must have seen my bafflement.

"Would *you* want to carve out more time with Ted if you didn't have to? And bear in mind I'd have to really work for it, he's usually at one of the vacation homes these days."

"No, definitely not. But—"

"My sister and I feel the same. Actually, she feels that *much* more intensely than I do," Theo said. "By the way, I decided to follow your lead and tell her the truth about us. It seemed like the best way to get her support. Besides, she genuinely *would* have been upset with me for not introducing you before now."

"Sure, okay." I nodded, ignoring the twinge of anxiety at the pit of my stomach. Technically, besides Bella, I *hadn't* told my family the entire truth. I might have mentioned "working together to get rid of Mangia" without adding unnecessary details like "as a fake couple. Fake-*engaged,* to be precise."

Those were future Ellie problems.

"I still don't get how you figure making Ted hate me was the *smart* play."

"Because you really are the last person he'd expect me to end up with."

"Wow. Really selling it, Theo."

"What I mean is . . . If I wanted a wife that's just an accessory, I'd have found her years ago. Ted knows that. But you're very clearly not going to play the role of happy helpmeet to the Taylor empire."

"He expects that for you? A . . . *helpmeet?*" The word practically *tasted* dusty, it was so antiquated.

"He might want it for me, but I've made it very clear I'm not going to be carrying on the family tradition there." Theo's gaze drifted to some unknowably distant point on the night-dark street. I had to repress the almost physical urge to ask for more details. "The point is, for me to tell him I'm serious with someone who's so obviously not the person he imagined . . . I think it made him nervous."

"So he was extra shitty to me because I'm the anti-Marta?"

"He was extra shitty to you because deep down, some part of him *believes* this whole thing."

I sat back in the stupidly comfortable leatherette seat, turning it over in my head. It made a weird sort of sense. Ted Taylor was clearly used to getting his way . . . but whatever had happened with the other women Theo had been with, the proverbial deal had never been sealed. I was starting to get the sense that Theo didn't outright stand up to Ted very often—if working at the family company wasn't proof enough, the dinner was a pretty clear demonstration—so for him to throw *me* in Ted's face . . .

Tingly excitement fizzed through me. Theo was right, Ted would see it as the equivalent of a full frontal assault, a battle so obviously guaranteed to be bloody that his son would never waste precious resources on it without good reason. Impulsively, I reached for Theo's hand, grinning widely as I squeezed it. He glanced down, raising an eyebrow, but for the second time in the last few minutes, he didn't pull his hand away.

The static electricity that skittered up my arm at the touch was probably just nervous tension over realizing he thought it was strange. Nothing more.

"You really think we've convinced him?" I said, releasing his hand, determined not to let this feel weird.

"I think tonight was a *very* good start." His soft smile loosened the anxiety coiling through me. "But it's only that. A start. He needs to believe in this totally for Mangia to come off the table." Theo faced forward again, putting the car in Drive and pulling out onto the road in one smooth motion, one hand on the wheel, the other engaged in making his points. "Our next step has to be convincing other people."

"Sir, yes sir."

Theo's mouth tightened, but he didn't turn to me.

"I'm serious, Ellie. Like I said, appearances matter to Ted. It's one thing to resent the Taylors for doing well, it's another to have *proof* that Ted's mercenary enough to drive his own future family out of business. Closing down Greco's Deli might not bother him now, but if you *were* a Taylor? Think how that would *look*." He pulled a faux-scandalized expression, eyes flashing appreciatively when I laughed.

"Whoa there. You know I'm not taking your name, right? Like . . . ever." Theo's mouth twisted in amusement. It was amazing how much more interesting it made his otherwise almost aggressively Ken-doll features.

"Oh? And why's that?"

"You said we need people to believe this. They'd never buy me taking *anyone's* name unless I'd taken the blow to the head."

"Noted. Just don't tell Ted until you absolutely have to. You're far enough down his shit list without adding feminist to your tally of offenses."

"Don't worry, I plan to avoid ever speaking to Ted again unless you force me to. Which maybe . . . there's no reason to go there?" Theo threw me a single-raised-eyebrow, *Good fucking luck*. "Fiiine. Then just as long as I can avoid it, I suppose."

"Always the best plan with Ted," Theo confirmed, nodding sagely.

"Okay, now I *have* to ask. 'Ted'?"

"Come on." Theo lowered his eyelids conspiratorially. "Can you really see *that* man as a 'Dad'?"

I couldn't help but laugh.

"Okay, but when did it *start*? I have to believe there was some point when you called him Dad."

"I suppose it started . . . around six years ago." Theo didn't look at me, didn't shift his expression, but his posture went a hair more rigid, as though he was bracing his entire body.

"Six years? Like the amount of time you *actually* lost at the hospital?" I said slowly, testing with each word how safe the ice was that I could feel us stepping out onto.

"I suppose so, yes."

I chewed my lower lip. It was none of my business what had changed then. What had been important enough that it not only marked a clear breaking point in Theo's relationship with his father, but a break in his *mind*.

But I was supposed to be his fiancée, right? I should know the major turning points in his life.

"What happened six years ago, Theo?"

"I'd rather not talk about it." His hands gripped the steering wheel infinitesimally tighter.

"If we're going to pull this off, you have to—"

"I don't *have* to do anything, Ellie," he snapped. In the close confines of the car, his voice sounded painfully loud. *And a little like Ted's.*

"Okay, no, you don't have to." I inched forward even more slowly than before, a single toe on the next foot of ice, that much farther from whatever shoreline we'd so suddenly abandoned. "But if we're going to convince people that this is real, knowing more about each other would help."

"No," he said, eyes narrowing at the road.

"Excuse me?"

"It's a simple word." His tone dripped condescension, and I could feel anger ballooning in my chest. "No, you don't need to know every detail of my private life."

"You're the one who just said we need to convince *everyone* we're engaged. How am I supposed to do that if you won't be honest with me?"

"There's a difference between dishonesty and simply not disclosing something. Which I'm certain you, of all people, are aware of," he spat, upper lip curling scornfully. The fact that he was right only made the sting of the words that much more irritating.

"I came clean with you as soon as I had the chance. If we're going to be partners, you owe me at least that much in return."

"This is a business arrangement, Ellie, nothing more. As my *business* partner, I owe you transparency on what affects our plan. I *don't* owe you my life story."

I stuck my tongue in my cheek, searching for some retort. I wasn't that eager to learn whatever he was hiding anymore—the urgency had dimmed beneath the neon flare of annoyance at the return of his patronizing *It's my world and you just live in it* Trip Taylor arrogance.

But I couldn't think of anything that would convince him to

trust me with it. Besides, he was right. Reaching the same end goal didn't require real *intimacy*.

For some reason that thought felt like a lead weight hooked to my sternum, tugging me down painfully for the rest of the silent drive home.

Eleven

I'd just finished cooking the penne for the feta, olive, and sun-dried tomato salad that had been a staple of Greco's for as long as *I'd* been there, when I heard the faint strains of the song coming through the speakers in the front room of the deli:

Do-dee-do-do-DEE-do-DEE-do, Do-dee-do-do-DEE-do-DEE-do . . .

That legendary opening guitar solo, tone high and wailing, that kicked off the Guns N' Roses classic. I smiled softly, darting my head out to make sure the shop was empty before I turned my eyes to the ceiling and whispered *"Dad and daughter dance party."*

I gave the pasta another quick stir under the cold water before turning off the tap and lifting the slotted spoon to my mouth to sing "my" line. Dad took the first half of every verse, I took the second.

Then I moved the spoon between myself and the ceiling for the chorus—we *always* teamed up for the choruses—emphasizing the breaks between each of the however many syllables Axl managed to wring out of one *oh.*

I couldn't remember when the dance parties had started, or why my dad had latched on to "Sweet Child o' Mine" as our song, but for as long as I could remember, they'd been a thing. Whenever we were together and the song came on—which was pretty damn often, my dad kept the radio at the deli tuned to the oldies station, and it *was* Guns N' Roses' biggest banger—he'd grab hold of whatever utensil was close at hand and use it alternately as a guitar, baring his teeth as he "shredded" along with Slash, and as a microphone, keening into it in a way that was very un-Dad. As a Greco man he was usually soft-spoken, used to letting the women in his life be the stars of the show.

It had occurred to me in the years since his death that maybe that was the point of the sing-alongs (there wasn't a lot of dancing, whatever Dad called them, unless you counted frantic hair whipping). Encouraging *me* to make myself the center of attention, to belt out the lyrics without particularly good pitch but with excessive enthusiasm, had to have motivated his making a fool of himself with those nasal wails. He'd kept it up even through my teenage years, when the call-and-response of the song usually went something like <*Dad sings his line*> followed by me groaning about how embarrassing he was, my drawn-out whine unwittingly Axlesque.

I made it through another verse "swapping" lines with Dad—I could hear him so clearly in my mind, it almost didn't matter that he wasn't there to sing them aloud—then dumped the pasta into the gigantic mixing bowl, whisking up the dressing and drizzling it over the top as I whistled along to the guitar solo, hips swaying to the beat.

I'd just made it through Axl's triumphant postsolo *Oh-oh-oh-OH-OH* when I heard it.

A slow, loud clapping.

My eyes whipped open as I poked my head through the door between the prep room and the deli proper.

Standing in the center of the tiled floor, once again dressed like an ad campaign come to life, lips twisted in amusement, was Theo.

I didn't have to glance at the shiny surface of the paper towel dispenser to know my entire face and neck had gone a blazing red—I could *feel* the heat emanating off the rapidly spreading wildfire of my mortification.

"Did you just . . . *apparate* or something?"

"I think the dulcet strains of your song might have covered the sound of the bell," Theo said. "But please. You're missing the bridge."

I realized I was still holding the spoon near my mouth and dropped it to my side.

"Do you *need* something?" I said, jaw jutting defiantly. Looking like an idiot didn't bother me in theory—it wasn't the first time I'd been caught belting out the oldies. But there was something about being caught out by Theo particularly, seeing him laugh at me when it was my *Dad song,* that immediately raised my hackles. We'd exchanged a few texts since Saturday's dinner-triumph-turned-ice-out, but despite the initial urgency of "getting the word out," neither of us had gone so far as to plan a meetup.

"Aren't I allowed to drop in on my fiancée? Share these truly adorable moments of joy with her?" His eyes went extra wide with feigned excitement. "Ooh, maybe this is where I encourage you to try out for *Sing.* Other people might not think you could be the world's next big pop star, but we *believe* in each other."

"If you just came to make fun of me, Theo, I really don't need it," I snapped, the inside of my nose starting to prickle painfully. I hated that this was making me emotional, but I always felt a little smooshy when Dad's song came on, even if it was quite possibly the single piece of music *least* conducive to producing surges of tenderness.

Theo's smirk disappeared so fast it felt like some unseen fly operator had dropped a curtain over his face.

"I really wasn't trying to make fun of you," he said, voice low, any trace of mirth gone. "I didn't . . ." Theo licked his upper lip, trying to find the words. "Does that song mean something special to you?"

"It was my song with my dad, not that it's any of your business," I spat, turning back to grab the pasta bowl and move it to the prep counter as I blinked rapidly. I ducked down to open the cupboard with all the salad platters to buy myself extra time to regain control. "And yes, I know it's stupid, I don't need *you* to tell me that, but . . . it always makes me think of him." Dammit, now the tears were welling up again. I sucked a few breaths through my tightly o'ed mouth, pinching my eyes tight. Was I starting my period or something?

"I don't think that's stupid," Theo murmured. I risked a glance over my shoulder. His eyebrows had lowered with remorse, and he couldn't hold my gaze for more than a couple seconds. "I wouldn't have said anything if I'd known what it meant to you."

And now the tears were surging so hard I could only gulp and nod. Theo wasn't supposed to creep into that part of my life. Hell, he wasn't even supposed to know it existed.

I carefully scooped the salad onto the platter and topped it with chiffonaded herbs, the minimal focus the task required enough to allow me to finally get a handle on myself.

"Anyway," I said when the dish was ready, crossing to pull the nearly empty platter out of the deli case to make the swap, "I'm assuming you came here for a reason?"

"Right, yes." Theo nodded, clearly relieved to move on to other topics. "I thought we could get dinner tonight."

"And you felt the need to deliver this news in person . . . why?"

"So you'd say yes. It's more difficult to disappoint someone face-to-face." A tiny twinkle returned to his eyes.

"Are you saying you'd be deeply disappointed if I said no?" I scooped the remaining pasta from the old platter into a quart container and moved to the scale to weigh and label it for the pre-packed fridge I'd installed at the front of the store, near the breads and dried pastas. It was one of my more successful additions; a surprising number of customers shopped from it almost exclusively.

"As your *fiancé*? Yes. I expect at least one date night a week. You know, to keep the spark alive."

"What if I have plans? It's"—I glanced at the wall clock—"almost six o'clock. Bit late to issue a dinner invitation."

"*Do* you?" Theo raised one eyebrow. It gave him a rakish look, like he was about to suggest something that could get us sent to the principal's office. "Have plans?"

"I mean . . . I could." I planted my hands on my hips. Technically, opening a bottle of wine and texting Bella with some reality show on in the background wasn't a *firm* plan, but I had been *planning* to do it.

"Which means you don't." His lips curled in that specifically Theo show of triumph. Annoyance coiled through me. "So. Dinner."

"Why tonight? No, scratch that, why at all? You can't expect me to put on my game face for some new friend or family member we have to convince with no warning."

"But I can expect you to sit across from me somewhere that a few people might see us together," he said, voice halfway to scolding.

"Theo, we don't have to—"

"Yes, we have to." He tipped his chin down, the better to stare at me from beneath his lowered brow, clearly preparing to educate me. My annoyance twisted tighter. "We can't rely on my building manager to get the word out to the entire town. We only bought ourselves so much time, and we agreed that the story has to have legs outside of direct conversations with Ted."

I inhaled sharply. I wasn't even sure why I was resisting so hard. Maybe I just resented Theo's supreme confidence that I'd agree. That, and the singing incident had left a lingering feeling of having my ribs cracked open for Theo to poke around inside.

"Fine, I close in twenty minutes, we can go then," I ground out.

"To your apartment, to change."

"Excuse me?"

"No offense, Ellie, but taking you to some burrito joint isn't going to yield the results we're after."

"Plenty of couples like burritos." With most of my exes, that had counted as splashing out.

"Then we'll do burritos tomorrow. Tonight we have reservations at Post."

Post was Milborough's most prominent foray into fine dining, a farm-to-table spot housed in the decommissioned post office. The grand interior—with clever details like a dividing wall of old PO boxes and the kitchen visible behind the still intact customer service counter—drew crowds of chic, attractive people eager for a taste of city-level luxury. It had appeared on regional "best of" lists for years. I think it was even up for some fancy award recently, though I had no idea whether it won.

Maybe because I'd never actually *been* there. I walked by regularly, had even paused to peer at menus full of heritage meats garnished with pickled seasonal slaws and produce varietals you could picture without having actually eaten them, like chervil. But Post? Who was I going to bring, the drummer from the crappy local punk band I slept with off and on last summer?

"If you have a reservation *there,* you could have given me some warning," I sputtered. Even on weekdays the restaurant booked out well in advance.

"I got it on the drive over, otherwise I would have." I squinted, disbelieving. "I'm friends with the beverage director," Theo said, glancing back at the clock. "It's now even *closer* to six, and I'm sure you have plenty to do before closing. The reservation's at seven-thirty, if you want a shower . . ." His eyes elevatored me.

"Fine, flip the sign to Closed," I said, gritting my teeth. At least if I had to put up with Theo's arrogance for another night, I'd get a good meal out of it.

"So, uh . . . sorry things are messy, I didn't expect anyone." I glanced over my shoulder as I jiggled the key in my apartment door—it always stuck at first.

"I don't care, we're just here to get you ready," Theo said with a terse nod.

He'd insisted on staying with me at the deli, posting up at a bistro table near the window with his laptop until I'd finished my closing routine. Having him there was vaguely irritating—what was I going to do, try to make a break for it?—but I didn't have a good reason why he should leave, so I just focused on wrapping meats and salads, slotting things into their walk-in spots, cleaning the slicer, running the sanitizer, mopping the floors, the mundanity of the checklist soothing me . . . slightly.

But now he was at my apartment. Somehow it hadn't occurred to me when he'd announced this plan that he'd actually *see* it. I bit my lip as the key finally turned and I pushed open the door.

I crossed to the coat closet—as if I used it on the daily—using the shield of the door to hide my assessing glance. It wasn't *that* messy, barring a wine glass on the coffee table and a couple coats heaped on the corner of the sewing table, but it felt . . . *dingy*. The walls were painted greige before I moved in, and hadn't been touched since; I could see smudges here and there, scuffs that were suddenly stark against the backdrop of blandness. The smattering of framed show bills and family photos I'd managed to hang before running out of steam somehow just made the walls feel barer. The floors were hardwood, but they were already dull and scuffed when I signed the lease, and the handful of mismatched area rugs I'd thrown around were faded and worn, the ratio of trampling to vacuuming clearly skewing toward "ground-in dirt." I couldn't see the kitchen from where I was standing, but I knew the cupboards and countertops hadn't been updated since the eighties, when ivory melamine with oak trim—curved exaggeratedly to be all space-age and handle-free—was the height of interior design. And then there was the furniture, a combination of hand-me-downs and curbside freebies that not only had no unifying aesthetic, it all *looked* like stuff someone with an actual plan for their place would unload. The only piece that was even remotely nice was the sewing table, an antique trapdoor model Mimi had outfitted with a new machine during my high school years, and which was hidden under my one pile of actual junk.

At least he wouldn't have to see the state of the bathroom tiles, unless he couldn't hold it for the twenty minutes I planned to use to get ready. Until I'd moved in, I hadn't realized they made those seventies-style interlocking-rectangles-and-squares floor tiles in lavender. Though it was distinctly grayed now.

"Can I . . . take your coat?" I scanned Theo's face for some sign of what he was thinking. Wordlessly, he slipped it off and handed it to me, leaving the scarf around his neck. "I have wine. And stuff to make Manhattans. Also there should be some Polars in the fridge." I was babbling, but it helped distract me from the low-level anxiety skittering around my rib cage. Was he *judging* my place? Why did I care if he was?

"Thanks. I'll be fine." He threw me an unreadable look, then settled onto the couch with a creak of the ancient springs. Was it just me, or was he trying to hold himself away from the back? "I'll wait here, you get ready."

Grimacing, I hurried off to shower and apply the bare minimum amount of makeup I could get away with. Mascara and a little lip gloss? Maybe some cream blush? Most days I swiped tinted moisturizer over my face and called it good.

By the time I was dressing I felt less tense, more defiant. So what if he didn't like my place? Not all of us were brought up in literal *mansions*. Not all of us tried to carve out a personality via the things we adorned our spaces with. And frankly, my focus was on the deli, not an apartment that existed primarily as a place to sleep, eat, and shower. It's not who I *was*. Theo might model both his wardrobe and his mindset after country club rules, but his "fiancée" definitely did not. Laughing under my breath, I pulled a top out of the closet that I'd only worn once since I moved back from New York. It didn't fit into my usual routine of deli, family dinners, and the occasional night out somewhere casual. But for *Post* . . .

I emerged eighteen minutes after our arrival, skin tight with the need to leave.

"Ready," I announced. Theo glanced over at me from the

couch—he was more recumbent now, arm stretched along the back as he flicked through his phone. A bemused look stole over his face.

"*That's* an interesting top."

"I think so," I replied tartly.

"I meant it as a compliment."

"Is that what 'interesting' means?"

"In this case, it's definitely a compliment. Though it's also quite *attractive,* if that makes you feel better." He approached me, eyes narrowing as he examined the blouse more closely. "Where'd you even get this?"

"Why?" My spine locked in, preparing me for battle.

"Because it's really exquisite." His eyes flicked up to mine. "If you'd worn it to dinner Saturday, you could have had Marta taking passive-aggressive swipes at you too. It's the kind of thing she'd try to buy out at Neiman's so no one else could manage to re-create her *particular* sense of style."

"Oh, well . . . I, uh . . . made it."

I couldn't hold his gaze, eyes drifting to the corner of the room as I finished the sentence, my closet-facing bravado withering under actual scrutiny, muscle memory I'd thought had long atrophied kicking in unexpectedly.

I'd never been good at the rejection part during my time in New York, and it never seemed to matter if the director or producer I'd met with was letting me down gently, a string of compliments bookending their eventual "no," or dripping disdain as they brushed aside my portfolio of sketches and handful of sample garments; I felt the exact same blend of shame and despair every time I was told my work *isn't what we're looking for* or that they *need someone with more experience.* How can you *get* any experience if you keep making your way down the ladder and even the scrappier, altogether unglamorous productions won't hire you? At least toward the end, when the number of offs-Broadway grew too high to bother counting, I'd more often get the excuse of *Don't have the time and budget for custom costumes* than an objection to my vision or qualifications. Though if that had really been *true,* my protests that my way was actually cheaper, and that I'd gladly make up the difference by taking a lower fee if my budgets were wrong, should have worked.

The blouse I was wearing was from the middle of my extended Failure Period, when I still believed I might eventually land a truly impressive gig if I just showed them how *right* I was. I'd made it for a revival of *The Importance of Being Earnest,* one of the seemingly endless string of shows that opted to modernize the physical trappings—set and costume design, the occasional place reference—while otherwise keeping the book intact. I'd never really understood that impulse—if they're speaking Shakespearean English or reaching for smelling salts every few scenes, a couple leather coats won't make it feel super *contemporary*—but others seemed to, and I was distinctly in the category of beggars, not choosers.

I usually didn't make costumes for the show I was hoping to get hired onto—even I knew that was too eager—but I'd been so enchanted with the design I'd come up with for Gwendolyn, the shallow, appearances-obsessed lead, that I couldn't help myself. The blouse was closely fitted, with a small peplum, modified leg-of-mutton sleeves, a high neckline, and explosions of lace around the cuffs and collar, thick swaths of ribbon fixing the frills in place. The bodice and sleeves were a stunning peacock-green moiré sateen, the lace was a gentle tea-stained color, the ribbons a deep navy, and the buttons and seaming were teal to complete the color palette. I wanted to evoke the Victorian era in the shape and Gwendolyn's personality in the colors, and I'd spent an entire week of late nights and early mornings—really all the hours I wasn't waitressing—perfecting it.

If I'd been hired, the blouse might have been altered to fit one of the actresses and wound up in the theater company's wardrobe closet, but I'd never made it anywhere close. The director only met me as a formality; he'd already agreed to hire the producer's niece, a recent RISD graduate, to keep the relationship sweet.

Instead, it remained perfectly tailored to me—years of sewing in high school had given me an instinctive ability to pattern for my own measurements—and had hung in my closet ever since. The one time I'd worn it out in New York, for my roommate's birthday, the compliments I'd received felt like a gut punch—if it was so stunning, why hadn't it worked? If I was actually good at this, why couldn't I land a single fucking job? And my life in Milborough was much more suited to my never-ending parade of reworked T-shirts and off-the-rack jeans—with the occasional addition of a vintage look I'd tailored to fit better for the vanishingly rare events I attended—than to a highly structural sateen blouse. That wasn't who I *was* here—even if it had come out of my head and I still went a little fluttery when I fingered the fabrics—but I couldn't convince myself to part with it, still too proud, deep down, of the beautiful thing I'd created. Letting it go would have felt like *really* giving up on the dream I'd known for some time I wasn't going back to. Like giving up on some vital part of myself.

"You're kidding," Theo said, taking the cuff between his long, slim fingers, frank disbelief on his face. "You made *this*?"

"I make most of my clothes. Or at least rework them. I've been doing it for years."

"I remember you doing that in high school, but I didn't realize . . ." He looked up, a slight flush in his cheeks. "Don't take this the wrong way, but I had no idea you were this *good*."

I exhaled a laugh.

"I'm guessing that's also a compliment." I crossed to the hall closet, shuffling the coats until I could tamp down my stupid grin. *Theo* certainly didn't need to know how thirsty I was. Once I'd managed my face, I handed him his coat, shrugging into one of my less utilitarian options, a slim black wool and faux fur number from the sixties that I'd darted through the midsection, swapping out the dingy plastic buttons for oversized gleaming-gold replacements. We *were* going to Post, after all.

Theo held open the door as I slid into the heeled booties I wore on special occasions, read: pretty much never.

"Are you saying I look the part of your fiancée?"

"You certainly look like someone I'd be lucky to be seen with."
His lips curled lazily at the corners, eyes going slightly hooded as he
gazed at me. It was a remarkably sultry stare, and for a moment it
left me feeling like a shaken soda, fizzy from top to toe. At least
until I managed to remember there was nothing between us besides
a shared business interest. "I'm certain no one in that restaurant
will be able to tear their eyes away. Which is better than fitting their
preconceived notions of who I might choose, don't you think?"

"Oh, *infinitely* better. You know me. There's nothing I love more
than being the center of attention."

Warmth flared through my chest at his appreciative laugh.
Theo might not be my ideal man, especially not on paper (in person
I had to admit he showed occasional glimpses of an interesting
personality), but I was shocked to realize that, on some level, we
seemed to understand each other.

"So?" He gestured through the door. "Shall we?"

"Lead the way, *darling*."

And for a moment, as we emerged into the chilly winter night,
Theo's arm slung casually around my waist as he guided me down
the slick sidewalk, it almost didn't feel like playing a part.

Twelve

After the bustle of coat-taking, Theo suggested a spot "with a view of the kitchen, it's my fiancée's first time here, I want her to have the full experience" so smoothly that I truly didn't realize until we'd been deposited in the center of the restaurant that he'd directed the hostess toward the spot where we'd be likeliest to be seen. She clearly hadn't either, her entire bright-eyed demeanor stuck on Theo's *Let me charm you* smile. It had been such a distracting combination of bustling and fawning—Theo seemed to inspire everyone around him to want to meet his unstated needs—that it wasn't until we'd ordered cocktails that it occurred to me.

What were we going to talk about for an entire dinner?

Not just any dinner, Post was the sort of place, as our server *Jaden-I'll-be-guiding-your-dining-experience-tonight* slickly informed us, where they were *happy* to course out the meal, ensuring diners had time to savor each dish. Which, frankly, was the least they could do. I saw the "wood-grilled artichoke with citrus coulis" head out to a nearby table as he explained the menu. The plate was pristine, true, but it couldn't have been more than four bites, and it was the cheapest appetizer *at eighteen fucking dollars*.

"Anything jump out?" Theo took a sip of his cocktail, a smoky concoction of Scotch and various liqueurs that had almost tempted me away from the rye-and-various-other-liqueurs drink they'd specifically labeled as *our spin on a classic Manhattan.*

"Besides the fact that this dinner is going to gut my bank account?"

"Don't be ridiculous, I'm paying," Theo said with a wave of his hand.

"I mean . . . I can afford it." I felt my spine stiffen. *Which* why, *Ellie?* What completely idiotic trace code would make me fight for the privilege of spending an arm and a leg on some pretentious meal when the rich kid across the table was *offering to pay?*

"I just saw where you live, remember? The fact that you *can* pay isn't the point."

"Wow. Okay." I sat back hard, unexpectedly stung. He *had* been judging me. Theo shook his head once, exhaling heavily.

"That's not what I meant. Just . . . I'm in commercial real estate, Ellie, I know average rents all over town. Especially if you've been in that place a while . . . ?"

"Five years," I muttered.

"Then I'm betting you have a hell of a deal on rent. Which is fantastic, it's got everything you need, you're saving money, and it gives you the freedom to keep doing what you love."

I squinted at him, unsure what he meant.

"Running the deli?" He tilted his head to the side in question. "I have to imagine having more capital available is useful, right?"

"Right," I slid out between clenched teeth. "But forgive me if I'm not quite buying it. Remember, I've also seen *your* apartment." I willed my cheeks not to flush. Even if he was bullshitting me, what did I care what Theo thought of my apartment?

He took another slow sip, gaze steady on mine, the shifting depths of his blue eyes unreadable.

"I only moved in a few years ago, you know. Before that I lived in a studio near Thief River where I could tell you what the neighbors ate for dinner every night. Specifically because I could smell it through the walls."

"Why did you live there?" Thief River wasn't exactly *rough*—there weren't any genuinely scary sections of Milborough—but it was definitely seedy, a densely packed warren of run-down three-families with lovely views of the grimy seventies-era power plant that hunched along the border with Burnton. It was the last place you'd imagine someone like Theo calling home, unless it was as some sort of long-term gentrification plan.

"To save up for a down payment." Theo shrugged. "I didn't want to mortgage a lot, so it took a few years."

"How nice for you not to have to deal with tedious things like debt," I snipped. "Maybe I should move somewhere with even *lower* 'average rents.'"

"Hey. I'm sorry."

I startled at Theo's fingers closing over mine, glancing up at him in spite of myself. He was leaning across the table, genuine remorse tugging at his features. Warmth spread up my arm and swirled through my chest, stirring up all sorts of fairy dust I'd frankly prefer he left alone.

"I promise, all I meant was you're clearly on top of it. You wouldn't have such a successful business if you weren't smart with money."

I nodded, the best I could do with this stupid lump in my throat blocking all clever retorts. After a few seconds, I managed to gulp it back down.

"Then we should split the bill." I tugged my hand back. Dear lord, it wasn't just trace code, it was clearly some sort of mental malware I'd unwittingly downloaded.

"No, no way." Theo shook his head for emphasis. "Whoever picks the place covers the tab. *Especially* if they pick a place with twenty-eight-dollar salads."

"Yeah, that lettuce better be dipped in fucking gold."

"Or at least sprinkled with real saffron."

I decided to let that mollify me (there was a lot of coursed for you ahead of us, after all), then turned to the menu, losing myself in the details of the obscure foodstuffs that had been shaved, whipped, flash-fried, and sprinkled over the top of a protein so deeply heritage, so emphatically sourced, that I was half-surprised we didn't get a list of hobbies alongside the details of the farm or coastline it had previously called home.

Before long, the server returned and we traded picks until we'd filled our quota. Once he'd slid off toward the kitchen—the staff seemed to undulate through the restaurant more than walk—we fell into a not quite companionable, but at least not tense silence. I looked around, wondering whether any of the well-dressed people holding forks up to one another's mouths and exclaiming over the handmade pastas would be familiar.

"I still can't get over that shirt," Theo said. I turned, surprised to find his gaze hooked on my collar, the most intricately detailed section of my peacock creation. I'd imagined it as the petals of a daffodil when I'd drawn the pattern, the inner lace layer tightly frilled while the moiré surrounding it opened into a wider, more languid bloom.

"Is it really that surprising that I'm capable of more than slicing meat?" I said, a bit more sharply than I'd intended.

"Of course not. But this isn't hobbyist level." Theo leaned back as Jaden placed a plate of house-cured duck prosciutto with a local honey drizzle, tart Maine blueberry preserves, and homemade sourdough toast points. I busied myself assembling the perfect bite so I wouldn't have to meet Theo's eyes. "Was that what you moved to New York for? Fashion design?"

"Not precisely." I took a dainty nibble. "Jesus *fuck* that's good." I stared in open shock at the half-eaten morsel in my hand. Theo flashed a self-satisfied grin.

"Rethinking your stance on this place?"

"I wouldn't go that far. You forget that you're talking to not just a hobbyist seamstress, but a charcuterie *master*."

"Clearly you've been holding out on me."

"Future meat hopes are the only thing I have to keep you coming back for more." I grinned as I stuffed the rest of the toast in my mouth.

"I think that's supposed to be *my* ace in the hole." Theo leaned closer, a conspiratorial look on his face. "Full disclosure, I've been told it tastes just like jamón ibérico."

My laugh was so barky that all the diners nearby turned to stare. Theo flashed a self-satisfied grin as I sipped my water to tamp down the residual giggles. I knew Theo could be funny when he wanted, but that sounded more like, well . . . *my* kind of joke.

"You said not precisely," he said, taking a bite.

"Sorry?"

"You weren't *precisely* doing fashion design. What were you doing?"

I stared at him, trying to decide if I could trust him with all that. Him knowing about my year and change of trying—really, mostly failing—to kick-start an artistic career felt like it would leave me vulnerable, even all these years after I'd (admit it, Ellie) given up. But he seemed genuinely interested, and honestly . . . it was almost embarrassing how good it felt, even now, to hear someone praise my work. I might have abandoned the idea of ever finding a wider audience for my creations—many of them far too fantastical for me to even consider wearing in public—but it didn't mean I'd stopped *caring*.

"I was trying to break into costuming. For theater?"

"Right, you mentioned that when we left the hospital." Theo nodded slowly. "Were you always a theater kid? I don't remember you in any of the high school shows."

"Why would you? I know for a fact you weren't a theater kid."

"Why so certain? I've been told I have *several* leading man qualities."

"I'm sure you have, but you didn't use them in any Milborough High productions. Besides, lacrosse season overlapped pretty much entirely with the spring musical."

He rolled his eyes skyward in a half-rueful *You got me.*

"I wasn't ever in the shows. But Maritza was in all of them, so I went to a lot."

"You were friends with Maritza?" She was two years above me, something of a golden god in the theater-kid scene, friendly even to freshmen, with a killer voice and genuine acting ability. She was *always* cast as a lead.

"We dated for almost a year when I was a sophomore. And stayed friends after."

"Oh." I tried to process this. Dating Bella was easily explained—she'd never been popular, but she was unfailingly sweet, and pretty enough that a toe in the water of "girls presumed not to be on the Trip-Taylor-crew radar" made sense. But Maritza, while attractive, was very obviously *weird*. She sang show tunes aloud during passing time, usually with accompanying choreography, and had a tendency toward accessories that looked like they'd been made by a kindergartner (I still remembered the soda-tab necklace she'd spatter-painted with nail polish). If she didn't wind up pursuing acting, it would be easy to imagine her finding her calling as an elementary school art teacher.

Theo's look of mild amusement made me feel like he could see every thought moving through my head.

"Well, I was. A theater kid, I mean. I just happened to be one of the mole people with no interest in the spotlight."

"Clearly you knew your strengths."

We both leaned back as the next two dishes appeared, with an elaborate explanation from Jaden.

"Are you still trying to break in? To costuming, I mean?" Theo shifted a pile of little gem lettuce and about twenty-five other accent items onto his plate.

"It's been . . . on hold since I got back."

One eyebrow shot up. He didn't have to say what we were both thinking: *That was five years ago.*

"Don't you miss it?" Theo finally said.

I stabbed a few leaves aggressively. Of *course* I missed it. Did he think weighing pasta salad and flipping through catalogs of specialty canned goods with distributors and mixing up the same sauces and side dishes week in and week out *fulfilled* me?

But then . . . why wouldn't he? Occasionally—specifically when I'd had a drink too many—I was able to admit to myself that, mixed in with the grief and shock and anger after Dad died, there had been a significant amount of relief. I didn't have to keep trying to do this thing that I couldn't seem to crack no matter how many ways I came at it, didn't have to keep baring myself to strangers armed with the razor-sharp blade of *no,* didn't have to force myself to build up yet another layer of emotional scar tissue, then rally and do it all again. I missed the feeling I got when I had a *really* amazing idea for a garment, the barest wisps of a design spinning out of my head into this beautiful *real* thing, like fairy-tale magic. But I didn't miss the constant pendulum swings of intense hope and grief shot through with shame, the motion more nauseating every time. The deli wasn't challenging, it wasn't creative, but it was *safe.* Or it had been until Mangia breached the surface of Milborough like some Leviathan of old.

All of that was definitely too much underbelly to show *anyone,* let alone this relative stranger sitting across from me playing pretend, so I settled on the explanation I'd given my New York friends, the one I'd tried for five years to convince myself of but never quite managed to:

"Some of us wind up in the family business by choice, some of us wind up there because we have to."

I dropped my eyes to my plate, focusing on the za'atar croutons so I wouldn't have to catch Theo's eyes, afraid I might find disbelief there, or worse, pity.

"Trust me, *that* I understand," Theo muttered.

"Really?" I frowned at a tiny edible flower, not quite believing it.

"You've met Ted. You really think I wanted to work for him?"

"I mean . . . it's not like things would go under if you didn't."

"That's not the only version of obligation," Theo said, voice low.

Now it was my turn to stare.

"So . . . why, then? I have to believe you had other options."

His jaw worked like he was physically chewing over my question.

"Does it matter?"

"It matters to me. For one thing, it would make this whole 'Help Ellie try to keep Mangia out of Milborough' stance easier to trust if I knew *why* you'd be willing to go against Ted. Fuck, against your own interests. You must stand to make more money if the deal goes through."

"You don't need to know why to trust me, just that you *can* trust me." Theo's gaze hardened. "And believe it or not, money isn't my sole motivating factor."

"That might be true, but I don't actually know you, which makes it pretty hard to take your word for it." I folded my arms over my chest, glaring. "I told you how I ended up here. The very least you could do is show me the same courtesy. If for no other reason than knowing more than the crib sheet version of each other's lives can only help this thing work."

He stared at me for a few long seconds, then sighed, the sharp lines of his handsome face sagging under the weight of some unspoken pain.

"I started working for the company right out of college," Theo started, voice low and rough. He twisted his rocks glass slowly as he spoke. "I realized it was . . . not the best fit about nine months later." The corner of his mouth quirked in a suggestion of a wry smile that didn't quite fulfill its promise. "I'd hoped that if I worked my way up the ladder—Ted was imposing a half-assed version of the 'learn the whole business from the inside out' regimen, but he was too impatient to check out himself to leave me doing menial work for long—I'd have a chance to put *my* ideas into play. But it became clearer and clearer that the actual plan was for me to stand in for his way of thinking."

"What didn't you agree about?"

"Mostly little stuff. I wanted to invest more in our properties between tenants, find ways to make them shine. There are so many beautiful old buildings in Milborough, but it's easier and cheaper to get rid of what makes them special. Replace it with a 'fresh, modern' look that winds up feeling . . ."

"Antiseptic."

Theo nodded rapidly, something like gratitude skipping across the surface of those deep blue eyes.

"Exactly. Vinyl plank flooring is easy, but it has no personality. But, in Ted's words, *Character costs too much.* And that was just a couple thousand this way or that on properties we already owned— there was no *way* he was going to hear me out on new directions for the business." Theo shook his head, lost for a moment in memory. "Anyway, it was clear I wasn't going to get to try anything different at Taylor Properties, so I was figuring out what else to do. I'd gotten as far as requesting applications for architecture school, and then . . ."

He licked his lip slowly, staring at the ice so hard I was surprised it didn't melt.

"And then what?"

"Chase died, and I couldn't do it." Theo's Adam's apple bobbed.

"Chase?" A hint of memory nipped at the back of my brain.

"My brother." His voice was chipped slate. "He was the year below you, but he wound up at Benedictine after freshman year. His grades weren't good—Ted seemed to think dyslexia was a cheap excuse—so they sent him to private school to 'get more individualized attention.'"

"Did it help?"

"He graduated with a decent GPA. Made it into UMass Amherst, though I think Ted's donations were a big part of that." Theo shrugged.

"How did he die?"

"On one of our building sites. He was there after hours, and . . . I don't want to go into it." His hand went clawlike on his glass.

"How long ago was it?"

"It'll be six years this summer," he murmured, gaze sliding to the floor. He didn't have to say it: *almost the exact amount of time he'd lost in the hospital.* And his brief bout of amnesia came just after an accident—or a near accident—on a building site. God, no *wonder* he'd lost his shit with Jaime.

Heart aching for Theo, I reached across the table and took his free hand in both of mine, squeezing gently as I stared into his startled eyes.

"I'm so sorry, Theo."

He swallowed hard as his fingers curled around the edge of my hand.

"Anyway . . . it was hard on all of us, I didn't feel like I could leave the business *then,* and by the time things started to feel less . . . chaotic . . ." He rolled his eyes, weariness hanging heavy on every feature. "I don't know, it just felt too hard."

"What about now?" I said, releasing his hand but leaving mine nearby. Fully pulling away felt too callous, somehow.

"What do you mean?"

"Are you looking to make a change now? To leave?"

He chewed his lower lip.

"Now . . . I'm trying to make changes from the inside. I have more clout than when I started, and Ted's much less involved. But if he brings Mangia in, we'll lose the chance to rethink one of our most valuable assets for years, maybe decades." He closed his eyes, taking a deep breath. When he opened them again, his usual steely self-control had returned. "So to answer your question, you can trust me because this is my last real chance to do something I *care* about. If Mangia comes in . . . I either have to find a new line of business, or, more likely, I'm doomed to serve in Ted's trenches indefinitely."

"Oh. Well . . . okay, then." I wasn't sure what else to say. The Theo across the table was the same man I'd walked in with, in the same crisp shirt and slim-fit trousers that I could tell from a single glance were high end, with the same commandingly handsome face, but he suddenly felt different in a million indefinable ways, as if someone had slid a filter over the lens I'd been seeing him through, or maybe pulled one off. Somehow it had never occurred to me that his relationship to what he did could be so complicated. That his high-sheen polish might just be a veneer.

And I felt flat-out terrible that I hadn't known. Had Ma told me when it happened? I could conjure the conversation: a call home from New York, her hushed tone as she relayed a stranger's heartbreak, voice equal parts empathy for that other family and relief that tragedy had spared *us*. But that wasn't a memory, it was just the reflection of one Frankensteined from a hundred other phone calls filled with tidbits of hometown gossip meant to remind me that I was still tied to this place. I'd griped to friends in New York about how often she called, but really, it had been a lifeline. It wasn't just the failure that made New York so hard, it was the sense of dislocation. The absolute certainty that this city didn't belong to me—that I wasn't really a part of it, that the people around me didn't know or care what happened to the short, dark-haired girl in the dingy walk-up—had brought on a loneliness I'd never experienced before or since.

We spent the next few courses focusing on the food. I tried to make jokes about various foams, draw Theo's attention to the customer rearranging her entire table in search of the perfect photo while her overpriced entrées congealed, but I only eked out a few dutiful replies and the vaguest approximations of pleasant expressions. Eventually, I decided to just stick to eating.

I was staring at the reflection of the room in the floor-to-ceiling windows, wavery and glittering, strangely ethereal, when a voice boomed out from over my shoulder.

"Theo, my man! Sorry I couldn't get over to check on you two sooner."

The man was dressed in a crisp black suit that didn't quite hide his burgeoning belly, thick horn-rimmed glasses amplifying the genial expression creasing his boyishly pudgy face. He was vaguely familiar, in the way half the population of Milborough around my age was.

"Andy, thanks again for squeezing us in," Theo said, photo-shoot smile firmly in place as he reached for Andy's hand. "Ellie and I have been meaning to get here for months. After the accident she forced some carpe diem on me." Theo grinned ruefully.

"How *are* you, by the way? I mean, you look good, but I heard you were in the hospital?" Andy stared at Theo's head as though its topography might fill in the details.

"I was, but I'm fine now, thank god." Theo reached for my hand in a way that looked absent, but which I knew was *highly* deliber-ate. Maybe he should have been a theater kid. "But it really put things in perspective. I can't wait until Ellie and I tie the knot. I realize even more now how lucky I am to have her." He gazed lov-ingly at me.

"Tie the . . . Fuck, congratulations!" Andy smiled widely. "I didn't even realize you two were together."

"It all happened so fast," I said, beaming. "We just got engaged a week ago." I flashed the ring, catching Theo's appreciative smile out of the corner of my eye.

"In that case, let me get your dinner."

"Oh, you don't have to—"

"No, no, it's the least I can do. Besides, if you're hitching your wagon to Theo, it won't be the last time I see the two of you in here."

"Not if I have any say in it. The duck prosciutto was a revela-tion."

"That's high praise coming from Ellie," Theo said, leaning in conspiratorially. "Greco's Deli has the best cured meats in town."

"Of course, you're Ellie *Greco*. I've been meaning to get in touch." Andy gave me a look of real interest. He reached into his pocket and plucked out a card. "We'd love to partner on sourcing ingredients. Involving local producers and suppliers is a big part of our mission. Shoot me an email? We're looking to revamp our charcuterie selections for spring."

"I'll be in touch." I bit down a surge of excitement. I'd never thought about partnering with Post, but if the weekday crowd was any indicator, it could become a very reliable order. Even with a lower markup, that would be a nice safety net.

"Always good to see you, Theo. And wonderful to meet you, Ellie. We'll talk soon."

With that, he bustled away to another table, stopping only to flag our server and whisper something in his ear before turning on the charm for the next couple. We finished our drinks, left a generous tip, and made our way to the hostess stand, where Theo handed over a ten-dollar bill for the privilege of getting our coats back. No wonder they liked him here. While she was downstairs, he leaned close, lowering his voice.

"Don't jump, okay?"

Before I could process that, his hand was at my waist, warm through the silk of my blouse, his nose practically in my hair. A shiver ran through me as Theo whispered again.

"What would you say to activating rule two?"

"Which one's rule two?" A devilish grin overtook me. Something about standing there, pressed up against Theo, felt deliciously naughty. I couldn't tell whether the restaurant was watching our little performance, but it *felt* like they were . . . and like it was working.

"The one where I kiss you on the cheek. For effect, obviously."

"Obviously." I twisted to take him in. He was gazing at me with that hooded stare I'd seen during our final practice session in his father's driveway. The one that, for the life of me, I couldn't spot as fake. "Do we have a big enough audience to make it worth your while?"

"We certainly have the *right* audience. Andy knows a lot of people, and he likes being the man with information. Besides, you really do look incredible in that blouse."

"In that case, it would be foolish *not* to activate it," I whispered, pulse starting to throb in anticipation, the heat from his hand blooming from the base of my spine through my whole body, pooling in my belly.

"My thoughts exactly," he murmured, the words getting lost as his lips pressed against me, warm and soft, the hand gripping my waist pulling me ever so slightly closer as we lingered, skin to skin. My breath caught in my throat as he pulled away, a tingle running to the roots of my hair in a way I hadn't felt in . . . I honestly couldn't remember feeling it, actually.

And then the hostess returned with our coats, her bright smile tightening as she turned to me, and the moment was over. Theo held my coat up, sliding me into it with practiced ease before moving his hand to the small of my back again to lead me out. I risked a glance back and spotted Andy, at the side of some table, eyes fixed on us as we disappeared into the night. Theo's hand stayed on my back as we made our way to the car.

"Do you think he really wants to partner with me?" I said, picking my way around a patch of ice.

"Absolutely. That's their whole shtick." He grinned. "Besides, Andy is *very* solicitous of your fiancé. It's why he's always comping apps when I eat there."

"And tonight's whole meal? I demand another dinner as repayment."

"Your wish is my command." He flashed me an intimate look, hand tightening against my body again.

And the strangest thing was, as we walked down the sidewalk— Theo's hand warm on my back, the glow of the meal and the drinks pulsing through me, the string lights the city ran between the old-fashioned lampposts downtown catching patches of ice and flecks of mica in the sidewalks, turning the world to a glittery snow globe—I felt genuinely excited about the prospect.

Thirteen

"Annnd a quart of the minestrone. Anything else for you today, Loretta?"

Loretta Bownes squinted at the deli case through her purple cat's-eye glasses. She owned one of those vaguely hippie stores filled with linen tunics and hand-beaded necklaces, seemingly designed exclusively for women in late middle age who'd gotten really into gardening and/or birding. Loretta wasn't everyone's cup of (herbal, thought to have calming properties) tea—she was an inveterate oversharer, both of her own personal trials and her opinions about whoever she was speaking to—but I got a kick out of her. She reminded me of a younger, more patchouli-scented Mimi.

"I'm tempted to get a pint of the red pepper ricotta, but it gives me such gas. Last time we ate it, Brian had to sleep in the guest room."

I glanced sideways at Bella, sipping an Orangina at one of the tables in the window, her entire face pursed with repressed mirth.

"Well, it'll be here the next time he's got a business trip."

I rang Loretta up, she wished me a "peace-filled day," then

swept out of the store in a swirl of bright felted patchwork over-coat.

"Dear lord, I think it was worth coming into town early just for that," Bella said.

"Loretta's definitely a bonus."

"What's the main event?" She slipped a bookmark into the thriller she'd been reading and turned to face me.

"I was hoping . . . that is, I thought maybe you knew . . ."

I thrust my tongue into my cheek, trying to root out the words. At first I'd planned to just sort through things over text the way Bella and I usually did—I'd written one when I got home from Post a few nights ago, but somehow, seeing it in digital black and white, it felt too cold. After a few failed attempts to frame my questions in a way that rang less stony-hearted, I deleted the whole thing. Apparently family tragedy was on my list of in-person topics.

"Spit it out, Ellie. Mimi will tear me a new one if I'm late." Bella's eyelids lowered in familiar *I see you* exasperation. This was why I needed her here in person. So I couldn't wriggle away from it.

"So I'm realizing . . . there's a lot Theo and I don't know about each other . . ."

"You're realizing this *now*?"

"I'm becoming more aware of it," I said, ignoring her exaggerated disbelief. We both knew Bella thought the plan was terrible, there was no need to get sidetracked. "Don't get me wrong, I think we've got enough info to pull this off, but . . . you know. I don't want to get blindsided by anything."

Bella took a long sip of soda, raising a skeptical eyebrow.

"Like?"

"Like . . . how his brother died," I murmured, dropping my gaze to the countertop.

"Ohhh." Bella nodded slowly as this sank in. "How'd that come up?"

"Just in conversation a few nights ago."

"In conversation? Are you guys having nightly check-ins or something?"

"Theo was talking about how he wound up in the family business at dinner . . ." Bella's eyebrow shot almost to her hairline—I suppose I hadn't actually *told* her about Theo's impromptu "Let's be seen out as a couple" night—so I circled my hand through the air, *Let's not get hung up on that.* "The point is I didn't know anything about it, and I wanted to be . . . sensitive? It's clearly really tough for him."

"*You* want to be *sensitive.* To *Theo.*"

"Is that so hard to believe?"

"Do I need to answer that?"

I folded my arms across my chest, huffing exasperatedly.

"Yes, fine, we all know I'm the heartless cynic of the family. Can we get past the scolding to the part where you tell me what happened?"

Bella's face softened and she set the drink down, folding her hands on her lap.

"I'm happy to tell you what I know, Ellie, I'm just surprised you're that worried about Theo's feelings."

Heat rose to my cheeks. "I'm just trying to avoid pissing him off so royally that he walks out on our deal, okay? Are you going to help with that, or . . . ?"

Bella's lips twisted into a knowing smirk—annoying—but then she sucked in a long breath, eyes tilting skyward in her *thinking it over* face, so I decided to let it go.

"Okay, so . . . What *do* you know about Chase?"

"That he was a couple years below me in school, but at Benedictine. And that he died almost six years ago at a company construction site. Do you know more?"

"Pretty sure alcohol was involved, though none of the kids who were with him ever admitted it." I frowned and Bella bit her lower lip, her expansive empathy making this hard for her to talk about. "He and some friends were there after hours. He'd been interning for his dad that summer, probably to be closer to Theo, so he was able to snag the keys somehow. There was scaffolding all along the outside of the building, and they were swinging off it, daring each other to do parkour, just stupid college boy shit, you know? And I guess Chase just . . . fell." She shook her head, eyes glistening. "Theo and I were still in okay touch then, I came in from Boston for the funeral. It destroyed him. The whole family, really. I think Cat wound up taking a gap year."

"He and Chase were close?" I ventured, half-fearing the answer.

"I think Theo was Chase's hero. We were dating when Chase started playing lacrosse, and Theo acted all exasperated about it— *He seriously needs to get his own thing* or whatever—but deep down he loved it. Having his brother look up to him that way. I think . . ." Bella blinked rapidly, eyes shinier now. "I think Theo blamed himself for what happened."

"What? Why?" My entire face scrunched with disbelief.

"Not directly, obviously—he wasn't even there—but Chase worshipped Theo. And honestly . . . it's the kind of thing Theo would've done at Chase's age. Fooling around on a job site, like he was invincible. I think Theo felt . . . like Chase was acting the way he thought Theo would have. And of course, Chase never would have worked for their dad in the first place if Theo hadn't been there."

"But that's ridiculous." I slapped my cleaning towel down on the counter, jaw jutting with indignation. "Theo didn't force Chase to play lacrosse, or intern at the company. And he sure as shit didn't tell him to get wasted and climb around on scaffolding."

"Of course not," Bella said gently. "And logically, I'm sure Theo knows that. But since when do emotions have anything to do with logic?" Bella twirled her bottle slowly, the glass clinking rhythmically against the mosaic surface of the table. "I'm not saying it's how Theo *should* feel, but I think it's how he *does* feel."

"Fuck," I murmured.

"I know," Bella said. "Still . . . it's good you know about it."

"You sure about that? You should have seen Theo's face when he was telling me."

"But he *did* tell you." Bella twirled the bottle again, eyes fixed on the label. "Even a couple weeks after it happened, he shut down about Chase. He's a really private person. The fact that he trusted you with that . . . It has to be a good sign."

I sniffed out a laugh.

"You make it sound like this is an *actual* relationship, Bella."

"It is. Maybe not a romantic one, but it's clearly real. Which honestly makes me way less worried about what you've gotten yourself into."

I was working out a retort when the bell over the door rang and in walked . . .

"Theo, hey. Is it six already?"

"Quarter to. But I figured we could go over the game plan. The wine bar we're going to is owned by . . ." He stopped as he registered Bella at the table, eyes widening almost imperceptibly. "Bella, hey. Ellie didn't say you'd be joining."

"I'm just in town for family dinner. You two lovebirds can hit the wine bar alone," Bella said sweetly, crossing her legs as she smiled at Theo. Her eyes caught mine, mischief flickering there. "But don't let me interrupt." She gestured between the two of us. "You probably missed each other. And being engaged is so exhilarating. Go on, I don't mind if you kiss."

Theo's eyes flitted from Bella to me, panic brewing on their surface. He reached across the counter to take my hand.

"It is hard to be apart these days . . . But we can control ourselves. You know how Ellie is about PDAs."

"Ellie said she *loves* how physical you get. That it makes her feel . . . what was the word you used, El? *Safe*."

"That's nice," Theo said vaguely, Adam's apple working. He started leaning across the counter. Something in my chest tightened mutinously.

"Oh for god's . . . she's *fucking* with you, Theo." I rolled my eyes, stepping back and tugging my hand away. "I told you from the beginning I was telling my family the truth." Though I *may* have strategically planned tonight's "date" to avoid the family dinner gauntlet that would be coming now that I'd finally followed through on that promise. Details.

"It's not like we followed up on that," he muttered as Bella tried to cover her laughter with a hand.

"I'm sorry, I just couldn't help it," she said between giggles. "You should have seen the looks on your faces."

"I'm glad we amuse you." Theo's brow was low, aiming for annoyance, but the corners of his lips were quirked. Bella picked up her Orangina and took a delicate sip through the straw.

"Anyway, I should get going. Mimi's cooking her famous cacciatore. And I promised I'd pay in details about how your little 'arrangement' is progressing." Bella grinned wickedly as she shrugged into her coat. "After all, Ellie's almost as good at fooling herself as you are, Taylor." With an emphatic eyebrow raise, Bella sauntered out.

"What did *that* mean?" Theo asked. "She's still fucking with us, right?"

"She just loves messing with people," I said. "It's her thing."

But it wasn't, and we both knew it. Which begged the question . . . What did she think we were fooling ourselves about?

The wine bar was surprisingly pleasant, so much so that I almost forgot we were there to "sell it" to the staff—all fixtures of Milborough's social scene—and the customers, apparently important in Theo's circles. Whenever a familiar face would appear, he'd take my hands in his, leaning in to whisper who the couple watching us from the back booth was, or urging me to smile "like I said something naughty. And show off your ring hand, but subtly." It all felt like some fun secret only the two of us were in on, which I suppose it was . . . and which must explain the tingly feeling that spread through me each time he'd pull me close, urging both of us to recommit to the parts we were playing.

"That was actually really fun," I said as Theo pulled up in front of my apartment afterward. "I think we were pretty convincing."

"Did you see the look on Erin Martinelli's face? We deserve Oscars." Theo grinned widely.

"Clearly all that time hanging out with the weird theater kids rubbed off on you."

"Maritza always was committed to . . . *the Method*." He waggled his eyebrows and I laughed in spite of myself. "Here, I'll walk you to the door."

"I'm perfectly capable of making it up a sidewalk by myself, Theo."

"I know."

Before I could retort, he was moving around to open my door, arm already out for me. Together, we walked the short path to my building's entrance. He paused just outside, turning toward me, close enough that I could smell a faint hint of his piny smell. For some reason, I didn't want to head inside just yet.

"So . . . what's next?"

"I was thinking it might be time to broach the topic of Mangia with Ted. I doubt he'll pull the plug on it right away, but we've been doing everything right. My friend Everett just texted to ream me out for not telling him about the engagement. This is *working*."

Theo reached for my left hand, lifting it so the ring caught the light from inside the building. It sparkled mesmerizingly. After a moment, he lifted his gaze to mine, eyes darkened by the night. My heart started thudding heavily, the warmth from his hand shooting through me, swirling around the base of my belly before it traveled lower to settle between my legs. I swallowed hard. Somehow here, away from anyone's assessing gaze, the residual glow of our mutual deception still flowing through my veins, I couldn't find a reason to pull my hand away. I drew my lower lip between my teeth, biting down hard in an effort to bring myself back to my senses. This made no sense at all, this was Theo Taylor, and yet . . .

"What can I say? We make a good team." My voice was just

above a whisper. Theo lowered my hand but didn't drop it. I still didn't pull away.

"You're not what I expected, Ellie." His thumb started rubbing absently over the inside of my palm, the soft graze of his skin on mine keeping time with the increasingly insistent pulse of my blood.

"Oh? What did you expect?"

"I'm not sure, but . . ." He licked his upper lip, drawing my attention to the perfect curves of its bow. "I feel more *open* around you than I have in a long time. Like . . . there are possibilities I hadn't considered before."

My lips parted slightly. Theo's eyes dropped to them.

"What sorts of possibilities?" I murmured. I couldn't tell if he was pulling closer to me or if I was being drawn into his orbit, but suddenly he was nearer, his breath warm on my cheek. My skin felt tingly, more sensitive, warm all over despite the late-winter chill in the air. If he moved his hand even an inch up my arm I felt like I might burst into flame, his touch turning my body incandescent.

"Do I really need to say?" He leaned closer still, voice going husky. "On that note . . . What would you say to modifying rule two?"

A tidal surge between my legs.

"Modifying it how, exactly?"

A hair's breadth closer. The outside of his coat grazed my hips, forming a little enclosure around our bodies, looping us into each other.

"It's important that people believe this is real, right?"

"Now more than ever."

"And if you *were* my fiancée . . . I probably wouldn't stop at kissing you here." He bent to press his lips to the line of my jaw. I tilted my head to the side, sucking in a sharp breath as the pressure of the kiss seemed to take hold of my entire body at once. He moved his mouth an inch lower, catching the curve where my jaw met my neck. "Don't you think?"

"Definitely not," I said breathily.

"People might start to wonder."

"A risk we can't take."

"My thoughts exactly." He pulled away, just a few inches, but the spot where his lips had been still felt sparkly, like he'd awakened something beneath the skin that hadn't quite settled back down.

"So if I did this . . ." His hand slipped around my waist, finding the small of my back and pulling me closer yet, the strength in his arm firm but gentle. ". . . that would be okay?"

"Smart, even."

"And what about if I did this?"

And then his mouth was on mine, soft and warm and insistent. Without any conscious thought my arms slipped around his shoulders, body pressing along the length of him as my lips parted. His tongue grazed over the soft inner curve of my lips, slowly, deliberately, and my breath hitched in my throat. My hand inched around to the nape of his neck, fingers tangling in the soft near-curls I knew nestled there . . .

. . . then a car door slammed in the parking lot behind my building.

Startled, I pulled away, breathing heavily, blinking as I stared at Theo. We stood frozen a few inches apart as one of my neighbors made his way past us. By the time the lobby door closed, the snow-globe swirl of glitter seemed to have settled. I swallowed hard, nodding slowly.

"I think that would be alright. To convince . . . other people."

"Of course. That's what all this is for."

We stood there a few more seconds. Finally, I took another deliberate step back, trying to ignore the collapsing feeling in my lungs that accompanied it.

"Anyway . . . good job tonight. It was very . . . convincing."

"Clearly the role was meant for me." Theo ducked his head ever so slightly, his eyes somber and locked on mine.

And then he was walking back down the path, and I hurried to the elevator, refusing to look over my shoulder, and before long I collapsed onto my sagging sofa with my coat still on, the same five words spooling through my head on repeat.

What the fuck just happened, what the fuck just happened, what the ever-loving fuck *just happened?*

Fourteen

It had to have been the wine.

Sure, I'd only had a couple glasses, and I'd woken up clear-headed, barring the confusion swirling around my head like a cloud of midges, tiny specifics—his hand pressing against the base of my spine, the intoxicating smell of his skin, those lips, somehow even more perfect against my own than they were as a platonic visual ideal—darting in to nip at my brain quicker than I could swat them away. But I'd let Theo order, and he'd picked options that were pricey even for the chichi wine bar. Maybe rich-people wine was just more . . . effective?

Or maybe it was plain horniness. It had been almost five months since I broke up with Jake Makris, the bedroom-eyed, broody bartender at Mary Mallon's, the one bar in Milborough that could claim legitimacy as a music venue. With Jake, the sex had been good—really good, even—and there was a thrill in showing up to the occasional house party or show on the arm of one of the most desirable men in "the scene"—not that Milborough could boast much on that front. But within a few weeks it became apparent Jake wasn't the strong silent type so much as he had literally nothing to *say*. When he'd explained to me that the real reason twins freaked him out was *What if they mixed themselves up, how would they know what thoughts were theirs*, I hadn't been able to help myself, I'd laughed aloud. Which had killed the postcoital mood for both of us, and frankly, made it hard for me to feel particularly coital ever afterward.

After Jake, I'd deleted my dating apps. Winter was coming, I couldn't be bothered with the effort of primping for yet another first date with someone who turned out to be deeply devoted to CrossFit, or tried to tell me, straight-faced, all the reasons I just didn't *get* David Foster Wallace, let alone another six to ten weeks of hookups with a variation on Jake, the type of man I somehow kept returning to, long on style but lacking in just about everything that might carry us past the three-month mark.

Jesus, maybe Bella was right. Maybe I *had* been dating losers on purpose.

Either way, what happened with Theo had been *chemical*. For both of us—head injuries must have all kinds of side effects. It didn't mean anything. I was not falling for *Theo Taylor*. Sure, my "type" up until this point might not be the *most* conducive to long-term relationships, but that didn't mean the solution was jumping into the deep end of the country club pool. It had been a blip. A momentary out-of-brain experience. Some mix of wine, my underserved genitals sending up a flare, and the fact that, objectively, Theo was extremely good-looking. So were Ken dolls. So what?

The routines of the deli helped slightly, and by midafternoon I'd almost managed to stop worrying our mutual temporary insanity like a sore (throbbing, aching with need, *Do not go there, Ellie*) tooth. I didn't even think twice when the phone rang, tucking it against my shoulder as I dumped a generous amount of oregano into the red sauce I was preparing.

"Ellie. It's Theo."

And just like that, all the midges swooped back in, dive-bombing me with flashes of last night, heart fluttering at the on-slaught.

"Hey . . ." I said, cautious. Did he want to talk about what happened? Did *I* want to? What was this warm, puddly feeling going through my core just at the sound of his voice, this Pavlovian desire I had *not* approved but which was rapidly overtaking my ability to focus on something as simple as *measuring oregano*?

Dear lord, was this what Stockholm syndrome felt like? I'd never felt such sympathy for Patty Hearst.

"How are you?"

"Okay. Just . . . making sauce." Great. Now I sounded stupid to boot.

"Ring still on?"

"Yes, actually."

"Proud of you."

I laughed in spite of myself. It slightly calmed the stuttery nerve-jangles.

"Did you just call to check on your ancestral wealth, or was there something *meaningful* you wanted to interrupt my day with?"

"Actually . . . I have some good news." A hint of excitement crept in. "I just got off a conference call with the leadership team. We patched Ted in—"

"Totally normal form of communication with one's father."

"As I was *about* to say, the team had a call, and I brought up Mangia."

I hurried into the back corner of the back room, death-gripping the phone.

"And? Did he agree to call off the deal?"

"Not exactly."

I slumped against the walk-in, limbs immediately sandbagged.

"How is this good news, Theo?"

"I was *getting* there." I rolled my eyes. "He agreed to call a board meeting. But first, he wants to throw a party."

"A . . . what? Why?"

"For our engagement. He felt it was 'important to share the happy news before rethinking the Mangia relationship.' The board is entirely family."

"He's such a family man now?"

"That's how he'd like to *appear*. Which makes this a clear step in the right direction." Theo's voice lowered gleefully. "Publicizing this in the broader business community would make it almost *impossible* for him to move ahead with the deal."

"I'm sorry, our *engagement* party is going to be for the 'broader business community'?"

"If we're lucky. We want this to be Ted's affair. It ups our odds."

"Yes, but that means maximum *Ted*."

"Trust me, I know. And he wants to have the party soon, most likely this weekend—he's adamant about it happening before we convene the board, and we have a limited window for that if we really are going to nix the Mangia deal. So . . . are you free tonight to plan our attack? I know it's last-minute, but I can be flexible on timing . . ."

Theo's offer opened a valve on some previously dammed reserve of nervous excitement, the feeling bursting from my center all the way to the tips of my fingers. Somewhere at the back of my mind a red flag was waving frantically, *You can't trust yourself around him,* but that was idiotic—the kiss had been a fluke. The giddy, floaty feeling overtaking me wasn't about seeing *Theo,* it was about how close we were to getting what we wanted. It was starting to look like the deli might actually survive. And whatever else he was—and he wasn't anything to *me,* just a genetic lottery winner with a more interesting personality than I'd previously given him credit for, which wasn't saying much, considering I'd previously assumed Theo's essence was composed entirely of golfing tips, canvas belts with sailboats on them, and a generous sprinkle of *Let them eat cake*—Theo was a good teammate in Operation Keep Mangia Out.

Plus, it was probably like . . . ninety-two percent the wine.

"Tonight works. This is important."

"I knew you'd understand. Meet at mine around seven? I'll order food."

"It's a date," I said, cheeks heating as I hung up. He knew that was just a phrase, right? Because that was definitely all I'd meant by it.

The excitement kept me buoyant through the slow hours of the afternoon. I even cheerily offered Ruth Pinsky a taste of the new farro salad recipe I was working on, which seemed to shock her even more than it did me. I was finally in the last-hour stretch, prematurely wrapping the meats people bought less often so closing would go faster, when the bell over the door tinkled. I looked up, smiling brightly—was this what it felt like to be Bella?—but my smile froze when I realized it was . . .

"Sam?"

"Hey, Ellie. So this is the deli, huh?" She turned in a slow circle, looking it over. "It's charming. Not that I'm surprised, you're so stylish." She moved over to a shelf, turning a bottle of balsamic around to read the label. "Do people realize how hard it is to get your hands on some of this stuff?"

"Definitely not," I said, pride welling in my chest. Sam complimenting the deli—and calling *me* stylish—definitely felt higher-value just because of the source.

"Maybe you should start keeping it behind the counter."

"Or ask for a special password."

"Totally. Instead of speakeasy you'd have a speak-cheesy."

"That's terrible . . . but also yes, I'm all in." I grabbed a mortadella out of the case to wrap as she put down the vinegar. "What are you doing here, by the way? In Milborough, I mean?"

"Oh, business things." She waved one hand through the air as she peered at a squat jar of preserved lemons. "And personal, I suppose. Which is where you come in, actually."

"Oh?"

She slid the jar neatly back into place and turned to me.

"Be honest. You and Theo aren't really together, are you?"

I blinked, mouth hanging open slightly.

"Sorry . . . what?"

"At the very least you're not engaged."

My heart pinballed around my chest. I licked my lips slowly, putting on an annoyed frown, while the siren blare of *How does she know?* grew so loud in my brain I was almost convinced she'd hear it.

"I don't know where this is coming from, but I don't appreciate—"

She raised a hand, fingers long and slender, studded with tastefully simple rings.

"Honestly? I think it's kind of a baller move—though I don't know how you ever convinced *Theo* to come on board. Was it to keep Mangia out?" My head jerked back, I was so startled, and a tiny, triumphant smile curled her crimsoned lips. "I thought so. Ted's a pompous ass, but even *he* wouldn't put Theo's fiancée out of business. It's kinda brilliant, actually."

My limbs and head felt too light, like they might detach and float off in different directions. How did she know? More important, what was she going to do? Also, was it possible that an incredibly tiny part of me liked Sam even more right now? I'd known she was a shark the moment she'd slid into Theo's hospital room, all smooth skin and barely concealed power, but I hadn't realized she was Sharklock fucking *Holmes*.

I had to make one last-ditch effort.

"Sam, I don't know why you're saying this, but it's inappropri—"

"The *regattas,* Ellie."

"Excuse me?"

"You told me Theo was planning his next sailing regatta? At Ted's."

"Right . . ." Oh fuck. I should have *known* that was a trap. But she'd thrown it out so casually, and Theo was beyond the type to pay thousands a year for the privilege of docking some tiny polished-wood boat in the marina over at Thornvale . . .

"Theo doesn't sail."

I sniffed exaggeratedly.

"I know you two have history, but Theo has changed in the last few—"

"He's terrified of it. Ever since he was a kid and Cat fell overboard from his grandpa's boat. I buy that he's developed some new hobbies since we were together, but there's no way he's taken up *sailing regattas.*"

I could keep denying it, but what was the point? I was checkmated and we both knew it. Besides, part of me was more than a little relieved. Lying to people like Sam—people who actually cared about at least one of us—was the part of this whole charade that still had me feeling morally queasy. The fear on her face in the hospital . . . Didn't she *deserve* the truth? Especially now, when maintaining the lie was pointless? I blew out a breath so large it inflated my cheeks, collapsing onto my elbows on the counter and burying my face in my hands.

"For what it's worth, we're not planning to keep it up forever. In the meantime . . . are you planning to out us?"

"*Out* you?"

"To Ted. Will you tell him?" I looked up at her, my body taut with anxiety. We'd been so *close* to pulling this off.

She stared at me, brown eyes narrowing slightly . . .

. . . then she laughed.

"Fuck no. Jesus, *no*. What do you take me for?"

"A woman who set a trap for me the second time we met?" I muttered. Sam grimaced.

"Fair. I just had this feeling after the hospital—something about the way you talked about Chase—and I wanted to be sure I wasn't . . . grasping at straws, you know?" She grimaced apologetically. "But I'd never tell Ted. Like . . . forget what a complete dick he is, he *should* ditch the Mangia deal. I hate the idea of him sucking all the charm out of Milborough—other cities would kill for a downtown like ours. Besides, it's short-term thinking. Half this town's in the Taylor portfolio—the better play is to develop that building in a way that ups Milborough's overall appeal, bring in higher-income individuals from Boston, once their money's being spent here start raising your commercial rents, blah blah blah, you know the drill."

No.

"Totally."

"But Ted's always been a sucker for the profit motive, the shorter-term the better. He doesn't care if Milborough winds up a clone of Burnton and all the other upscale big-box-burbs around here, as long as there's another zero on the check. And clearly he doesn't care about how much that building means to Theo, which is . . . disappointingly expected, but *should* count for something. It's not like he has that many spots that can bring his brother back to life for him." She sighed heavily as recognition jolted through me. I knew Theo and I had more in common than I'd realized but this felt . . . uncomfortably close. "Anyway, the plan's gonna change if I have any say in it."

I squeezed my eyes closed, trying to block out at least one stimulus so I could *think*.

"So you just . . . wanted to let me know you cracked our secret?" My forehead furrowed. "Congrats, I guess?"

"Be real, it *was* kinda impressive."

I fixed her with a glare. She shrugged, relenting.

"Sorry, annoying, I know. I keep telling my therapist I want to stop doing that, but I never actually stop." She moved closer, glancing over her shoulder and lowering her voice. "As it happens, I have an idea of my own. What would you say to helping me fix things with Theo? He . . . well, he's always been the one that got away."

Her face took on a tight, anxious look, and she leaned forward, clearly hanging on my response. Theo's ex wanted me, his now admittedly fake fiancée, to set *her* up with him? It was so patently ridiculous I barked out a laugh. She simply raised an eyebrow.

"I'm sorry, you're *serious*?"

"I wouldn't be here otherwise."

"For all I know you were just really craving an Italian sub."

"I mean, I wouldn't say no to one. But for the record, yes, I'm serious."

"But *why*? No, nix that—how? You just sleuthed us out, you know better than anyone that there's nothing *between* me and Theo."

His hands on my back, pulling me against him, his lips fervent, hungry, the full-body electricity that shot through me at his touch. *No. Bad Ellie.* None of that was real. It was just wine-fueled idiocy. And it was absolutely *not* happening again. Trying to force the mental image back into the box it should have known better than to crawl out of, I added:

"Honestly, I don't think he even likes me."

"Oh come *on,* Ellie." She lifted her eyebrow in elegant scorn.

"I'm sorry, can *you* imagine someone less like Theo than me?" She laughed slightly, then her expression turned thoughtful.

"I don't know about that, but I *do* know he trusts you."

"You want to tell him that? Because every third sentence out of his mouth is some variation on 'Don't screw this up for us.'"

"Yeah, for *us.* He's willing to do this with you, tell this massive lie—to Ted, of all people, which puts it on a whole other level. There isn't a single person I could imagine convincing him to agree to something like this—which is wildly out of character, if you weren't aware. But somehow, *you* did."

I opened my mouth to protest . . . but she was right, wasn't she? The person I'd assumed Theo was before we wound up in this frankly ridiculous situation had dozens of fancy acquaintances, casual friendships with the people who attended Milborough's most glittering affairs, a rotating cast of beautiful people surrounding him. Still, if he had any intimate friendships, a Bella so to speak, I had a feeling that it was a position he, like me, reserved for one individual at a time.

I nibbled my lower lip. Why shouldn't I help them get together? Sam was burnished with the same patrician patina as Theo, but like him (or as I'd recently realized about him), she seemed far more interesting than most congenitally gilded people I'd met. It was almost too easy to imagine the two of them walking into Ted's mansion arm in arm, presiding over a gorgeous holiday party in Theo's condo, chatting with another unfairly attractive couple over dinner at Post. The fact that the image twisted my lungs tight was probably just generalized jealousy—my dating habits clearly didn't put me on track for anything like *that* in the near future—right?

Right. Definitely right. *Wine-based insanity, Ellie. He is* not *your type.*

"Let's say I'm considering this," I finally said, unable to find a good reason not to, but equally unable to agree. "Why would I help you? No offense, just . . . it's kind of a lot to ask from someone you don't even know."

Sam's eyes twinkled with glee at the miniature concession.

"First off, that can change. Our knowing each other, I mean. Genuinely, all this aside, you seem like my kind of people."

"Oh? Is it my glamorous lifestyle?" I gestured around the room with a bologna.

"More that. The sense of humor. It's harder to find than people think. And the style, glamorous or not. But anyway, you're right, we don't know each other, at least not yet. Which is why I'd never *dream* of asking if I didn't think I could scratch your back too. You're doing this to keep Mangia out, right?"

I tilted my head to one side, not quite a concession, but definitely not a denial.

"I could help with that. Throw my weight behind ending the deal . . ."

"Sorry, but . . . what weight?" I crinkled my nose, skeptical. "I know you have some extremely high-powered job, and *clearly* Ted's a fan, but that doesn't mean he's going to make major business decisions based on your recommendation."

"Maybe not now, but trust me . . . I could help you *very* soon. And in a major way."

"And I suppose if I don't agree you'll make sure my very *stylish* deli goes the way of the dodo?" I narrowed my eyes.

"Definitely not. I was being genuine, Ellie. I think this place is what Milborough needs *more* of. Mangia . . . it's exactly the wrong direction. If you say no, I'll be disappointed, obviously, and I can't promise I'll try to cash in the chips I have for your sake, but I'm not going to get in the way." She licked her upper lip, eyes flitting to the side in uncharacteristic uncertainty. "Also . . . I know the engagement isn't real, but if there's something between you and Theo that I just totally blew by, *please* pretend I never said anything. I had my chance and I screwed it up. That's not something you should pay for. There wouldn't be any hard feelings."

"Really? You just offered a Faustian bargain where my half would be getting you two together."

"Yes, but I'm not here to break anyone up, I'm here because I'm *assuming* there's nothing to come between in the first place. If there is . . . then this conversation never happened." She shrugged. "I'm not one of those women who view everyone else who was born with ovaries as competition. I mean . . . I think you're cool, why shouldn't Theo?"

"That's because I *am* cool," I deadpanned.

"See? Proving my point." A genuine grin overtook her face, then it went more somber. "Seriously, though, if you and Theo are the real deal, forget I said anything. But if you're not . . . It took me too long to realize I messed up when I let him go. I want to try again. I feel *ready* to try again. So if this whole thing is just about Mangia . . . think it over, yeah? There's a way everyone could come out of this getting what they want."

And with that she hurried out, leaving me in a swirl of her undoubtedly expensive perfume, and an even more tumultuous tornado of confusion.

Could I really help her and Theo get back together? Double-cross *him* even as he and I were trying to double-cross the entire town?

Also . . . was it even what I wanted?

My brain kept screaming *Yes, focus on saving the deli, he's so not for you,* but every time I imagined the way his lips grazed my jaw . . .

On the other hand, could I afford to say no?

Fifteen

I hadn't untangled the Gordian knot of Sam's proposition by the time I showed up at Theo's door, so I decided to push it to the back of my mind and focus on the more immediate concern: It was imperative that Ted be willing to at least *call* the board meeting that could set things in motion. Which meant nailing our party plan.

I shifted the focaccia and whipped red pepper ricotta to one hand to hit the elevator button for Theo's floor—he'd given me a fob after our first study session. I hadn't even managed to fix my hair when the door opened not on the empty hallway I'd been expecting, but on Theo, eyes bright. His hair had freed itself from its business confines, flopping over his forehead in a way that evoked his teenaged self, and he'd swapped out his usual checked button-down for a faded Milborough Lacrosse T-shirt that probably hung off his lanky frame once, but that now pulled tight across his broad shoulders, highlighting the muscles of his arms and chest and somehow turning his chiseled good looks younger, and sweeter. More like the kind of guy I usually found myself swiping—

Nope. Hard nope. Not happening.

"Were you just waiting outside the elevator door?" I said, voice a little too tart in my effort to silence my unwelcome internal monologue.

"We get alerts when someone's entering our unit. As a safety feature?"

"Oh. Right, well . . . here." I thrust the bread and spread at him.

"You didn't need to bring anything . . ."

"Yes, I did. Generations of Italian ghosts would haunt me if I showed up empty-handed. Besides, this is like . . . the best thing we have in the deli."

"High praise." He waggled his eyebrows and I laughed, shoulders lowering as I pushed past him. It was just *Theo,* not some nuclear sex bomb I'd set off if I got too close. Imagining all the various special-edition Topsiders he probably owned could shut off any unwelcome libido. Besides, he clearly wasn't worried about *me.* "So? We're on a timeline, we should get started, right?"

"I love how we've never lost the romance," he deadpanned as he trailed after me into the kitchen, laying the bread and cheese down to start searching for a cutting board.

"When people think of me, the first word that comes to mind is 'romantic.'"

"Oh? For me it's 'salami.'"

"Shhh, don't be vulgar, I haven't even had wine yet."

I took a stool at the counter, sniffing the air. A familiar smell tickled my nostrils, making my mouth water . . .

"Before I slice into this, I want to make sure you're okay with doubling down on bread and cheese." He pulled open the oven. My eyes went wide.

"Oh my god, Theo . . . you got *Veschio's?* Are you a hero?"

"I called for pizza delivery, Ellie, I didn't cure cancer."

"They deliver to you?"

He laughed, shaking his head as he slid the box out and pressed the button to turn off the warmer.

"Consider it motivation to move out of that apartment." Before I could work up a suitably fiery response—I *knew* he'd been judging my place, and what gave him the right?—he was sliding the box onto the island. "Anyway, you were so emphatic about it, I had to see if it was any good."

"*Any good?* I think you forget you're speaking to a food industry *professional*. Who's also Italian. And probably eats way more pizza than you. You know, since I'm down-market enough to live where I do."

"It wasn't a gauntlet." Theo raised his hands in mock surrender. "I'm looking forward to this being my new go-to spot. But I need an answer, focaccia or pizza?"

"Ugh, I can't believe I'm slighting the focaccia this way, but . . . definitely pizza." I pointed at the bread, lowering my eyebrows menacingly. "But eat that for breakfast tomorrow, otherwise it'll start being less good."

"Yes, ma'am."

We made plates and crossed to the loveseat near the dramatic fireplace, the realistic crackling sounds almost tricking me into thinking it was wood-burning. A bottle of bubbly waited in a frosty ice bucket on the intricate (and probably authentic) midcentury coffee table.

"Classy. Who were you expecting?" Theo rolled his eyes as he pulled the bottle out.

"It's a terrible pairing for pizza, but . . . I thought we should celebrate. We haven't pulled it off yet, but this party is a major step." He carefully removed the foil and cage, expertly twisting the cork out of what I could see was genuine France-would-approve Champagne. He slid a pair of delicate flutes out from behind the bucket and poured. "Besides, my therapist is always trying to get me to appreciate the small wins more."

"You have a therapist?" I raised an eyebrow as I set the pizza down.

"Why wouldn't I?"

"I don't know. Your family seems more . . . stiff upper lip. Or whatever the New England WASP version of that is."

"All the more reason I should be in therapy."

"Fair point."

"Anyway"—he raised his glass, eyes softening as he gazed at me over the whisper-thin rim—"to us. I don't think either of us would have guessed it, but we make a really good team."

I clinked my glass against his, cheeks heating as I took a sip. The champagne exploded over my tongue, dry and crisp, the effervescence seeping into me as I swallowed. And still his eyes on mine. I took a big gulp and dropped my gaze to the pizza, praying I wasn't actually blushing.

"On that note, what's the plan? Do you want me to try to be more . . . Ted-approved at the party? I can't promise I'll achieve that, but intentions count for something . . ."

"No need. We're past the point of winning Ted over. Besides, the folks he'll invite to boost his ego will get a kick out of you."

"Since I'm not about to blight *their* family trees?"

Theo shrugged acknowledgment.

"You're clever, you're attractive—the fact that you say things polite company might be thinking but isn't expressing makes you that much more charming."

I gulped more champagne. The bubbles fizzed through my entire body, releasing their wealth of sequestered sunlight. Theo topped off my glass, then his own.

"Then what is there to plan, exactly?"

"We have to introduce our families, for one thing." Theo put his pizza down, angling toward me. His knee grazed mine, the heat of him palpable through the fabric.

"Really?" I squeaked. "Why?"

"We're supposed to be engaged, Ellie. Our families would at least *meet* at this point. And I have a sense that your grandmother might not be as on board with this plan as you led me to believe."

"What makes you—"

"I asked Bella point-blank."

I pursed my lips, annoyed at her unfailing honesty.

"I promise, Mimi will toe the line if I ask."

"Still, I'd prefer a quick tête-à-tête before we head into the lion's den."

"Trust but verify?"

"Something like that. Plus, you should show her this. So she doesn't act surprised by it, I mean." His hand moved across the loveseat to mine, and he lifted it slightly, glancing down at the ring as he rubbed his thumb over my knuckles. A shiver worked its way down my spine, lodging itself between my legs. "More importantly, I want her to believe I'm on her side. That I'm on *your* side." His eyes, heavy and hooded, firelight flickering over their surface, caught mine.

"Why does it matter?"

"At least one of our families should seem excited about this." His voice had gone rough. It activated some sort of magnet in my chest, one polarized to him. "About *us*."

"And then people will believe it?" I whispered. "You . . . and me?"

"I think they'll wonder why they didn't see it before."

And now *he* was leaning closer. The shivery feeling at my core started spreading outward, warmth flooding me.

I shouldn't do this. Shouldn't let myself slide into him so easily a second time. Shouldn't let his lips trace the line of my throat, his hands slide over the curves of my body, feel the strength in those muscled arms as he pulled me up onto his lap . . .

Why shouldn't I do this?

I flung around desperately for an answer, but I couldn't find one, every nerve, every inch of skin begging me to give in to his touch, pregnant with possibility even as he barely grazed the tips of my fingers.

Sam. She'd shown again and again that she really cared about Theo. Put herself on the line today because there was something *real* between them, or at least there could be. After the accident, she'd dropped everything and come running, and I'd . . . lied for my own self-interest. I still wasn't sure if there was a trick in her offer I hadn't spotted, but I at least owed her a fair hearing, right? Owed it to *myself* to know the full story before I blustered in and made a mess of not only my life, but Theo's, and hers?

Sucking in a sharp breath, I forced myself to sit back, sipping the champagne to give myself something to focus on besides the curves of Theo's lips.

"Before we go there, I have to know . . ."

"Yes?" I could feel his eyes burning over the skin of my neck. He was leaning closer, quickly closing the gap I'd tried to create.

"What happened with you and Sam?"

He blinked a few times. Sat up.

"What do you mean?"

"She clearly cares about you."

"And I care about her, but there's nothing *romantic* between us."

"But there was, right? Before?" He squeezed his eyes shut, exhaling heavily through his nose. "I'm just saying . . . if we're going to sell this, I can't be blindsided by her, or by someone's idea of her. Ted, his friends . . . they'd expect me to at least *know*."

"I suppose that's true." Theo drained his glass in one gulp. "First, refills."

Once he'd topped us off again, he reclined into the loveseat, idly reaching for my hand once more, but safely slack. My heartbeat started to slow back to normal. The champagne was giving me a pleasant, warm, buzzy feeling.

"The truth is . . . Sam and I were engaged."

"When?" My eyes widened with genuine shock.

"For about a year. I proposed on her twenty-third birthday, we were in Turks and Caicos. It was all very . . ." He pursed his lips.

"Instagramworthy?"

"Exactly." He laughed, rueful.

"Twenty-three. That's pretty young."

"It seems young now, but back then . . . We'd been together since sophomore year in college, everyone seemed to be expecting it . . ." He turned his gaze to the ceiling, body tensing defensively. "And we were in love. Or I thought we were."

I swallowed hard, ignoring the ache the words opened up just beneath my sternum.

"Anyway, you've met Sam. She's always known exactly what she wants."

"Was she planning some over-the-top wedding?"

"The opposite. Sam wanted us to run off to Vegas specifically to *avoid* that. Her mom's not like Ted—she actually means well—but she's very . . . traditional. True old money, 'There's a way things are done' and all that. There was never going to be a version of that wedding that Kate didn't completely dominate."

"So . . . what happened?"

"I told you about the doubts I was having. About working for Ted, I mean."

"Right . . ."

"Sam was very much Team Leave the Company. She was the one who started bringing home applications to architecture schools."

"Shouldn't that have been your choice?"

"Yes . . . and no." Theo canted his head, considering. "To her it was just . . . simple. I wasn't happy, I wouldn't be able to grow there, so the only logical thing was to leave as soon as possible and do the thing that had a chance of *making* me happy."

"I guess that makes sense. Still . . . it's *your* life."

"But we were planning to build a life together." Theo's lips twisted at my grimace. "Like I said, we were young. Honestly, I think she saw it as supporting me, not pressuring me. I told her it was what I wanted."

"I suppose . . ." I could just about see my way to her meaning well, but still . . . it felt perilously close to assuming you can just *rework* people into the shape you'd prefer.

"Anyway, I was getting started with the applications and then . . . Chase." Theo's brow clouded. "When he died . . . everything just went sideways." He shook his head sharply, Adam's apple bobbing as he blinked away a shimmer of tears. I squeezed his fingers a little tighter, throat thickening sympathetically. Soon, though, that feeling was consumed in a spurt of fiery indignation.

"Wait . . . she left because your brother *died*?"

"What? No. God no." Theo shook his head rapidly. "Sam was incredible through all that. I'm not sure I'd have made it through without her."

"Oh. Well . . . that's good." I tried to ignore the prickling thorn of jealousy growing out of my fury ashes. "But then . . . what happened?"

"I just . . . took too long." Theo shrugged. "There was no way I was going to abandon Ted right after that. I'm not sure I could have held it together through the applications process anyway. But after a few months, things started going back to normal, at least with work, and all the same problems reappeared. Sam started pushing me to apply again, but I flat-out refused. It was too soon, it would kill my father, blah blah blah."

"I mean . . . that sounds legit to me."

"It wasn't completely off base, but it was an excuse, and we both knew it. To her credit she dropped the subject for a few more months. But when she brought it up at the next round of application deadlines—this would have been almost a year after Chase died—it didn't go over as well." Theo sighed heavily and took another long sip of champagne. "She didn't actually *say* I was using it as an excuse, but I knew that's what she was thinking. And I blew up. It turned into one of those fights where you say all kinds of things you've been holding on to for too long, things you don't even mean, just because you're feeling defensive. I really laid into her, told her she was heartless, that she'd never loved *me*, just the on-paper version. Now, of course, I realize she was right."

I felt for both of them. It sounded like Sam had been genuinely trying to help, even if she didn't go about it well. And Theo could intellectualize it *now*, but he must have still been reeling from grief. That kind of loss didn't disappear so much as it became normalized, like a scar from childhood you'd gotten used to. Or maybe more a limb that's been lopped off, the pain reigniting every time you take a step into empty air and realize anew that it's gone.

If they'd been five years older when it happened, or if Chase had lived . . . the only question would have been whether Kate got her way about her daughter's lavish wedding. And Sam couldn't have been clearer: She was still in love with Theo, even now.

A heavy, wrung-out feeling overtook me. The idea of him and Sam, a Greek tragedy that could still avert the inevitable ending, dug sharp claws into the part of me that had felt vaguely guilty since we'd started this charade. Theo couldn't be further from my type, but I couldn't keep pretending that he was just an overpriced oxford and a jawline. The question seemed to percolate through me of its own accord, buoyed on champagne and guilt and the vast ocean of long-buried emotions I'd thrown Theo into with this conversation.

"Have you ever thought . . . that maybe you should give it another shot?" I whispered. "With Sam, I mean."

"Of course I've thought about it." He gazed straight into my eyes. "But when I say there's nothing there . . . I mean it, Ellie. I feel bad about how things ended, but in a way, I think everything we went through just proved we were never really right for each other. And lately . . ." His eyes dropped to my mouth, and the air between us crackled again, prickling through the hairs at the nape of my neck.

"Lately . . . what?"

He set his champagne down very deliberately, then reached for my glass. I released it, obedient, lips parting of their own accord.

"Lately I've realized that maybe I've never given the right thing a real shot. Or the right person."

"Oh?" My breath hitched as I raised my eyes to his. The intensity of his stare felt like a brand on my skin. "And who might that be?"

"Someone who challenges me . . ." He leaned closer. "Someone who isn't *like* me so much as they complement me." Closer yet. His eyelids went heavy, the firelight flickering across his skin. "Someone like . . . well, *you,* Ellie."

I wasn't sure who moved first, but within seconds his lips were on mine, strong arms slipping around my back, pulling me to him. I wriggled onto his lap, wrapping my legs around his waist, mouth level with his now, moaning low as his fingers traced the furrow of my spine, slipped over the curves of my ass, gripping me tight as his tongue slid between my lips. Some distant corner of my brain sent up a flare—*Bad idea*—but it felt unimportant, the urgency of his mouth, his hands, too much to ignore.

I reached down blindly to tug his shirt up, broke the kiss to pull it over his head. I ran my fingertips over the hard ridges of his stomach muscles, biting my lower lip as I grazed the skin there, relishing the shiver that ran through him as my hand moved lower, to where the sharp lines of his pelvis dipped beneath the waist of his jeans. In an instant, his hand was cupping my nape, pulling me in for another hungry kiss before he released me to hurriedly tug my shirt over my head.

"Jesus, Ellie," he murmured, thumb grazing along my collarbone then down toward the extremely gentle curves of my breasts. I sent up a tiny prayer of gratitude that I was wearing my "good" bra, simple black with lace trim, but actually fitted to my almost-a-chest.

"I know, they're tiny."

Theo's eyes lifted to mine.

"They're perfect. You're so incredibly sexy."

And then we were on each other again, my teeth scraping the inside of his lower lip, testing its softness and give, his hands loosing my bra deftly, one palm sliding past the dip of my waist and up my stomach to lightly cup my breast, his thumb moving over my nipple in a way that made me groan aloud. I fumbled at his belt, need throbbing through me, radiating outward from my core, heightening every sensation.

Theo put both hands around my waist, lifting me off him easily, then tugged his belt free, fumbling his fly open with one hand, the other still on me. I wriggled out of my jeans, kicking them aside unceremoniously as Theo stood to tug his pants down. I could see him straining against the fabric of his boxer briefs, and a new thrill went through me. *Look how much he wants you.* I ran my hand over his length and he pulsed gently against my palm, eyes closing. He drew in a sharp breath, head tilting back slightly as I swirled my thumb over the tip.

"Fuck, Ellie . . ." he said, voice rough. "That's . . . *Fuck.*" He gripped my wrist, eyes blazing with intensity as he urged me back along the couch, moving over me in one smooth motion. I slipped the fingers of my free hand beneath the waistband of his underwear, running them along the sharp vee of his pelvic line and back up slowly. A flicker of amusement passed over his face.

"Are you trying to torture me?"

"Maybe a little."

With a grin, he lowered himself over me, hips grinding against my own as he kissed me deeply on the mouth, then along my jaw, then down the length of my throat, my head dropping back to give him access. One hand moved back to my breast, gently squeezing as his thumb flicked over my nipple, the motions rougher now, more urgent. My hips bucked up against him and he pushed up, staring into my eyes.

"Is this okay?"

"God, yes," I said, the words coming out in a breathy rush, body speaking before the rest of me. His fingers slid over my stomach, my back arching as they moved lower, lower still, until they were tracing slow circles over me through the fabric of my underwear. Every nerve in me flared to life at once, concentrating their electric energy at my core. My skin tingled all over, the effervescence of the champagne buzz intensifying every touch. Theo bent over the side of the couch to fumble a condom out of his pants pocket. I laughed aloud.

"You were *planning* this?"

The twist of his lips, sultry and knowing, sent a new swirl of heat through my belly.

"I was a Boy Scout, Ellie. I believe in *always* being prepared."

"Of course you were."

He raised an eyebrow, then tugged his underwear down.

"Take those off," he growled, pointing at mine.

"Aren't *we* demanding," I said as I arched up to tug them free.

"When I know what I want."

He lowered himself back over me and I took him in hand, guiding him against me, letting the friction of skin on skin stoke the fire that was spreading from my center over every inch of my body. Finally, when it felt like something inside me might burst from need, I slid my hand around to the small of his back, guiding him in. He moaned, thrusting into me slowly at first, then more quickly, his body taking over.

"You feel incredible, Ellie."

"Harder," I said, voice a breathy whisper.

And then he was moving against me, into me, *through* me somehow, every thrust of his hips adding to the pressure building inside, my skin growing hotter every moment, and I was arching up to meet him, hips rolling with his, fingernails digging into his back like I might tumble into oblivion otherwise, breath coming in little pants as this swell of want kept growing . . .

"Ellie . . . I—I can't—"

"Go. Go now," I commanded, thrusting my hips hard against his. Dimly, I felt his muscles shudder, heard him cry out, but the intensity of the pleasure crashing over my body blurred my senses, stripping away everything but the explosion at my core, a starburst of sensation that faded only slowly, leaving a pleasant glow in its wake, the still-warm embers of the fire that had raged through me so suddenly.

Theo rolled onto his side, body pressed along the length of mine, and reached a hand up to cup my cheek. There was a tenderness in his gaze I'd never seen before, his whole face softer as he stroked my cheek absently with his thumb.

"That was . . ."

"Good," I supplied.

"Incredible," he returned with an open grin. "That thing you did with your hips . . ."

"What can I say? I'm kind of a prodigy." Warmth unfurled through me at the sound of his laugh.

He drew me in for one last, soft kiss, then pushed himself up, scooting around to perch on the edge of the couch. He reached for our champagne flutes, and I propped myself on an elbow to take mine. There was something deliciously indulgent about lying naked on an expensive sofa, sipping champagne in front of a roaring fire. After a few more seconds, I stretched over to search for my underwear. I'd barely made a dent in the pizza, and it felt strange to eat it *totally* naked. Theo followed suit, pulling his boxer briefs back on. The firelight carved out the lean muscles of his stomach, shoulders, and arms. The sight of him, totally unselfconscious as he bent to clothe himself, reignited the heat between my legs. He settled onto a cushion near me, reaching over to thread his fingers between mine.

"I'm sure you know what this means." Theo gave me a mock-serious look.

"You're going to need to reheat the pizza?"

"That . . . and we're going to have to rethink rule two." He squeezed my hand lightly.

My whole body went tense. With the last traces of postorgasmic glow fading, the words hit like cold water, dousing whatever coals had still been burning inside.

You have complicated things massively. *This is a business arrangement. You are the absolute opposite of each other's type. Nothing is ever going to happen here, other than things getting very, very messy. Were you really that sex-starved, Ellie? Because this was a* huge fuckup.

Dammit, why was the little voice so much louder *now*, when it was too late for me to listen?

"Oh?" I loosed my hand and reached for the red pepper flakes.

"I'm not saying we grope each other in public, just that we expand the boundaries slightly. After all, the biggest concern was that we'd be too awkward, right? That the lack of chemistry would be obvious?" Theo grinned at me then reached for another slice. "I think we can feel confident that that's not a problem anymore."

"True . . ." The rush of cold water was solidifying into ice, clamping cold around my spine and vital organs. "But if it's not broke . . . We're so close, right?"

"Disagree. The last quarter isn't a time to play it safe. You leave it all on the field."

"Well, you're the lacrosse player." I tried to grin naturally, but it felt too tight. *You fucked this up you fucked this up you fucked this up.* "Speaking of, I should probably go get some rest. If Ted's set on throwing the party this weekend, we both need to be on our A-game. And this went . . . longer than I expected."

"Oh . . . sure, of course." A flicker of hurt creased Theo's brow briefly, but just as quickly disappeared. He slid his plate onto the coffee table, grabbed the pizza box, and strode over to the kitchen. "At least take some pizza for the road. There's no way I'll eat all the leftovers."

"Don't blaspheme, Theo, it offends my delicate sensibilities." He grinned over his shoulder as he fished out a roll of aluminum foil, any lingering tension fading from his face.

"You'd be more offended if I let the focaccia go to waste, no?"

"Good point. On second thought . . . load me up."

As Theo wrapped a few slices, I quickly dressed and gathered my things. By the time he was done, I had joined him in the kitchen. He set the packet of pizza on the counter and slipped a hand beneath my coat, cupping it around my waist. My body reacted before my mind could, leaning into him, the intimacy of the touch short-circuiting the same vital switch that had already failed me once tonight.

"Text me that you made it home safe?" Theo said, voice lowering. I swallowed hard, the tenderness of his gaze equally thrilling and terrifying.

"Pretty sure I can manage. We didn't even finish the champagne."

"Still. It would make me feel better."

"Fine." I rolled my eyes, trying to dissipate some of the tension crackling between us. But Theo just squeezed my waist, and my breath caught somewhere in the middle of my chest, and my eyes shot to his lips before I could stop them.

"Thank you. For that and . . . for tonight." He leaned closer, stopping a few inches from my mouth. "We really do make a good team."

And then his hand wrapped all the way around to my back, and I was giving in to the kiss before I really knew what was happening. After a few long seconds, he pulled away.

"Talk tomorrow?" I said, physically stepping back. Apparently my body couldn't be trusted otherwise.

"As long as you text me that you've made it home safe." He smirked.

"Good-*bye,* Theo."

"Sweet dreams, *darling.*" His voice was heavy with sarcasm, but there was . . . *something* beneath the words. Something that sent my internal temperature plummeting again. I smiled vaguely and hurried to the elevator, suddenly desperate to be out of there, knowing—and hating—that I couldn't trust myself to stick to even the most basic rules if I stayed in his presence.

I made it all the way home before I leaned my head against the steering wheel and groaned.

What had I been *thinking*? No, nix that, why had thinking completely abandoned me in the most critical moment?

Champagne. Dammit, how had I let myself be tricked by rich-people wine *again*?

After a few long seconds, I sat up, forcing myself to sort through my thoughts.

We'd made a mistake. Obviously. But it was just that—a mistake. We were both so caught up in pulling this off that we'd lost touch with reality. It didn't have to happen again. No, nix that, it *wouldn't* happen again, no arguments this time, clitoris, you had your chance to lead this wagon train and you sent us over the edge of a goddamned cliff.

I'd just . . . keep my distance. Stick to public appearances. That wouldn't be hard; after the party we'd basically be done, right?

I could not seriously entertain the idea of *Theo Taylor* in my life. My phone pinged.

FROM: Little Lord Doucheleroy

Home yet?

The words squeezed around my heart, threatening to thaw the protective ice layer I'd built up—when was the last time someone had cared enough to check that I was safe?

Stop it. That's not logic, it's your genitals trying to mount a rear attack.

Yup! Talk tomorrow.

Can't wait.

The words released a burst of tenderness I hadn't even known my ice-heart held, and I had to throw the phone onto the passenger seat to keep myself from texting back something moony and ridiculous. I groaned again, dropping my face into my hands.

Dear lord, how had I let this spin so far out of control?

Sixteen

I stared at my closet, physically paralyzed by the decision. *It's just an outfit* . . . and also my armor for the party that would hopefully tilt the war against Ted in our favor. Plus, Theo would practically be required to keep his eyes on me as we worked the crowd. Which shouldn't affect me—it was just sex, not some courtly romance where the knight wears my fucking flower into battle—and yet . . .

Wanting to look good was just the smart move. For the *plan*. Nothing more.

I pulled the peacock blouse free, running my fingers over the iridescent silk. Theo had said it would impress his family . . . but he might assume I was wearing it for him, which wasn't the message I wanted to convey right now. If he was similarly Stockholmed, things might get even messier.

I flipped through options until I saw the answer: a knee-length cocktail dress in delicate silver-threaded lace, the plunging shoulder-to-waist vee of the neckline vaguely Grecian, the capelet whimsically beautiful. I'd whipped it up out of scraps for a myths-and-legends-themed party my roommate's friends threw one Halloween, but looking at it now . . . it felt like something Marta might wear. Besides, I *was* playing a part.

I threw it on before I could second-guess myself, pulled my hair into a messy topknot, and turned in the mirror to admire the result. I looked like a more glamorous version of myself, the silvery dress a delicate chain mail protecting me.

Dame Ellie the Mendacious, prepared for battle.

Theo got stuck in a meeting and told me to meet him at Belle Glen, *Do* not *go inside without me, we have to present a united front.*

I rolled up the club's long, winding drive, old-growth trees on either side shielding the view of the building. I'd half-expected alarms to go off at the gates at the sight of my Camry—could security systems recognize poor cars?—but the teenager inside the booth barely looked up when he asked why I was there.

After one final turn, the club appeared at the top of a massive cul-de-sac, the patch of lawn it enclosed regimentally manicured. The building was a behemoth in white stone, uplights along the front adding to its palatial drama. A valet stand marked the entrance, the red glow of a heat lamp dyeing the face of the vested attendant.

I spotted Theo across the vast sea of the lower parking lot—of course he'd snagged a spot several rows nearer the club—and tottered over in my heels.

"Ready for this?"

"As I'll ever be."

"You're going to nail it." He flashed me a private, almost tender smile. "I couldn't have asked for a better partner."

"In crime," I said under my breath, trying to ignore the shimmery swirl that his words, his look, stirred up in the pit of my stomach. *This was just for show, we weren't* real.

Inside, the ceilings soared, at least fifteen feet in the entryway, with frothy swirls of molding at the edges. Carefully placed and spit-shined antique furniture was topped with the sorts of *objets*—heavy mantel clocks, weighty brass bookends propping up a few leather-bound tomes, old-fashioned croquet mallets mounted over black-and-white photos of Victorian ladies playing the game—that almost *smelled* like money. Theo helped me out of my coat, handing it to the attendant as I took it all in.

"Wow," I murmured. He allowed his eyes to drift around the space. I had a feeling he hadn't really seen it in years.

"Not too shabby, right?"

"You don't really want me to answer that."

He chuckled as he took the tags from the attendant—I wondered, briefly, how many people the club employed just as various attendants—and held out his arm.

"Sorry we don't have time for a tour. The restaurant and bar are that way. Locker rooms are upstairs. Tonight, however, we'll be in the ballroom."

We made our way down a broad hallway. Windows to my right overlooked the drive, the grounds and golf course opening up beyond a wall of trees I hadn't been able to see past on my drive in. Both were covered in a pristine layer of snow, like something out of a 1940s Christmas movie. *Somehow even the weather here is just shinier.*

We turned left through the first of several sets of double doors and stepped into a gigantic ballroom. Windows on three sides offered views of a large, empty pool deck, and beyond that, the rolling wooded hills of the Milborough nature preserve, a popular hiking destination for "the other half" who didn't inhabit spaces like this. Circular tables topped with towering flower arrangements clung to the edges of the room, and a long series of buffet tables, ornate silver chafing dishes already marching along them, curved around the nearest corner. Between the sets of doors, a tower of empty champagne coupes awaited their big moment.

A large bar dominated the far back corner of the long room, and leaning against it, chatting with a prim-looking woman in sensible pumps and a sheath dress, stood Ted, a crystal lowball of most-likely-Scotch in one hand.

"There's the happy couple," he called out. "I was starting to wonder if you'd make it."

"Sorry, my meeting with the Briccolis went late," Theo said.

"Marty Briccoli *is* a talker," Ted said with an easy grin, setting the Scotch down to take my hand. He lifted it to the side, making a show of taking me in. "Don't you look a picture. Susan, I'm sure you'll agree my son has found the loveliest fiancée this side of the Mississippi."

"You look wonderful. Both of you." Susan—presumably a party coordinator of some variety—flashed a perfunctory smile, pressing a leather folder to her chest. I could see the Belle Glen logo embossed on the back.

"Marta's going to love that getup. You two will have to go shopping soon. She'll want to steal all your fashion secrets," Ted said with an avuncular chuckle.

My eyes darted to Theo's, blaring a *What the fuck?* signal. He threw the briefest of glances at Susan. *Audience.* Right, of course. This was the Taylor Family Variety Show, and we were all just players in the spectacle of Gee Aren't We So Wholesome.

"Guests will start arriving in about twenty minutes." Susan glanced at her delicate gold watch. "Ellie, when do you expect your family?"

"Soon." I'd promised Mimi a chance to "give this Theo the once-over" before they officially arrived, but I wanted to get my own sense of what we were facing before I subjected them to Ted. "Sorry, my mom couldn't take the day off on such short notice, but she'll be here as soon as she's cleaned up after her shift."

Susan nodded, supremely unruffled.

"Perfect. In that case, Theo, why don't you show Ellie the lay of the land. Be back here no later than ten to." Theo nodded, then reached for my hand, leading me back into the hallway. He managed to point out the nearest bathrooms before Ma texted that she and Mimi had arrived. We met them at the entrance, Ma looking a bit overawed, Mimi's jaw jutting with preemptive defiance.

"Do we look alright?" Ma said, worry spidering the corners of her eyes. She gestured to the simple V-necked navy dress she was wearing, one I'd seen at half a dozen weddings and christenings. "You said a cocktail dress would be fine . . ." Her frown deepened as she noticed a woman behind her handing off a mink.

"You look beautiful, Ma. You too, Mimi," I said, tilting my head at her soft cashmere cardigan—a Christmas gift from Bella and me she'd protested was *far* too nice for her—and silk slacks.

"Speaking of looks," Mimi said, eyes raking slowly over Theo, "you are the spitting image of your prick father."

"Mimi." Ma's eyes were wide with shock. She turned anxiously to the attendant, who, fortunately, couldn't care less what we were muttering about.

"I'm just saying what anyone with eyes can see," she said with a shrug. "Clearly there are *some* differences between them if this one's willing to help us. You *are,* aren't you? Helping us?" Mimi fixed Theo with one of her deadliest glares.

"As best I can."

"And why should I trust you?"

"Because Ellie and I want the same thing." Theo smirked. "As the prick's son, surely I'd look after my own self-interest, yes?" Mimi sniffed out something approximating a laugh.

"I'd imagine selling out to Mangia would take care of that self-interest quite nicely."

"It would if what I wanted was money."

"I'm supposed to believe it's not?" Mimi's eyebrow shot to her hairline. Theo rolled his eyes.

"If you must know, I have a soft spot for the old Taylor's building. When we were kids, my brother Chase and I practically lived there. It was almost like our clubhouse."

"Hell of a way to play Swiss Family Robinson," Mimi spat.

"More like . . ." Theo squinted.

"The Mixed-up Files of Mrs. Basil E. Frankweiler!" I said, excitement raising the pitch of my voice. Theo smiled softly.

"That's the one where the kids camp out in the Met, right?" I nodded. "Then yes, that's a perfect comparison. It felt like there were a million places to explore, or hide. We'd spend hours in there, making up games I can't even remember now . . . And the building itself has always been gorgeous."

"And you're expecting me to buy that you'll pass up millions for nostalgia?"

"I don't expect you to 'buy' anything. I *do* expect you to play along if you're going to join us. Not for my sake, of course—for Ellie's. After all, she's the one who wanted you here." He raised his eyebrow right back at Mimi. Her eyes narrowed, but I could see a hint of game-recognizes-game in the set of her mouth.

"Fine. Let's get this over with," Mimi conceded. "There had better be drinks."

"Allow me to lead you to the open bar," Theo said. "Ellie said you preferred reds? I hope Barolo's alright."

"The king of wines? If you're trying to bribe us, you're off to a great start," Mimi said with a genuine grin.

I hung back with Ma and Mimi as we made our way back to Ted.

"Quick recap, you're thrilled for us, yes?"

"Definitely. Theo's a gem, treats you so well," Ma parroted gamely.

"But it was all a whirlwind for you too," I prompted.

"That's just how you are!" Ma said, a genuine smile easing the tension on her face. "Trust me, that's an easy sell."

"And you're going to play nice with Ted? *No* mentions of Mangia."

"The word won't cross my lips, Ellie, but if some of that Barolo *doesn't* cross them soon, I can't be responsible for what happens next," Mimi said sharply.

"Okay, then . . . here we go." We crossed to where Ted was still leaning against the bar, Marta now smiling at his shoulder, white wine in hand.

"Ted, this is my mother, Linda, and my grandmother, Mimi." Ma extended her hand, which Ted took with a smooth smile.

"Thank you so much for hosting, Ted. The space is lovely."

"Yes, we *would* have hosted something, since usually that's up to the bride's family, but you were just so quick off the mark," Mimi added, eyes narrowing as Ted turned to her. "We'd barely processed the news."

"What can I say, we were just so excited," he said, sipping his Scotch. "Though I must say I'm relieved to hear I'm not the only one who found this match a bit . . . surprising. One day my son's playing the field, the next he shows up with a fiancée I've never even heard of. It's almost enough to make a man suspicious." He flashed Ma a vulpine smile, clearly sensing the weaker target. She gulped, but Mimi leaned in, laying a craggy hand on Ted's suit sleeve.

"Don't worry, I gave Ellie her first pack of birth control pills when she was in high school. No shotguns pointing Theo's way from our direction."

Ted frowned, clearly uncertain how to play this, but Mimi just smiled genially.

"Of course I *do* hope they get started on that front soon. I'd love to meet my great-grandbaby before I go. And they'd make such stunning children together, don't you think?"

"Why rush? Especially when it's already been such a whirlwind." Mimi shrugged, impervious to the eye daggers Ted was whipping at her.

"Different strokes, I suppose." She glanced around the room. "Oh, are those crab cakes they're bringing out? You certainly spared no expense."

"When it comes to family, I never do," Ted said. "I hope I didn't step on any toes."

"Of course not," Ma said. "Anyway, we'll *all* be family soon."

"Mmm," Ted sneered. Mimi's brows lowered in a way that set off an alarm in my head. Time to cut this off before real knives came out. Like mine, Mimi's intentions were often better than her follow-through.

"It looks like guests are starting to arrive. We'll leave you to your hosting duties," I said. "I just wanted to make sure I introduced you all first. Ma, Mimi, why don't we get you some food?"

"I just hope it agrees with me," Mimi said, eyes narrowing at Ted. "Everything looks so *rich*."

"Theo and I should say some hellos, but the buffet's in the corner. Meet you there?" With that, we made our separate escapes just as a middle-aged sports coat approached Ted. Theo and I moved to the smaller bar at the front to order a pair of double bourbons.

"Hopefully they just . . . avoid each other," I said under my breath.

"But they're about to be *family*, darling," he said, dripping sarcasm.

"You know, I don't think Ted loved when Ma dropped that word?"

"And you told me Mimi was the one to watch out for." His eyes sparkled with repressed glee. "Remind me to send Linda a really nice bottle of wine."

The next half hour was a whirlwind of introductions, polite expressions of interest, and (thankfully) occasional refueling from the serving staff. Before long, Theo split off with Josh and Everett, two high school friends I vaguely recognized, leaving me with the Turcottes, a couple a few years older than Ma who had been coming into the deli for decades, and whose dental practice I'd never realized occupied one of the Taylor Group's many properties around town.

"We're just so happy for you, Ellie," Gail said, eyes misty as she gripped my hand in both of hers. "It's too bad your father couldn't be here to share this moment."

"Oh . . . yeah. Thanks," I said, smiling queasily. This party was supposed to stay firmly on Theo's side of the moral gray zone. But surely they wouldn't be *genuinely* upset to learn we'd called it off, whenever we got to that point . . . right? We weren't *close*. They'd probably just say *Oh, that's too bad. Where's that torture pik? Lots of buildup on this one . . .* and move on to the next topic of conversation. Still, it didn't feel good to lie to them, especially after Gail mentioned my father. Glancing over my shoulder, I made a show of waving across the room. "That's my cue, but thanks so much for coming."

"We wouldn't have missed it for the world, dear."

I strode away with feigned purpose, but Theo was clearly in the middle of some hilarious story with his friends—the unguarded look on his face as he guffawed at something Everett said was something I hadn't seen before. I flung around for another option, then darted to the buffet before I could be dragged into another queasy-making congratulation, or, more likely, another thinly veiled interrogation. Turned out Ted wasn't the only one skeptical of my sudden appearance on the scene (though to be fair, most people had been gracious, even warm, including some whose only ties to Ted were through the country club we were standing in).

I was deciding whether to try to squeeze more truffled mac and cheese onto my cocktail plate—I'd clearly gone in too hard on the charcuterie platter before I'd realized what was on offer—when a voice at my shoulder startled me out of my thoughts.

"Ellie. Long time no see."

It took me a moment to place the woman. She was pretty, in an unremarkable way—largish brown eyes set in a pleasing but slightly forgettable face, straight brown hair just past shoulder length pulled into a simple half-up, wearing a boat-necked black cocktail dress that fit her well but would have been hard to pick out of a lineup. The only unexpected element was a small red clutch fashioned to look like an antique book, complete with a scroll-heavy gilt title I couldn't make out. Her amused look when I looked up from it finally clicked things into place.

"Jenna DiSousa?"

Jenna was on the periphery of my high school crowd: someone Bella hung out with in groups; friendly with the theater kids but never involved in the productions; briefly the girlfriend of one of the guys in my first boyfriend, Jonathan's, postpunk band. She'd been pleasant but quiet, sipping a drink in the corner of the basement or hanging just outside the circle around the campfire, observing . . . or maybe just too shy to speak up.

"I was wondering if you'd recognize me." She reached for a brioche bun heaped with lobster salad. "It's been a minute."

"Seriously. What are you even doing here?" She half-smiled. "Sorry, that came out weird. I mean . . . do you know Theo, or . . . ?"

"I suppose you could say that." Jenna sipped her elaborate-looking dark liquor cocktail and moved to a nearby high-top. "We had golf and tennis lessons together as kids. More family friends, though." She tilted her head toward a middle-aged couple—the woman recognizably similar to Jenna, down to her sensible-but-upscale ensemble—chatting with a handful of people I recognized as Belle Glenners.

"Wait . . . you *go* here?"

She laughed at my obvious incredulity. But like . . . *seriously*? The Belle Glen kids were like Theo—athletes and dance team captains, conspicuous in their shiny new cars and brand-name clothes. I'd never spent much time considering Jenna's financial situation—even if I'd been wired to care about those things, she was just far enough outside my circle that it wouldn't have registered—but I suppose I'd assumed that, in the perennial shakeout of Milborough's longtime residents, she'd have sifted into my side of things: if not blue collar, exactly, then definitively middle class.

"I used to. My parents can't understand why I won't let them sponsor me as a junior member. Luckily, my salary makes most of the argument for me." Her eyes snapped back to mine, a brightness in them I hadn't noticed before. "Thanks, though. I'd kind of hate to think you *did* assume I was a Belle Glen type. By the way, I love your dress."

"Oh . . . thanks. I uh . . . I made it."

"So now we're best friends and as such you're going to become my personal stylist and couturier. Awesome. I love that about us." She grinned and I quickly mirrored it. I hadn't expected to find someone I enjoyed talking to at this thing, let alone someone whose sense of humor seemed to mesh so well with my own. Had Jenna always been this wryly funny?

"You're running your family's deli now, right?"

"That's right."

"I always loved that place. We ate there at least twice a week senior year. Your dad would give us freebies since we came in with Bella." She smiled fondly at the memory. A little swell of pride filled me. Things like this were why I couldn't let the deli go under—people's happy memories of my dad, the way it had woven itself into our town over decades. I wasn't the only one who would be devastated to see it go. Or, well . . . sad, at least.

But would Dad be proud of me today? Of what I was doing to keep the deli alive? Or would he be disappointed that I'd given up on my costuming dream to do it?

"What are you doing these days, anyway?" I said, needing a change of subject *stat*. "I didn't even know you were back in Milborough."

"It's pretty recent. Just since last year."

"What brought you back?"

"A job. At Winnfield?" She cocked her head as she named the nearby arts college, tiny, but well-respected in New England. "I'm teaching fiction writing."

"Oh yeah? How'd you wind up there?"

"Mostly lucky timing. I'd just sold my first book when they posted the position, and I knew their last poet-in-residence from my MFA program, she put in a good word." Jenna shrugged. "I never *planned* to teach, but it's a decent way to pay the bills. Literary fiction definitely doesn't. Especially when you're managing a novel about every five years." She smiled ruefully.

Something like jealousy momentarily needled into me. Jenna

DiSousa was publishing novels? It wasn't something I wanted for myself, but there was something undeniably impressive about the fact that she had a creative career, even if it wasn't a bill-paying one.

"Wow, congratulations," I finally managed. "About the novel, I mean. Is it out yet?"

"Next spring. My agent claims that's actually fast for publishing." She rolled her eyes. "Until then I'm stuck in the land of thinly veiled coming-of-age autofiction by writers who have yet to actually come of age."

"It can't be worse than slinging salami."

"If that's not the name of a porno, it should be." I guffawed and she rewarded me with a knowing smile. "And honestly . . . I love my baby writers. I should go, my mother has that *look* in her eye." She threw side-eye in her mother's general direction. "It was really good to see you. Let's grab a drink sometime, I need to make an effort to have actual friends here. And congratulations."

With that, she disappeared into the crowd, leaving me feeling simultaneously glowy and a little embarrassed. A drink with Jenna actually sounded fun . . . which made me realize just how little effort I'd put into finding *my* actual friends since I'd moved back. Why had I assumed that no one in Milborough would click with me?

I glanced at Theo, still standing with Everett and a crowd of other vaguely familiar, generically handsome men, and was surprised to find his gaze already on me. He raised his bourbon and eyebrow simultaneously, mouthing *Need one?* before glancing meaningfully at Ted, surrounded by a few of his more pompous cronies. Laughing, I shook my head. He smiled easily. I was about to make my way over—in the wake of Jenna, it didn't seem so impossible to imagine actually enjoying his friends—when Mimi sidled up next to me.

"Don't waste space on the burrata, no flavor at all," she said.

"Good looking out, Mimi. So? How are we doing so far?"

"I'd say you're selling it. The prick wouldn't have been so snippy otherwise." She waggled her eyebrows and I laughed. "I'm just glad you let *us* know the truth. Otherwise . . ." She shook her head slowly. My heart stuttered.

"What do you mean?"

"Just . . . all this," she gestured at the grand space, the vests-and-bowties staff hunching obsequiously as they offered delicacies that the artificially youthful attendees waved away without making eye contact. "Theo seems like a smart cookie, which I'll admit was a pleasant surprise, but this isn't *us*. If I thought you were really hitching your wagon to it?" She chortled. "I'd be rolling in my grave, Eleanor."

"You're not dead yet," I said, trying to keep my face neutral. It was hard with my lips going suddenly numb.

"Exactly." She patted my shoulder affectionately. "But I'll let you get back to it. Need to make sure you really sell it tonight, right? Then you can wrap this whole charade up and we can get back to our lives. *Without* the Taylors, thank Pete."

"Right," I murmured. With one more gentle squeeze, she snatched an olive and moved off to find Ma, leaving me stranded there, heart beating wildly.

She was right, of course. Mimi knew me better than almost anyone on earth, barring Bella. This world, these people . . . I could *never* be a part of it. I'd suffocate inside of a week. And since that was true . . .

What was I holding out for with Theo? The chance to make it a two-night stand? Another fancy meal? The longer I strung this out, let the two of us fall under the easy, hypnotic sway of novelty and hormones, the more painful it would be when we both had to admit to ourselves that fundamentally there was nothing there. Hell, the fact that he was so profoundly different from anyone I'd ever gone for made me even more vulnerable. Already I'd let him insinuate himself much too far, simply because I didn't realize I needed to worry about him in the first place.

The only reason I was resisting Sam's plan was attraction—the stupid "Look at those *lips*" kind—and taking this place in through Mimi's eyes . . . I realized how flimsy that excuse was. Feeling stifled by its grandeur, I beat a quick retreat from the ballroom. I needed to get my head on straight before I started up the act again.

The stream in and out of the bathroom was too constant to risk, so I ducked into the darkened après-golf casual restaurant next to the function room, moving to the nearest table and collapsing into a chair.

"Sorry, I'll just . . ."

I startled at the voice from the far corner. It wasn't until my eyes adjusted that I realized it was . . .

"Sam?"

"Guilty." She grimaced, gaze darting to the door. "Sorry, I just needed a second to catch my breath, and the pub is always closed this time of year . . ." She shrugged, the combination of her natural beauty and the high-necked satin slip dress that clung in all the right places somehow turning the gesture elegant. "I'll give you some space."

"Actually, no. Wait a second." I squeezed my eyes shut, trying to regain control of my thoughts. "I've been . . . thinking about your proposal."

"Okay . . ." She perched on the edge of a seat, body taut, intent on my face. "And?"

"And we would have to work out the details, obviously. I can't go at it full force while Theo and I are still working on *our* plan." I swallowed hard. Why was it so hard to just say yes?

"I wouldn't want you to."

"But . . . it makes sense," I finally choked out. "So, you know . . . I'm in or whatever."

Her eyes lit up with glee.

"Oh my god, *incredible*. This is . . . Okay, I have *so* many ideas about this. Obviously tonight is about you guys, we need to keep that clean." Her hands wove designs in the air as she picked up speed. "But once you've survived the gauntlet, we should get together and make real plans. What days do you work? I can meet you at closing, maybe, and—"

"Slow down," I said, raising both hands and chuckling in spite of myself. Sam's obvious enthusiasm didn't completely eradicate the heaviness in the pit of my stomach, but it *was* endearing. It reminded me of Bella, actually—scratch the polished veneer and you'd find a gushing, slightly neurotic weirdo just waiting to get out. Plus, the fact that she'd been holding out this much hope was reassuring. Clearly Sam cared more about Theo than I ever could. Our entire *thing* so far was built on attraction and mutual self-interest. He was objectively hot, and I was probably . . . exotic to him, somehow. The thrill of trading out caviar for the sinful pleasure of a Big Mac. But that didn't make a *future*.

"Testing . . . Are we good?"

Sam's head jerked at the echoey voice from next door, amplified by the speaker system.

"We should get back in there. But more soon, yeah?"

"Definitely." I managed what I was almost sure was a passable smile. Sam stood, grinning widely, then strode out of the room, leaving me in the dark. I closed my eyes for a moment, trying to regulate my breathing. It was the right choice. Even without Mimi's input, I knew deep down that Theo and I weren't meant to be. This would be better for everyone. The lingering leadenness was just the sudden deadweight of extinguished lust mixing with that mac and cheese.

I made it back to the ballroom just in time to see Sam moving up next to Theo near the dais at the back. Ted was chatting with the DJ, hand over the mic. He nodded once and turned to the crowd. Catching sight of me, Ted tapped Theo's arm, who gestured me over before turning back to Sam. Mirth danced over both their faces at whatever he whispered, forming a bubble of intimacy around them. I swallowed hard as Sam casually rested a hand on Theo's arm, shaking her head.

They really do look good together.

And judging by the easy, carefree smile on Theo's face, one I'd only seen a few times, and then fleetingly, Sam wasn't crazy to think there could be something there. We might have chemistry—intense chemistry, even—but they clearly had the real thing. And even if I'd wanted it, we never could. How could I be serious about anyone my family was against? Which meant I owed them a shot . . . right?

Sam pulled away as I approached, turning her wide smile on me.

"Ellie, hi!" She wrapped me in a lightly perfumed hug. "You look *gorgeous*," she said, raising her eyebrows for emphasis, so convincing I almost believed we hadn't spoken less than two minutes ago. "You'd better not let her out of your sight, Theo. Someone else might snake you."

"I'll keep that in mind." He slid an arm around my waist casually. I knew it was for show—Ted was clearly gearing up for some sort of speech—but the warmth of his hand on the curve of my hip, the solidity of him along the entire length of my body, shot off tiny fireworks inside me.

Even more reason to push them together. Your vagina is threatening to overtake your reason.

"If I could say a few words?"

Ted's voice boomed through the room, quieting all lingering chatter.

"First off, thank you for being here. I know I speak for the whole family when I say how much it means that you turned out for Theo's unexpected announcement." He raised his glass. "I always knew my son would marry someday. As a father, I'm biased, but he's quite the catch, don't you think? No way the women of the world would let him off the hook forever." Cheers broke out. "And it looks like Miss Ellie Greco is the one to finally catch him. Well done, Ellie." He doffed an imaginary cap at me.

"As many of you know, Theo and Ellie are very different people. And theirs was the definition of a whirlwind romance. Theo's always been private, but he really took us by surprise when he told us that, after all these years, he's finally ready to take the plunge after mere months." Ted's eyes narrowed, and though he was still smiling, the heat behind his stare practically singed my skin. The pause drew out. I tilted my chin a bit higher, fixing my smile more firmly in place, ignoring the crawly feeling of all the eyes in the room on us. "But you know what they say, opposites attract. Strongly, in my son's case."

Chuckles rippled through the crowd. I made a show of turning an adoring gaze on Theo. His fingers dug more sharply into my side.

"I'll be honest, seeing him take such a *huge* leap of faith . . . it surprised me. And it made me realize my little boy's all grown up. He's forging his own path now, venturing into the unknown. I'm sure we all applaud that." He smiled at the crowd, but judging from the awkward throat-clearing, they could hear the tepidness of the . . . honestly, it wasn't really even a compliment. "So let's all raise a glass. To Theo and Ellie, jumping in with both feet. I hope you both get everything you deserve."

I lifted my glass along with Theo. Once his was at his lips, he murmured, "Asshole."

Then we both took a smiling sip, basking in the applause.

"Oh, and while I have you . . . This is a big night for the Taylor family in more ways than one. I'm sure Theo won't begrudge me one more little announcement."

The room stuttered back to silence. I glanced at Theo, but his brows were knitted with genuine confusion. Next to him, Sam's eyes were wide with something like horror. She shook her head rapidly at Ted, but he wasn't looking at her.

"I'm thrilled to welcome yet another member into our family today, a woman as brilliant as she is beautiful. Many of you know Samantha Lindsay . . ."

The room turned to Sam, who managed a deer-in-the-headlights version of a smile. Ted cleared his throat and her eyes darted to me. *I'm so sorry,* she mouthed. I blinked, still confused.

"I'm thrilled—no, honored—to say that she'll *also* be joining the Taylor family soon." Ted paused for a long moment, waiting until the whispers began to gather strength. His smile at Theo and me was positively serpentine. "The Taylor *property* family, of course. Sam has agreed to come on as our new CFO."

There was some polite applause, but the mood had shifted. Ted couldn't have broadcast a clearer *Fuck this engagement* if he'd tried. Actually . . . he was definitely trying.

"To new beginnings, in business and in love," Ted said, raising his glass again. "There's a lot of change on the horizon, but I'm starting to realize in my old age . . . change might not be such a bad thing. But for now, let's stick to what we know and enjoy the drinks, hmm?"

Relieved laughter broke out as he passed off the microphone, and within moments, Sam was swarmed by people—her people, I couldn't help but notice—eager to congratulate her. It was absurd—I was already planning to help her resume her rightful spot as Theo's actually loving fiancée—but a little kernel of hurt was taking root near the base of my spine.

"Do you need a drink as badly as I do?" Theo bent to whisper the words directly in my ear, and the tickle of his breath over the sensitive skin there ran through me, prickling the hairs on the nape of my neck.

"Theo, this entire night is just one big 'Damn, you need a drink' for me."

He laughed and snagged us refills before ushering me to a little nook half-protected by the edge of the bar, turning his back to the room. It bought us a brief respite from the flow of guests.

"That was pretty aggressive, even for Ted," I started. "But I guess it makes sense for him to announce it when he already has a room filled with his entire network. Did he tell you he was planning to give Sam such a major role?"

"Of course not. We rarely talk. Plus, he must have known I'd see through him." I raised an eyebrow in question. "Come on. You don't really believe he hired her for her *skills*?"

"That's not fair. Sam's really good at what she does, right?" I realized I wasn't exactly aware of *what* Sam did, but her air of supreme competence had to come from somewhere. Plus, even if the plan wasn't fully under way yet, it didn't seem great to encourage him to neg her.

"Oh, absolutely. But we weren't even looking for a CFO." Theo bit his lower lip, shaking his head slowly. "This hire has nothing to do with the company."

"Then . . . what's it about?"

"Isn't it obvious? Ted's never gotten over how I 'let the best thing that ever happened to me get away,'" Theo scoffed. "I'm guessing in his mind, announcing her role *here* will help everyone else see it his way. Make them think the two of us ought to be together."

My stomach twisted. Ted definitely wasn't the only person in the room who felt that way.

"Why was he so set on her? You've dated other girls since you and Sam . . . ended things."

"But none of those girls were *quite* as impressive in Ted's eyes." Theo sighed, dragging his eyes back to me with effort. I couldn't help but notice they'd been on Sam. *Which was good . . . right?* God, why wouldn't my mind and the pit of my stomach just get on the same page?

She and Ted were chatting animatedly with a handful of older men, all of them the sort of worn-driving-shoes shabby that, in *this* room, actually indicated a higher stratosphere of wealth and influence than sharp, expensive suits. There was an eagerness on Ted's face that I hadn't seen before. If I had any doubts about what Theo was saying, the hunger in Ted's eyes quickly dispelled them.

"Still," I said, thoughtful, "what does it matter?"

"What do you mean?"

"It's too little, too late, right? Ted can try to engineer a happy ending for you and Sam all he wants—he can even get it for all I care." Theo's face twisted briefly. "It won't hurt *us,* right?"

"We're clear on how this plan works, aren't we, Ellie?"

"Of course. But we're not planning to actually make it to the altar, *Theo.*" I rolled my eyes, trying to ignore the tightness beneath my sternum as I voiced the words. *Focus on the plan . . .* or, plans, at this point. "Step one: sell the engagement" was already on the road to completion, which meant it was time to deploy the recently added "Step two: set Theo up with the girl he *should* wind up with."

"Let Ted think he's pulling off some devious plot," I said, flippant. "By the time he realizes he was fighting a straw man, Mangia will already be neck deep in a deal with whoever runs the commercial property racket in Burnton."

"God, it would serve them right," Theo said. "I think I'd rather die than live in Burnton."

"Be honest, that's just deep-seated lacrosse rivalry coming out."

"That, and the fact that the entire place feels like you could buy it out of a West Elm catalog."

"Oooh, sick burn on the bougie home goods store."

"Not on the *store*. On the store as a substitute identity." Theo grinned. "I'll take a town full of scrappy deli owners who can turn fabric remnants into fairy dust over a hundred thousand Anthropologie clones any day."

He reached over to twist the hem of my capelet between his fingers, drawing me ever so slightly nearer as he looked first at the sparkly fabric, then into my eyes. The shadows where we stood had turned his deep and oceanic. There was something stirring there, something that was forming an answering whirlpool at my core. I could feel myself getting sucked into it . . .

"Sorry to interrupt." I startled at Ma's voice just over Theo's shoulder. She smiled apologetically. "They want us for pictures?"

"Of course." Theo slid an arm around me fluidly. "Lead the way, Linda."

We crossed to the dais, dutifully lining up in various formations of his family and mine, with a few highly posed photos of Theo and me tastefully wrapped in each other's arms thrown in for variety. Fortunately, the watchful gazes of Ted and Marta, the photographer and her assistant, not to mention half the room, kept me from descending into more bourbon-fueled bodily madness at his touch.

"You know, while we have you . . ." Ted glanced around the

room, and Theo and I moved apart. We'd been holding our chaste-cheek-kiss pose—*Look sideways at him, Ellie*—for so long I had a minor headache. "Let's grab a few pictures of the dream team. Sam's always impeccable, but catching both me and my son looking this nice on the same day is rare," Ted chuckled.

Before Theo could protest, Ted had maneuvered Sam to us.

"You don't mind, do you, Ellie?" he said, barely bothering to look at me.

"Of course not." I found a spot next to Marta as the photographer arranged Ted, Sam, and Theo.

"Get a couple with just the two of them," Ted said after the first few snaps. "The future of the company and all that." He threw a tiny smirk my way as he moved to one side. "Theo, put your arm around her. It has to look like we all like each other, after all."

I took a long sip of my drink as my fake fiancé and his very real ex took photo after photo, every one of them more convincing than anything Theo and I could possibly pull off.

It was so obvious they should wind up together. And now that our engagement was "official," it was time for me to make sure that was exactly what happened.

Seventeen

"Sorry I'm late, there was an accident on 95." Sam rolled her eyes hugely as she shrugged off her purse and coat.

"No worries." I glanced at the kitschy clock over the entrance to the coffee shop, which showed that Sam had arrived precisely four minutes past our planned meeting time. I'd never been here before, mainly because it was on the far side of Marshburg, one of the more charming towns within spitting distance of Milborough, but the sixties décor and home-baked pastries almost made it worth the drive.

"Have you ordered yet? My treat," she said.

"Oh, umm . . . I was thinking maybe a scone and a latte, but you don't need to do that."

"This whole thing is my ridiculous scheme, a latte is the least I can do. Back in a flash."

Soon she was settling in across from me, three scones laid out between us.

"I couldn't decide."

"I knew I liked you."

Sam grinned, sipped her drink, then leaned forward, face suddenly serious.

"First off, I hope you know I had *nothing* to do with Ted's little . . . whatever the fuck that was." She winced. "I only sent over the contract the day before, I don't think he even told the board yet." She sighed heavily, breaking a corner off the cinnamon chip scone. "Beyond tacky. Though I can't pretend I'm surprised."

"You're the one who wants him as a father-in-law."

Sam scrunched her nose in disgust.

"I suppose we all have to make sacrifices."

"Either way, don't worry about it." I sipped my latte, good enough that it almost made me wish I was willing to travel for life's little luxuries. "The timing might have been a little . . . I mean, tacky really is the word for it, but it teed things up pretty well for this." I gestured between us. "The important part was that he announced the engagement, not that he acted psyched about it, right?"

"Good point," Sam said. "Jesus, this scone is ridiculous."

"Maybe I'll see if they want to partner with the deli. We don't have a lot of breakfast options."

"Oh my god, *do that*," she said, eyes wide. "Like . . . I was going to do what I could to help already, but if you bring these in? I'll sell my eyeteeth to keep Greco's open."

"Luckily, you don't need eyeteeth to enjoy scones."

"This day is seriously coming up Sam." She lifted her drink in a mock toast. "By the way, now that the cat's out of the bag, I figured you might want a little more info on the whole 'How could Sam possibly help kill the deal?' front. Full disclosure, I can't just walk in and tell everyone to scrap it. That said, Ted already sent over Mangia's opening offer. I need to dig into the numbers, but it seems low, probably because they're planning a total gut job, possibly even a teardown."

"What?" I stopped with the blueberry scone halfway to my mouth. How could anyone tear down such a stunning old building?

"I guess there's nowhere near enough square footage for their 'standard store model,' so they'd be looking to expand the foot-print. There's all kinds of inside baseball stuff I could go into on comps for commercial real estate, carrying costs of leases versus the profits from a sale . . ." She rolled her hand through the air, miming all the details I allegedly understood. "Point is, there's almost definitely a strong business argument for passing on their offer, or at least looking around to see what else might be out there."

"I guess that's reassuring?"

"Trust me, it is. At the very least it'll buy some time." She popped a bite of scone into her mouth, raising her eyebrows. "But enough boring business stuff. You said you had an idea?"

It had struck me in the middle of the night, as I lay awake staring at the popcorn ceiling in my shitty apartment, the buzz from the engagement party finally worn off enough for me to stop feeling sorry for myself—over a man I *didn't even want,* mind you. Lord knows I'd been around the block enough times to realize sexual chemistry did not a solid relationship make, and everything else about us was just . . . mismatched. Mimi could see that. Up until the last week or so I *had* seen that.

But with my brain firmly back in the driver's seat my genitals had briefly hijacked, I'd realized the perfect way to jump-start Sam's plan, one so well suited to Theo's *and* my needs, there was no way it would raise alarm bells.

"Everett's single, right?"

"As far as I know."

"Be honest: Has he ever been into you?"

I was ninety percent sure I knew the answer—I'd seen the way his eyes trailed Sam at the party, how his face lit up when she joined the group.

"Maybe? We met when Theo and I were together, it's not like he ever made a move."

"Real talk, though?"

"Yeah, probably." Sam shrugged and looked off to the side.

"So if you were to ask him to hang out . . ."

"He'd probably say yes. But what's the angle. Jealousy?" Sam frowned as she considered this. "He might not even *tell* Theo, especially if things don't lead anywhere. And like . . . Everett's hot, obviously, but I hadn't planned on hooking up with other people for this."

"You won't have to hook up with him. Unless you want to." I smirked, leaning forward, conspiratorial. "And I think we can guarantee Theo sees you two together. Here's what I'm thinking . . ."

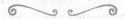

"Not that I'm not thrilled to spend the morning with my gorgeous fiancée, but why tennis?" Theo slid into one of the spots near Belle Glen's enclosed courts, throwing the car into Park before turning to me.

"Would you prefer golf?" I gestured at the snow-covered grounds.

"There's always the driving range."

"*Fah* too down-market," I said in my best *Downton Abbey* voice. "The range is *public, dah-ling.*" Theo grinned impishly.

"Which means that many more people would see us together." He leaned across the console, eyelids going heavy as he neared me. My heart started ping-ponging dangerously. "All the better to put on a show, no?"

Nope, no way. Not the point, not of today, not of this entire arrangement. I rolled my eyes and opened my door.

"As far as this plan is concerned, there's people and there's *people*. After all, don't you want Ted's friends to think I'm all in on becoming a Taylor? Regular Belle Glen appearances are practically a requirement."

We made our way into the vast geodesic bubble that enclosed three courts, ball hoppers, and an automatic serving machine scattered around the edges. On the benches nearest the door, Everett hunched over his phone, tapping furiously, gym bag forgotten at his side.

"Everything okay?" Theo said, dropping his bag and shedding his jacket. Everett looked up, smiling with genuine warmth. He was handsome, if in a less obvious way than Theo, his even, open features verging on baby-faced despite the deliberately maintained two-day scruff. His dark brown hair was cropped close, and he had the broad, muscled look of a former athlete who made some effort with upkeep.

"Just another junior analyst trying to prove how much overtime they're working."

"Are you still good to play?" Theo asked.

"Definitely. Dude *loves* getting grunt work delegated to him." Everett held up a finger, quickly finished his message, and slipped his phone back into his bag, then turned to me. "So, Ellie. Big tennis player?"

"Hardly. I think the last time I held a racket was in high school gym class." I hadn't been half bad . . . but I hadn't been on a court since.

"Are you trying to get me to go easy on you?" Everett's eyes sparkled. "Because I don't really *do* that, ask Theo."

"God no. I'm trying to get you to run Theo ragged while I look cute in my tennis skirt. He's had it too easy lately. Or . . . always, really."

Everett bellowed out a laugh.

"Theo, I *like* her." He slapped both thighs, then pulled his racket out of his bag. "Especially because I might actually beat you today."

"Only if I'm not a handicap." Sam's voice sang out from the open doorway. Her long blond hair was up in a jaunty ponytail, and the cold had pinked her cheeks prettily. "Sorry I'm late, I was sitting in the parking lot for the last ten minutes trying to wrap up a call with Ted."

Just like we'd planned. Her showing up last guaranteed all eyes would be on her, including, hopefully, Theo's. She made her way to Everett first, stretching up to give him a hug that went on *just* a moment too long.

"Thanks for suggesting this, Ev. It's *exactly* what I needed." Her eyes dropped to his lips for a few seconds before she stepped back, lingering a moment before she turned to Theo and me. God, she was *good* at this. Was that practiced, or just part of the genetic package people like Sam were gifted at birth? "And thanks to you two for being willing to play doubles. Pretty sure trying to destroy each other on the court isn't the best path to future dates."

I watched Theo for a reaction, but he just flashed his trademark sardonic half-smile.

"Plus, it gave you a reason to end a Ted call. My deepest sympathies, by the way."

"Don't worry, I knew what I was getting into." She smiled slyly at him over her shoulder, then bent to wriggle out of the fitted sweats she was wearing over her tennis skirt. I couldn't help but notice Theo's eyes catching on her legs, impossibly long and smooth beneath the short hem.

Which was good. Definitely the goal. I tugged my own sweats down, smoothing the pleated skirt I'd picked up the day before. Compared to Sam's clingy spandex, it felt old-fashioned, and vaguely fussy. I pulled out the racket Theo had lent me, tucked my pants into my gym bag, then bounced anxiously from foot to foot on the springy green court as Theo, Everett, and Sam stretched and took a few practice swings. I'd told Sam I'd try to find a way to push her and Theo together . . .

"Should we warm up?" I squeaked. "I think I'll need it."

"Good idea. Should we take the far side?" Theo looked at me expectantly.

"Actually, didn't you say Everett's the best player?" Theo frowned. "I thought I could try to steal his secrets while we warm up, then maybe I won't embarrass you *quite* as badly when we actually play a set."

"We can lob you a few easy balls while you get the rust off," Sam said, smiling pleasantly. "It's been a long time for me, too. Some easy volleys would definitely help."

"As if any of us believe *that*." Everett raised an eyebrow at Sam, then turned to me. "She was all-state in high school."

"High school was a long time ago." Sam smiled coquettishly at him. Theo glanced back and forth between them, expression unreadable.

"Shall we?" Theo finally said.

"Sir, yes sir!" Everett said, mock-saluting and setting off for the far side of the court. I followed, leaving Sam and Theo to drift to the opposite baseline together.

"So, Everett. We've barely had a chance to meet. What's your deal?"

"My *deal*?" His eyes flashed with humor.

"You know, what you do, things you like, the basics." On the opposite side of the court, Theo mimed tossing a ball in the air, practicing what looked like an extremely competent serve. I could hear Sam saying something teasing. He gestured for her to demonstrate. She mimed her own serve, the sharp swish of the racket audible all the way across the court. Theo mock-bowed and she playfully pushed his shoulder, the sort of gesture of physical comfort with each other I couldn't ever remember reaching with any of my recent . . . "boyfriends" didn't feel like the right term anymore. More like bedwarmers.

I tried a fake serve of my own, trying to focus on my pretend-ball instead of the warmth on Theo and Sam's faces. *This is working, it's what you want, don't fuck it up.*

"Like for me . . . own a deli, so I always smell like cured meat—I know, erotic—love a good dive bar, which I guess means I love a *bad* dive bar? And . . . I sew. Clothes, mostly." The last felt almost like a lie—when had I last made a totally new piece?—but the recent appreciation for my library pieces made it feel like something I was at least allowed to mention. Which was surprisingly . . . nice.

"I suppose my deal is . . . finance bro, but I try *really* hard not to be a douche?"

"That's a start. If it's your whole deal, though, expect me to have a lot of previous plans whenever you and Theo want to hang."

Everett laughed loudly. I noticed Theo's head twitch our way.

"Okay, I hear you. Give me a prompt. I work better with parameters."

"Hobbies? Please don't say finance 'coz that's just heartbreaking."

"I learned how to bake bread in the pandemic, does that count? It works well with my low-level OCD. I'm anal enough to be like . . . really into perfecting that now."

"I'm listening. Slash hungry."

"Pairs well with your erotic meat smells. Oh, I've got one. Cat guy." He thumbed his chest. "Like . . . who wants a pet that's hard-wired to love you already? Way too easy." He flashed a goofy grin.

"Now we're getting somewhere." I tried my fake serve again. Tried not to notice Sam's furrowed confusion as she took it in. "So . . . you and Sam?" Everett's eyes narrowed, assessing, but he said nothing. "It sounds like it's a new thing?"

"Not sure I'd go so far as to call it a *thing*," he said, lips twisting with amusement as he took a practice serve, which looked—and sounded—alarmingly professional.

"Did I misunderstand? She made it sound like this was a double date."

"No, it is. But Sam's . . ." He scrunched his nose. It made his youthful face look even younger. "Don't get me wrong, she's awesome. Gorgeous, obviously—sorry if it's offensive to lead with that, but it's kinda hard not to notice."

"Completely agreed."

"And funny. And she's a total baller at work, which I love. But she and I *both* know she's out of my league." There was wistfulness in his eyes as he stared across the court at Sam. It tugged at my heart a little—how much collateral damage would I have racked up by the time I finally managed to drive Mangia out of town? *Not your problem, Ellie. Focus on the goal.* Everett shrugged. "Let's just say I'm not expecting anything." He rolled his shoulders, trying one more fake serve. "Though, for the record, I *did* respect bro code before I said yes. Because of their, well . . ." He reddened.

"*Gotta* respect bro code," I agreed with a solemn nod, and Everett exhaled, clearly relieved not to have to continue shoving his foot down his throat. With that, he turned to the net, stuck two fingers in his mouth, and whistled shrilly.

"Are we warming up or what?" He bent to grab a ball. "If I don't at least call in to my ten o'clock, the junior associates are going to swarm me."

Everett served first, the ball traveling back and forth until Sam hit it near me and I doinked it off the tip of my racket into the geodesic-dome-o-sphere.

"Sorry." I grimaced.

"No worries," Theo said, expression gentle. "That's why we're warming up. I'll serve next?"

He hit an easy lob my way. I just managed to scoop it back over the net toward Sam. She rocketed it at Everett, and he shot it back, the ball dropping just inches before the baseline. Sam stretched but didn't quite reach it with her backhand.

"Still your weak side, Sam?" he said, looking triumphant.

"I don't *have* a weak side," she snipped, but there was a sparkliness in her features that hadn't been there a few moments before.

"Wow, so glad we're keeping things casual during the warm-up." Theo flashed me a private look of amusement.

A few more balls went back and forth, most of the volleys ending with me. I panted as I tried—and failed—to reach Sam's latest return.

"Should we start?" Everett said. "I want to make sure we have enough time to fit in a set."

"Just hit it to Ellie and we'll be done in no time," Sam said, grinning widely as she bent to pick up a few stray balls, tucking them into hidden pockets at the back of her skirt.

"Wow, *that* was unnecessary," Theo said, frowning hard. Sam's eyes darted to his, mouth opening to retort, then she caught herself.

"Sorry, you're right. But I was only joking. Ellie knows that."

"Totally. Plus, we all know it's true. I'm definitely the weak link."

"So we've had more practice. You'll get there," Theo said, eyes intent on mine as Sam and I passed each other at the net.

"Absolutely. Sorry, Ellie, I didn't mean to be an asshole. I tend to get a little . . . competitive, I guess." She shrugged.

"We all remember," Theo said, voice flat. Sam's eyebrows knitted together.

"Nothing to apologize for. Playing above my level will help me get better, right?" Sam smiled gratefully and we both retreated to our sides of the court.

"You wanna take first serve, Ellie?" Everett said as I neared Theo. "I promise, I'll keep Sam at bay. Or at least try to prove my valor by getting as many returns as humanly possible."

"Sounds good."

I moved to the baseline and Theo approached, a few balls in hand. His hand caught mine as he passed me one.

"Don't let her get to you, okay? She's always been *way* too competitive." He side-eyed Sam over the net. Warmth radiated from somewhere beneath my sternum at the tender, protective look that had settled on his brow. But . . . this wasn't what was supposed to be happening. The speed with which Theo had accepted the invitation proved Sam's claim: He loved tennis. Who wouldn't want a partner that shared that passion?

"Don't worry, Theo. I'm a big girl." I pulled my hand away, ignoring the tingle of his touch, and moved into position. "Okay, so . . . love-love. That's what you say, right?" Everett nodded. With a deep breath, I pulled my racket back, tossed the ball overhead, swung through the air . . .

And whiffed.

"No worries, El. Try to toss from your shoulder. And once it reaches the top of the throw, that's when you swing," Theo said, miming the motions.

"Right. Okay, got it." Somehow I'd thought this would come

back to me more easily. Yes, Sam was supposed to shine by comparison, but I hadn't thought I'd be *quite* so terrible. Heart beating a little faster, I tried again. This time, the serve connected, sailing high over the net and onto Everett's side of the court . . . just outside the sideline.

"Out," he called.

"I think it hit the line," Theo said.

"Oh come *on*, Theo," Sam snorted. "That was definitely out." Theo's jaw tightened, but he nodded once.

"Alright, Ellie, switch sides," Theo said, walking over to my half of the court. Obediently, I moved to the other corner, served again . . . and slammed the ball into the net.

"Fault," Everett called.

"Yes, we noticed, Ev." Theo raised an eyebrow. Everett shrugged good-naturedly. I tried again and managed to hit it into the right quadrant. Sam swatted the ball toward Theo. The ball whipped back and forth for a few rounds, then Sam, brow lowering, twisted her wrist, directing it straight at me. I ran, reached . . .

"Sorry." I sagged a bit as the ball flew past.

"It's okay, you did great." Theo moved over to give me a quick shoulder squeeze before resuming his position.

We managed to eke out the next point—I say we, but it was definitely all Theo—but after a particularly hard-fought volley for the next, Everett hit the ball just past Theo's reach, into what should have been my territory. I flailed at it with a backhand . . . and missed.

"Nice one, Ev. I never realized you were such an ace!" Sam raised her hand, and he grinned widely as he high-fived her. "Next point's game," she crowed across the net, forehead glistening with sweat, a preemptive look of triumph settling on her pretty features.

"We're well aware, Sam," Theo said tightly. "Give us a sec?"

He moved over to me, taking my hand in his and lowering his voice.

"Hey . . . you okay?"

"Of course. It's just a game, right?" I smiled weakly. I didn't actually care about tennis, but being the obvious weak link didn't feel *great*.

"Absolutely. Not that some people remember that." He flicked a narrow-eyed gaze across the net.

Shit. Somehow my total inability to keep up meant that instead of reminding him how fun this thing he'd shared with Sam had been, how fun *they* had been as a couple, it was making Theo feel protective of *me*.

"I'm sure they're just trying to make sure I don't feel . . . patronized." I blinked, not particularly convincing even to myself. "Clearly I'm not going to be wowing Belle Glen with how well I fit in anytime soon, huh?" That would *have* to register with Theo, wouldn't it? That the person who actually fitted into his life, his world, was less than a hundred feet away?

"I don't know about that. Can I show you something? About your backhand?"

"Oh, uh . . . sure, okay."

"So, you're using a two-handed backhand, which is fine, but your hips aren't really rotating into the shot, so it's not going where you want."

"When I even manage to connect."

Theo smiled gently.

"You're getting better. Anyway, when you *do* connect, you want to really nail it, right? Right now you're doing this." He demonstrated. "But you should do this." Theo demonstrated the "right" move, then showed both actions again. I squinted. Maybe his hips swiveled slightly more?

"So . . . like this?" I tried to mirror what he'd done. Theo shook his head.

"Let me show you." He moved up behind me, pressing himself along the length of my back. My breath caught in my throat at the sudden contact, pulse quickening traitorously. My brain could wrap itself around how wrong Theo and I were for each other, how little we had in common, but the hairs rising at the nape of my neck, and the suddenly hypercharged surface of my skin, could only seem to focus on the feel of him, the memory of the carved muscles I could feel through the thin fabric between us, his body limned by firelight, poised over me, me arching up to urge him deeper inside . . .

He bent over my shoulder, speaking low in my ear.

"Hold it like this, the right grip is everything." His breath skimmed across the soft skin of my cheek, sending a shiver through my entire body as he placed his hands over mine, shifted them into place, the quiet strength in his arms restrained but evident as they circled me. The hard planes of his chest pressed into my shoulders, and his faint piny scent wafted over me, the heat from his exercise-warmed skin turning it deeper, and somehow even more intoxicating.

"Okay," I said, voice barely a whisper. Could he feel how hard my heart was pounding? See my pulse jumping? The image of him bending over the delicate skin between my jaw and my neck, pressing his lips to it, then along my throat, shot into my mind unbidden, and I had to physically restrain myself from tilting my head to present myself to him. When he spoke again, his voice was rougher.

"The whole swing has to come from your hips. Like this."

One hand still over mine on the racket, he moved the other around to my front, pressing me back against him, swiveling my hips with his own as he moved my arm through space. Heat swirled through me, condensing between my legs in a throbbing ache.

"Am I doing it right?" I pressed back against him, rolling my hips ever so slightly, craving the friction. Theo made a low sound in his throat. I could feel him stiffening against my back. I swallowed hard, skin tingling everywhere his body touched mine.

"Yes," he growled, hips pressing into me hard. "That's perfect . . ."

"You think you've got it, Ellie? I wasn't kidding about that ten o'clock," Everett called out from across the court. I startled, suddenly remembering myself, and had to force myself not to spring away. It shouldn't be strange for Theo to touch me, even intimately, even in public—Bella had made a point of mentioning his physical-ity, after all. Or it wouldn't be strange if our relationship were *real*.

God, how had that felt so real? I needed to get a fucking *grip*. And not just on my tennis racket.

"Yup!" I said, voice tight and high. "Or at least I'm not getting any better before the next point."

I took a step away from Theo.

"Thanks for that." His gaze locked onto mine, the fire I'd felt flaring between us still flickering in his eyes.

"We can have a private lesson later." His sly smile promised so much more than study. I licked my lips and nodded once, not trust-ing myself with more words. When I looked at Sam, she was watch-ing the two of us, face totally blank. I hurried back to the baseline.

But my nerves were still sparking crazily with pent-up desire. I managed to get my serve into the right section, but it was high and slow, and Everett slashed it to the far back corner of the court be-fore I even realized what was happening.

"That's game," he said, grinning widely. "Sam, you want to serve first for us? I'm dying to see that killer instinct in action."

The next three games were a blur of rocket-speed shots from Sam and Everett, valiant efforts by Theo to keep us competitive, and truly pitiful play on my part, which somehow still left me pant-ing by the time Everett set up for his final serve. Sweat prickled my hairline, and the muscles in my legs were on fire from my mostly futile attempts to reach the balls that Sam and Everett—but mostly Sam, she clearly hadn't been joking about exploiting me as the weak link—kept sending my way. *Maybe she's just pissed at you for turning this plan in entirely the wrong direction.*

His serve shot over the net to Theo, who hit it right down the middle of the court. Everett made a show of just barely missing it with his outstretched racket. I could tell he was holding back, not that it did us much good; Everett half-trying was still twice the player I was. But Sam was already sprinting across the court behind him, arm back as she neared the ball. With a loud *thwack* she con-nected, sending it just past me, my startled attempt to catch it with a backhand half a second too late. The ball soared over the adjoining court, thudding to a stop against the curves of the white domed wall.

"That's set," she said, the sweat glistening on her skin only highlighting her high cheekbones, the obvious triumph in her eyes mirroring their sparkle. "Good effort, guys, really," she added, locking onto Theo.

"Next time, maybe we can focus a little less on the win and give Ellie a chance to learn the game," he said as we all drifted back to the benches. "It doesn't *always* have to be so competitive."

"Sure, but that's what makes it fun." Sam's tone was light, but I could see the hint of something darker tugging at the corners of her eyes. *God, she must hate me.* Which sucked on two levels; I didn't just want her help with Mangia (though that was *hugely* important), I really just . . . liked her. Learning she was moving to Milborough had been unexpectedly exciting. She'd hardly make an effort at friendship if I actively salted her on this.

"Maybe for some people." Theo turned to me as I tugged my sweatpants up. I couldn't help but notice the full-on barrier of back he'd put between himself and Sam. Judging by her pained expression, she caught it too. "Do you mind if we head out, El? I need to squeeze in a shower before my first meeting, and the club locker rooms have terrible water pressure."

"Sure. Of course." I hoisted my bag onto my shoulder, and Theo moved with me, sliding his arm around my waist, pressing me against his hip. I tried to eye-apologize to Sam, but I wasn't sure it transmitted right. "Thanks so much for putting up with me. Maybe next time you all should find a different fourth. At least until I can up my game a little."

"It was fun," Everett said, wiping his face with a towel and tossing it into his bag, grinning widely. "And why would we do that? I *like* winning."

"Well, glad I could help." He laughed his warm, open laugh, leaning in to give me a quick back-patting hug. Then he turned to Sam, body going infinitesimally stiffer.

"I would love to do this again, though. Maybe a singles match? See who's really carrying the team?"

Sam frowned, tearing her eyes away from Theo to flash Everett a weak smile.

"Absolutely. Beating you will be even more fun than playing with you."

"Oh, it's *on*."

Theo and I made our way across town in silence. Just as we were pulling up to my apartment, he reached across the console to take my hand.

"Hey. I'm sorry."

"Why?" I blinked, genuinely confused.

"I'm sure that wasn't fun for you." His eyebrows tented with concern.

"It was fine. So I suck at tennis. I could have told you that before."

"Well, for the record, I appreciate it." He leaned closer. "You putting yourself through that just for the two of us . . ." Closer yet.

"I mean . . . we have to sell this thing."

"On that note . . ."

And before I could think to move away, his mouth was on mine, hand cupping the back of my head, his tongue gently parting my lips, and my brain just shut down, leaving only this, the feel of him, the soft pressure of his skin on mine. I sucked his lower lip between my teeth, nibbling lightly, and he tangled his fingers in my hair, mouth growing hungrier against mine.

When he pulled away, I was dizzy with the intensity of it, body so taut with desire it felt like a single touch in the right place could shatter me into a million pieces.

Theo tilted his forehead against mine, thumb softly caressing the back of my head as he spoke.

"I'm going to be pretty tied up this week with work stuff. There's an event I want you to come to, but . . . sorry in advance if you don't hear much from me in the interim."

"I'll try to hold it together," I said, smirking.

He leaned in to press one more kiss to my lips, the gentleness of it somehow . . . tender? I couldn't be certain, it had been so long since anyone had kissed me that way, not with urgency, just sweetly, like they were looking for attachment, nothing more.

"Until then . . . I'll be thinking of you, Ellie." Theo pulled away, and my breath slowly returned to my body, eventually reaching my brain.

"Should I be worried?" I fussed with my gym bag so I wouldn't have to meet Theo's smoldering stare, afraid of what I might do if I did.

"Only if you get rid of that tennis skirt before I see you next. I will personally undertake your training *solely* to keep seeing you in it."

"Ha," I barked, unsure how else to respond, frothy delight filling my chest. I hadn't even noticed him looking . . . "Sounds like you should make that shower cold."

Theo tilted his head in playful acknowledgment, and I took the opportunity to get out of the car and its inexplicably potent atmosphere of sex. Probably something to do with all the leather trim.

Theo waited at the curb until I made it into the lobby, making me too aware of my body to process . . . well, *anything* that had just happened. It wasn't until I was safely in the confines of my living room, the familiar dinge an antidote to all twittery feelings, that it struck me.

I had fucked this up *so bad*. I knew what I had to do, knew it was better in the long run—and even the short run, going softcore in front of Sam was *not* going to convince her to hold up her end of the Mangia bargain—and in the moment, none of that had mattered. My body had taken over, responding to Theo's scent, the intensity of his eyes, the intoxicating feeling of him against me— I shivered a little, imagining it again—and it had somehow entirely short-circuited my brain.

At least Theo's busy week was a reprieve—I would *not* give in to the achy sensation in my chest that the prospect was bringing on. I'd use the time to get my shit together and get things back on track.

As if in answer to my thoughts, my phone pinged inside my gym bag.

From: Samantha Lindsay

> I think we need a debrief. Drinks tonight?

I winced. I knew things had gone badly, but if Sam was clearing her schedule to discuss just *how* badly . . . that couldn't be good. Stomach sinking, I texted back.

> Sounds good, just tell me where to be.

Maybe the week would be a chance to get things back on track.

Or maybe all of this was going to end sooner than I'd planned . . . and not in the way I'd been hoping.

Eighteen

"Oh you have *got* to be fucking kidding me," I muttered aloud as I pulled up to the maps pin for the Boston restaurant Sam had chosen, Amicizia.

I'd noticed the high ratings and how close it was to 93 when I pulled it up, and I'd quickly responded with an enthusiastic yes. What *hadn't* been immediately apparent was the fact that the restaurant was located inside Mangia.

Gritting my teeth, I turned in to the attached parking lot. I hadn't taken Sam for the passive-aggressive type—she seemed to fall into the "no bullshit" bin I personally occupied—but maybe in her mind she was fighting fire with fire. Being felt up by the very man I'd promised to help her repair things with probably wasn't raising me in her estimation any.

At least they validated parking.

I made my way through the rococo entryway, all Easter-egg-colored scrollwork and splashes of gilt. Inside, things changed.

The first floor was expansive, divided into half a dozen hyper-specific markets. The Negozio di Aceto, stocked with hundreds of varieties of vinegar for every taste and price point, shouldered up next to the Uliveti, the outpost for all things olive, from oils separated by purpose—this one for cooking, that one for salads, this other for finishing a soup or pasta—to squat jars packed with the glistening fruits, their detailed placards explaining the varietal's characteristics, specific terroir, and the unique techniques the producer used to distinguish it from the next ridiculously expensive jar. Then there was the dried fruits and nuts store, the tinned fish store, the dried pastas store, a helpful sign near its entrance noting that *fresh* pastas were on floor 3. Each subsection had a specific flavor— rustic woods and terra-cotta tones for the olives; geometric shapes in bright reds, oranges, and greens for the pastas; an earthy-bordering-boho vibe for the dried fruits and nuts—but the space as a *whole* was blindingly modern, with industrial-loft ductwork snaking around the ceilings, bright white walls, and blond woods turning all the communal spaces that vaguely Scandinavian flavor of antiseptic that somehow reassured people buying food.

As I glanced around the hangar-sized space, it was immediately apparent that Sam was right. The old Taylor's building was large, but the upper floors were divided into approximations of smaller rooms, intimate enclaves designed so the experience of buying perfume, or hosiery, or linens, could feel thrillingly specific and important, a holdover from when the entire concept of the department store was new and luxurious. On top of that, it was simply too small. I wasn't great with guessing square footage, but the entire footprint couldn't be half the size of this building's.

Plus, the sheer *number* of floors was daunting. At the escalator I found a helpful building plan: The second floor was for dolci, with subsections for pastries, gelato, confectionery, and home baking; the third was for fresh meats, fish, cheeses, and pastas; the fourth was wines, spirits, aperitifs and digestifs, limoncello (apparently that merited its own section), and soft drinks; the fifth held everything you'd need to outfit an extremely high-end kitchen, from pasta makers to stand mixers to fussy little olive pitters no one actually *used*.

It wasn't until the sixth and seventh floors that you hit the restaurants. In addition to Amicizia, a "true Italian bistro," there was Napoli (for pizza), Salamoia (seafood, apparently), Affogatto (a café), and Carne (their white tablecloth steakhouse).

When I reached the bistro, Sam was already nestled in a booth at the back; she waved me over and I picked my way between low tables topped with cheery red-checked cloths. Her smile looked genuine . . . Still, my stomach clenched preemptively as I slid in across from her.

"Thanks for coming into town on such short notice," she said, glancing at the cocktails menu briefly before handing it to me. "I'm still wrapping up a lot of stuff at my old job, there was no way I could get out early enough to make it back to Milborough at a reasonable hour."

"No problem," I said, using the menu as an excuse to find the precise words I wanted. "I could beat around the bush, but I don't think either of us are fans of bullshit." Sam frowned slightly, then nodded, urging me on. "Was this some kind of fuck you?" I gestured around the space. "I know this morning didn't go how we'd hoped, but—"

"A fuck . . . ? *No.*" Sam shook her head, emphatic. "Didn't you get my text?" She pulled her phone out, scrolling rapidly to find our message history. "Dammit. I was going into the tunnel. It said I still had bars . . ." She turned it to face me. The little red exclamation point next to the last message in the chain showed it hadn't gone through: *Full disclosure the restaurant is inside Mangia. Know your enemy, right?*

"So you're not pissed at me?"

"Pissed at *you*? I figured you'd be pissed at *me*." Sam's eyes widened in disbelief.

"Why?"

"For wasting your time. And ruining a pretty solid plan. Theo getting all protective was predictable, honestly. I'm guessing it was in response to how badly *I* fucked things up this morning."

"Clearly we have very different takes on this morning." The

server came by and we ordered cocktails and apps. When she was gone, I bit the end off a spindly breadstick, then pointed it at Sam. "What do you even think you fucked up?"

"Not sure if you noticed, but I really like *winning*." Sam scrunched her nose and reached for her own breadstick, cracking it in half thoughtfully. "I don't think I'm a particularly bad loser, but I get pretty competitive. Everett's the same, which definitely didn't help."

I thought back to Theo's aside that morning, his barely repressed annoyance as he'd noted the trait in Sam. It wasn't until that moment that he'd turned "protective," as Sam put it . . . which of course had turned things in a different direction entirely. Heat rose to my cheeks as I remembered the feeling of him growing stiff with desire against my back . . .

"Isn't Theo competitive?" I said, trying to divert my thoughts from the gutter they'd sloshed into.

"Sort of . . ." Sam drew circles in a dish of oil with her breadstick. "He likes to be the best *he* can be at things. But he's got a soft spot for an underdog, like . . . pretty much always?" She shrugged. The cocktails arrived and she took a long, thoughtful sip of her negroni. "I suppose it isn't a *bad* trait. I'd just forgotten how much less passionate he was about the little things. And the big things, sometimes . . ." She swirled the glass, watching the vivid pink shimmer on the surface of the alcohol.

Relief flooded me. Sam might be wrong—I was at *least* as much to blame as she was—but that wasn't the point. So far, I hadn't royally fucked everything up, either with the Mangia plan or the less-well-formed "Maybe Sam becomes your actual friend" plan that had recently sprouted up between its roots.

"So next double date we try something I don't absolutely suck at. I'll tell you right now, I can *school* you in bowling."

She grinned.

"Worth a shot. Though . . . maybe we just avoid games entirely. I'm not sure I can turn that part of me *off*. Or that Theo can turn it on." She grimaced.

"Then we eat, or drink." I shrugged. "Everyone's friendlier when they drink."

"As long as we're not drinking and playing Cards Against Humanity." Sam grimaced. "I think I might be worse with that game than I am with tennis."

"Honestly . . . this morning wasn't a total disaster," I said slowly, thinking through it. Knowing Sam wasn't holding it against me seemed to have cleared away some fog. "Theo was definitely *very* aware of you and Everett hitting it off."

"Anyone can hit it off with Everett, he's just a genuinely good guy," Sam said, face softening into fondness. "We always called him the litmus test back in the day. If Everett can't find anything nice to say about you, there really *must* be something wrong."

"I'm surprised he's still single."

"Bad luck, I think." Sam smeared a blob of gooey cheese onto a crostino. "He got together with this girl Kari maybe . . . five years ago? She was great, super funny, a filmmaker. Her friends were all so interesting."

"What happened?"

"Everett's always wanted kids, Kari realized she was never going to get there. They broke up a while ago, but Everett was pretty messed up by it. At least that's what mutual friends said. I wasn't super in the loop." Sam shrugged. "Anyway, I'm sure he won't be single for long. I mean . . . he's objectively a catch."

"You're making me think we should just swap them out once this is over."

"You could do a hell of a lot worse." Sam's expression turned devilish. "Plus, from what I hear, he's *extremely* giving in bed. Holdover from being the nerdy kid who hung around the athletes in high school. Apparently he spent most of junior year perfecting his oral technique with the goal of consistently being able to give women double orgasms." She waggled her eyebrows.

"Okay, how do you even know that?"

"Kari was a very open person. Besides, that's the kind of info all women *should* share."

"Did he succeed? At the double orgasm technique?"

"Everett's nothing if not *extremely* driven."

We both burst into giggles. When they finally subsided, I looked out over the restaurant. On the opposite side of a central register, dozens of undoubtedly tempting smalls arranged on its shelves, was another *entire restaurant*. The fish one, judging by the washy blue walls. I sighed heavily, swirling my cocktail.

"So this is what I'm up against, huh?" I took a huge swig of the drink, the walnut liqueur somewhere in the mix lingering pleasantly. "Kinda makes you want to throw in the towel now."

"There's no way you can compete with Mangia directly, we both know that." Sam propped an elbow on the table, cradling her chin. "Even if you could figure out a way to snag the bulk discounts they're getting—which is pretty much impossible—they'd always just have more *options*."

"Wow, you're *really* making me feel better about this."

"Sorry, side effect of the job. There's no room for blowing smoke when you're the one in charge of the financials." Sam's head swiveled, neck elongating. "But you do have something Mangia never will."

"Besides higher costs per unit?"

"Yup. You've got *intimacy*." Sam tipped her drink to the room. "You can see them trying to create it here, with all the micro concepts, the staff trained to greet you informally, but it doesn't really *jell*. All you have to do is raise your sight line and you remember you're in a food warehouse. And honestly? Having fifty thousand choices for each type of good doesn't lead to more purchases, there's solid research on it."

"So, what, I'm gonna win on lack of choice and scrappiness?"

"What *we're* gonna do is make sure you're never actually in direct competition." Sam raised an eyebrow meaningfully. "But in the meantime, it wouldn't hurt to steal the things that are working. The recommendation cards, maybe, or the way they group goods into little sections, so people have the sense that they're being really discerning about what are totally non-necessity purchases."

"Just don't make me start offering gift wrap."

"Okay, heard, but have you ever considered gift *baskets* at the holidays? I'm definitely not the only person who's too lazy to plan ahead."

"That's . . . a really good idea." I blinked rapidly, head whirling with possibilities. "You could actually do them for special events year-round. Housewarmings. Maybe a date night package? Like . . . everything you need for a picnic."

"Oh my god, *yes*." Sam's eyes went saucer-wide. "Every dude in a hundred-mile radius would pay a premium for that. 'I just thought a picnic would be romantic, sweetie,' but without any effort whatsoever."

Excitement sprouted deep in my chest. I'd been making changes to the deli since I got back, some of them fringy, some larger, but this was one of the first that felt like it wouldn't just improve the bottom line, it would be *fun*. And it wouldn't require any new machinery or product lines, just some creativity on my end. I could even whip up some simple checked picnic blankets, maybe throw in matching napkins, your entire evening both planned out and social-media-ready with one artfully arranged purchase.

Actually . . . napkins would be smart, period. Offer a mix of designs, tie them up in sets of four with butcher's twine, and handwrite a fancy tag on card stock to complete the picture. If I started with scrap fabric when I got home, I could have a dozen within an hour. And aprons were pretty easy, too. Plus, a mix of fabric patterns would make them feel festive . . .

I grinned. It had never occurred to me that I could use my sewing skills *for* the deli, but the possibilities were limitless. And kind of exhilarating.

"I know you just got a pretty fancy offer from Ted, but are you *sure* you wouldn't rather work as an adviser to an extremely small deli? Once we drive out the excessively large mega-deli-plus-everything-else-ever, that is?"

"Hmm. Tempting." Sam curled her forefinger around her chin, feigning deep consideration.

"Let me sweeten the pot: I can pay you in salami. The *good* stuff."

"Bonuses in dry goods, I'm assuming."

"Obviously. We offer all the standard benefits at Greco's."

"Let me run some numbers. I am *very* intrigued by this opportunity."

The rest of the evening sped by, a blur of overpriced snacks and drinks, laughter, and that sparkling, effortless stream of conversation that I hadn't found with a *new* friend in . . . longer than I could remember.

For the moment, it drove the scheme, the increasingly confusing situation with Theo, even the looming threat of Mangia, out of my mind. Maybe it wasn't too much to hope that we could somehow pull this off.

In fact . . . maybe things would turn out even better because of it.

Nineteen

I'd gone an entire week without getting Pinskied. I suppose I was
overdue. Ruth was bent so low over the cheese section her breath
fogged the glass.

"The provolone's always reliable, but I wonder if cheddar
wouldn't be better with ham . . . and Jimmy does like a Muen-
ster . . ."

I returned to the sketch I'd been playing around with during
downtime all morning, a mod-influenced dress, all bell shapes, but
instead of classic seam piping, seam-*vines* wriggled up the skirt from
multiple directions and snaked around each sleeve, undulating sinu-
ously before bursting into cascading arrays of flowers around the
neckline and sleeve openings. I was imagining it in shades of green,
a foresty base color with new-growth-bright vines unfurling over it,
perfect for spring days that *weren't* just around the corner—New
England winters were as stolidly enduring as our Puritan forebears—
but that were finally starting to feel possible, now that we'd clawed
our way through the worst of winter to days when sunset was later
than four-thirty.

I always imagined clothes on myself first; it was long habit to pattern for the measurements I knew best. But for some reason, every time I imagined the reality of *this* garment—which fabrics would hang right, what lines would be the most flattering—I was imagining Theo *seeing* me in the dress. I'd already tweaked the design, picturing the furrow of his brow as he took in the drift of flowers on one shoulder. And shortened the hem, remembering the heat in his gaze when he talked about my tennis skirt . . .

"Did you hear me, Ellie? A half pound of the cheddar."

"Right, sorry, Ruth." I moved over to slice the cheese, trying to push the unwanted thoughts from my mind. *Theo's off-limits, dummy. Because you want him to be.* "So the ham, the cheese . . . anything else for you today?"

"That's all." She moved to the register as I wrapped her slices in wax paper. "Oh . . . these are new."

She picked up one of the five sets of cloth napkins I'd managed to whip up since the drinks debrief. The gift baskets would take a little planning yet—turned out half my suppliers carried woven baskets, but I wanted to find ones that matched the *feel* of each concept: date night, housewarming, and an "anytime" option for thank-you gifts or birthdays.

Ruth turned the set over in her hands, peering at the mixed geometric patterns in bright orange and red—remnants from curtains I'd made for Ma years ago—tugging at the corners to see each individual napkin.

"Is this price for the whole set?" She flipped the tag toward me, as though I hadn't written it myself just yesterday morning.

"Yup. Four napkins for sixteen dollars."

Her eyebrows went up.

"You'd pay twice that at Crate and Barrel. Maybe more."

"Making them myself saves a lot on shipping."

"Making . . . *no*." Her mouth dropped open into a little o. "You *made* these, Ellie? But they look so professional!"

"I'm a woman of many talents, Mrs. Pinsky."

"You really are," she said with a dazed smile, turning the set over in her hands again before tossing the napkins onto the counter. "Well, I suppose I'll have to take those too. It's always nice to have a little something you can use as a gift tucked away. Especially if it's made locally. Everyone seems to love that these days."

"I, for one, am very glad people feel that way. It's what keeps the lights on."

"Oh, we'd never go anywhere else, Ellie. But you know that."

My throat thickened with tenderness as I rang up her order. Jesus, whoever thought *Ruth Pinsky* would induce that?

I managed to hold back the full-on grin until she'd exited with a little tinkle of the bell. Yes, it was just one sale, and not even a *large* sale, but I couldn't help but feel excited. This was the first change I'd made that felt like it brought *me* into play. In fact, it merged parts of me I'd always thought couldn't coexist, the Ellie who loved this place more than anything, who deeply wanted—*needed*—it to succeed, and the creative person I worried was suffocating beneath practical Ellie's daily routines.

And this was just napkins. Tablecloths were practically as easy, and if you paired one with a napkin set that didn't match so much as complement, you had instant character for a dining table. And I hadn't forgotten the apron idea; cute fabrics and vintage inspiration could really make them pop. Carried on by enthusiasm, I shot Sam a quick text.

TO: Samantha Lindsay

> Sold the first set of napkins

> I was thinking tablecloth+napkin sets.
> And aprons?

Oh my god DEF do aprons

What if you had different seasonal designs?

And they could be kinda flirty

So like sexy santa vibes

Or were you thinking more sexy Jack-O'Lantern?

You can do a lot with the placement of those eye cutouts

Don't forget sexy arbor day

The most celebrated and sex-focused holiday obvs

Legit tho aprons are brilliant

Also, I know it's basic, but tea towels?

Could also be seasonal

Welp that's tonight's sewing project decided

Feel free to pay my finder's fee in the deli meats of your choice

I was wiping the counters idly, one eye on the phone to see if Sam would message back, when Bella walked in. I frowned at the clock.

"Afternoon get away from you?" she said as she shrugged out of her coat.

"Something like that." I bent over the deli case, quickly wrapping each of the meats. After a few seconds Bella moved around the counter to start in on the cheeses. I'd just made it to the salads when I heard her little exhalation of surprise. When I looked over she was holding the sketch. I had to restrain the immediate impulse to snatch it out of her hands, that full-body-clenching sensation of offering myself up for judgment dizzying in its intensity after so many years of avoiding it.

"I was just fucking around," I said, tugging a tray out of the case, simultaneously unable to meet her eyes and to stop myself from stealing tiny glances her way to gauge her reaction. "Slow day."

Bella's lips parted slightly as she tilted the drawing in her hands.

"You should have more slow days," she finally said, replacing it on the counter. "This is *gorgeous,* Ellie."

"I mean . . . it's pretty basic. A lot of the details would be appliqués. I wouldn't even be making them, really."

"You'd sew the flowers yourself."

"Probably, yeah."

"Doesn't sound very basic to me."

I returned her soft smile, relief dissolving the tension in my muscles.

"Maybe I'll try patterning it. My wardrobe could use an update."

"You should. But . . . what brought this on?"

"What do you mean?"

"It's been a while since you designed anything new. Which isn't a criticism," she held up a hand, forehead crinkling with preemptive concern. "I'm just wondering what inspired you."

The look in Theo's eyes if he saw me in it. His fingers tracing the narrow channel of my spine as he zipped me into . . . or out of it.

"Too much pent-up creative energy?" Sure. That's the kind of energy that was driving me. "And . . . I don't know, I was talking with Jenna DiSousa at the engagement party—did you know she writes novels now?"

"Really? Good for her."

"Yeah, I guess hearing that she's got this whole, like . . . creative *career* lit a fire under me."

"I always liked Jenna. Now I like her even more. Is she back in Milborough? You two should get together."

"Maybe. It was just one conversation." An unexpected wave of nerves rolled through me. What was I going to do, call her up for a blind friend date? "At *Belle Glen*. Proof positive that we don't have much in common."

"You can't know that without ever hanging out," Bella said evenly. I shrugged, and she rolled her eyes, dropping the point. "What about broccoli salad for tonight? I think Mimi's going with gnocchi, we should probably get a vegetable in somewhere."

We'd just managed to pack everything away when my phone pinged on the counter.

FROM: Little Lord Doucheleroy

> last minute but are you around Thursday night?

> > I think so. Why, what's up?

> Dinner with the board

> Mostly ironing out Sam's role rn but I think we'll switch over to Mangia by then

> Aunt Cheryl flew back from Turks & Caicos for the meetings

> > Aunt Cheryl? Turks and CAICOS? This must be serious

> If you knew Cheryl you'd realize that's not a joke

> Having you there won't decide anything but it can't hurt

> Plus it's a good excuse to ask you to dress up for me

My cheeks heated.

> I think I can squeeze you in if you ask REALLY nicely

> Forget the ask what if I promise an incredible afterparty at my place?

> Very exclusive guest list. You're the only person on it actually

Warmth pooled between my legs.

But Sam.

She'd be at the dinner. I could *not* risk another fiasco like the tennis game; Sam might have blamed herself, but she was way too smart not to spot the pattern if it happened a second time.

But actually . . . maybe this was the safest version of seeing Theo. She'd be there, a constant reminder to behave, and the board's presence would mean that even if Theo wanted to play up the so-in-love-fiancés angle, he couldn't go *too* far. Besides, until Mangia was officially off the table, I had to keep up the appearance of our engagement. Ted was suspicious enough of it.

> Count me in for dinner

> The rest we can negotiate

> I love when you talk dirty to me

Smirking, I made to slip the phone into my back pocket . . . and finally noticed Bella standing just behind me, worry written all over her delicate features.

"Did you . . . read those?"

"I didn't realize I wasn't supposed to," she said slowly. "Real talk, Ellie, when did this turn into an actual *thing*?"

"What?" I scoffed, moving past her to grab my coat. Bella was one person I'd never been good at lying to. "You must know how ridiculous that sounds."

"Why is it ridiculous?" She snapped a lid onto the container of broccoli salad, turning one of those deep, insightful Bella looks on me.

"Theo Taylor and me? Come on. We're nothing alike, you said it yourself."

"I never said that. I *wouldn't* say it. You've both got dark senses of humor, you're both *more* than happy to offer your opinions, even if you know they won't land with your audience."

"So assholes flock together. Thanks, Bell."

"You know that's not what I meant. Anyway, I wasn't finished. Both of you are no bullshit on the outside, but deep down, you care deeply about the things that matter to you. Family especially."

"You always have been my soft marshmallow center."

"And both of you shut people out so you won't have to be vulnerable. But you'd both be better off if you let someone past the wall."

"Are we done with the armchair analysis?" Bella shrugged acquiescence. "Good. Because all of that explains why I don't hate Theo as much as I expected to. I'll admit he has *some* good qualities. But he's light-years away from my type . . ."

"Strongest recommendation yet," Bella muttered.

"*And* I'm not looking for anything serious."

"Okay, let's say I take you at your word. When *are* you planning to look for something serious?"

"Excuse me?"

"Ellie, come on. We both know your 'type' didn't land on sexy losers because you think there's real potential there. It's because you know there's *not*."

"Jesus, Bella, did I do something to piss you off?"

"I just want you to . . . not even be happy, just like, be *willing* to be happy?" She threw her hands up, exasperated. "So Theo isn't your usual type. So what? He's a really good guy, he's stable—which is a good thing, by the way—and he makes you laugh. How many of the guys that you've slept with in the last ten years have done that, Ellie? And laughing *at* them doesn't count." I closed my mouth again. "If there's something there, why not pursue it? Or at least not actively push it away."

Because real relationships imply real roots. Because giving up the part of me that still wanted an artist's life in New York—or pretended to—felt like failure, even if the idea of going back to that made my stomach sink. Because I wasn't supposed to be okay with this life, back in my hometown, falling into a role that had been predetermined for me. Shouldn't I at least *want* to want more?

Plus, just because we both grew up here, that didn't mean Theo and I were from the same world. And what about Sam? I owed her this now, didn't I?

I pinched my eyes shut, shaking my head.

"But there *isn't* something there. We get along, that's it. End of story."

Bella sighed heavily.

"Okay. In that case I'll drop it."

"Halle*lu*jah."

"But I'm signing you up for Bumble once this is over, no arguments."

"You can drag a horse to water, but you can't make her swipe."

"Oh, did I not mention? I'll be running the account."

With that, we made our way out into the night, the topic dropped for the time being (Bella was nothing if not true to her word). Still, it made me wonder: If even Bella could see that this was slipping out of my control, how could I possibly keep it going without someone getting really hurt? Someone like . . . me?

Twenty

"Ellie! So good to see you again. Let me take your coat. I'll show you to the private room."

I dutifully let Andy slide the coat off my shoulders, trying not to enjoy the annoyance twisting the face of the prissy woman he'd ignored in favor of me. At least not *too* much.

Andy whisked me across the restaurant to a room at the back, the walls of which were constructed entirely of antique cubbies, decades of hands passing in and out of them patinaing their surfaces.

"You're the first to arrive," Andy said. "Can I get you something to drink while you wait?"

I longed for a cocktail—the prospect of meeting with the board had been slowly incrementing my anxiety all day. The fact that I'd have to juggle both the parts I'd decided to play—Theo's loving fiancée and Sam's self-appointed matchmaker—only made it worse. But looking like a lush wouldn't help anything, especially since the board might be the last thing between me and the end of this increasingly difficult-to-balance high-wire act. Which was the best thing for everyone involved . . . right?

"I'm fine for now."

With a perfunctory smile, Andy hurried out, leaving me to try to manufacture interest in the room's décor: rubber stamps still set to dates in the 1920s, a dusty telegraph signaler that was objectively cool but currently registered as "lots of wires and metal on wood."

Luckily, I didn't have to wait long. Minutes later, Andy reappeared with the entire crew. Ted barked something over his shoulder as he stepped through, trailed by Marta, Theo, Sam, and a middle-aged man and woman I didn't recognize. Theo moved over to me immediately, sliding an arm around my waist and bending to my ear.

"Did we keep you waiting long?"

"Not particularly."

His eyelids went heavier, and he leaned closer, creating a tiny pocket of intimacy, but before he could say whatever was turning his gaze so sultry—Jesus, when had I started thinking of Commercial Real Estate Ken as *sultry*?—Ted cleared his throat loudly.

"Ellie, glad to see you're on time tonight. My soon-to-be daughter-in-law shares Theo's . . . flexible sense of scheduling," he said to the unfamiliar man, who smiled tolerantly. I choked down my annoyance. "Why don't we get started. I know everyone's eager to meet you."

Theo pulled out a chair for me directly across from Sam, seating himself across from the woman I presumed was Aunt Cheryl. Marta, Ted, and the unknown man curved around the head of the table.

Theo's hand moved toward mine beneath the table as he turned to his father, fingers lacing between my own so naturally I almost didn't notice the gesture. He squeezed once and I turned, intercepting an unexpectedly tender smile that sent my heart straight to my throat. I forced myself to look away—now was not the time. In fact, never, *that* was the time for this. Plain never.

That's when I caught Sam's eyes, narrowing as they flitted between my face and our joined hands. Swallowing hard, I loosed my fingers, folding them in my lap as I waited for Ted to continue.

"I know there's a lot more business to get through, so I'll make this brief. This is the mysterious Ellie Greco, the woman who somehow turned my son into a romantic." Ted gestured at me, his smile close to a sneer. "Ellie, you know Marta and Samantha. Let me introduce my sister, Cheryl, and my brother, Paul. Along with myself, they make up the board of Taylor Property Management. Though we may create more seats, now that we have an official CFO." Ted smiled indulgently at Sam.

"So nice to meet you." I turned to Cheryl and Paul in turn. Cheryl had steel-gray hair coiffed into a neat bob, and was trim in her winter-white bouclé skirt suit. I could see the resemblance to Ted; her features were softer, but they shared the same strong bone structure and brow, and there was a shrewdness in her blue eyes that felt familiar, if slightly less predatory. Paul had the general Taylor face as well, but his entire body felt blurred and a bit rumpled—jaw gone jowly, slight paunch straining against the sweater vest he wore beneath his navy sports coat—as though the edges of the mold had eroded with time. If it weren't for the III after Theo's name, I'd have assumed Paul was the oldest, but judging from the burst capillaries around his nose and cheeks, he was simply aging at an alcohol-increased rate.

Cheryl gave me a polite, unreadable smile. Paul's was distinctly curdled.

"So lovely to meet you, Ellie. I hope we won't bore you with too much family business talk," Cheryl said. "If Paul and I could stay longer, I'd say we should shelve it for the night, but you know how it is."

"Of course. Pretend I'm not here—I know how much you all have to cover."

They took me at my word. As soon as drink orders were in, they launched into analysis of all things Taylor Properties, the conversation jumping around quickly, relying on a shorthand I didn't understand. From what I could gather, Cheryl was interested in specifics about both projected annual returns and carrying costs on the current portfolio, peppering her replies to Ted's blustering predictions—all positive, of course—with information about market trends and percentage yield talk that I'd have needed a printout to keep up with. Paul piped in occasionally with a snide comment but otherwise focused most of his attention on his Burgundy. Sam and Theo added the context, facts, and figures. It quickly became clear that Theo hadn't been joking—Ted's name might still get top billing, but he clearly wasn't conversant with the day-to-day operations the way Theo and Sam were.

I was completely superfluous. Luckily, Andy had left a copy of the menu, so I at least had something to focus on. I lingered over the cheese and charcuterie selections, mentally drafting a list of alternatives *I* could supply.

"So another long-term lease is out of the question?" Cheryl asked Sam, who tilted her head to the side, thoughtful. I perked up a little—the conversation had spiraled inward from high-level revenue, growth, and carrying costs to focus specifically on the old Taylor's building.

"It's not impossible, of course." Sam swirled her wine. "But the space just doesn't fit many retail mandates in this market. It's too large even for local chains. I asked Phil Bray for his financials from the last decade to get a sense of where to look for competitive offers, and the store barely broke even that entire time. Theoretically you could subdivide the building, but it's hard to rent retail space without a street-level entrance. We never even managed to keep the top-floor offices at full occupancy, and *none* of those were retail."

"So it seems like Ted's right, selling to Mangia is the smartest play."

"Maybe . . . but they're likely to either gut or tear down the building. It could be years before they're operational."

"Forgive me if I'm being dense, Samantha, but I'm not sure how that's our problem?" Cheryl lifted an eyebrow.

"My thoughts exactly." Ted raised his glass to his sister.

"Short-term, it wouldn't be. The company would get a large

infusion of capital and your dividends would increase for the year. But if the project drags on, it has the potential to depress business in other portfolio properties. Most of them, if traffic gets rerouted for construction. South Street is a major artery for downtown. I need to run more projections, but I'm not sure it's a smart move, just from a dollars and cents perspective. And of course there's the reputation cost."

"Reputation *cost*? For pulling off a major deal with Mangia? Maybe we shouldn't have approved Sam's appointment so quickly," Paul scoffed. Sam's face tightened almost imperceptibly, but her expression stayed pleasantly neutral.

"I'm sure Ted told you that Mangia would compete directly with Ellie's family business, and other businesses like it. But hers is the most relevant, since she'll be *joining* your family. Financial savvy is absolutely a mark in the pros column, but a reputation for ruthlessness won't do us any favors. Particularly since a good chunk of the portfolio sinks or swims based on local sentiment," Sam said.

"Ellie's family . . . I'm sorry, I don't believe Ted mentioned that." Cheryl turned her intense gaze on me. "What is it you do?"

"Oh, I . . . run a deli?" She caught me midsip and I gulped, the alcohol singeing my sinuses. "Greco's Deli? It's just downtown."

"That sounds vaguely familiar." Cheryl frowned, pensive. "It's been so long since I lived here. So. A deli." She sat back, smirking in a way that must be habitual, judging by the deep lines parentheseeing one side of her mouth. "I assumed you worked in something trendy. PR, maybe, or magazines. I'm not used to seeing deli owners dressed so chicly. Who made that blouse, if you don't mind my asking?"

I was wearing an ivory blouse I'd made during a "play with volume" period from the end of my time in New York. The shape was classic, with curve-hugging seams and a tie-necked Peter Pan collar. The most noticeably "different" element was the sleeves, exaggerated balloons of ethereal sheer silk. Of course the scalloped black edging along the placket, collar, and cuffs had been incredibly fussy,

and figuring out how to attach the sleeves so they'd hang *just* right
had taken me half a dozen not-quite-there attempts, but the overall
design was hardly revolutionary; the glamour was in the details.

"I did, actually." Cheryl's expression of polite interest sharp-
ened.

"No. May I?" She leaned across the table, and I let her take the
sleeve between her outstretched fingers. "The workmanship is incredible."

"You made this *too*?" Marta blinked, mouth o'ing. "Cheryl, you
should have seen the dress she wore to the engagement party. It
was perfection."

"I'm betting she made the pants, too," Theo said, a proud look
on his face that I couldn't remember seeing before. "Ellie's incredibly talented. Who knows, maybe by our first anniversary she'll be
running two businesses. Then I can be a househusband." He
slipped an arm around my shoulders, squeezing me against him and
pressing his lips gently to my temple.

"I mean . . . yes, I made the pants, but the design's *very* simple."
I rolled my eyes, simultaneously uncomfortable with the attention
and pulsing with a sweet, all-enveloping ache that made it impossible not to lean into Theo's warmth. He squeezed me a little tighter,
kissing the top of my head, and my eyes closed of their own accord, a contented-cat feeling overtaking me.

"Maybe bringing Mangia in would be doing you a favor, Ellie,"
Paul said, his lazy, half-amused tone tugging me back to earth. I
straightened, but Theo's arm stayed around me, tightening as
though he was ready to come to my defense.

"How do you mean?" I said, working hard to keep my tone
polite.

"Clearly you have a calling." Paul gestured up and down my
body with his wine glass. "A *deli* sounds like a waste of your talents."
He took a sip, sneering sideways at his brother. "Hell, if she sells
now, all our problems would be solved."

The basic sentiment—that I was wasting my life, my skills, my *time* at the deli—I'd bemoaned to Bella countless times since my return. It was my pet complaint when Mimi couldn't keep herself from commenting (negatively) on changes I'd made to the inventory, layout, or marketing, and my go-to gripe whenever a particularly difficult regular salted my mood. Once, in a moment that still made me cringe with shame whenever I peered at its reflection in my memory pool, I'd even lost it with Ma. It had been a particularly grueling holiday shift, but even though she'd already put in a full day at the hospital, she was wiping down counters after nine o'clock beside me, my obviously foul mood throwing her peacemaker instincts into hyperdrive. She'd made some offhand remark, the sort of silver-lining comment she always defaulted to when someone she loved was in pain—the helplessness she felt in those moments made her pathologically focused on finding bright sides, her small attempt at righting the world for the people whose hearts were threaded all through her own. I, of course, was having none of it, and I'd laid into her: *Who* gives *a fuck that it was a good sales day, I'm wasting my entire life slicing meat for townies. How is that a* success, *Ma? How is that anything but* sad?

The hurt in her eyes was immediate, and worse . . . there was real disappointment there, a sorrow that went deeper than the sting of my acid tone. I could see that in that moment, she thought less of me. But all she'd said was *I'm sorry you feel that way. For the record, I don't see that as a wasted life.*

She hadn't had to voice the subtext: Dad. I wasn't just writing off a quiet, small-town life for myself, I was saying his life, his path, hadn't mattered. Of course I'd felt terrible, but I'd just mumbled an apology for my mood, unable to deny my underlying frustration. Sure, it had been good enough for Dad, but that didn't mean it was what *I* was supposed to be doing.

But somehow, hearing this smarmy middle-aged trust fund kid voice the same thought I'd muttered to myself in a hundred moments of frustration set my teeth on edge. What the hell did he know about *callings*? Judging from the makeup of the board, his great achievement in life had been his last name. How could he possibly understand what the deli—the embodiment not only of my family's history, our love for one another, but of a version of community that *mattered*—meant to people? How could he understand that there could be something deeply fulfilling in weaving yourself into a larger story, creating something not just for yourself, like all my cleverly constructed blouses, but for the people and places that were your whole heart?

A quiet internal voice noted that I'd been avoiding that precise understanding for *years,* but the fury alarm going off in my brain drowned it out.

"I don't see it that way at *all.*" I dug my fingertips into my knees, forcing myself to keep my expression neutral. "I'm extremely proud of what my family has built. And I feel lucky that I get to carry on their legacy. Design is important to me, and it's fulfilling in a very different way, but if it were the *most* important thing, I wouldn't be here now."

Paul threw up his hands, even his expression of shock indolent.

"No need to get worked up. It's sweet that you care about the place."

Pressure started building behind my eyes. The need to lay into this rich schmuck was creating a physical pain in my chest. Then Theo's hand moved onto my thigh, and he squeezed once. When I glanced over, there was a warning in his lowered brow, but also something else: fierce protectiveness. I could almost hear him: *Don't say something you'll regret, Ellie.*

Sucking in a deep breath, I turned back to Paul.

"Of course. If you'll excuse me, I need the restroom." With a grimace I hoped approximated politeness, I strode out without a backward glance.

I was leaning heavily on the sink, breathing deeply in an effort to recenter myself, when Sam walked in. She made no pretense of going to the bathroom, instead catching my eye through our reflections.

"Are you okay? Paul's a congenital asshole, but no one takes him seriously. Which probably just makes him act like a bigger dick, to be honest."

I exhaled a thin laugh.

"I'm fine. Sorry, that just . . . struck a nerve, clearly."

"No need to apologize." Sam flipped on the sink to wash her hands, turning back and forth to examine her makeup in the mirror. "Before we go back out there, I have to ask . . . Are you *sure* there's nothing between you and Theo?"

A mix of fear and guilt geysered up my throat. Sam had just proven she was my best ally—if she told the Taylor clan that selling to Mangia was a bad move, they'd probably listen. And if she didn't . . .

And Jesus, the first thing she'd done when she came in was to check how I was doing. She wasn't just my ally, she was the first person I actually *wanted* to be my friend in longer than I could remember. What in god's name was wrong with me lately?

"Obviously I can't speak for Theo, but I think it's a combination of us both wanting to sell the engagement and just . . . getting along. As friends, I mean."

"Things seem a little more than friendly . . ."

"That's how we want them to seem, right? People have to believe we're real. And from what I've heard, Theo's into PDAs."

"That's true," Sam said with a small laugh. She flicked off the water and caught me full in the eye again. "But be honest: You're *sure* that's all it is? Because I meant what I said before, if there's something there, I have zero interest in coming between you. Theo and I might not even work, I'm not about to break up something real just to test the waters. If that's what's happening, we can call this off. Hell, I could even help *you* get him."

She flashed a quick smile, but she still had that guarded, unreadable quality, the perfect mask whether you're in a boardroom or trying to get a straight answer out of a hopefully-eventually-friend. Somehow it was more anxiety-inducing than if she'd expressed annoyance; cold control wasn't something I knew how to manage, and I had the feeling it was less easy to move past than the more explosive brand of disagreement I was used to.

As much as the idea of writing Theo off entirely plucked at something deep inside that I hadn't expected it to, there was only one right answer: *Do whatever it takes to save the deli.* Whatever was screwing with my hormones was *not* the point. And who's to say I even wanted something serious, not just with Theo, but at all? I'd just realized anew how important the deli was to me, to my family . . . With Sam's help, I'd even started coming up with changes that genuinely excited me. For the first time in I couldn't remember how long, my sewing machine was at the ready, my work table covered with fabric scraps and thread spools, and on top of all that, I was even designing new outfits. Somehow, accepting that the deli actually mattered to me seemed to have unblocked me creatively. Maybe because it took the pressure off; with the deli as priority number one, design could return to being the thing that drew me to it in the first place, tricking me into believing I was supposed to turn it into a lifelong calling: It was fun again.

I couldn't give all that up for some *man*. Especially a man my family didn't like for me—that guaranteed we'd fizzle eventually. Sure, we'd probably burn hot and strong at first, but what was a few months of sexual pleasure compared to a lifelong plan that finally, for the first time *ever,* felt like exactly what I was supposed to be doing?

I turned to look Sam straight in the eye. She needed to see how sincere I was; in a way, she was my most important audience in this whole thing.

"Theo and I are partners in crime, and I'm thrilled you think we're pulling this off, but that's the extent of it. Meeting his extended family . . . It's a huge night, especially since they have final say over Mangia. So yes, we're playing to the bleachers. But you don't need to worry about us, I promise. We both know where we stand, and that hasn't changed since we agreed to this."

Sam bit her lower lip, anxiety narrowing her eyes, then she nodded resolutely, turning to reach for a hand towel.

"In that case, let's go drag ourselves through the rest of this dinner." She bent to wrap me in an impromptu hug. "You're doing an incredible job, by the way. I really think this will work out perfectly."

"I hope you're right."

And I did.

I just had to keep telling myself that I did.

Twenty-One

"Ellie, I'll walk you to your car?"

I startled at Theo's voice, low and close to my ear. By the time Sam and I returned from the bathroom, Paul and Ted were deep in a discussion of winter golfing destinations and Cheryl was telling Marta about a recent Paris trip. If anything, I'd felt even more out of my element than when they'd been digging into financials.

"We can wait. For everyone to be ready, I mean."

"No, you lovebirds get going." Cheryl smiled in a way that she probably meant to be indulgent; the strong lines of her face didn't really lend themselves to the softer expressions. "I'm heading out any minute. I can't keep up with my brothers once they've started on the cognac. Ellie, I want you two to visit me in Palm Beach next month. I'll take you to all the best restaurants and we can talk more about your brilliant designs. I know more than a few women who would spend a very pretty penny for bespoke looks."

"That sounds lovely," I sputtered. Playing tailor to the uber-wealthy was in no way a goal of mine, but the idea that I *could* was flattering.

"I'll see you tomorrow, Aunt Cheryl." Theo leaned over the

table to kiss her cheek, real affection warming both their faces, then rose, raising two fingers in a perfunctory wave. "Back at it at eight sharp, yeah?"

"Make it ten," Paul said. "There are a lot more cognacs on that list I want to try."

With that, Theo ushered me out. I looked back across the restaurant, catching Sam's eyes, laser-focused on Theo's hand at the small of my back.

It was the perfect reminder: The tingly feeling radiating from that point, hugging my center, wasn't worth the risk of losing everything Sam was trying to help me secure. This feeling was passing, the intense high of a short-lived drug; saving the deli would be for the rest of my *life*.

"Where'd you park?" Theo said once we were on the sidewalk, arm slipping around my waist unconsciously, pulling me against him for warmth.

"I walked. I didn't want to deal with finding parking."

"We must be at least a mile from your apartment." Theo frowned in concern.

"*Maybe* two-thirds of a mile. Also, walking a mile isn't some major endeavor." I raised an eyebrow. "How many sit-ups do you do in a day?"

"I do them with my trainer in a heated gym." He grinned. "But this is good. Now I have an excuse to drive back to yours." He twisted me around, so my chest pressed against him, then reached up to tuck a loose strand of hair behind my ear. The shiver that ran through me had nothing to do with the chilly night. "On that note . . . shall we?"

His gaze dropped to my lips, eyelids going heavy as his arm tightened almost imperceptibly around me. I could feel my breath hitch as he leaned ever so slightly closer, my lips starting to part of their own accord.

No, Ellie, for Christ's sake no. This is not the plan, and in fact has every likelihood of completely destroying what's left of the actual plan.

I pulled away, tugging my coat around me deliberately.

"What are we waiting for? I'm not getting any warmer standing here."

Theo's lips curled in amusement, and he extended an arm.

"Right this way."

I followed him to his car, where I made a show of fiddling with the seat-heating controls so I wouldn't have to catch his eye.

"Were you planning on driving anytime soon?" I held my hands up to the air vent. It was imperative that I keep ignoring the heat between my thighs, pulsing and insistent in a way I couldn't blame on the car's luxury features.

"Someone's impatient." Theo took my hands between his own, rubbing the outsides slowly. Against my will, I caught his gaze. In the dark interior of the car, it crackled with barely repressed need. "What precisely are we rushing back to your place for, Ellie?"

"Sleep. Don't try to tell me that wasn't exhausting."

"Oh, it was." He gently lowered my hands to my lap, then ran a finger up the inside of my thigh. I drew in a sharp breath, biting my lower lip as a steady alarm blare of need at my center throbbed in response. Theo's lips curled as he wrapped his entire hand around my thigh, fingers stopping *just* below where my legs met. "Strangely enough, I'm not feeling that tired."

He slipped his other hand inside my coat, sliding it up my side until he reached the curve of my breast. He ran his fingers over the side slowly, back and forth, thumb whispering over the surface of my nipple. It hardened immediately beneath his touch, and my back arched involuntarily. His breathing grew heavier and he squeezed lightly, drawing a gasp. Through the thin silk of my blouse, I could feel him *feel* my body respond.

I should be stopping this.

"Theo . . . someone will see," I murmured, voice breathy.

"Doubtful. We're one of the only cars parked here." He slid his hand the last few inches up my thigh, rubbing his fingers over me through my pants, the fabric making the sensation that much more intense. I could feel myself going slick beneath his touch, my body practically begging for more. "Besides . . . I kind of *like* the idea of someone watching, don't you?" His voice was a throaty growl as his fingers moved over me more roughly. He dropped his hand from my breast to rub himself through his pants. I could see him growing harder with each stroke. Blood throbbed through me in response.

"Fuck," I murmured as his fingers kept working me, first slowly, then fast, softer, then harder.

"Great idea."

Before I fully realized what was happening, Theo was opening his door, moving around the car to open mine, pulling me out of the seat and roughly against his body, one hand slipping between us as the other wrapped around the nape of my neck, pulling me into the feral kiss he was already pressing to my mouth. My lips parted, hungry for more of him, and I bucked against his fingers rhythmically. He groaned.

"Get in the back," he said, yanking open the door.

"I want to be on top." I grinned, feeling devilish. His eyes blazed as he squeezed my nape a little tighter.

"I was hoping you weren't kidding about that."

He shrugged off his coat, tossed it onto my seat, and eased mine off before climbing into the back of the car. I slid in after him, shivering as I tugged the door closed against the frigid night air.

I didn't have long to be cold, though, because Theo's hands were on me again, gently tugging my blouse free, then unbuttoning it from the bottom up. He bent to kiss his way along my neck as he slid it from my shoulders, the combination of his mouth moving to the hollow of my throat and the fabric's silky caress sending goosebumps over me. I reached for his collar, but he pushed my hand away, leaning back just long enough to tug his shirt over his head and toss it over the front seat. Pressing his shoulders into the seat for leverage as he unbuckled his belt, he lifted his hips and slid his pants down to his ankles. The muscles of his abs stood out starkly, a distant streetlight carving each individual line. My fingers drifted to his stomach, trailing lightly down the front. He grinned sideways at me as he gripped me on either side of my waist, pulling me roughly onto his lap. I wriggled out of my pants with his help and bent to take his lower lip between my teeth, biting lightly. He tugged me down onto his hips, his hard length running along my folds through the thin fabric of our underwear, a promise of things to come.

"You're so fucking beautiful," he murmured, the words skittering over the skin of my jaw as his mouth moved along its line to my ear. My breath hitched as he took the lobe gently between his teeth, one hand slipping between my legs again. "Oh my god," he growled as he felt my wetness. *"God."*

Then he was sliding his fingers beneath the elastic of my underwear, thrusting them inside, but it wasn't enough, and I ground against his hand, trying to deepen the sensation, breath ragged.

"I need you *now*," he said, running my hands down to his waistband, my head still thrown back in ecstasy as his fingers moved inside me. I started tugging his underwear down. He pushed up again to help me, and suddenly he was freed, his entire length pressing against the inside of my thigh insistently, and I had to tug his hand out, wrapping my fingers around him and stroking once, twice, before slipping him inside.

"Oh god," I whispered, thrusting down onto him, stars shooting off behind my eyes as I rocked forward, feeling every inch deep in my center. *"Fuck."*

My body took over then, hips moving faster and faster against Theo, breath coming in gasps as he took one nipple into his mouth, then the other, electricity crackling over my skin, heating every inch of me. He moved his hand over me as I continued to ride him, rubbing insistently, his own need too great now for it to be anything but rough, but I *wanted* the roughness, I *needed* it, and I was bucking against his hand, and his hips were thrusting up to meet mine, each movement perfectly timed to stoke the flame burning hotter and hotter inside me, and then suddenly, with one final grind of my hips, my pleasure burst through the last barrier, spilling over my edges, sweeping through every inch of me. I shuddered against him, wave after wave pulsing through me, intensifying anew as I heard his murmured *"god"* and felt him thrust deeper, felt his own release merging with my own . . .

When it finally let go of me, I felt wrung out, body shaky with spent need, and I collapsed onto Theo, face nestling where his neck met his broad shoulders. His arms wrapped around me tightly, head twisting to press a gentle kiss to my thicket of sex-mussed hair. I purred against Theo's throat, a delicious sleepy feeling overtaking me in the wake of the explosions.

"Looks like Paul was right," he said with a low chuckle.

My shoulders tensed. Somehow everything that had preceded the last frantic several minutes had washed away on the tsunami of orgasm.

Back now, though.

"What do you mean?" I said carefully.

"Oh, I was just telling him about you on the way to dinner." Theo's hand moved up and down my back absently. Part of me wanted to press into it, but the rest of me was starting to settle back into my body. Starting to realize what we'd just done . . . again. "He said you sounded like a wildcat."

"Like a . . . What did you *tell* him?" I rolled off him onto the next seat, body going tight. His eyebrows knitted as I bent to find my bra and top, actions jerky with fury.

"Just the basics. How we 'met,' what you do . . ."

"So he decided I'm some feral sex fiend because . . . why, exactly? I have a down-market job?"

"What? No!" Theo's face twisted in disbelief. "I just said you kept me on my toes!"

"It makes sense." Shame was heating my skin even more effectively than Theo had just minutes before. "Why *else* would you go after someone like me, right?"

"Ellie, don't get this way."

"*What* way?"

"All . . . defensive." Theo rolled his eyes, slowly tugging his pants up. "Paul's always been a douche, it's just . . . *him,* okay?"

"Would he call Sam that?"

"What? What does Sam have to do with it?"

"Or any of your other exes? Are any of them *wildcats*? Or does it make sense to him that you'd be with them *without* weird assumptions about your sex life?"

"Ellie, where is this coming from?"

I thrust my arms into the blouse forcefully. Sex was exactly the wrong thing to do, I'd *known* that, and didn't it just prove Paul right? I couldn't even control myself long enough to make it home from dinner. Sam's face in the mirror, genuine concern for me on every feature, flashed in front of my eyes, and I had to bite back a groan. I was screwing this up every chance I got.

"Just . . . take me home," I spat, throwing the car door open and sliding into the front seat, awkwardly wriggling into my coat while I waited for Theo to dress. I folded my arms firmly across my chest, staring at the foggy interior of the windshield as he finally buckled in. He reached for my hand across the console, but I yanked it away.

"Hey," he said, anxiety creeping in. "I'm sorry I said anything, okay? Paul was out of line."

"It doesn't matter," I muttered through a clenched jaw. "He's not wrong. You'd need *some* reason to be with someone like me."

"I see plenty," he said, voice low, as he started the car. A stupid wave of tenderness pulsed through me and *Fuck, this was exactly what I was trying to avoid.* I dug my fingernails into the butts of my hands, trying to get ahold of myself. The goal wasn't Theo, it had *never* been Theo. The goal was saving the deli. I'd let myself lose sight of it, possibly spike my last, best chance at it, to *fuck him in the backseat of his car.*

"Is that why he prefers Mangia? Because he thinks I'm . . . cheap?" I ground out.

"No one called you cheap, Ellie."

"I may not speak rich person fluently, but I know you don't call someone classy a fucking *wildcat*."

We were stopped at a light, and he glanced over, worry furrowing his strong brow, softening those absolutely perfect lips.

"I'm sorry if I made you feel that way just now. I shouldn't have said anything."

Theo's voice was so sorrowful, so guilty-sounding, that my chest tightened painfully, and I had to slip my hand beneath my thigh to keep myself from lifting it to his cheek, reassuring him with a touch.

But Sam wasn't going to stand for my delaying things much longer—she'd already guessed things weren't as casual as I'd made out, and there was no way I'd be able to sell the "We're just *really* good actors" bit again. She'd *said* she didn't plan to run me out of business if I wasn't willing to push her and Theo onto the path to happily ever after . . . but that was before I'd promised I would. And getting a good feeling about someone doesn't mean you can guess how they'll react. It would only take one careful, just-worried-enough remark in Cheryl's ear to move everyone into Camp Mangia . . .

If I couldn't rely on myself to maintain the boundaries, I had to enforce them some other way, otherwise my *wildcat* instincts were going to tank this in spite of me.

"Listen," Theo said as he pulled through the light, "Paul's an ass, that's established, but I still think he'll see reason . . ."

I took a deep breath, steeling myself. I had to do this for real, *now,* otherwise I might never be able to muster the strength.

"It's not about Paul, Theo, it's about *you*." His shoulders tensed visibly. We were barely a minute from my apartment, but part of me wondered whether it was wise to have started this conversation in a moving vehicle.

"What did *I* do?" he said, voice low and even. His jaw gave away just how hard he was fighting to keep it that way.

This was it, the moment to tear off the Band-Aid, to put the two of us back where we belonged. My throat tightened traitor-ously and I forced myself to imagine the scornful expressions on the faces of the off-off-off-Broadway directors rejecting me, Paul's superior sneer, Ted's scorn when he more than implied I was a money-grubber—anything that could manufacture real anger.

"It's what you *haven't* done," I said, frowning out the windshield to try to retrofit the emotion. "We've been doing this for weeks now, you keep trotting me out at parties and family dinners—which are miserable, by the way, I know I wasn't raised by country club staff but I'm not some barely literate piece of trash."

"No one thinks that."

I could hear the pain in his voice, but I was finally hitting my stride.

"Except Paul. And half of Ted's Belle Glen friends. And I know it's what I signed up for, but the point was that this thing would *work*. That we would find a way to make sure I'm not driven out of business. I know the deli isn't important enough to register on Cheryl's memory, but it's my family legacy, Theo. It *matters* to me."

"I promise, I know that."

Theo slid to a stop at my curb, throwing the car into Park so quickly the brakes whined in protest. He turned to me, reaching into my lap to take both my hands in his.

"Ellie, I know how hard this is for you." He shook his head, frowning. "Actually, no, I have no idea how hard this is. Obviously I have skin in the game, but it's nothing compared to what's on the line for you. I get that. And I know tonight probably didn't feel like progress—"

"You think? You *promised* that the optics would be enough to keep your family from pushing this through. Instead, Paul and Ted are joking about how you're in this for the sex and tag-teaming about me finding some new fucking calling."

"I didn't promise, Ellie. And I can't promise now. But you have to believe me, we *are* making progress. Cheryl's coming around, I can tell, and Paul will do whatever she says in the end. It doesn't hurt that Sam's got the numbers to back this up; it's the smarter play on a lot of fronts. Does that mean I'm a hundred percent certain everything will go the way we want? Of course not. But I'd wager a hell of a lot of money on it." He squeezed my hands, tugging me slightly to face him. His brows were tented with worry, lip almost trembling as he looked me straight in the eye. My breath caught. *Don't touch him. Don't kiss him. You have to see this through.* The warning was there, but getting fainter . . .

Theo must have seen me wavering, because he leaned in until his forehead rested against my own, dropping one of my hands to cup the nape of my neck gently. His voice dropped to a whisper.

"I know it's hard feeling like this is still up in the air, but please trust me. You know you can by now, don't you?"

"Why?" I murmured, my will starting to dissolve in the wave of emotion swirling through me. "You said it yourself, you don't have as much skin in the game."

"Maybe not on the business front, but Ellie . . ." His thumb started caressing the spot where my neck met my hairline, the touch tingling through me, faint echoes of the pulsing desire from just minutes ago starting up again. "When this started, I know we both thought it was just going to be . . . transactional. But now . . . don't you think . . ."

He paused for breath, and I could do it now, I could lean forward just a fraction of an inch and press my lips to his, drag my nails across his back until he gasped against my mouth, until he was pulling me onto his lap again. I could practically still *feel* all his touches, the way they lit me from the inside . . .

And then . . . what? If I gave in to this feeling, what happened next?

Not just tomorrow morning, when I'd still owe Sam what I'd promised, and the deli's future would still be hanging by a thread, but in the minutes and seconds after, the tenderness that had already been creeping into Theo's gestures, gazes, words, flooding through me too, telling me to ignore reason and throw myself away on him. And when it all eventually crumbled—he remembered who he was, what kind of person he wanted by his side in life, not just waking up next to him in bed, and I woke up to how completely wrong we were for each other, both too strong-willed, both too tender beneath the thorny exteriors, banter turning to bickering and power struggles as the honeymoon-period hormones receded— what then? Would I have anything left? Or would I have thrown it all away for this need that felt real now, but that couldn't be, not really, or at least wouldn't be enough to sustain us?

I jerked away, real anger flooding me, not at Theo and his painful sweetness, but at myself for finding a way to complicate this, for the stupid longing squeezing my lungs and heart.

"What are you *talking* about, Theo?"

His mouth dropped open, pure shock slackening his face. Within moments his eyes narrowed, wary. I dug my nails into my palms again. No turning back now.

"I mean, we've had fun, sure, but it's just sex, for Christ's sake."

"Just . . . what?"

"I figured you were just doing what we said—selling this, remember? But I guess I'm the only one that's bothering with follow-through."

Theo's lips pinched tight, brow lowering dangerously.

"I'm sorry if I misread things."

I barked out a laugh. His whole body tensed.

"Me too. Because while you've been living in some ridiculous fantasy, my business has been on the line."

"Living in some— What do you think that meeting was? I'm sorry if you didn't realize this when you agreed to the deal, Ellie, but businesses with a bit more clout than yours don't just turn on a dime. You have to lay *groundwork*."

"And we've done that. And yet from where I'm standing, nothing has actually changed. Has anyone reached out to Mangia to even, like . . . start a conversation about this not happening?"

"That's not what's *done,* we—"

"Just answer the question, Theo."

"No, of course not. Because that would be not only premature but *irresponsible.* This isn't something you can just plow your way through, Ellie."

"And it's not something where *you* can just keep taking a back seat in your own fucking life, *Theo.* That might be fine for you, but it's not gonna work for me."

His eyes went so wide the whites showed all the way around.

"Excuse me?" His voice was so low it was almost a growl. But my blood was high now, the lingering sex flurries mixing with my anxiety over the business, a heavy pour of five-years-of-feeling-stuck topping it all off. I bared my teeth.

"Have you told Ted this deal can't happen?"

"What?" He scoffed. "We've discussed this, the plan—"

"No, enough bullshit, I'm not one of your clients. Have you shown even the most *basic* amount of spine with him?"

Theo's nostrils flared, hands tightening into fists on the console.

"You're calling me a coward."

"If the shoe fits."

He sniffed out a laugh, the disdain on every feature eerily reminiscent of Ted.

"You want to talk about cowards, Ellie? Look in the fucking mirror."

Now it was my turn to reel. My spine stiffened, body trying to defend against the blows I knew were still coming.

"I'm the one actually working to pull this off."

"And why? Why even bother?"

"You *know* why, it's my family's legacy, the deli is—"

"No, fuck your family, Ellie, why are *you* doing this? Why even leave New York in the first place?"

"You know I had no choice."

"Maybe at the beginning. But I've seen your books, you could have hired more staff years ago and you'd still clear a profit. At the very least you'd keep the lights on. You could be following your *real* dream. So why aren't you?"

I guppied for an answer, but it wouldn't come.

"Either you're too afraid to go after the thing you really want—which is sad, you know?" His pitying sneer lanced through me. "Or maybe—and this is what *I* think is going on, for the record—you're too chickenshit to admit that *this* is what you want."

"I'm fighting for this, remember? In what world is that pretending it doesn't matter?"

"You're still whining that you were forced into it. Still living in a shitty apartment—I mean damn, I've seen college *dorms* with better furnishings—just so you can keep pretending to yourself that all this, your entire fucking *life,* is just some temporary way station."

I *knew* he was judging my apartment.

"You're fucking insane," I murmured, throat feeling like it might swell shut, like I couldn't even breathe, because how had he seen that so clearly? How had I only just seen it myself when he'd spotted it from the start?

"And you're fucking lying to yourself. I think you were *thrilled* you got to give up the whole 'trying to make it in the big city' act. You're just too embarrassed to say so because then you might have to admit you were actually *wrong* about something. Besides, it's not like you really failed if the party line is that you were robbed of your chance to try, right?"

The edges of my vision were blurring, heart beating so hard it was all I could hear, my pulse palpable in my neck, my temple, the taut suspension of my breath. Rage burned through me, sucking up the oxygen, ravaging the barriers between my darkest thoughts and my words, because how *dare* he reduce me to that? Even if he wasn't entirely wrong—no, *because* he wasn't entirely wrong.

"Thanks for the armchair psychology, *Ted.* Really means a lot coming from the man whose head is stuck so far up his father's ass he can't even see what he wants for himself." My lip curled with disgust. "I can't even imagine how disappointed Chase would be if he could see you now."

The air in the car seemed to go solid around us, and for just a moment, it felt as if we might linger there forever, amber-trapped by the viscous viciousness of my words. Then Theo turned away, Adam's apple working wildly as the rest of his body practically shuddered with tension.

"Get out."

"Theo, listen, I didn't mean—"

"No, you meant it. You might even be right. I have to imagine your father would feel the same way."

And when he turned to me, the look in his eyes was one of such intense loathing that it made my skin sting.

Already a shoreline of mucky shame was appearing, inch by inch, as the flood of rage receded. I'd had to pull the Band-Aid off, sure, but I hadn't had to reach into the wound beneath and tear it open with filthy, wickedly sharp claws.

"Theo . . ."

"Please just go."

This time, he didn't wait for me to make it inside before driving away.

Upstairs, I threw my coat over the sewing chair, stepped out of my shoes, and beelined for the cabinet with the whiskey, pouring a generous glass and taking a swig, relishing the sinus burn. As the alcohol hit the muscles of my shoulders, pressing painfully on the tension there, I made my way into the living room, settling onto the sofa with a loud protest of the ancient springs.

I looked around, forcing myself to really take it in. The coffee table was scuffed, and ugly to begin with, a hulking mass of dark wood–look MDF, the cheapness of the materials even more obvious in the overwrought scrollwork at the edges. My "dining table" was Formica and bent metal, which I'd told myself was retro-chic when I found it on Craigslist, but where the surface wasn't stained, it had yellowed with age and neglect, and rust crept gangrenously up the legs. The kitchen wasn't just dated—half the cabinets didn't close right, and the linoleum was peeling at the corners. And the ratty, ancient inherited sofa wasn't even comfortable, just one more reason not to spend any more time here than I had to. Looking around at the mostly bare walls and random assortment of junk I'd accumulated to fill out the minimum requirements of an adult life, the only thing that really felt like *me* was the sewing table. And until very recently, it had been my makeshift coatrack. That is until Sam helped me see what should have been incredibly obvious ages ago: that the creative part of me didn't have to be stuffed down in one of the several boxes I still hadn't unpacked since I moved back from New York, it could be part of my life here, could make that life better, more successful, more my own. I mean fuck, napkins were *such a no-brainer.*

The whiskey was just making me more jittery. Leaving it on the coffee table, I hauled myself out of the maw of the couch and did the only thing I could think of that might help.

Bella picked up on the first ring.

"Everything okay?"

"It's . . . I mean, I think . . ."

And then I burst into tears. As if I needed any *more* humiliation tonight.

After some general soothing, Bella started pulling the story out of me, slowly at first—to explain why I'd gone nuclear, I had to own up to what was going on with Sam, which took a while. Bella didn't actually *say* she was judging, but I knew her too well to tell myself otherwise. Soon it all started gushing out—how things had shifted between Theo and me even before that first kiss on my doorstep, the night we spent together on his couch, how badly wrong the tennis game had gone, the fiasco at the restaurant . . . and after.

"Oh, El," Bella said, voice low and pained.

"I know," I whispered. "I don't know why I said it. I know I'm not like . . . Becky Sunshine, but it was just cruel, Bell."

"I mean . . . yeah, it was. But you obviously lashed out that way because you care."

"That doesn't even make sense."

She sighed heavily, and I swear I could *hear* her pinching the bridge of her nose.

"Ellie, think about it. You wouldn't have to push him away so damn hard otherwise. If what happened—twice—was really 'just sex,' you wouldn't be so afraid of it."

"Who says I'm afraid?"

"If we're gonna hash this out this late at night, you're not allowed to play dumb."

My shoulders slumped into a full-body wince. Dammit, was she right? Which meant . . . was *Theo* right? Was I the coward?

"Honestly, this is what I was worried about all along."

"That I'd fly off the handle and ruin everything at the most crucial juncture?"

"That you'd get hurt." My nostrils started stinging again, throat thickening alongside them, and I rubbed my nose vigorously to try to will the tears away as Bella went on. "I told you from the start, Theo's a good guy. Yes, I know there are a lot of surface differences between you two, but honestly . . . he's the kind of person I think would be really good for you."

"Seriously? You're shipping me with the yacht club crew?"

"We both know that's not who Theo is. Anyway, it's good to go outside your comfort zone. Especially for you."

"What's that supposed to mean?"

"It means you've basically run through all the age-appropriate losers in town and I was hoping that maybe, someday, you'd realize that well had run dry. Just because you like dive bars and wear the same clothes you did in high school most days, that doesn't mean that's all you are, Ellie."

"Man . . . why is everyone only telling me the stuff I should have realized sooner *now*?"

"Would you have listened sooner?"

"Okay, fair."

I sighed, squeezing my temples with one hand as I paced the small, dingy room. God, how had I lived in this apartment for so long?

"But Bella . . . what do I *do*?"

"What do you mean?"

"I mean putting all the . . . *right for me* stuff aside, what if Theo decides to tank this because of what I said?"

"He wouldn't."

"You didn't see his face."

"Well . . . there's not a lot you can do about that now. When will the board make a final decision?"

"They didn't say. Not immediately, I don't think. Everything's been moving pretty slowly."

"Good. Hopefully you'll both cool down in the next day or two and you'll at least be able to apologize. If he *does* decide to tank things out of spite . . . he's not the person I thought he was, but it's probably not anything you can stop. Theo's really sensitive, I don't think you can force him to get over this faster than he's ready to."

"So I did completely fuck everything up."

"Hey, *no*. I mean . . . you didn't act awesomely, okay? But everyone makes mistakes. Honestly, the fact that you let yourself be open enough to *need* to destroy him so thoroughly seems like a really good sign."

"That's an extremely fucked-up silver lining."

"I stand by it." Bella paused a moment, gathering her thoughts. "What's the actual worst case here?"

"Oh god, you think it's that bad?" My eyes pinched so tight the room blurred.

"No, I think once you know the worst-case scenario, anything *less* bad isn't so hard to handle. So . . . worst case, Theo and Sam get together."

"Actually, worst case is she winds up hating me too. She's the first cool person I've met since I moved here."

"Okay, next time you undertake an absolutely ludicrous scheme, you *really* need to keep me more updated on the progress. You two are friends?"

"Maybe. At least I thought we might become friends." I sighed. "Anyway, let's continue the exercise."

"So worst case, things fall apart with you and Theo *and* Sam, and he's still angry. And I guess she's also angry. Enough that the two of them decide to bring in Mangia, then ride off into the sunset together."

I could see them so clearly in my mind's eye, standing next to each other on the country club dais, laughing, exactly the people who were supposed to wind up together. It was hard to believe Bella's words were anything less than prophetic. Still, a tiny part of me felt relieved. Sam was a badass; even if she hated me, she deserved to wind up with someone who made her happy. And . . . so did Theo.

"What happens next?" Bella pressed.

My chest tightened.

"The deli closes," I whispered. "Maybe not right away, but eventually."

"Okay. And if that happens . . . would it really be so bad?"

"Are you serious?"

"No bullshitting, Ellie, it's late and I'm grumpy." Only Bella could make a therapeutic phone-hug out as grumpy. "The deli closes. You have to find something new. I know that would be incredibly hard, and I'm not trying to downplay that at *all*, but in a way . . . wouldn't that be for the best? You've had to put so much on hold for so long."

I longed to say yes, to lean into the comfort I knew I could find in the "Finally I can do what matters to *me*" narrative. But that's all it was: a story I'd been telling myself.

Yes, I'd resented it at *first*. Leaving New York had been so abrupt, and so tied up with grief over Dad, and the fact that everyone expected it made me bristle—which seemed juvenile in retrospect, but that "If you *tell* me to do it, I won't" reaction was hardwired, one of my many genetic inheritances from Mimi.

But Theo had said it just an hour ago, and if I was honest with myself, I'd been starting to realize it before that: having my family around me; having something I could call my own (and *make* my own, if I just bothered to see the possibilities); hell, even just feeling like my design didn't have to prove anything, like it could be something I loved but which didn't have to define all of me . . . that *was* what I wanted.

It wasn't just the rejection that had primed me to leave New York before I got that call from the hospital, it was the sense that I wasn't wholly myself there. The last few months, I hadn't even been designing things I liked, I'd just been trying to guess what someone else might want, what would crack the code. It wasn't *fun* anymore, it was me being too stubborn to admit that if this was what it looked like to build a career in costuming, it wasn't what I actually wanted. And the loneliness of the city, feeling invisible to almost everyone around me . . . some people thrived on that anonymity, but honestly, it felt like every day I faded a little, until one day I'd wake up and realize there wasn't any *me* left at all, just another trim young woman walking too fast down a city block, filling the empty spaces inside with busyness and expensive tastes and ambition for its own sake, the kind that, by definition, could never be truly satisfied.

I'd told myself I'd been forced to give up what I really wanted, whined about it to my family, not because it was *true,* but because allowing myself to want the life I'd grown up in felt like failure. But how was keeping the one thing alive that connected me to my father every single day a failure? Why did I think that what I'd done to make the deli more modern, more successful, more *me* was somehow meaningless? And how would cutting myself off from the place and the people that made me who I was, and meant more to me than anything else on earth, qualify as success? When I'd been in New York, I'd spoken to Ma and Bella almost every day.

After I left, I texted half-heartedly with two or three friends for a month, and when the threads fizzled out, all I felt was relief at not having to pretend to care about their dates and promotions, which restaurants they'd snagged seats at and what famous people they'd spotted. Even when I was there, all of that had seemed so hollow.

"Honestly, Bell? I think I've been lying to myself."

"We've established that."

"Not about Theo—about the deli. I don't need to save it for Ma or Mimi, I need to save it for *me*. I think . . . maybe I care more about this than I ever did about costuming."

"Ohhh . . . oh man, of *course*." I could imagine Bella's eyes going huge with comprehension.

"Right?"

"Well, in that case, I guess you're lucky there's something else you care about."

"Translation: I'm fucked."

"Not necessarily . . . but it's the actual worst case."

"So now all I have to do is convince the sensitive man I just annihilated to keep my family business open out of the goodness of his heart."

"Or you can focus on convincing his ex that you're fully on her team. Even if you and Sam don't become besties, it sounds like she wouldn't renege on a deal."

"I suppose there's that."

"Ellie, I need to sleep, but . . . are you going to be okay? Not with the deli stuff, with, you know . . . everything else?" Bella paused. "I know this isn't what you expected, and I know it hurts right now, but I promise, opening yourself up is a *good* thing, even if this is where it ends for you and Theo."

"We can debate that later. For now, I need to figure out the best way to eat crow."

"Okay. Keep me posted."

I was still too antsy to imagine sleeping, so I sat at the sewing table, laying out a fresh sheet of pattern paper with the intention of drafting a basic apron design. But before I even put pencil to paper, I paused, superstition pulsing through me—it felt like tempting fate to launch yet another project for the deli right now. Instead, I started tracing an exaggerated bell sleeve, then the gentle swoop of the wide neckline I'd need for the floral dress I'd been playing around with, pausing every few seconds to check a measurement, visualize how two sections might join, imagine the way this shape versus that would look for the shoulders. By the time I had a version I was satisfied with, the anxiety pulsing through me had faded slightly, and the clock told me it was past midnight.

I pulled out a roll of muslin, leaving it on the corner of the work table in an attempt to goad myself to keep going with the dress.

Before I slid in between the sheets, I pulled out my phone and tapped a couple of quick texts.

TO: Little Lord Doucheleroy

> I just wanted to say again that I'm really, really sorry

> I shouldn't have said that and I didn't mean it

But even though I stared at the screen long past the point when it had gone dark, there was no response.

Twenty-Two

I woke up over an hour before the alarm I'd set, and I'd showered, downed half a pot of coffee, and even finished cutting muslin for the sleeves by the time seven-thirty rolled around. If I didn't hear from Theo by eight—the time he'd expected to get back to work, even if Paul's cognac obsession meant it was unlikely the board would be present—I'd call.

I'd spent half the night lying awake, staring at the pebbled ceiling, thinking about what to say. Sorry, obviously and abjectly. Not that it would fix what I'd said. Calling him Ted I could chalk up to anger; telling him the brother whose death had rerouted his entire life would be ashamed of him? That was potentially unforgivable.

Which was why I had to tell him everything. The deal I'd made with Sam, the feelings I was only now acknowledging had been developing, how scared those feelings made me . . . and how right he was about me. About how deeply, and how long, I'd been lying to myself about who I was and what I wanted. It might not fix anything. For all I knew, it would just make him angrier. But he deserved the truth, at least.

I made it to 7:47. Theo's phone rang . . . and rang . . . and rang . . . and went to voicemail.

The second time I called we skipped the rings entirely.

I should listen to Bella. Wait until cooler heads prevailed, come in with a plan instead of a visceral need to relieve the guilt pressure swelling through me.

Instead, I waited about five minutes, then phoned his office.

"Ellie? Hey! How goes it, chica?" I'd only met Theo's assistant briefly at the engagement party, but she had that bubbly, we're-all-girlfriends brand of immediate intimacy I associated with cheer captains and game show hosts.

"Hey, Kayleigh. Things are good," I lied.

"I meant to ask, have you been dress shopping yet? Because my friend just got *the* most gorgeous gown at this adorable shop in Burnton. It like . . . makes me want to get back with my ex, that's how stunning it is. I should totally take you there."

"Uh . . . yeah, that sounds . . . so fun! And I really wish we could chat, but I actually need to get ahold of Theo. He let his cell die *again*."

"Oh my god, *so* annoying."

"Right? So . . . could you put him on?"

"Wish I could. He's at the old Taylor's building."

"What? With who?"

"Sam and the board. For some big meeting? Did he . . . not tell you?" A hint of incredulity crept into her voice.

"Right . . . he left so early, I guess I was still half-asleep." I bit my lip—the meeting wouldn't have started hours ago. "For the gym, I mean. You know how he is."

"I *wish* I could be that committed, but like . . . naw, girl." Kayleigh laughed far harder than her joke warranted. "Anyway, did you want to leave a message?"

"That's okay, I'll catch him later. Thanks, Kayleigh."

"Anytime, girl. Let me know about the dresses!"

I hung up, dashed over to the front of the store to hang the "back in fifteen minutes" sign—hopefully no one planned to show up the minute we opened to call me on it—and hurried to my car. Theo wouldn't be able to totally ignore me with the board there. An ambush was my best chance . . . and possibly my last one.

I walked into the grand first floor of the building, steeling myself against an immediate encounter with the Taylor clan, but the space was empty. The last of the Bray's paraphernalia had been cleared away, leaving nothing but a few stacks of building materials dotting the corners of the immense room. Dust motes danced through shafts of sunlight, softened by the soaped windows, giving the space a fairy-tale aspect, some grand ballroom that's been trapped in time by an evil witch's curse.

"I'm sorry, I was out of line, but I can explain," I murmured to myself, the mantra I'd been reciting the entire ride over, apparently hoping repetition would somehow manifest into Theo's giving me the time of day.

I didn't have long to work my magic; moments later, the elevator dinged, and Cheryl walked out.

". . . half a dozen concepts on this floor alone?" she said over her shoulder.

"That's right." My heart skipped a beat as Theo emerged behind his aunt, looking painfully handsome in a heathered gray suit. "It's one of Mangia's best ideas: creating individual retail spaces within a larger open market. A central register unifies the concepts without unnecessarily—"

He stopped short as he spotted me, so suddenly that the middle-aged man exiting the elevator behind him bumped into him. Sam only just managed not to create a pile-up. The man was unfamiliar, his close-fitted three-piece suit elegant and perfectly tailored to his tall, slim frame, heavy square glasses automatically conferring intellect upon his friendly, open features.

A Mangia executive, clearly. My stomach churned—I'd known Theo changing course because of our blowout was a possibility, but I'd hoped I'd have a *little* more time to plead my case.

"Whoa. Sorry, Theo." He frowned slightly before he spotted me.

"That's alright," Theo said absently, eyes narrowing as he held my gaze. "Chris, give me a minute." He'd recovered enough to flash his million-watt smile at the man. "It appears my fiancée needs me rather urgently. Sam, can you and Chris take point while I clear this up?"

"Of course. Chris, I always find a walk-through helpful—I'm not as spatial as Theo. We could start in the northwest corner? That's where the café would go, yes?"

"That's right. A classic European-style bistro would be ideal for . . ." The man's voice faded as they crossed the floor. Theo strode over to me, jaw tight. I took a shuddering breath and opened my mouth to deliver my mantra, but Theo got there first.

"What are you doing here?"

"You didn't respond to my texts. Or my calls . . ."

"Did you consider that that might be because I didn't want to speak to you?" His voice was a controlled whisper, but his eyes flashed fire. I swallowed hard.

"Right. Fair. I just . . . wanted to apologize." The simmering anger on his face drove my carefully planned opening out of my brain. "There's . . . um . . . there's more to this. I thought maybe—"

"This is *not* the time, Ellie." He glanced back at the group making their slow circuit of the floor. "This meeting is extremely important."

"I get that." My eyes darted to the polished executive, gesturing expansively as Cheryl hung on his every word. *Maybe this meeting wasn't Theo's doing.* I clung desperately to the thought. He'd called me his fiancée, after all. He wouldn't have done that if he'd already decided to explode things . . . right? And Cheryl clearly liked digging into the details . . . "Did Cheryl ask for it, or . . . ?"

"Sam did. I was surprised she pulled it together on such short notice, but . . . that's Sam." An affectionate look softened Theo's features as he looked at her.

I blinked, not quite processing.

"Sam? But why would she—"

"If it isn't Ellie Greco." Paul's voice boomed out from the elevator, his smile distinctly sneery as he and Ted emerged. "Theo didn't tell us you'd be here. Frankly, I'm not sure it's appropriate." He pulled a face at his brother. Ted was staring at us with narrowed eyes, no doubt weighing up my cringing posture, Theo's tightly controlled anger.

"Theo, Paul had a few questions about the build-out that I'd like you to walk him through. If you don't mind?" Ted raised an eyebrow expectantly and Theo nodded.

"Of course. Ellie was just going."

"Theo," I whispered, voice pleading. "Please let me—"

"I told you, Ellie, this isn't the time."

And without a backward glance, he followed his father and uncle to where Cheryl chatted with the Mangia executive while Sam tapped rapidly at her phone. The three men's long, confident strides were so similar it had to be a genetic inheritance.

I'd been dismissed; lingering would only heighten Ted's suspicion. And Theo clearly had no interest in hearing me out. Mustering what was left of my dignity, I headed outside, simultaneously sparking with anxiety and leaden-limbed.

I was standing in the cold next to my car, sucking my lips between my teeth, trying to formulate an alternate plan, when Sam emerged, phone to her ear, to pace the sidewalk near the entrance while she finished her call. On impulse, I scurried over, hovering a few feet away until she finished.

"Sam," I said the moment she lowered the phone. She startled. "Hey, sorry to scare you. Do you have a second to—"

"No, I don't." Her lips pursed around the tart utterance. "If you'll excuse me."

"Sam, wait! Please, I have to know—" I laid a hand on her arm to get her attention. She physically shook me off, glaring.

"Stop, Ellie. Just . . . stop." She shook her head once, tendons in her neck springing out. "I don't have time for this."

"Sam . . . what's going on?" My heart was beating hummingbird fast, comprehension dawning before she even spoke.

"I *saw* you, Ellie. In the parking lot." I reeled, the words landing like a physical blow, nearly knocking the wind out of me. "And before you say it, no, I do *not* believe that what happened in Theo's car was just you two playing your parts really, *really* convincingly."

"Sam . . . I didn't . . ."

"Save it. You lied to me, even after I gave you *multiple* opportunities to come clean." Her nostrils flared. "I have nothing to say to you right now. And neither does Theo."

"Wait . . . Sam, what did he say to you?"

"It's what I said to *him*. I told him, Ellie. Everything. After what I saw . . . I guess I was sick of all the lying." Her lips twisted with disgust. My heart started ricocheting around my chest as the import of her words sank in. "Luckily, he was willing to hear me out."

"Is that why you called the meeting?" My voice was barely a whisper.

"I called the meeting because it was the smart play. Theo agreed, obviously."

"But I thought . . . you said . . ."

"Just . . . stop, Ellie. I don't have the energy for this. Suffice to say neither of us wants to see you right now."

Even through the hammer blows of her revelation, that one little word—"us"—landed with painful finality.

"Sam, you have to understand—"

"I don't *have* to do anything. Not for someone who lied to my face over and over. Now. If you'll excuse me."

With that, she strode back inside, fury straightening her spine.

When Bella had talked me through the worst case, she really hadn't laid out the details clearly enough.

I dragged my way through the day at the deli, checking my phone compulsively, knowing the texts giving me an opening—or better yet, forgiveness—were never going to come in, but unable to stop myself from looking for them over, and over, and over.

By the time I got home, I felt like a wrung-out rag physically, but the overflow of anxiety made the idea of sleep frankly ludicrous. Even garbage reality TV wasn't enough to turn off the minor-key chorus at the back of my mind, *You fucked it up, you fucked it all up, you were cruel and stupid and you fucked it all up.*

Desperate, I turned to the dress pattern on the sewing table, letting the familiar rhythms soothe me: ironing, measuring, cutting, changing the seaming here, reshaping an opening there, tacking on scraps of fabric that would stand in for the flowers in the areas I was envisioning them to get a sense of how it would look completed. The focus it required was just enough to blunt the edge of shame and pain I was feeling.

It took me four nights to finish the dress in real fabrics—I'd let myself get rusty over the last few years, but my muscle memory hadn't entirely disappeared. I still hadn't heard anything from Theo or Sam, so I went with my old standby and texted a picture to Bella.

FROM: Bella

> Wow, that's GORGEOUS Ellie

> You should wear it on your date

> With who?

> I didn't hallucinate the part where I told you what happened with Theo, did I?

> With whoever I find for you on Bumble

> And don't argue, after all the Theo stuff, you know I'm right, you need to get out there

I sucked my lips between my teeth, searching for an excuse she would accept . . . but there weren't any. If I'd been even a *tiny* bit more self-aware, none of this—or at least the worst of it, where I eviscerated the first guy I had real feelings for in pretty much ever, which led directly to the end of the deli—wouldn't have happened. Even making the deal with Sam (peak denial, in hindsight) I could have probably come back from if I'd just been honest about what I was feeling. Sam had given me multiple chances to back out, and Theo and I probably could have sorted out the Mangia stuff without her; even if she hadn't thrown her weight behind us, I was pretty sure she wouldn't have tried to salt things.

The idea of a bunch of awkward drinks dates with strangers made my skin crawl a little, but Bella was right: I needed to actually put myself out there. And more important, Theo was right. My life here wasn't temporary, I didn't even *want* it to be. It was beyond time to be honest with myself about that.

Plus, I was going to need something to distract me when my entire professional life disappeared.

> Fine, sign me up

> . . . BUT I get veto power over anyone I don't like

> I'll agree to 5 no-explanations-necessary vetoes

10

> I accept your counteroffer

> I'll come out Saturday and we can set up your account

I put down the phone, feeling the tiniest bit better . . . but only the tiniest bit. I was coming to the painful conclusion that there was probably no world in which Theo and I could repair things. Still, I had to let him know why I said it, and how sorry I was.

Which would mean telling him the truth. The *whole* truth. Not just the bit about trying to help Sam that I'd been planning to divulge that morning at the Taylor's building, the part where I was falling for him, and it scared me shitless, and so I had done the only thing I could think of: I attacked.

It wouldn't fix things between us, but at least I'd have shown him something honest for once. And eventually, he'd just be an important lesson I learned, someone I could look back on wistfully, but gratefully.

Keep telling yourself that, Greco.

Twenty-Three

I bellied up to the bar at Major MacLeod's, drumming my fingers anxiously on its worn surface. Mimi had banished me from my own apartment the fifth time I'd taken the top off the simmering sauce to check how it was coming along, *Get out of here before you ruin the flavor with all your worrying,* so I'd opted to kill my nerves—or at least fifteen minutes—with a quick drink. My phone pinged as I waited for Kerry to pour the drink. But instead of the "All hope for this lasagna is lost" message I'd expected from Mimi, it was Bella.

FROM: Bella

> Okay, I think I have a real contender

> Make sure to swipe past the first picture before you try to nix him

I gritted my teeth, annoyed to be preempted so quickly. Sometimes it felt like Bella knew me *too* well.

But that wasn't always a bad thing. The man in the profile she'd sent leaned a little nerdy, his heavy glasses, carefully tended dark hair, and soft features like an emo song come to life. He was cute enough, but not particularly heart-stopping . . . but the third photo was a near-perfect recreation of the cover of *Marquee Moon,* with him and a series of wigs standing in as all four members of Television, presumably one of those early pandemic distractions we'd all gone in for. I sighed—I didn't really feel ready to "put myself out there" yet, but I'd promised Bella I'd at least *try* to try. And this guy had . . . potential. Maybe.

TO: Bella

> Fine. But if the first date doesn't go well, that's it

> No "you have to give him more of a chance" bs

I accept your terms.

But only because this is the first first date

If he's not your future husband I reserve the right to renegotiate

I sighed, taking a long pull of my drink. Why did personal growth have to be so damned unpleasant?

"Straight whiskey? Dare I ask?"

I startled at the amused voice at my elbow.

"Jenna, hey." I smiled, lifting my glass in her direction. "Don't judge, I only just escaped my grandmother. Which if you haven't met her . . . trust me, I earned this."

"I was just going to assume you had excellent taste." She grinned and poked the lime in her drink with her straw. "Does that mean you're free tonight? I'm here with a few work friends, you should join." She tilted her head to a corner booth that held a clutch of artsy-looking twenty- and thirty-somethings, none of them familiar. "You'd be doing me a huge favor, if I have to dissect the faculty meeting for another minute I might actually shrivel up and die."

"Sorry, this is literally a five-minute stop." Yes, Mimi had told me to be gone at least twenty minutes, but we both knew that was unreasonable.

"Oh, okay." She blinked, smiling wanly. "No worries. Have a good night."

Jesus Christ, Ellie, do you want *to have no friends forever?*

She was already halfway back to the table when I yelled out.

"Jenna, wait." She turned back, cocking an eyebrow. "Could we, uh . . . raincheck? I'd really love to hang out pretty much any other night. I'm not in very high demand these days."

My chest went fluttery with anxiety—I'd clearly forgotten how to make new friends, but it felt painfully close to asking out your high school crush. Fortunately, Jenna grinned at me almost immediately.

"Don't worry, I'm painfully available as well. Maybe Wednesday? This brutally pretentious kid in my seminar is up for critique that day. I'm guessing I'll need a drink."

We quickly exchanged details and went our separate ways. I was pretty sure the glowy warmth spreading through my chest as I unlocked my apartment door had nothing to do with the whiskey I'd downed—sure, we weren't besties yet, but Jenna was the first maybe-new-friend I'd made in longer than I could remember. It felt so good, it made me wonder why I hadn't made the effort sooner. Though "Why didn't I do X sooner" was kind of my whole *thing* these days.

"How's the sauce looking, Mimi?" I called out from the entryway.

"Fine, once you left it alone. No thanks to that stove. I have half a mind to call your landlord." Mimi's nose wrinkled with disgust.

"Don't worry, I won't be stuck with it for long. And I know you and Grandpa have plans. Go. I've got it from here."

"If you say so. But you text me if you have any questions, I didn't go to all this trouble for nothing, Missy."

We hugged and she made her way out, leaving me just enough time to pull out the other ingredients and click on a "new listing in your area" email. The condo was small—barely nine hundred square feet—but all the finishes were new, and the building was charming from the outside. Besides, I wasn't looking for anything fancy, just a one- or two-bedroom place not too far from my current spot. Something that would help me build equity (god, Theo really *had* rubbed off on me). More important, something that was *mine*, where I could build a life I actually wanted, not just the one I'd fallen into five years ago.

I emailed the listing to the realtor Ma had connected me with and turned back to the task at hand. It was quite possibly the last time I'd ever interact with Theo; I needed to make sure I got it right.

The lobby of Theo's building was empty, a small grace, and I still had my elevator fob. It was only when the doors opened directly into Theo's apartment that I realized this wasn't so much showing up on someone's doorstep as *in* their home.

"Umm . . . hello?" I called out, taking a tentative step. "Theo, are you home?"

Theo appeared at the end of the hallway. His dark blond hair was falling loose across his forehead, and his tight white T-shirt and slim-cut jeans seemed custom-made to accentuate his lean, muscular physique. My heart started thudding heavily, blood heating at the sight of him. Admitting to myself that I had caught feelings seemed to have supercharged the low-level thrum of desire I'd been feeling in his presence for weeks now.

"What are you doing here?"

The wary blankness in his face and voice was like an ice bucket challenge to the genitals.

"I, uh . . . I wanted to give you this." I thrust the lasagna in front of me, the gift bag perched on the lid wobbling perilously. He frowned as he took it, clearly confused. "It's a lasagna. *Mimi's* lasagna. So basically the best in show. Or . . . best in breed? Oh, and these are some napkins I made." I pulled them out of the bag. In a gigantic dose of sappiness I'd used the leftover green fabric I'd bought for the new dress . . . but he didn't need to know that part. "Throw them away if they're not your style. Or regift them, or whatever." I grimaced. Already this was going *awesome*.

"Thank you?" Theo blinked at the tray. "I'm sorry, you really came over to give me pasta?"

"Not pasta—Mimi's lasagna." If anything he just looked more confused. "I guess it's . . . symbolic."

"Of what?"

"Of me. And us." I raked my hand through my hair, forcing myself to focus. "Basically, I wanted to say I'm sorry again—because I'm really, *really* sorry. What I said . . . 'out of line' doesn't even begin to cover it. Not to mention it wasn't true. I was just lashing out. Because . . ." Here goes everything. My throat tightened painfully, even the idea of voicing this triggering a wave of anxiety. "Honestly, I was scared."

"Scared of what, exactly?"

"Of you." Theo's brows drew down. "Not in a bad way, just . . . I don't really *do* relationships. Ask anyone. So when things between us . . . *changed* . . ." I swallowed hard. The flutters in my stomach were getting so intense I was surprised they weren't shaking me from the inside out. "When I realized I had developed real feelings for you . . . basically, I freaked out. And that doesn't excuse what I said, but I want you to know *why* I was so horrible. It wasn't anything you did, it was just me being . . . broken, I guess. Some stupid animal-brain remnant was protecting me by pushing you away."

"So lasagna is what . . . the traditional Greco mea culpa?"

"Theo, this is *Mimi's lasagna.*"

"You keep saying that like it's supposed to mean something to me."

"This recipe means more to my family than pretty much anything—Mimi won't even write it down. 'If you don't learn this from me, you don't deserve to have it, Eleanor,'" I said, pulling my best Mimi frown. "My family is the truest part of me. They're the reason I'm here running the deli—not why I stayed, but why I came. They're my whole heart. And this lasagna . . . it's them. It's *me.*"

"And the napkins?" His face was totally still, revealing nothing.

"They're me too, but a different part. Like . . . family dinners, the lasagna, that's my past. It's the stuff that made me who I am. And in a way . . . these are my future?" I scrunched my nose, trying to find better words for it. "I know the deli is doomed, now that Mangia's coming in, and I know you probably can't forgive me, and I don't expect you to." Theo's frown deepened imperceptibly, but he didn't say anything. "But I wanted you to know that being with you helped me see things differently. It helped me really see *myself.* And I realized that these two sides of me don't really need to be at war, they're actually on the same continuum."

Jesus, this was going so far off the rails.

"The point is, even though what we had wasn't . . . well, it *was* real, at least to me, but it wasn't normal. But the point is, it changed me. For the better. I know I'll have to start over soon, but . . . that doesn't scare me like it would have a couple months ago. So . . . thank you."

"Ellie . . ." Theo ran his tongue over his lip, staring hard at the tray of lasagna, the spray of green napkins like new growth on its surface. Something playing in his eyes almost felt familiar . . .

Then we both startled at the sound of footsteps approaching.

"Theo, is everything al— Oh." Sam stopped a few feet behind Theo, blinking first at me, then at him. "Ellie," she finally said.

She was wearing high-waisted jeans, an oversized men's oxford tucked into the waistband. *It had to be one of Theo's.* And her feet were bare. Which meant . . .

"Hey, Sam," I said weakly, trying not to let the freefalling weight of my stomach physically pull me down. I hadn't realized until that moment that I'd still been holding out hope. But I'd been right all along—they *were* perfect for each other. I could hardly blame her for doing exactly what she'd told me she wanted to: getting him back. "I was just leaving. The, uh . . . the heating instructions are on the Post-it," I finished, desperate to get away. "If you don't like it . . . never say it aloud, I think Mimi would sense it and come to fight."

"Noted," Theo said, the first hint of a grin softening his mouth. It shot through me, electric, and suddenly the wanting in the pit of my stomach was so fierce I thought it might claw its way out.

"I'll, uh . . . see you later," I managed, stabbing the elevator button, desperate to retreat. Fortunately, it was still waiting on Theo's floor.

The last sight I had was of Sam reaching for the napkins while Theo stared over her shoulder at me, the elevator doors closing silently, but definitively, between us.

Twenty-Four

The text came in a week later, while I was elbows-deep in a vat of pasta salad.

FROM: Little Lord Doucheleroy

> There's a town council meeting Tuesday

> As a small business owner you might be interested

It took me four tries to figure out how to word a reply—the sharp smell of vinegar from the dressing wasn't helping my focus any. Was he trying to rub my nose in it? Or—the slightly more generous version—giving me a courtesy heads-up, so I wouldn't have to "officially" learn from a regular that my business was ending?

Finally I settled on:

> Thx for letting me know. Have you tried the lasagna yet?

I have. When I look in the fridge and
realize the leftovers are gone I cry
real tears

Mimi would be gratified

Always the goal

So? Will you be there?

Something fluttered in my chest. If he was planning on hating
me forever, he wouldn't care if I actually came, would he?

It's a date

No, it's a mostly tedious procedural
meeting

So you're saying bring the drinks in a
flask

I'm glad we understand each other

It wasn't exactly warm and fuzzy, but it felt, unexpectedly, like
a start.

The community center was much fuller than I expected when Mimi
and I walked in Tuesday night, a few dozen people milling around
the folding table topped with a coffee urn and a pitcher filled with a
highlighter-colored liquid I assumed was meant to be lemonade.

"Oh god, there's Loretta Bownes. If she comes over, run interference. She keeps nagging me to join her stupid tai chi class. I
know we're both old, but for Christ's sake, be less of a goddamned
caricature, Loretta," Mimi muttered.

"Don't worry. I'll fall on the sword of Brian's-bowel-updates in order to save you, Mimi."

"She really brings that up to you?"

"And whoever else happens to be in the shop."

"Maybe I should be the one running interference."

Luckily, we were both saved from Loretta's variety pack of inappropriate conversation topics by the town selectman stepping up to the podium and tapping gingerly at the mic.

"If we could all take our seats? We have a lot to get through."

I glanced around, but I didn't see Theo anywhere. Before long, a string of complaints about crosswalk placement and street repair schedules, approved vendors for the May Day festival and the state of the trash bins at Fulton Park, had shifted my focus entirely to trying to stay awake. How Mimi sat through these things was beyond me. I was about to call it a night—apparently this had been Theo taking revenge, which, points for creativity—when the selectman quieted the room again.

"That's our regular agenda business concluded. At this point, Theo Taylor would like to discuss upcoming plans for the old Taylor's building. Theo?"

He waved Theo up from where he'd been leaning against the back wall. Sam stood a few feet away, elegant in a long-sleeved black silk sheath that would read plain on anyone else but somehow seemed devastatingly chic on her.

They'd come together, clearly. I tried not to let disappointment take hold—I should be, if not over it, at least used to the fact of them as a couple. Still, seeing him stride by in his perfectly tailored suit, the slate-blue color making his eyes pop, was enough to make my breath stick in my throat. For just a moment, his eyes caught on mine, then he turned, sliding a piece of foam board onto an easel near the podium. It showed a blueprint of what I could just recognize as the Taylor's building . . . or part of it. Specifically the first floor, subdivided into smaller sections that vaguely mirrored the layouts of the floors above, all of them opening onto a large central space.

"Thanks for having me. I know it must feel like déjà vu to some of you." Theo paused for a laugh that didn't come. Smirking, he glanced at his notes and continued. "So. Last time I was here, it was to float the idea of Mangia purchasing the building. I'll cut right to the chase: That plan is no longer on the table."

Murmurs flew around the room as my heart rocketed into my throat. Had I heard him right? A woman behind us, middle-aged and vaguely familiar in the way half the town was, leaned forward, resting an arm on Mimi's shoulder.

"Good for you, Mimi."

"Hmmm," Mimi grunted distractedly, eyes fixed on me. I'd told her that Mangia was a sure thing—they'd been talking over where to place the café, for Christ's sake—but clearly I'd missed something. *No idea,* I mouthed at her, shrugging, before we both turned back to Theo, hanging on his every word now.

"The biggest argument for Mangia was that most businesses aren't able to occupy the entire building. Even the first floor is about five times the average retail space in Milborough today," Theo said, gesturing at the diagram.

"So you're planning to sell it to some medium-sized-box store instead?" Chet Beauport drawled from the third row. He was maybe fifteen years older than me and ran a CrossFit gym near the Burnton border. Actually, a gym would be the perfect tenant for a space that size.

"No. As it happens, the building's already been sold."

The buzz grew louder. *Weren't consulted . . . bad for small business . . . what about traffic?* Theo's mouth tightened with annoyance.

"Did you want to hear more about our actual plans? Or . . ." He raised an eyebrow, his trademark *I'm too busy for this* look settling on his handsome face. Something like nostalgia bloomed beneath my sternum.

"Wonderful. So, I know it's hard to make out details, but the space will be subdivided into seven small units, with a large central atrium. I'll be opening these to tenants this fall, once building repairs and maintenance are complete. Rents will be in line with other commercial properties in the city, and the central section will have additional space for permitted microbusinesses. Think single-item food stalls, or booths for artisans."

I glanced around, waiting for someone to ask the obvious question, but the buzz of conversation showed no sign of stopping. Feeling sheepish—I'd never been to one of these things before, so if there was a protocol, I didn't know *how* to follow it—I raised my hand.

"Yes?" Theo looked at me with the mild interest of a museum docent.

"This plan is for the first floor. What about the rest of the building?" Sam had said at the dinner that even leasing offices had been a problem—how were they going to attract four full floors of tiny businesses?

"That will be converted into housing."

"Great, more luxury condos? Just what Milborough needs," Mary Thornton spat. She'd always been sour.

"The current plan is for this to be converted to a single residence, though it's possible that will need to be rethought. Either way, to answer your . . . well, it wasn't really a *question,* but no, luxury condos aren't likely."

"And why should we approve this?" a man in the first row grumbled. "How will a fancy new house on top of a few shops help Milborough?"

"The plan doesn't *require* your approval," Theo said, mild amusement curving his lips. "The building's already zoned mixed-use, and the purchase is already under way." He raised a hand to shoulder height as the indignant murmurs rose in pitch. "I'm *here* because the buyer would like to involve the town in the plans for the retail portion. Nothing's set in stone yet, and the goal is to make this a self-sustaining space for years to come. So if any of you have thoughts on how it could be put to better use, I invite you to share them."

The room quieted for a few seconds, then a woman a few rows back raised a hand.

"Will there still be parking at the building?"

"Yes. With multiple businesses occupying the space, it felt important to the overall success of the project."

Another hand shot up.

"Are there limits to what kinds of businesses can go in? Like . . . will restaurants be considered?"

"At least one café or restaurant tenant would be preferred. It would add to the space's appeal as a destination."

From there, questions started flowing thick and fast, and while some were still salt-cured—griping seemed to be endemic to the existence of the town meeting—most showed genuine interest. After about ten minutes, the selectman moved up next to Theo again, and Theo stepped aside.

"Mr. Taylor has kindly agreed to take additional questions in the coming weeks. His email address is on the printout near the lemonade. He has also invited everyone to inspect the building plans, which he's happy to send out upon request. For now, we need to move on to the issue of unregulated firepits."

Twenty minutes later we were all rising from our uncomfortable folding chairs, chatting to neighbors as people started to drift out the door.

"I'm surprised no one asked the obvious question," Mimi said under her breath, wry amusement pulling out an alluvial fan of wrinkles on the flood plains of her cheeks.

"What's that?"

"Who bought the building, of course."

"Isn't it obvious?" I turned to find Sam at my shoulder, smiling conspiratorially at Mimi.

"If I had to bet money, I'd say it was the same man who was telling us all about the brilliant new vision for the 'European Market.'"

"You should go to Vegas, Mrs. Greco. I bet you'd clean up."

"I always do. Speaking of, I'm going to snag one of those cookies before the vultures take them all." Mimi patted my arm once before beelining for the refreshments.

"Wait, *Theo* bought the building?" I blinked at Sam, mouth dropping open, too shocked to remember that we weren't really speaking.

"Are you really that surprised?" She gazed at him, pinned near the front of the auditorium by a trio of older women talking over one another. If it weren't for the tension in his jaw, you'd never know he was dying to break free.

"After you two were bringing the Mangia exec through that morning? Yeah."

Sam frowned at me, then shook her head, realization dawning.

"That wasn't . . . Actually, no, I'll let Theo tell you. I'm sure he'd rather share the news himself."

"And . . . are the two of you doing well?" I finally said. "I'm glad everything worked out for you, by the way."

"No, you're not." Sam smirked.

"No, I'm not. But for the record, I really did plan to help you. Things just . . . spun out of control, I guess. Either way . . . I'm sorry. I didn't mean to lie to you."

"But you did. Lie to me. Which really pissed me off, Ellie. I *liked* you." Sam's eyes narrowed in obvious annoyance.

"I liked you too. I *still* like you. For what it's worth, I was lying to myself even harder."

"I actually believe that." Her face softened slightly. "And honestly, I still like you too. But I'm also still pissed. It's gonna take a *lot* of salami to make it up to me."

I grinned, relief coursing through me. Sam and I were holding ourselves stiffly, the tension between us palpable, but maybe, if I worked at it, there was still a chance at friendship there.

"All your top-shelf charcuterie is comped . . . forever, honestly. Just say the word." I glanced over her shoulder at Theo, heart squeezing tight for a moment. Sam was great, but she wasn't the person I most wanted to make up with at this thing. "Anyway . . . it seems like things worked out the way they were supposed to in the end?"

Sam nibbled her lower lip, then seemed to make a decision.

"That's still TBD. I *can* tell you that Theo and I . . . we're just colleagues."

"What? But I thought . . ." I frowned, trying to sort my thoughts. "You were at his house the other night. Barefoot."

"Believe it or not, even I take my heels off when we're pulling an all-nighter sorting out contracts." Sam smiled slyly.

"Did you just . . . change your mind?"

"You could say that." She sighed, gazing across the room at Theo. "After I explained things to Theo, we did try it on for size. And I think we both gave it a genuine effort. At least I did. But it turns out, sometimes they're 'the one that got away' for a reason." She turned back to me, clocked the look on my face. "Don't get me wrong, Theo's an incredible guy. And a part of me is always going to wonder if we didn't make a mistake giving up when we did. But we've both changed since then. The people we are now . . . they're not right for each other. Honestly . . . we loved each other, but we might never have really been the right fit."

"Oh?" My breath was coming faster, excitement bubbling through me.

"Even then I was trying to change him into . . . well, someone more like me."

"Let me guess, you want the dual C-suite household?"

"That's the dream. Or rather . . . that's *my* dream. But Theo's always wanted something different. He's more sentimental. I know he wants a family . . ." She shook her head, gaze going distant. "I was going through a whole *thing* being my college roommate's bridesmaid. It made me think about what we had, probably made me rose-colored-glasses our relationship a little. I'll always love him, but we're not each other's person. At least not anymore."

"But then . . . are you regretting taking the job? Won't it be awkward working with him?"

"No. Or at least not for long. Besides, I've been . . . hanging out with someone who'll force us all to get past the awkward pretty damn fast."

Before I could ask what she meant, Everett glided up beside her.

"Hey, Ellie. How goes it? Are you considering calling off the engagement now that Theo's decided to sink all his funds into dodgy real estate schemes? The man's basically an ogre if you take away the massive inheritance."

"Actually, it was the sleep farts that did me in."

"Oh, word. Those are a relationship killer for sure," Everett said, mock serious. "I'd love to dissect *all* the reasons you should be aiming higher, but I actually have to steal Sam away." He turned to her. "Reservation is in twenty. I'd say we can show up late, but this speakeasy is *very* pretentious."

"My favorite kind," she grinned, eyes turning sparkly. "Ellie, I'll text you. I think you and I should . . . reboot, let's say." She leaned in as Everett shook out her coat behind her, the perfect gentleman, and lowered her voice. "Plus, I know someone who would be a way better fit for our mutual friend. A successful local entrepreneur and fashion designer? That is if she's interested . . ."

Before I could protest, Everett had slid the coat onto Sam's shoulders and, after a quick goodbye, started guiding her out of the room. I was still staring after them, mildly shocked, when Theo broke away from the trio of interrogators to join me.

"So? What did you think of the plan?" Theo's pose was nonchalant, but his eyes were avid as he waited for me to speak.

"I think it sounds like a great idea . . . but I have no clue what could have possibly convinced Ted to agree to it."

"He didn't have a choice," Theo said, grinning triumphantly. "Getting Cheryl and Paul to vote against Mangia was pretty straightforward, at least once I activated the emotional blackmail card. It was hard for even Paul to vote *for* Mangia once I reminded them of what the building had always meant to me and Chase. Plus, I was offering the same amount, and they have to see me at the holidays."

"Offering . . . Theo, where the hell did you get that kind of money?"

"I decimated my trust," he said casually. "I haven't touched it in a decade. Why just let it sit there making money when it could actually do some good?"

"Wait . . . are *you* planning to move in to the building?"

"Eventually. First, I'm planning on using it as a sort of apprenticeship." He stiffened a little, chest thrusting forward as though to ward off a blow. "There's an architect we've used a few times on other projects, I plan to . . . half hire him, half take classes with him. Turning the building into a family home would be . . ."

"Your training grounds?"

"More or less." He sniffed out a laugh. "Architecture school would be cheaper, but honestly . . . what really interests me is preserving and updating historic buildings. I figure if this goes well, I'll have a great portfolio piece for future jobs. And if it doesn't . . . then I'll find something else instead."

"That's incredible, Theo." Tenderness gripped my chest. Apparently I actually meant it. "Why now?"

"Someone reminded me that I should have been doing what made *me* happy all along," he said, voice roughening. "Her delivery might have been a little . . . harsh, but she wasn't wrong. I spent way too long living the life Ted wanted for me. And I have the ability to change that. I just had to . . . take the leap."

I colored, still embarrassed by what I'd said that night, but it was clear from the look on Theo's face that he didn't want to discuss it further at the moment.

"So that guy I saw at the building the day after the dinner . . . he wasn't from Mangia?"

"He was not. In fact, that was Chris, the architect I'll be working with. After our . . . discussion, I reached out to see if he'd be willing to talk through possibilities with Cheryl. She's very hands-on."

"But wait . . ." Pieces started clicking into place. "You *knew* I thought that Mangia was coming in. When I brought you the lasagna." He shrugged acknowledgment. "What the fuck, Theo?"

"Oh come on, Ellie. I accept your apology—the lasagna did a lot of the work for you, by the way—but you deserved to sweat a *little* more than that."

He flashed a languid smirk. I pursed my lips, annoyed, but the man had a point. There was only one question left.

"And things between you and Sam are . . . good?" She might be over Theo, at least for now, but that was no guarantee he was truly over *her*. Maybe having her around so much more had brought up old feelings . . . and their date might have rekindled something . . .

"They are. No thanks to your little stunt. I never knew it was possible to have such a bad first date with someone you once planned to marry." He rolled his eyes. "Honestly, what were you thinking with all that? Sam I get—thinking she can strong-arm us back to what we had is her all over—but why would *you* think we'd be good together?"

"I don't know." It did seem a little ridiculous in retrospect. "I guess I figured your mutual love for tennis would carry you through."

"Luckily, Everett loves it even more than I do. Plus, he can turn drinking soda into a competition. They're perfect for each other." Theo turned his deep blue eyes on me, then frowned slightly, presumably catching the worry on my face. "What? And don't try to dodge it, we've both done enough of that lately."

"There's really nothing there?" I whispered. "You'll be working together every day, and you have so much in common . . ."

"Which is awesome, for the company and for me. Sam knows her shit like no one else. And she's really loyal, underneath the corporate cutthroat act. She knows better than anyone what the Taylor's building means to me." Theo's gaze darted over my shoulder for a moment, Adam's apple working. "When I called her that night to tell her I was considering making an offer, she worked overtime to help me pull together all the information I'd need to get it past Aunt Cheryl. She's . . . a really good friend."

"Right." I swallowed, trying to ignore the fluttery feeling in my chest, hardly daring to hope . . .

"But that's not who I am anymore, Ellie. And . . . it's not who I want." He lifted a hand to my shoulder. My breath caught as my eyes drifted up to his.

"And who do you want?" I murmured.

"I think you know that already." His hand tightened around my shoulder as the other drifted to my waist, then snaked around to the base of my spine. The heat of his touch started blooming inside me. His gaze lowered to my lips and I felt myself drifting closer, my entire body caught in his orbit, magnetized to his poles.

Oh god, now I was thinking about his *poles*.

"And you're willing to forgive me?" My voice came out breathy.

"I think I could see my way to that," Theo said, perfect lips curling languidly as he leaned half an inch closer. "If *you* were willing to go out on a first date. A real one, no act to keep up, nothing we need from each other."

"Really? There's *nothing* you need from me?"

"Want and need aren't the same thing, Ellie."

"Well . . . I *suppose* I could be persuaded. After all, I've always had a soft spot for jamón ibérico—"

And suddenly Theo's arms were around me, and he was pulling me against his body, and my lips had found his, arms circling his broad shoulders as I stretched up to meet the soft pressure of his mouth, stars exploding through my whole body at his touch, thrillingly new and yet somehow familiar, almost like I was coming home. We must have been lost in each other for longer than I realized when the cough behind me startled me back to reality.

"Not that I have anything against young love, but can you two put a hold on that?" Mimi's eyes narrowed at Theo. "Some of us have a bottle of wine waiting, and I need a word with my granddaughter."

"I wouldn't dare come between you and *that*," Theo said. "Ellie, I'll just wait for you over here." He tilted his head toward the doors before making his retreat.

Once he was out of earshot, Mimi took my hand in both of hers.

"Thank god you finally saw sense."

"Is that what you think I'm doing?"

"You don't get to be my age without learning how to spot the obvious, Eleanor."

"But . . . you said we'd never work. At the engagement party."

"I said that *place* is not us, and I stand by that. But . . . it may not be Theo, either. At the very least you should find out for yourself." She squeezed my hand tenderly, then her face turned grave. "There's just one thing I need to say to you, and I want you to listen very closely. It's important."

"Okay . . ."

"There is no way on god's green earth that I will *ever* share a holiday with Ted Taylor. Are we clear?"

"Crystal."

"Good. In that case . . . I suppose we'll have to pray that being a prick doesn't skip a generation. Now. Get going, before you make me lose my bet with your aunt Susan." She pecked me lightly on the cheek and strode out, nodding sharply at Theo as she pushed through the doors.

Theo slid his arm through mine as we emerged into the chilly night. I was so used to his opening the door for me that it barely registered. I sighed contentedly as the seat heater wrapped me in its warm, full-body hug.

"So? Where are we headed?" Theo turned to me. "I'd say that speakeasy Everett likes, but that might be a little awkward. But the bar at Post is nice. Or we could head into Boston, I know a great little wine bar in Back Bay."

"We're going to Major MacLeod's, obviously."

"Really?" Theo raised an eyebrow in disbelief. "I know you're saving for a condo, but I'm happy to float the drinks."

"How do you know that?"

"It's been great getting to know Bella again," he said, grinning wryly. "So? The world is your oyster."

"And I'm choosing the oysters at Major MacLeod's. But not on the weekends. There's a reason they do the dollar Sunday special."

"Okaaay"—Theo started the car and pulled out—"I'll humor you. That is, if you tell me *why* we're going there."

"We've already established the meet-cute, Theo. Get ready to lose at pool."

Acknowledgments

With every subsequent book, I become increasingly aware of how very lucky I am to be surrounded by all the brilliant, thoughtful, hardworking people who have decided to take a chance on me as an author. With this book—a *serious* change of pace from my recent thrillers—I feel more grateful than ever that I'm taking this journey with people I trust completely.

An absolutely gigantic heartfelt thanks to Anne Speyer—you're not only an incredible, insightful editor, you're an absolute joy to work with. Thank you for taking a very hard left with me into the world of happy endings.

I couldn't possibly ask for a better agent than Taylor Haggerty. Our brainstorming sessions are my absolute favorite thing that I get to call work, and you always manage to ask the exact right questions (not to mention come up with the perfect solutions) to tease out the best version of an idea. Thanks, too, to Jasmine Brown. Your ability to perfect a plot and deepen a character is unrivaled.

I'm so grateful to the team at Bantam Dell for everything they do to get my books in front of readers. Particular thanks to Katie

Horn, Kathleen Quinlan, and Emma Thomasch: Your hard work is so deeply appreciated!

My writing group has been there for me through all the highs and lows (and crises of confidence). Lana Harper, Adriana Mather, and Chelsea Sedoti: You are some of the most talented writers I know, and your insights are invaluable to me. I am so lucky to have found you.

I would never have been able to chase the dream of writing books, let alone achieve it, without the love and support of my incredible family. Thanks for putting up with me longer than literally anyone else.

Thank you to Signe for bringing a level of joy into my life that I didn't know I could experience. There is nothing you could ever do that would make me love you less.

And thank you, always, Danny, for everything you do to support me and our family. You're the reason I believe in happy endings in the first place.

Love You,
Mean It

Jilly Gagnon

Random
House
Book Club

Because
Stories Are
Better Shared ™

BOOK CLUB KIT

Letter from the Author

Dear Reader,

I have a secret: I'm not a very nice person.

Of course, if you met me, you likely wouldn't agree. I'm Midwestern, specifically Minnesotan, and "Minnesota nice" isn't just descriptive, it's practically a requirement. Good manners, holding the door open for the person behind you, pleasantly chit-chatting with the rowmate on the airplane who tortures you by wanting to talk a lot—I have all this in spades, which adds up to the appearance of nice, at least at first glance.

But beneath my pleasant smiles and octave-higher-for-strangers cheery timbre, I'm muttering an embittered "You're welcome" when an entire string of people stroll into the shop like this is Downton Abbey and "door holder" is a vital rung on the service ladder. I'm annoyed at having to fake-smile through yet another photo of this Boomer stranger's dog Halloween parade, possibly even live-texting a friend snide remarks about the many ways Shirley from Gainesville could better spend her retirement than forcing her poor chihuahua into a Dorothy costume complete with four glittering red slippers. Get to know me better and you'll hear my off-color jokes, my snarky retorts, and my elaborate imagined petty revenges.

The salty, the smart-alecks, the sarcastic: These are my true people. And if you ask me, they deserve happy endings at least as much as, if not more than, the rest of us. Think about it—the genuinely good-spirited who go around actually seeing the best in people and . . . I don't know, talking to forest animals? They're already having a great life, and there's nothing you can throw at them that will make them think otherwise.

This is my love story to, and for, those of us who sometimes wake up on the wrong side of the bed. Fight it as much as you want: Sometimes you just wind up in a love story. And dammit . . . it might be just what you needed.

xx,
Jilly

Discussion Questions

1. Bella and Ellie are often described as having different personalities—sugar and spice. Who are you more like?

2. Family is an important theme in this novel and heavily influences the actions of Ellie and Theo. What are the positive and negative impacts of family seen in this novel?

3. Mimi is an important matriarch in the Greco clan. How are she and Ellie alike?

4. Ellie's and Theo's relationships with their respective families are vastly different. How would you describe Ellie's relationship to her family? How would you describe Theo's?

5. One of the key themes in this story is grief. Consider Ellie's grief about her father and Theo's about Chase. How did their loss of loved ones influence the decisions they make in this story?

6. The story takes place in the setting of Ellie's small hometown, Milborough. What was your impression of the town and the townspeople? How did the setting add to the story?

7. While navigating business and romantic issues, Ellie also undergoes moments of self-discovery. How did being a small business owner of her family's legacy impact her sense of worth? How does her opinion about owning the deli change throughout the novel?

8. The deli was significant to Ellie as it reminded her of her father, her childhood, and her family. Do you have a similar place that feels like home? What emotions do you feel when you visit or think of your home-away-from-home?

9. Theo and Ellie quickly realize they are good at working as a team. Why do you think they worked so well as partners (in crime) despite coming from different worlds?

10. As the story is told in her POV, through Ellie's internal thoughts, we get to see how she viewed Theo and their interactions. Though she was in denial, her thoughts and actions reveal her true feelings about Theo. In what moment between them did it become clear they cared about each other? Who began to care for the other first—Ellie or Theo?

11. How do Ellie's memories and descriptions of her past life in New York compare to her current life in Milborough? What do they reveal about her? How do her thoughts about the two places change throughout the novel?

12. Both characters struggle to maintain family expectations while pursuing their own passions. What does this look like for Ellie? What does this look like for Theo?

13. As they become closer, Ellie starts to realize that Theo is not the same boy she remembered from high school. She eventually realizes that she has also grown and changed from high school. To self-reflect, consider how you have changed from high school. Are there any parts of you that are still the same?

JILLY GAGNON is the author of *All Dressed Up, Scenes of the Crime,* and the young adult novel *#famous.* Her humor writing, personal essays, and op-eds have appeared in *Newsweek, Elle, Vanity Fair, Boston* magazine, *McSweeney's Internet Tendency, The Toast,* and *The Hairpin,* among others. She lives in Salem, Massachusetts, with her family and two black cats.

jillygagnon.com
Twitter: @jillygagnon
Instagram: @jillygagnon

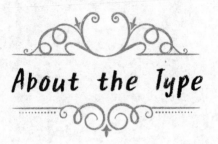

About the Type

This book was set in Garamond, a typeface originally designed by the Parisian type cutter Claude Garamond (c. 1500–61). This version of Garamond was modeled on a 1592 specimen sheet from the Egenolff-Berner foundry, which was produced from types assumed to have been brought to Frankfurt by the punch cutter Jacques Sabon (c. 1520–80).

Claude Garamond's distinguished romans and italics first appeared in *Opera Ciceronis* in 1543–44. The Garamond types are clear, open, and elegant.